By My Sword Alone

BY MY SWORD ALONE

DAVID BLACK

LUME BOOKS

LUME BOOKS

Published in 2021 by Lume Books
30 Great Guildford Street,
Borough, SE1 0HS

ISBN 978-1-83901-218-1

Typeset using Atomik ePublisher from Easypress Technologies

www.lumebooks.co.uk

About the Author

David Black is the author of the best-selling Harry Gilmour series set in the Royal Navy submarine service during World War Two.

He also wrote the novella *All the Freshness of the Morning*, a fictionalized account of President John F. Kennedy's epic World War Two service as Skipper of the US Navy torpedo boat PT-109 in South Pacific.

Black is a former UK national newspaper journalist and TV documentary producer. He now lives in Argyll and writes full time.

Learn more about him and his books by visiting his website: www.theblackscribe.co.uk

To my old school friend, Gerry, one of the
genuine latter-day Scots *wild geese*.

1

The Battle of Glenshiel, 1719

From all the gold lace, and the feathers in his hat, even from a distance you could not help but assume the red-coated man on his white charger must be a general. Even against the solid ranks of the other red-coated soldiers he stood out, as he cantered to the head of their column, to where another officer was conferring with the troop of light horse who'd been riding picket. It was a beautiful late spring day; bright, crisp and fresh as only the West Highlands could display. And not for the first time this man, so finely accoutred, ruminated on how a just God could have suffered such beauty to be squandered on such a benighted people as the Scots.

And even though you were viewing from a distance, you could not help but see why the general didn't need to be told why he'd been summoned, or why his column of troops had halted. Ahead of this mass of redcoats was the drovers' road to Loch Duich, curving gently to the right, following the contour of a hill. Where it emerged from shadow, the mouth of a glen opened up on a splendid vista of bald, grey rock and heather scrub; treeless and rugged.

Strung across that mouth, from the deep-sided scar of the River Shiel on one side, over broken ground to a steep, scree-covered escarpment on the other, was a defensive line of troops. It appeared that the rebels this general had been sent to hunt down, had decided to present themselves to him instead.

The general pulled a long telescope from his saddle and in an un-hurried pan of the valley mouth, took in the enemy dispositions. If the force facing him had been a modern European army, his professional eye – sharpened by many, many years of campaigning – would have told him their line was unassailable.

Their left, on the river, was not only anchored on the deep gorge that channelled the fast running water, but on a steep, trackless precipice that even a Barbary ape would have trouble traversing, which rose from its far bank. No way around that.

Their right clung to the rise of that scree escarpment, a position the enemy had fortified further by erecting a series of stone dykes as cover for their marksmen, allowing them to fire down on any advancing foe, while remaining impervious to any return fire behind slabs of slate and whinstone.

The general's name was Joseph Wightman and he had faced men like these before, however; not least four years prior at Sheriffmuir, where he had helped fight a vastly superior Highland army to a standstill. So he was not unduly perturbed. He knew this rabble was no modern European army. And despite the formidable nature of their position, they would be eminently beatable.

The white coats and yellow facings of the immaculate ranks barring the broken ground in the middle, however – they were another matter. These must be the Spanish he'd been warned about. Regular line infantry. And rather a lot of them, lent by the King of Spain to fight in the Stuart cause. He lowered his telescope to scratch his chin. On this terrain, they would be formidable. But a plan was already forming. He ordered his aides to his side, and began to make *his* dispositions.

Even with all the energy of his tender years, and pumped by all those dreams of impending glory the young fool feels before his first battle, James Lindsay was starting to flag. For three days now he'd been seldom out of his saddle. Riding to and fro, galloping with written orders, folded safe, close to his breast; sheet upon sheet of them, issuing from the army's general. Orders of march for the entire host; orders specific to each and every detachment and then once considered, refinements to those orders, then revisions. Orders affecting the assembling of the army; then the army's ten-mile march from the castle, down the north shore of the loch and to the far end of the glen. The building of the fortifications upon which the Hanoverian usurper's troops were to be encouraged to impale themselves, and then further orders, a constant stream of orders, back and forth, regarding the troops' dispositions and what was to be their conduct in each and every sundry scenario the general and his staff could conceive. And then the notes returning from all those officers commanding lesser formations, some concurring, some disputing. To and fro, back and forward; gallop, gallop, gallop. Even for a lad so deep in the thrall of events, he couldn't help but feel his generals were a chatty crowd for supposed men of decision.

James was galloping now, behind three lines of Spanish infantry, on their feet since the enemy column had suddenly marched into sight. If James stole a glance over his shoulder, he could see the red-coated enemy plainly, in the process of debouching from the road he knew ran here all the way from Inverness. A number of the Spanish officers were waving to him as he sped past, Irishmen in the King of Spain's service, who had befriended James during the weeks of waiting that had preceded this latest great convulsion of activity. In him they'd divined a lively, intelligent lad; fearless. And as they watched him rush dispatches from one end of their lines to the other, they admired the dash he displayed.

General Wightman couldn't help but notice him, too. Crouched for speed over the neck of his elegant grey; a junior officer no doubt, in a bottle green small coat, lapels taped and cuffs faced in maroon and cut in the fashion of a French dragoon – no flapping tails to clutter his hand's easy reach to his light cavalry sabre or the carbine holstered on his saddle. Also, he wore no hat, nor wig, and that allowed a luxuriant tangle of reddish brown hair to flow out, like a banner to measure the wind of his passing. And young, thought Wightman. Only a young man could ride with such verve. The range, however, was too great for him to perceive just how young. All that was discernible was that he appeared to be an aide, a mere messenger, a minor link in these rebels' chain of command, which was probably why this flaunting of his bravado irritated the general. Who the hell did he think he was? The whippersnapper!

'Hadden!' bellowed Wightman, and a young officer from his own detachment of cavalry cantered forward. 'See that young blade over there, all tricked out like a Frenchie and going hell for leather?'

'General Wightman, sah! Yes, sah!' said Hadden.

'He's being far too energetic for his own good. Take that machine you have there …' Wightman gestured to an elegant, rifled carbine holstered on Hadden's saddle – a weapon obviously designed less for warfare than for the sporting field – 'and see if you cannot put him at his ease.'

'General Wightman, sah! Yes, sah!' said Hadden. Reaching down, he produced the weapon with a flourish, and cantered forwards to a hummock in the broken ground that would give him an easier shot at the galloping rebel aide de camp in the green dragoon coat.

While Hadden was cantering forward, James was reining in; he had espied the man he was seeking. Lord George Murray, commander of the army's right flank, sat on one of a tumble of rocks on the lip of a steep-banked burn that ran down and away from the field. His lordship was deep in counsel with his subordinates. James had a dispatch for him; he'd even watched it being written by a more senior aide at the dictation of the Marquess of Tullibardine, their general. James had been too far away to hear the orders dictated, but close enough to witness the time they took to record, obviously a long and detailed scenario for the battle to come. James' throat was tight with pride that he served alongside such men.

That pride was still with him as he dismounted. Before he'd first joined the king over the water's army, all those weeks ago at the head of Loch Duich, he had never seen such a gathering of men; the ranks of fearsome Highlanders in dun jerkin and plaid, and the disciplined majesty of the scrubbed and blanco-ed Spaniards. And now, over there, was another host, a sea of marching red. The army of the Hanoverian usurper, King George I, filling the mouth of this ancient, usually silent Highland glen with the noise and hubbub of their bellowed orders, drummer boys and the pounding of their marching feet – and this was all before the sound of musketry had begun.

Lord George Murray had been his father's friend since James could remember, a familiar face at the table. But James, full of the gravity of the hour, was sensible not use his customary greeting – 'Uncle Geordie!' – as he stepped forward.

'My lord,' he said, freeing the folded paper from inside his waistcoat. 'A dispatch from the marquess, sir.'

Murray acknowledged the lad's salute and took the folded paper. 'Aye, Jaimie, how fare ye, laddie? Ye'll have seen the wee German lairdie's men have come to accept our invitation, eh?' said Murray, gesturing over his shoulder with the hand that held his orders, before clapping James on the shoulder with his other.

James grinned at that initial, familiar greeting, but after it he heard not another word, his senses stunned by what he was witnessing. Murray, after a cursory glance at the scribbled address on the front of the dispatch, had held it out, unread, for his own aide to take and thrust into a satchel stuffed with similar documents, all of them still folded too.

When James turned back to his lordship, he was walking away to where his aide was already holding out a telescope. Dismissed, and trying to compose his tumbled thoughts – could such a thing have happened? A general throwing his orders into a bag, unread? – James distractedly slipped the reins of his filly, Sophie, from her saddle pommel with one hand, and brought them to his side. Then he lifted his left foot up into the stirrup. Later, he would remember hearing the crack of the carbine, and thinking nothing of it; then the two heartbeats, and then the punch that hit the back of his fist, and the searing slash across the top of his thigh, and Sophie's fearsome whinny as she reared, flung him to the ground; and bolted.

This was, when he looked back on it, the moment James Lindsay stopped seeing the world through a child's eyes and embarked upon the long, laborious and frequently demoralising task of learning how to think like a man.

For ever after it, he only had to look at his left hand to be reminded; the stumpy gaps where the third finger and pinkie used to be, now gone at their first joints. He had to drop his breeches however, if he wanted to see the gouge the onward passage of the bullet had made across his leg. Still, they were his first honourable wounds, won in battle, and on the day, they had painted a heroic picture in blood.

Events then passed in a blur. James was aware of faces looking down on him, and then figures bundling him away, down the ravine and then up again on a soldier's back to where the army's meagre detachment of cavalry stood idle. The wounds were already hurting, but that pain was as nothing compared to the searing, sudden agony when the cavalry's farrier cleansed and cauterised his finger stumps with an iron from his brazier. His hand was then tightly bound, as another bustling figure whipped the torn breeches off him and laid bare the slash on his leg. The sight of it rendered poor James momentarily faint, but he roused himself to watch as the farrier packed it with a foul-looking poultice that appeared concocted from warm mud and nettles and stank of vinegar.

Poor, poor James; he'd never felt so far from glory.

They propped him up against saddles, and gave him a flask of spirits, urging him to drink hearty. When he could unscrew his eyes from the first hit the fiery liquid delivered to his chest, he was suddenly aware that from his perch, halfway up the side of the glen, he had an almost perfect view of the battlefield, and the fight that was to come.

He had to admit to himself, the British soldiers did look magnificent – he also had to admit they were British, not just English. For the detachments of Mackays and Munroes, loyal to King George, were all too evident.

The first shots came from the British side, directed against Murray's troops below him, and they provided an explanation for the four

14

queer-looking stretchers that he'd watched being carried from a couple of tumbrils rolled up just behind the enemy's front line of infantry. The devices looked like plump brass toads, and once individually arrayed, became the centre of much activity. Then, the first puff of white smoke made all too plain what they were; belching, first from one, then from the others, and the bangs that belatedly echoed across the glen. Some crude form of artillery.

But wasn't the bangs that stunned James, it was that he was suddenly aware he could see the balls fired from these devices as they climbed lazily into the air, describing parabolas agonizingly slowly until over the top, at which point they began plunging rapidly earthwards to land among Murray's infantry lines, where they bounced, fizzing, and then exploded, one by one, in brief flashes and smoke. It was only after a scream wafted up from within the meagre clouds, that James realised their potential lethality.

He would learn later the devices were coehorn mortars; stumpy, angled barrels designed to lob shells as plunging fire, and the fizzing he'd seen was each ball's fuse, lit before firing and designed to detonate them once they'd fallen amongst an enemy. Against the Highlanders' piled stone defences, they were ideal weapons, better than ordinary artillery which could only fire ball on a level trajectory. You might say James' slack-jawed gaze of wonderment, right then, was the beginning of his tactical education.

The bombardment proceeded unabated for a while, and to James, looking down from his perch on his own lines, it did not seem as if the enemy were wreaking much actual physical havoc among them. Yet he could see the men shuffling, restless under the fire. Despite the distance, it was as if he could feel them flinch at every bang.

Musketry could be heard from the centre now, and when he looked to the white-uniformed ranks of Spaniards, he could see they were exchanging volleys, at extreme range, with ranks of red coats. The officers on both sides however, appeared to show no inclination to bring their fight to bayonet point and were concentrating instead on keeping their lines regular, and in seeing the odd gap re-filled when any soldier fell, wounded. However, in the still of the evening – it was now almost 7 o' clock, according to James' timepiece – the powder smoke began to thicken into fog and its intensely evocative reek to fill the air.

James Lindsay, third son of the Earl of Branter, had celebrated his thirteenth birthday barely two months before, which made him the youngest fellow in the Marquess of Tullibardine's army that day. One might have reasonably assumed that no mother would have allowed a son so young to march off to war, but James' mother had died of smallpox when he was but three years old, and given that the Lindsays were a family fiercely loyal to the cause of the king over the water, James Francis Edward Stuart – King James III, as by divine right – no-one had thought to stand in the boy's way when he announced that he too would rally to the Royal Stuart standard.

Loyal as the family might be, however, James Lindsay's father, the earl, was not on the field this day, to see his son wounded in the cause. Instead, he was still in hiding after the previous rising, four years before, having been stripped of his title and most of his lands by a Westminster bill of attainder in the reprisals that followed. Nor was the family's oldest son, Archibald, present. In the wake of that previous rising, by family agreement, instead of going on the run with his father the earl Archibald had stepped forward to petition King George for his own pardon, renouncing all loyalty to the Stuart cause, with his fingers firmly crossed behind his back. He had not been alone. Half a generation of first sons had so opted, preparing to bide their time in pragmatism, awaiting the next time.

And so Archibald was in Edinburgh, preserving what little was left of the Lindsay estate. But the middle son, David, was there in Glenshiel, commanding a file of their own clansmen under another of James' father's friends, George Keith, the Earl Marischal.

As the crackle of musketry rose and fell, and the long Highland evening wore on, even a youth as callow as James could sense all chance of decision in this encounter was slipping away. The red coats advanced to fire volleys, then retired. The Highlanders returned their fire, but made no move to advance from their defences. And the small cluster of lace-trimmed coats and feathered tricornes that was Tullibardine's command group sat stuck to the same patch of hillside, doing nothing.

The inaction let James' mind wander back down the road to where this enterprise had begun for him, amidst so much hope and enthusiasm, in the hall at Eilean Donan Castle – with the hired ships that had brought the news, as well as troops and powder and guns from Spain, still riding in the bay opposite.

James had been in the hall for all the councils of war, an aide de camp on the staff of the Earl Marischal, while his brother spent all his time outside with the men he would command in battle. At first James had been jealous and resentful. David would be in the front line, and he would not. But he soon realised, that there, in the hall, was the very centre; and being there had been excitement beyond imagining.

He heard everything.

But it was only on this sun-dappled hillside, with his wounds throbbing and his inexperienced mind starting to swim in the brandy they'd been plying him with, that he'd had leisure to reflect, and for awareness to dawn that lessons are not just things you are taught in a schoolroom.

Growing up in the Lindsay household, the righteousness of the Stuart cause was the truth of the world. The talk at table was of the punitive taxes and duties imposed on Scotland after the union of the parliaments, the de-basing of the Scottish pound and the blatant bribery used to seduce an impoverished Scots gentry into the venal ways of the Whigs and the 'wee German lairdie'. And how the wrong king was on the throne.

All the fine words.

And then, in those first days at Eilean Donan, James, with hairs standing on the back of his head, could not help but feel that here, at last, was action. That here was the stage upon which all that noble aspiration would be made manifest. Because here were the great men of the cause, pooling their wisdom and genius to reverse history and restore divine right again to these islands.

For the great news the ships had brought, by the hand of the Earl Marischal himself, direct from Madrid, was that the King of Spain had thrown the power of his empire behind the claim of King James VIII of Scotland, and III of Great Britain. An expedition was about to set sail from Corunna; 6,000 men under the Duke of Ormonde, to land near Bristol, whereupon they would raise the pro-Stuart population of the whole of the west country and march on London. Meanwhile the Earl Marischal would raise the Highlands and march south to join them, collecting on the way every disaffected, right-thinking soul, of whom it was claimed, there were legion.

And the young James Lindsay had been in the hall when the Marischal announced that the first step towards victory, for the men gathered at the mouth of Loch Duich, would be to march the seventy-odd miles to Inverness, and reduce the Hanoverian garrison there.

'I have sound intelligence that they are but three hundred men,' the Marischal had said, in tones of great gravity, that first night round the long table in hall. The fire was roaring in the grate, and the host of guttering candles sending all manner of portentous shadows dancing.

The Marischal's commission as major general, in King James' own hand, had sat on the table before him, among all the claret glasses. He was, he said, the senior officer in the room, and thus in command. A letter from the king's own hand, this very minute in the copying, would be sent out summoning all the clans to his standard. Spanish muskets, and Spanish powder was this very hour being unloaded to arm them. They would march on Inverness within the week.

Young James Lindsay remembered how he'd thrilled to those words. But that had been before subsequent interventions.

The afternoon before that grand conference convened, the Marquess of Tullibardine, Murray and the Earl of Seaforth had arrived also, in a tiny barque from their exile in France. And at the conference Tullibardine had had some things to say regarding this march on Inverness. Where in the king's letter was there an authorisation? Was such a precipitous movement wise? Tullibardine wanted sight of the document. Once it was finished copying, he was told. A debate had ensued, lasting long into the night and becoming more fractious the more decanters they drained.

James had gone to bed believing that a wise decision must eventually be settled upon, after all that exercising of wisdom.

The next day he spent chatting to some of the Irish officers in the Spanish service as they transformed the castle into a magazine, then in the evening he had returned to the hall. Tullibardine made an entrance, brandishing two documents, and requesting an audience with the Marischal. James had found it all regally flamboyant and formal, but he was only thirteen years old, after all, and could not suspect what was afoot.

'This letter, my Earl Marischal,' Tullibardine had said, brandishing one of the documents, 'makes no mention of a descent on Inverness. Not only that, but it proscribes all movement until Ormonde is confirmed ashore at Bristol, and the west country has risen.'

The document had been the king's appeal. And what followed was Tullibardine's response. He counselled that not only should the march on Inverness be abandoned, but that all the troops now ashore should re-embark.

More decanters were summoned for the table, and the debate resumed. The points made and the language had been easy to follow, but James could not fathom the thrust of it all, the end to be achieved.

Stalemate.

Then, Tullibardine slipped the second letter across the table to the Marischal. It was Tullibardine's own king's commission, and it pre-dated the Marischal's by two years, having been issued at the time of some previous still-born tilt at restoring the Stuarts. More importantly, however, it conferred the rank of lieutenant general on Tullibardine, making him superior to the Marischal.

As George Keith read it, Tullibardine had embarked on a convoluted speech, emphasising that although undoubtedly the Earl Marischal had commanded the King of Spain's expedition to Scotland, now that it had arrived, it must be King James' will that those forces should fall under the command of his most senior general in the country. Namely, Tullibardine.

Young James Lindsay had hung on every cut and thrust of this fencing.

The facts could not be gainsaid, admitted the Marischal, but he counselled against the force re-embarking. British cruisers were known to prowl this coast hunting any Jacobite vessel (that label being a Hanoverian one, as in *Jacobus*, the Latin for James, their so-called king). Should a squadron appear, their naval force might be compromised where it lay, embayed and trapped, or worse still, brought to battle and destroyed with the army aboard, denying it any chance to strike a blow. And also, as the marquess had so pertinently pointed out, he, the Earl Marischal, was still in command of the Spanish expedition and its ships.

Young James remembered hearing Lord George Murray banging the table and saying he just wanted to fight, that was why they were all here, and could they all just get on with it? And then James' eyes had started to droop again, and he'd retreated to bed once more. When he awoke the next day, the Spanish ships had sailed in the night, empty. James simply thought a mutual decision must have been arrived at on the issue of re-embarkation. Only later did he discover it was the Marischal's alone.

If Tullibardine had been angry, he didn't bother to show it publicly, because the following night, it emerged that there were other 'issues' to debate. Was it time to send out the king's letter summoning the clans? Or did that too have to await news of Ormonde?

Poor young James, his head was left spinning at so much wisdom on display. Lying there against his saddles now, he recalled that it had taken his betters over a week to decide that the king's appeal must indeed go forth to the clans.

It was then that young James' revelry was disturbed by figures emerging from the smoke; a ragged cluster of them carrying a body slung in a cloak. The body was Murray, badly wounded. James went to stand up, but realised he couldn't, without opening his own wounded leg.

Down below the musketry and the booms of the coehorn mortars had abated and the smoke was eddying and dissipating. He watched the men carry Murray past him to a cart, and then wheel him away back towards the drover road and the loch. He called to the men, and others

20

who had gone to join the crowd around Murray. 'My lord? How badly is he hurt?' James yelled. 'How goes the fight? Are the English repulsed?'

Nobody answered him. And when he turned back to look down the hill, he saw a sight that shut him up. The Highlanders were walking out the powder smoke, up the hill towards him, away from their defensive line of stones. And not in an orderly way either, but in rabble clumps, some assisting the few walking wounded. Little staggering knots of dun and plaid, that against the heather and tussock looked more like camouflage than proud colours. Dismaying enough, but nowhere near as crushing as the vista he beheld behind them, emerging from the thinning smoke – their abandoned stone palisades, and not a red coat near.

It was obvious. There could be no mistake. The Highlanders, on this flank at least, had simply decided they were going home.

Watching them go, that evening on the side of Glenshiel, James' boyish dreams of glory and the nobility of their cause were stripped away. He lay there, impotent, as every castle he'd ever built in the air came tumbling down.

'I see no reason you shouldn't head home, Jaimie, lad,' a weary Earl Marischal told him after the sun had set on that battle that never really was. With his leg tightly swaddled in bandage, and leaning his weight on Sophie, now shamefacedly returned to her master, James had hobbled down to where the Marischal and some of his retainers gathered, behind the lines of the Spanish infantry, still standing-to and facing their front.

James had found it hard to follow what was being said, so engulfed had he been in that soldier's desolation when he first realises he is no longer on his army's strength; that he doesn't belong anymore, because he has crossed the line between the fit and the wounded. He was too dazed to argue, too drained to put up a fight. And that was how he departed the king across the water's army at Glenshiel. His brother David went off with what was left, heading for the coast and boats to carry them to the continent and exile; and James went home.

And what was home?

Kirkspindie Mearns was a moss and stone stronghold, tucked into a strategic little kink in a meandering glen worn out of the landscape by Spindie Burn over millennia, as it made its way to the River Tay. You could only come upon the castle, for that was what it was, by accident. It lay in verdant slumber below the skyline and was on a road to nowhere now, but for 400 years it had sat here, denying this strategic defile in and out of the land of Breadalbane to any uninvited interloper. It was also James Lindsay's family home, and where he had come after what was now being called the Battle of Glenshiel.

When he finally arrived, there was only the family factor Mr Cowie there to greet him. It was a Sunday, and as the factor was of the Catholic taste, he had nowhere else to be, the last chapel thereabouts having disappeared long ago. The other very few family retainers left at Kirkspindie had all been at the kirk.

James had come hobbling up the drive, leading Sophie because the wound she'd received – from the bullet that had taken her master's two fingers and the gouge out of his thigh – was still healing and that had made her too tight on her flank to ride for long.

'Oh, I see yer back, then,' was all Mr Cowie had to say to him.

James hadn't expected more. Kirkspindie had always been a cold, dislocated place, and with him now about to be the only Lindsay under its roof for the foreseeable future, it never occurred to him that would change. All he could look forward to was a household full of strangers – whom he'd lived with all his life.

There was a cook and a scullery maid; a farrier and a stable boy, and a gardener who saw to the orchard and vegetable plots. The cook was a short, fat, monosyllabic old woman – the only fat person for miles around – with a dark, saturnine nature and a collection of warts. The maid, on the other hand, was a scrawny, whipped and charmless little creature who seemed to spend her life endlessly trying to efface herself from the world. As for the gardener, James hardly ever remembered seeing him face to face. He was just a bent back, with a bent head haloed in manic tendrils of flyaway grey hair, always disappearing round a corner.

But then there was Gideon, the farrier.

One of the bevvy of platitudinous aunties who populated the fringes of James' early life had once assured him that 'a man who is capable of love, will always have something about him deserving of love.' It had stuck in his head as utter guff, until he considered Gideon.

Gideon had been his father's man, when his father fought with Marlborough's army, from the upper Danube to the low countries. And Gideon loved horses.

Gideon had always been there. Gideon, with the carrot hair and the gap-toothed grin. Gideon, who had sat the baby James on his first horse, before the little boy had learned to walk. When James thought about Gideon, it was always with a smile.

The summer passed. And James spent much of the time with his thoughts.

Then his brother Archibald arrived from Edinburgh, and his father's notary, Mr McKay, from Perth, to discuss the family's prospects.

Both had immediately gone into a huddle, hardly saying hello to James, or asking 'how d'you do?' Discussions had taken place – about the politics of the country now, then about the current law, as it viewed the Lindsays in the aftermath of their most recent treasons. Discussions to which James was not invited. Not that he cared, at first. He'd had a bellyful of the discussions and disputations of great men by then. It was only when the issue turned to James' own future that his attention was pricked.

Up until then, James had spent his days riding Sophie and then yarning with Gideon afterwards; or in his father's extensive library, where he had embarked on Suetonius' *History of the Twelve Caesars*.

There had been a lot of wonderment to be had at richness of the ancient world, but also a lot that was vainglorious. It had left him wondering – if James Francis Edward Stuart had really wanted to be King James III so much, why hadn't he been there that day in Glenshiel, where not a few of his future subjects had shed their blood for him, and even more had ruined their families' futures?

Indeed, his memories of the battle were never far away – the confusion of it and the disorienting sense of unleashed chaos. The seeming powerlessness of those in command to control it had chastened him, and the overwhelming impressions of pointlessness and waste had left him crying at times with frustration.

And it hadn't just been his own blood he'd seen that day. So not surprisingly, it had all felt like a rite of passage, and as if, as a result, he had become a man of parts. A person who should no longer be taken lightly.

And now, here was Archibald.

'It is time we turned to the matter of your education, James,' his eldest brother had pronounced one morning as James sat to his porridge. 'And to your future. You cannot languish here forever.'

James had not thought himself lacking in the matter of education. He had been able to read and write since he was five years old, the chance to learn being a gift his late mother had bequeathed him before her untimely death. For written into her estate had been a codicil setting aside money, ring-fenced from her husband's predatory dabbling, that would provide for a tutor to be hired and overseen by Mr McKay.

Mr McKay's choice had been an impecunious Huguenot scholar James knew as only as M'sieur Eugene, whose family had tried to remain in France even after the revocation of the Edict of Nantes had removed tolerance of their protestant religion, but who in the end had suffered one too many of Louis XIV's regular dragonnades and finally fled. The dragonnades being King Louis' exquisitely malicious policy of arbitrarily billeting unruly troops on protestant households as a way of persuading them to return to the Catholic faith, or leave France altogether.

M'sieur Eugene's flight had taken him as far as Montrose, and thence through Mr McKay's good offices, to Kirkspindie. James remembered a tall, spare, enigmatic character, a man of many parts, who never explained how he came by them. Or discussed his family, or what had happened to them, or indeed himself. So total was his reticence that no-one in the Lindsay family had ever questioned why those significant parts had not propelled him to far a greater status, on a more impressive stage, than a mere tutor to the third son of a minor aristocrat in an obscure corner of a not very significant European power.

But here he had remained; to all intents and purposes a happy man, seeing to James' letters; and thence to his Latin and French. And when he hadn't been busy in the schoolroom with the boy, he cultivated in him courtly manners, polished his rough, rural accent and developed in him a certain talent for dancing in the French fashion. And all of it, he made fun, instilling in the boy a love of reading, and through it the prospect of a whole, wide world beyond his own damp, dreich home.

'Use your brain, James,' M'sieur Eugene used to say him, tapping his head. 'Of all God's gifts it is the most divine. So don't be like …' and here M'sieur Eugene would range off on yet another disparaging allusion for the mass of mankind, each one more convoluted and hilarious than the one before, frequently reducing James, and then himself, to uncontrollable giggles in the middle of the most serious lessons.

However, as far as James was concerned, the best times with his unassuming tutor were the fencing lessons, where the young James displayed an early, and not to be sneered at dexterity with the épée.

Then, a little less than a year ago, M'sieur Eugene had departed without so much as a goodbye. As Archibald was in charge, only he would have known why, but Archibald said nothing.

Indeed, Archibald had sought to enlighten James about little in those days. Reasonable questions, such as how they'd managed to retain Kirkspindie house and immediate grounds if all else had been forfeit to the crown? Or where the monies came for its upkeep, or to put meat on the table?

James and Archibald. James, the late child – the 'mistake', if you like – and Archibald, the obligatory heir. They were not close. Archibald, still in his early twenties, invariably passed for a man much older, and his ubiquitous dark fustian suits didn't help. Archibald had been careful never to come out for the king over the water. Yet their father had come out, in no uncertain terms. He had been there for the '15

25

rising, or 'rebellion' as those damned Whigs called it, and had fought at Sheriffmuir before having to flee into exile with a price on his head, and King George's men all over his lands and policies with the king's bill of attainder in their hands, while Archibald had remained with his books at Edinburgh University.

But no schism had arisen between father and heir.

Archibald had been reading law at Edinburgh because he had to. First it had been the Act of Union, and all the taxes and tariffs that then encumbered a no-longer-separate Scotland. They left no wealth in the land for the gentry to live off, so that all young men of good family were forced to earn a living by means other than collecting rents.

Then there had been the reckoning for the '15.

And that was where Archibald's legal knowledge paid off.

He had picked for loopholes in the legal assault on their family estates and found a tract of land had been passed to him personally, through his mother. As the courts had decided in the wake of the '15 that Archibald had committed no treason, that bequest had been safe. And the rents from it had helped sustain what was left of the House of Branter and kept Kirkspindie Mearns.

And now Archibald was back here, to disrupt his life.

'Your father has instructed that you go to university,' continued Archibald, in his high tone. 'And I agree. You are too young to sit about this house, unsupervised.'

James had been ready to bridle, but the news he was to go to university, so suddenly sprung, just as suddenly gripped him in a fever of excitement. Until a thought occurred to him.

'How do you know what father instructs?' he asked.

Archibald looked at him as if he were stupid. 'We write, clandestinely. Do not interrupt. I have other matters to relate. And most important, and most sensitive they are too, so I require you to pay attention.'

Their father was returning to Kirkspindie. Something else sprung upon him, but he wasn't so sure that was quite as exciting.

The earl made his entrance a few days later. James did not step out to meet him. He'd taken to carrying whatever book he was reading to the far side of the orchards every day after breakfast, and hiding out there until dinner was called.

Also, while out on his perambles, the lad had systematically scouted all avenues of escape from the estate. He thought it only prudent given that his father, the earl, was a known fugitive, and in the event he was trailing a troop of pursuing king's dragoons in his wake, how would young James explain away his wounds? Glenshiel had not been so long ago.

It was while James was on one of those expeditions that Archibald had to send Gideon out to fetch him back.

'Does he look hunted, Gideon?' James beseeched the farrier for some hint as to what he might expect.

'Och no, maister. He's in fine feckle. Full o' it, like he always is. And demanding tae ken yer whereaboots, so pround o' ye he is.'

James suspected that last bit was a lie.

However, it was obvious that Archibald was eager for his presence, and not because he was proud. 'Sometimes I wonder whether you're not too old yet, tae merit a clip,' Archibald had hissed at young James, after Gideon had ushered him into the scullery, where Archibald was pacing. 'I'd ask where ye've been if I cared, all I know is you were no' where ye should've been!'

Upstairs, his father was in confab with McKay, the notary, and Mr Cowie. On reaching the head of the staircase, James recognised his father instantly, despite the passage of time. The earl, dressed in dowdy, country clothes and a scratch wig, still managed to outshine his more expensively, but soberly, attired men of business. He was a big, expansive man; a pumped out, greyer version of Archibald, occupying far more space and filling that space with far more noise than his heir ever would.

'Och, there ye are Archie!' he bellowed, as his eldest son preceded James across the room. Everything about his father, right down to the theatrical heartiness, was as young James remembered. 'Stop yer scuttling about and get to the table. McKay here has the Act of Indemnity papers, and Cowie's here tae be ma other witness when I sign.'

Archibald took his seat, revealing the presence of James behind him. Even then, his father did not bother to notice his youngest son. Instead, James was left in peace to watch this little bit of history unfold, as his father's pen scratched across a fine legal document, and the others solemnly added their signatures.

The Act of Indemnity, passed by both Houses of Parliament at Westminster two years previous, had granted full pardon to all who were prepared to re-swear allegiance to the House of Hanover, and thus spared from the scaffold many noblemen who had come out in the Stuart cause.

However, right then, young James had no idea what the document portended. Even so, he was mildly surprised that he was actually watching his father doing something, instead of just talking about it.

As McKay blotted the paper, the earl sat back clasping his hands over his stretched waistcoat. 'Now. A decanter of malmsey, d'ye think, gentlemen? Tae mark whit them in Westminster think's a surrender, when we ken it's mair a declaration o' warr!'

Only then did the earl deign to look over to where James stood.

'And that'll be you, eh. Wee Jaimie. Whit are ye daein' skulkin' aboot in the corners? Come intae the room laddie and let's get a look at ye. I heard ye left bit's o' yersel up in that glen. Show yer faither.'

James stepped forward and held up his hand.

'Ach, ye've still enough o' them left tae get yersel fankled in a lassie's drawers ... now where's that malmsey?' said the earl, banging the table for the scullery maid and his drink as if he'd never been away.

And that was it for James, after three years' separation from his only surviving parent. No embrace, no closer enquiry after his health, nor even a demand to hear recounted his heroic deeds on the day.

Much later, back in the scullery, Archibald had the maid fix James a glass of cordial. James was wondering what new deficiency had been detected in his conduct, and so was surprised to see his brother looking contrite.

'We have things we are going to expect from you James,' said Archibald, at last. When he used his full name, James knew his brother was about to address matters that went beyond mere filial niceties. 'Therefore, even though you are still little more than a child, you are deserving of an explanation. The king over the water has written to our father. In his own hand. There are plans in motion, in which King James expects our father to play a role. That is why he has ordered the earl to take up the offer of the Indemnity Act.'

Archibald, deep in thought, had taken to leaving long spaces between his words. James found it disconcerting.

'The country is riven with tittle-tattlers,' continued Archibald. 'The word abroad is that two sons of Branter were at Glenshiel. The government already has proofs that father was not at Glenshiel. So the earl is safe from any renewed Hanover vengeance. Everybody knows David was there. But he is already gone to Spain …'

'David is safe!' cried James. 'In Spain! He made it! Nobody told me.'

Archibald pursed his lips at the interruption, then furrowed his brow. 'Yes. I'm sorry. But I could not write and tell you, James. Letters are not safe. And as it is to be my case that I am not out, I should not know. And nor should you. Which brings me to my point. Father and I agree we want you to have no part in our great enterprise. So that if you are ever interrogated, we want it to be that you know nothing of our … commitment. And that must continue if the king's plan is to proceed.'

'If I am interrogated, dear brother, no interrogator is going to miss my wounds.' James held up his ruined left hand. 'He will want to know how I came by them.'

Archibald was becoming impatient. 'Have you been run through with a pike, Jaimie? Lost your leg to a cannonball? Two fingertips gone is all there is to be seen. People don't remember the unmemorable. They wounds might have stung like the devil when you got them, Jaimie, but they are not such as to create a stir abroad. "Have ye seen wee Jaimie Lindsay? Twa fingertips clean gone, man! It must've been some fierce battle!" If it is a man being telt, he'll already be contemplating the pie he's havin' for dinner, and if he is of a witty disposition, hoping the fingers won't be in it. And if a wummin, she'll already be lookin' at that

29

dress in the shop opposite. So will you wheesht now Jaimie and let me finish! Going to university at Glasgow will get you out the way, not because of some trifling scratches, but because I have to create a myth, and your presence might leave it open to doubt. You are likely to hear things, even as far as Glasgow. Feign total ignorance if you do. You have always looked a dizzy cheel, it will not be over difficult.'

James ignored the jibe; he was used to them. 'What things?' he asked.

'Two Branters at Glenshiel. I must let the rumour spread that the other one was me. And then dash it. It is risky but by far the easiest way to deflect attention from you. People's minds do not dwell on confusion if there is a plausible alternative. They will know that David was there, and they will be led to assume that the other was me. Then, once the notion has traction, I will be at pains to deny it. Aided by my alibis … my appearances before the bench, in the university library, at kirk. Two versions of the same tale … only one can be true. But as everyone knows, all tittle-tattler tales are prone to inflation in the re-telling. Was it two brothers? Or just one? Maybe the first witness had had a dunt from a redcoat grenadier and was seeing double …'

'All that trouble to go to, for me?'

Archibald lifted a finger for hush. 'You are my brother. Also, you are young. If they come to you, you might not know what you might give away to a professional questioner. But mostly, the cause needs you clean. For who knows when a grown James Lindsay's services might be needed?'

That was why monies had been found to pay for a place at Glasgow. And why Mr McKay had been in communication with the university senate.

James listened, all too aware that nobody in the family had ever discussed with him the cause, or inquired if he wished pledge his loyalty to it – and all too aware of the presumption of his brother in this matter, that he would.

So, he had rallied to the standard at Glenshiel – but it would have been nice to be asked if he could continue to be counted on. He wasn't saying it to himself at the time, but it would prove to be another seed of resentment.

Archibald did not deign to notice the expression on James' face as he continued. 'You are young yet to matriculate, but Mr McKay assured the senate despite your tender years you are competent enough in Latin to comprehend the lectures – all the teaching is in that language. Anyway, that and the heavy clink of a full purse was enough to secure the university's complaisance. I have arranged rooms not far from the High Street. You leave at the end of the week.'

His remaining days at Kirkspindie saw him wander its full extent, drinking in the only place he'd ever known as home. Apart from his recent cross-country march to war, which he now looked upon more as some holiday adventure, this trip to Glasgow would be the first time he'd ever really left.

And over everything hung the presence of his father. James was still too young to have the necessary vocabulary for his own description of the man, but he could easily recall apposite passages from M'sieur Eugene's teaching. 'Full of sound and fury, signifying nothing …' was one that fitted the bill, he remembered, penned by that English play-wright in his Scottish play.

For the earl was indeed a bellicose ranter, with a predilection for procrastination. And if he had been constant in his character, even unto that, his might have been a life lived free of turmoil. But he was not constant. There was a cycle to his behaviour that every now and then saw the procrastination torn asunder by sudden bursts of intense activity, nearly always ill-judged and invariably misguided.

Even at his tender age, James did not like to think what that cycle might portend for the cause of the king over the water.

2

Pushed to Flight

'I know not what intrigue they are up to now,' James said, running his fingers through a tousle of hair, 'but I'm damned but they've implicated me in it. I'm sure of it. And I'm a dither what to do, dear Davy. And that's why I'm here in the town, pinning your ear.'

James Lindsay and his friend David Hume sat huddled in the snug of a tavern in one of the many stinking wynds off the Royal Mile. Outside was a labyrinth of twelve-storey high tenement canyons, smeared in rain-runnelled soot; the night sky a merely a darker tier, high above in the permanent shadow into which the drizzle seemed to cling more than fall, like over-saturated air. And below, all manner of human waste puddled the ground in the tiny courtyards and narrow closes between.

The tavern, however, was a lit haven of warmth. The homely heat from a fire in an open grate, and the cosy fug in the air from a surfeit of candles that complemented the smoke from over a dozen pipes of quietly puffing customers in its tap room. Round a corner, in the snug, it was more intimate, with just our two sat together over a pint of claret – not their first.

'It sounds ominous the way ye tell it, James,' Hume was saying, as he stuffed his own pipe. 'But it could just as weel be yer imagination. Yer no' beyond a flight o' fancy, yersel, ye know.'

'It was Master Hutcheson himself who told me,' said James. 'A man in dapper coat, and handsome top boots, asking, "This fellow Lindsay on your student register? Is he a man of parts? With many friends coming from here and there to confer with him? Is he often seen in huddles?" And of course Master Hutcheson told me himself, his reply. "Are ye daft, my man? James Lindsay is not but a boy. Parts? Hoots, toots! The only *parts* he can afford must come out of his aunties' allowances, and that's no' grand, sir, I assure ye! Why are ye asking?" And with that, Master Top Boots was gone, next to be heard of inquiring of me in another quarter. I don't like it, Davy. I know my family and I don't like it.'

'You suspect Top Boots to be a government man?' asked Davy Hume.

'What other shadow could he have stepped from? Someone's whispered something and he is gathering information. I said it before and I say it again, I know my family and I don't like it. I smell blood in the air.'

Two young men, still in their teens. Students, not wealthy to look at, but adorned with the various devices of dress that announced their learned status. In the normal course they might never have met, but David Hume, an Edinburgh man, had paid a visit to Glasgow early in his student days, out of curiosity, to hear one Francis Hutcheson lecture there. Hutcheson, who had been gaining notoriety for his new dissenting philosophies, happened to be tutor to a young student from the north by the name of James Lindsay, of whom no-one had ever heard. Being the youngest students in the lecture hall to hear Hutcheson on that fateful day, the two young lads had gravitated together, and found there was much upon which they agreed – the principal being the examination of how to be virtuous in a world of political disorder and moral decay.

But that was not their topic for tonight, it was not why James Lindsay had parted with scarce pennies to spend thirteen hours on a bumping, malodorous coach to travel here to Edinburgh. The lad was worried. Master Top Boots hadn't been the first to seek him out. There had been that damn priest.

Religion had been a settled matter in the Lindsay house for all of James' life – but it had not always been so. The earl had been baptised a Catholic, but had renounced his faith during the religious warfare of the last century. Apparently, for a time, there'd been tumult, but his father's decision to embrace the covenant had accorded with the people who called him laird; so, growing up, there had been no disgruntlement abroad for James to sense.

That was not to say he grew up unaware of the influence of the Catholic church, or its priesthood. Priests would from time to time turn up, as if by chance, at Kirkspindie, seeking audiences with the earl.

'They don't like it if ye jump the dyke, Jaimie lad,' Gideon had explained after one such visitation. 'He's here to call yer faither back to the king's true religion.'

'But the true king doesn't mind which a man calls his true religion,' observed a nit-pickety thirteen-year-old James. 'He's said so.'

And what had Gideon to say about that? 'Aye. And whit kings say and whit they do, Jaimie,' delivered with one of his grins and one of his winks.

But what James had pointed out was true. Unlike his father, James II, who had thrown away his throne in religion's name, James Francis Edward Stuart was showing himself to be more flexible. While not exactly renouncing his Catholicism, the son, whom they now called the pretender, had indeed sworn that after his restoration every man would have freedom of worship. Yet the schism between Rome and protestant still would not heal, neither in the pretender's court abroad, nor in this realm he wished to reclaim.

Most of it went over the head of young James Lindsay; all such theological warfare seemed to him so much noise. But when that priest had accosted him in Glasgow, a mere few weeks ago, outside the university's High Street gate, it had been more than matters of theology at stake.

At first, James thought the priest had been carrying some message from his father. But no. Once James had stopped to listen, he heard the man accuse him of being at Glenshiel.

'He said everybody knew,' said James. 'That I was out for King James … trying to hide it, yes. But everybody knew. But how did they know, Davy? When there is nothing to know!'

'What else did he say? What did he want?'

'Oh, some rambling nonsense about the importance of my father returning to the true faith *before* the coming restoration, so he could help force the new King James to renounce all previous commitments and establish the Catholic church once again on his sovereign soil. And some other nonsense about how it was time for me to confess the sins I must have committed on that day at Glenshiel, but for which I would surely be forgiven by a grateful God. I told him, "The only sin I've committed, man, is listening to fools like you and worse … and for that it's not God I need to seek forgiveness from, it is myself!" And I pushed him away and fled. If people know, then people have talked. It is the government come after me, Davy, for something I know not what. What must I do?'

James looked across his jug of claret at the gaunt countenance of his friend, the mischief-twinkly eyes, and the mangey appearance of his scholar's wig.

'The thing is,' said James, at length, calm again, 'if, as I know they must be, my family are again embroiled in another plot against the House of Hanover, am I to come out with them? Where does my own heart lie? Indeed, where should it? And what wisdom or judgement should dictate the answer? And what desserts might await me, either way? That is why I am here, friend Davy, to lay it all before you, whether to follow the old ways, or my own star … and to hear you pronounce.'

From the set of Davy Hume's face, all angles and planes in the dancing candlelight, James knew a discourse was coming on. But then, that was what he had come for.

'We stand at the dawn of a new age,' said Davy, puffing ruminatively on his pipe for effect. James wasn't going to be disappointed. 'An age of reason and enlightenment. The discoveries of science and the study of the natural world are showing us that creation and our place in it, is far wider, more profound and more magnificent than mere canonical dogma can ever contain. But we're still at the beginning … we might have thrown off that yoke … but where has it got us so far, James? Into the jungle of Hobbes' *Leviathan* …'

Thomas Hobbes was the bête noir of their revered tutor, Francis Hutcheson. Hobbes, whose philosophical treatise written at the time of the last century's English war cast a dark shadow. Both James and Davy Hume knew all about Hobbes and his *Leviathan*; how he'd argued that man, in his state of nature, was a selfish, brutish creature, a degenerate concerned only in satisfying his base appetites. That he had survived so far only through the constraints of religion – so if you threw that off, then only the tyranny of a totalitarian state could save you from the jungle; from a perpetual, 'war of all, against all'. They also both knew that Hutcheson believed man deserved a significantly better destiny, and was working to define it and encouraging his students to follow suit.

'So when it comes to what path you choose, I suppose you have to ask yourself, James,' continued Davy, 'which is the nobler pursuit? That of learning, and the ascent of man? Or, who gets to plant his arse on a throne in London?'

'I agree, of course I agree,' said James. 'When you put it like that … great issues are in play.'

As older men, they would scoff at this debate, but now they were both young, still in their teens, so everything was a 'great issue', and they saw themselves centre stage in it.

'But I cannot deny my daily anger at all this oppressive Whiggery,' continued James, 'and the preposterous figure this King George cuts upon the world. Sometimes I just want to feel the heft of a sabre in my hand again …'

Davy smiled to himself. It amused him to notice how his friend James was not above romanticising his deeds on that day at Glenshiel.

'And you are oppressed, how?' Davy interrupted again. 'Dragged from your bed each night and beaten? Your purse confiscated by any passing redcoat who takes the notion? Where is the tyranny here? I'll tell you. It is in the general poverty of folk, and the chaos that blights all our lives. Not because of whose arse is on the throne, but brought about by something more fundamental. By man's failure to see things as they really are. Man survives. We know that. The very fact that we have history tells us. But if we are to prosper, if we are to find our way to our God-given potential, it is the duty of men like us to enquire ever more deeply into the soul of man … to name and label and so bring to heel all the forces that drive us. It is nothing less than a new moral firmament that we seek … to define a new polity and guide the hands that will write its laws. A process, I think you'll find, James, that you and I are already embarked upon.'

James was nodding, sagaciously – weighing these great profundities, as young men do – when there was a commotion, and raised voices from the tap room. A grubby, unshaven face appeared round the corner of the snug.

'Is on'y o' ye a scholarly weesitor fae the Glasgow?' it asked.

'Aye, and who is it askin'?' said Davy, suddenly alert.

The face ignored the question. 'Cuz there's a pairty o' militia stompin' aboot the wynds, askin' fer sic, sayin' he's a spy and recruiter fer the king o'er the watter … and they're fair set oan carryin' him aff tae the toll-booth … where nae doubt there'll be a noose waitin' fer 'im lang syne.'

'On yer feet, James!' cried Davy, grasping his friend's arm. From his pocket, he produced a handful of coins, and pressing them into the unshaven man's hand, he said softly, 'Tell the militia, aye ye did, and say you saw him heading up the Royal Mile for Borthwick's Close.'

Davy bundled James out into the wynd, and pushed him the other way, heading through back courts for Fleshmarket Close, and the steps down to the Nor' Loch.

'How could they ha' known?' hissed James as he stepped out smartly. They neither of them ran, not wishing to draw attention.

'Man, ye came on the bluidy coach!' Davy hissed back. 'Its arrival is practically an event for every cut-purse in the town, and an extra penny for the first one to tell the militia who was on it. Anyway, you have your answer. Your family is demonstrably involved in another

37

intrigue, and like to get you hung whether you want to come out with them or not.'

They reached the bottom of the steps, where the reek of the loch was strong.

'I leave you here, James,' said Davy, turning his friend to him; their faces just pale smudges to each other against the dark loom of stone that vaulted upwards on either side of them, up into the drizzle.

'You're not leaving me, surely!' cried James. 'I only have what I stand up in … a purse with little more than dross in it and not even a short sword to defend myself. And where am I here? I could be in Timbuctoo, for all I know!'

'Your way lies across the bog, and once over it, down the hill to Leith, even in the dark, it'll not take you much more than a brace of hours at a stiff pace,' said Davy, ignoring his friend's fright, and scrabbling in his pocket to produce a notebook and pencil. 'I'd not fain join you on the scaffold, my friend,' added Davy as he scribbled, 'and anyways, it's your safe passage from danger I'm off to arrange. Now when you get to Leith, head to the docks then turn left and take the Newhaven road, you will see a house at this address … it's a door where I am known … by the mistress of the place.'

'The place? What place?'

'It is an … establishment, James. Where it is … friendly to young men. Now shut up and listen. You will need more money, and some kind of passport.'

'Passport? What do you mean a passport, why do I need a pa …?'

'Will ye no' shut up! With muskets and bayonets on yer tail, I fear your options to linger in this country are done. And if you are to take ship abroad, then you'll need a letter, something notarised, signed by a person of substance, identifying you to foreign officialdom … in other words, a passport. It is a necessary document in this age, for travel. Or even better, a letter of introduction to some grand person in the country to where you are bound. Of course! One who will then speak for you. I will be thinking …'

'Dear God!' breathed James. 'That a fellow's life can turn in a blink! Well, let's be at it, man! What are my instructions?'

'They're starting to drain this sink in front of us, at last, so the path across it is safe enough, but tread carefully man, and don't stray off the path by even one step, or you're like tae never be seen again. Smell it. The run-offs from tanneries and slaughterhouses and aw the chamber pots o' every hoose … it's been the cess hole for the old town for 300 years, and ye don't want to know what unspeakable abominations must now lurk in its depths, and I mean depths. So go canny. Right?'

'Right!'

'And when ye get to Mistress Cantly's place, say you are a friend to Mr Hume of the university and give her this note. I will see you tomorrow. Now, speed … but no' too much, 'til ye get to the other side o' the loch!'

And with that, Davy vanished into the night.

The darkness was not complete; candles in windows, lanterns above taverns or under the arched entrances to closes leaked light upwards and were weakly reflected off the mist that clung to all these slime-soaked tenement bluffs. James stepped out onto the path across the loch, and found it not quite as dry under foot as Davy had said. He began picking his way across, and had barely gone a dozen yards when he encountered a crone coming the other way, a basket on her back filled with kindling. She gurned something unintelligible at him as she elbowed past him, forcing him to step off the path, and instantly his right foot sank to his shin in filth. He turned to remonstrate, but his voice died in his throat. A light, waving from out the gloom at the foot of the tenement walls was moving towards the path end. Voices.

He finally managed to free his foot from the suction, but his shoe remained in the mire.

'Hell! Damn and blast!' he muttered to himself, at a loss. He dropped to his knees – nothing else for it – and plunged his arm into the collapsing hole where his foot had come from. The cloying, stinking wet made his gorge rise as he groped for his shoe; no walk to Leith could follow, unless he freed it.

Voices again, and this time the crone's was added to the babble. He looked back, and in the wash of the lantern waving behind him, he could dimly see three figures. Two were obviously militia, the red of their coats could just be made out, but it was the barrels of their slung muskets, jutting above their shoulders, that said all that was needed. That, and the crone pointing back down the path to where he crouched.

One of the militia separated, and James could just make out his back tearing up the Fleshmarket steps, obviously going for assistance. And then the lantern began to advance on him. He felt his fingers squelch sickeningly in the ooze, groping for … and then they closed round the metal of a buckle, and he wrenched. The shoe, full of filth, shot free. James could have wept for his fine stockings, worn specially for his trip to Edinburgh. The right one at least must end in the fire after this.

'You there, on the path!' The voice came out of the night. 'I command ye tae halt where ye are, in the name o' the watch!' A tired, angry, uncouth voice, in no mood for putting up with any trouble. If the militia man could have seen beyond the spill of his lantern, would have beheld a figure crouching like a wild animal, head jerking here, there, looking for escape. And not finding any.

The militia man unshouldered his musket. 'Ah'll shoot ye deid, if ye dinnae show yersel'!'

James jumped to his feet, turned and ran. He heard the man growl, 'baistert!' and then the pounding of a heavy man's feet as he took after him, yelling his lungs out. 'Ah've fun' 'im! Ah've fun' 'im! He's here! He's here!'

James ran on in blind instinct, headlong into darkness, hoping his gut would plant each footfall on solid-ish path and not the ooze on either side. He didn't dare to look back.

And then there was a brief flash seen out a corner of an eye, and a loud explosion; the militia man had fired his musket. James had no idea where the ball went, it certainly came nowhere near him. The militia man renewed his pursuit, his lantern's light jolting wildly and spilling all over the place. 'Ah'll huv' this bayonet in yer tripes, ya baistert!'

And suddenly one of James' feet hit ground that was more sodden tussock than beaten earth. He jerked, almost over-balancing. And stopped. There was no path ahead. He stooped, peered, and saw that it was not a dead end, but a dog-leg. At first it wasn't clear … and then the lantern's spill bouncing closer, cast a shadow on the path's kink. He took off again, sharply to his left, following the veering ribbon of beaten earth that the light had revealed, and as he did, the militia man got good sight of him, and veered to left too, running hard to take advantage of the angle now opening to cut him off, as if he was following the hypotenuse of the triangle the pursuit was now describing on the ground – except it wasn't ground that the militia man ran into, but ooze and filth.

A splash. A scream. James juddered to a halt and turned.

A gothic shadow-play presented itself, of endless shades of dark, and tiny splashes of dancing light. A mere few yards behind him, the militia man was sprawled in the mire, his lantern held but inches above the filth, its light dancing on its surface crust – his musket arm flung back as if in pointless hope there might be a hook on the end of his bayonet to drag himself back with – and his body, the entire bottom half gone under, and the upper part, wallowing in the ooze. Most of the red of his coat showed clear in the lantern light, but a slice of it, from waist to armpit, was black as he rolled to and fro like a walrus trying to emerge from a viscous sea.

Beyond the man, however, was a more alarming sight. A row of jingling lanterns. His fellows coming on fast.

'Help, man, fer pity's sake!' screamed the militia man. 'Ah'm goan' doon, man! Ah'm goan' under! Ah kin feel ma'sel' sinkin'!'

James could now see clearly in the waving lantern light, the man's bloated, surly, ill-natured face, skin etched across bone in sheer terror.

A premonition of what it would be like to drown in this pit crept across James' skin.

Shouts. Yells. From down the path. James stepped back and grasped the barrel of the militia man's musket.

'Lord bless ye! Lord bless ye!' the man began repeating, like it was an incantation. James pulled on the barrel, and felt the man's iron grip

41

on the other end. But the militia man's body barely moved a foot, and when James relaxed slightly for another heave, the ooze sucked it back.

'Oh Jesus! Oh Jesus!'

They both could hear the banging feet of the militia party clearly, and James could see the lights in file now, coming at him. There were yells. 'Haud 'im there, Shuggie! Haud 'im fast!'

The militia man's eyes bulged white in his head as he sensed James waver.

'It'll go easy oan ye' if ye save me!' hissed the man, trying to sound friendly through his choking panic. 'Ye'll see. They'll be pattin' yer back and giein' ye a dram, man. Jesus, the fucken sheriff hissel' 'll kiss ye!'

But even as the man beseeched, they both knew it was a lie.

If James let go of the musket, this man would die. If he didn't, then James would die. Not right now, not tonight. But the arrest warrant these militia must be carrying could only be for a capital charge, and in these times, that could only end on a gibbet.

The militia man guessed James' decision, even before he had made it himself.

The scream tore the night. James forced himself not to look into the man's eyes as he let go of the musket barrel. Then he turned and fled.

It was long past midday when Davy Hume found James, sitting propped on a pile of fresh hay in the small stables behind Mistress Cantly's establishment. Her one horse, a slight chestnut filly that served to pull her trap, was standing over him protectively as he fed her an apple.

'James,' said Davy, 'the mistress said she thought you'd be safer out here … but you don't seem too distressed by such plain surroundings, not with your lady horse for company.'

James looked up and said, 'What news of the militia man?'

'Here,' said Davy, handing James his shoes, all shiny as new, Mistress Cantly having assured James in the early hours that she'd have them polished for him. A fearsome woman at first encounter; all brusque and business-like and entirely without curiosity. But then she'd mellowed, and she'd been as good as her word about the shoes.

'As fer yer militia man. They're callin' it murder, James,' said Davy. He'd been on the point of asking what the hell had happened, but the look on James' face silenced him. He wasn't looking at the lad he'd left last night, but at a man's face; composed, still and eerily resolute.

A moment passed as the two friends regarded each other with maybe a fleeting thought as to the future nature of that friendship, now that one of them had so obviously changed. Then Davy said, 'I have a purse for you … it's no' much but it'll see your passage to the low countries. A Dutch buss sails for the Texel on the evening tide. Her skipper has agreed tae take ye as long as ye promise no' tae spend the voyage complaining. I'm givin' tae understand her accommodations are no' saloubrious. And here, take this letter. There was no passport tae be had, but this is a note fay my professor tae his correspondent at the University of Leiden … Professor Pfuffenkipper … a learned Rhenish gentleman who writes and lectures on aw' matters ethical … asking him to speak for you, and see ye on yer way. It should suffice to pacify any over nosey official. But tell me James, how are ye in yourself? You certainly look like you've been pondering on the gravity of this pass you've come to.'

'That I have,' said James. And then he gave Davy a taut, confident smile, and said no more on the matter, changing the subject entirely.

'My horse, Sophie,' he said. 'She's stabled at Glasgow. Here is the place,' and he handed Davy a card with a note scribbled on the back. 'Give this to the farrier and she is yours. Look after her, man, don't let her end at the knackers, for she's a lovely lass.'

Davy also had a small valise for him, with a change of linen and stockings, and a short sword they called a hanger. The stockings James immediately swapped for the coarse ones Mistress Cantly had loaned him last night, his other ones soiled by the Nor' Loch beyond saving.

It was dark down on the quay, where James took farewell of his friend, the same perpetual har roiling off the water, and the drizzle swaddling them as they shared a final embrace. Davy felt the force of James' last handshake and of the spare, heartfelt words James spoke to him in

43

thanks for everything he had done. 'We'll meet again, James,' he said in reply. 'I've a feeling God isn't finished with either of us.'

'Amen to that, my friend,' said James, and then he stepped aboard the charmless, fat-beamed trader that was to carry him to exile.

3

A Foreign Land

On the morning of James' fourth day at sea, he woke, body aching from the falling damps, and he took his first look over the *Hilde*'s gunnel. There had been no cabin for him aboard, and so, like the crew, he had spent his nights curled on the bare deck. What he saw to his right was a long, low, solid patina of light beginning to coalesce out of the dark, like a firm line between sea and sky, and dead ahead, a forest of trees, which in defiance of all logic, seemed to be growing directly out of the brightening sea. Alarmed, James looked up at the man on the tiller; the sailor remained impassive. But then in the course of this voyage, all of Captain Dros' crew had proved phlegmatic to a fault.

With the light came a nautical bustle, from which James had learned to absent himself – usually by perching on one of the hatch covers and remaining there, out of the way. It was turning into a bright day, but with a high, thin cloud through which no blue shone. When James looked around again, he was this time presented with a flat, featureless coast, and dead ahead, the forest had transformed itself. What he had taken to be trees, were masts, and he was gazing upon a crowded and busy anchorage, the likes of which he'd never seen before; a huge expanse of shipping, nearly all of them large sea-going merchant vessels, three-masted leviathans capable of taking on all the voyages of the world and a sea-going anthill of barges plying between them.

'The Rede van Texel,' said Captain Dros, nodding at the ships. Then he nodded at the land, and merely said, 'Texel.'

They hadn't been a very communicative crew, the *Hilde*'s, but then neither had they been unfriendly, sharing their food and the occasional dram of a clear spirit James never caught the name of, but that they assured him would, 'Tegen de kou,' which he gathered was something like, 'keep out the cold'.

His first sea voyage had passed with few incidents of contrary winds, and no serious bad weather. They had made good time – or that was what he thought the captain had tried to tell him earlier. Yet throughout the passage, there had been a feeling of apprehension that had never left him. What else were you supposed to feel, on discovering yourself to being a mere speck on a featureless landscape of water, bounded only by a flat horizon that never changed and confronted by your essential, utter nakedness before the elements and nature? It was an experience he was sure was in some way salutary. Complementary even, to his reflections on the events that had so recently overtaken him, and the decisions he had made.

A small town appeared, and as they drew closer, its port revealed itself, and a daisy chain of fishing boats emptying from between its breakwaters and heading to sea. Then the crew were furling the sails, and setting two huge sweeps to row the *Hilde* the final few yards into the harbour, and suddenly the voyage was over. Lines had been thrown ashore and secured, plank run onto a wooden quay and Captain Dros was nodding to him and saying something in his unintelligible Dutch tongue, and James, carrying all he owned in his valise, was ashore in a foreign land for the first time in his life.

He quickly learned the name of the small town was Oudeschild, and that there was nothing for him here. Whatever he asked for, everybody pointed to what appeared to be farm track, smiling and repeating, 'Den Burg'. He quickly gathered they were telling him that everything he needed would be found there.

Throughout these exchanges he was acutely aware of the letter in his pocket, and wondered how he could explain to any yokel of an official what it said, surmising that any official here was unlikely to read Latin, in which the letter was written, or understand him, as he spoke only English, French or Latin. But no official accosted him, so he set off up the track to Den Burg.

Flat, verdant grazing. Sheep on both sides as he walked, retracing his thoughts like he was conjugating a Latin verb in order to fix it in his head.

When he ran from the drowning militia man in Nor' Loch, he'd been repeating endlessly to himself, 'My God! My God!' and telling himself he had just caused a man's death. He had not meant to, never intended it – but had he not just done murder? Then, after being consigned to the stable's straw behind that Leith brothel, he had taken breath. Logic had formed part of his education. Facts. To be reviewed. And only then, decisions reached. So he had reviewed. And what had he learned? About the man who'd been pursuing him, intent on capturing him, ultimately to put a noose around his neck? A man who'd said he was going to plant his bayonet, 'in his tripes'?

That man had died because he cut a corner on a path that was narrow, knowing what lay on either side.

He, James Lindsay, hadn't killed him; the militia man's own choices and his own stupidity had.

It was only James' own horror at the manner of the death that awaited that wretched creature, a death that James had tried to prevent, that made him want to assume responsibility for it. Not because he'd inflicted it, but because he'd run.

'I refuse to accept the guilt,' he'd said out loud to the horse in the stable that night, instinctively knowing that if he did not shuck off that burden, there and then, it would dog him for the rest of his life. And the horse, in her silence, had seemed to agree with him.

He was not to know it then, but that rigour set in him a way of thinking that would last the rest of his days.

He'd fallen back on the straw after that, almost as if he was exhausted after the mental effort. Regrouping for the other changed circumstances in his life he must address. He knew it was going to be a long night, so what better way to use the time than to take stock?

The first thing he had had to face down was the dread nausea he'd felt at his own impotence in the face of all the forces out there, beyond his ken, marching. Lying in the straw, with only the horse as his confidante, he'd forced himself to review what he actually knew.

He lived in a troubled time. It didn't matter whether he was innocent of the crime the militia was pursuing him for; the family name of Lindsay was obviously wrapped up in another conspiracy of sedition against the existing Crown, and him having the Lindsay name would put him on the scaffold regardless. But even if he didn't hang, if he escaped, the whole sorry situation had still robbed him of his future as a scholar.

That such injustice could exist in his own country had filled him with rage. It seemed so personal, that some stupid German parvenu could indiscriminately steal his life so casually, without even knowing him – just because his German arse occupied a throne in London, a place where James had never even been, or wanted to go.

But the rage, and the ragged trains of thought running away with his head, were futile and nothing more than distractions. If he was going to survive, he was going to do it by dealing only in the logic of the now. Facts. Only facts. And the dealing with them.

One horse he could ride out of this calamity was to pledge himself wholly to the king over the water. Accept the direction of this runaway, and just go with it. He would not be the first to cast away all impediment and follow his king.

Except his king seemed never to be there; only sending courtiers and generals to do his bidding – and James had witnessed their performance in his cause at Glenshiel. He'd marched to that battle-that-never-was as a young man, full of faith, and had been rewarded by a vision of how things truly stood, saw it all with his own eyes.

However, he held one memory from that time; of the Irish officers in the service of the King of Spain. Proud, honourable men, yet exiles like he was about to become – denied their home by stupid old men, just as he had been. No cause left to follow, no country but their own path through life, just the integrity each one of them seemed to embody – of a decision made, and the determination to follow it by their sword alone.

Confronted that night by a dread future, it hadn't seemed such a bad choice for a young man to make, to follow those young Irishmen into the service of the King of Spain. He'd certainly never have to fear the drudge of domesticity, paying tradesmen's bills, the prospect of work, like his oldest brother. Instead, he'd be following his other sibling, David, to the life of a soldier. David, who was already in Madrid. Yes. *That* was where he would go, after Leiden. To Madrid, to a life in the service of the King of Spain.

Den Burg, when he got there, hit him with a dislocation he had not expected. From the solitude of the road, suddenly he was among a throng of people. A market spilled out across the town's narrow streets, the likes of which he'd never seen before. He'd been to a city, yes; more than one. Hugger-mugger, hovel-upon-hovel, crushed, stinking, narrow like Edinburgh or even Glasgow, that great spill of a place, sprawling its grandeur and commerce. But neither was like this tiny town. Toy houses, each one immaculate, bright with paint, clean, nudged together like genteel ladies at a dance, their finery on display, not in lace, but as wooden lattice and filigree. And the folk – all much taller, slimmer, in cleaner, finer clothes. The men's hats, like pill boxes with little skips at the front, or in the style of England in the previous age, as worn by Godly men, and the women's pointed bonnets with their strange, fly-away coifs. And the wooden shoes … but most especially, the cleanliness. Everything was so clean.

He must have walked like a retarded fellow for some distance, slack-jawed, stunned by the crowds' incomprehensible tongue. People were beginning to give him looks.

And then he was in what must be the centre. He was dimly aware also of the quality and profusion of what was on sale; earthenware and farm implements and fine cloth and other manufactured goods. For a moment, he wondered about the *Hilde*'s cargo, which he had not even glimpsed. What could Scotland have produced that would be wanted here? But mostly his thoughts were consumed by a smothering unease that left him feeling like a latter-day biblical pilgrim, stumbled upon some new Babel.

This new land, with nothing the same to what he knew, no familiar thing to cling to. He forced himself to be calm and think, but the shock of all the unfamiliarity unsteadied him. Randomly, his need for a horse suddenly seemed of paramount importance. He needed a mount if he was to get to Leiden. And tack for it, too. He knew the quality he needed, but what was the just price of it in a place like this?

The babble told him he had no hope of haggling here. And then, an idea struck him. He checked down every side alley until he saw the sign; 'Apotheker'. Apothecary, as good as dammit. Here was a chemist, and surely an educated man? If he didn't have English, or even French, then surely Latin?

He had Latin.

A friendly old man, neat in his fine-woven cloth, with an apron of rougher material. He welcomed the young Scots scholar to Texel and guessed he was on his way to one of the big universities in the south. Such young men as he came this way from time to time, he said. All thought it good such exchanges of learning could occur.

The chemist's willingness to help, the general wealth of his attire and the finesse of his manners made James acutely aware of his own threadbare state. He felt suddenly ill-bred in the chemist's company, even though he was conversing fluently with him in the language of the ancients. It took an effort of will to recover himself, and pay attention to the advice offered. And when he did, he had the impression the old chemist sensed his feeling of dislocation, and was being patient with him. That was reassuring, and slightly humiliating at the same time.

'Non emere equus hic,' he said to James. Don't buy a horse here. Adding, it wasn't that Texel did not have good horse flesh, but that he would have to transport the beast across the water to Den Helder. Then

50

he said, that as it was – and he lost the Latin at that point – 'Achttien? Achttien mijls.' It was the distance from Den Helder to Leiden.

'Mijls?' said James.

'Mijls. In English … leagues. A league, ja?'

A ride of eighteen leagues, they finally agreed, was a long way.

So, don't buy a horse at Den Helder either, he was told. A ride of eighteen leagues would knacker it! Laughter. There was a system run by stables, the chemist continued, he should use that instead. You hired your horse and tack, and rode it to the next stables along your route. Then you left the horse there, and hired a new one, until you got to where you wanted, and the stablers were left to swap and move their horses back and forward. Short rides, lots of rests in between. Everybody, and every horse, happy. James agreed it was the wisest course. And then he marvelled at the order and basic honesty of a society where such a commercial arrangement might actually be viable.

Then the chemist asked him, did he have a passport? Because folk, foreign folk that is, using the system, were often checked by the stables' owners and customs officials. Foreign folk often meant smugglers, who'd secrete huge bundles in bushes along the roads, and then load the poor unsuspecting nag where the stabler couldn't see. Officials took a dim view of unexcised goods passing illegally in and out of their towns, and the stablers, of unscrupulous riders who handed back spavined nags.

James laughed and said he had no heavy contraband, just what he carried, and then he produced his letter of introduction to Professor Pfuffenkipper, and the chemist was duly impressed. That would do nicely, he assured James.

It was only as James was walking south from the town, heading for the ferry, taking time to drink in the gentle countryside, that he understood the oppressive feelings that had been dogging him. It was the poverty and squalor of the land he had come from; that he had grown up in. He had never thought on it overmuch, because he had known nothing else. But this place of plenty and contentment had laid it bare for him. That such a land as this could exist. The counterpoint shone a light

51

on the narrowness of his own life until now; the general frayed grubbiness of his native society hung on him like a shame. However, each step he was taking was pulling him further away from it. He'd found something wanting, and he was acting to change it, now, as he always swore he would. It stood to reason, that was how you became the man you wanted to be. And that took all the sting out of the thought that he might never see his native country again.

4

Paris: An Apprenticeship in Calculation

Picture a cavern of opulence, the likes of which James Lindsay has never seen. A high ceiling, cornices and sculpted architraves, columns, shot-silk walls, mirrors, drapes, a cacophony of colour, and people, dozens of them, milling in a cloying fug of *parfum.* The chatter all but drowns out a quintet of musicians so that from the strings, only the low notes survive as rhythmic scraping, and the piano just manages a sonorous toll.

James Lindsay is here to be shown off by Mr Dillon, the Paris envoy of James Francis Edward Stuart, as the latest 'hero romantique' of usurped King James III's struggle to regain his throne. M'sieur Lindsay is tall, pale, young, with a luxuriant mane of dark, autumn-red hair that flows to his shoulders like a cavalier of the previous age – no need for a powdered wig here – and his muted, soldierly attire stands out amidst all the lace and fripperies of every other man present. M'sieur Lindsay even has wounds on display; a rather vulgar mutilation to his left hand, but fascinating, nonetheless.

James does not really want to be here, but the man who pays his bills, a fellow exiled Scot called Mr Crawford, has told James he has to attend these salons, especially if 'that man Dillon' asks him.

'It is the only way you are going to be recognised in Paris, and thus gain some suitable employ,' Mr Crawford has advised James – some weeks ago, not long after ensconcing him in spartan lodgings close to his own offices on the less than salubrious Rue de Quincampoix. 'Because,' Mr Crawford assured him, 'I am buggered if I am going to continue subsidising you any longer than I have to, out of my master's dwindling purse, in this city of extravagance.'

Dillon and James sip punch, or rather, James sips. Dillon is more enthusiastic, being far more familiar with how such events unfold.

This is the Paris of the new King Louis XV, newly past his majority at the age of thirteen, and his bottom barely warm on the throne. In the corridors of power however, the levers remain in the hands of the regent, the Duc de Orléans. As far as the aristocracy is concerned, it is still an age of indulgence and the pursuit of any new thing. The fate of the Stuart claim to the throne of Great Britain, and France's attitude to it, is of little concern at this new court. Not so for Mr Dillon. He works for the pretender's chief of staff, and his job is to keep France thinking about the pretender's claim, and to reverse the froideur of recent years.

France, originally a staunch supporter, has been persuaded to cease military aid to the Stuarts by the prospect of better relations with the existing incumbents on the British throne. They have banished the Stuart court in exile from France. So Mr Dillion is now alone in Paris, and having to work hard for his stipend. And he thinks that throwing another tragic Scots émigré onto the scales of aristocratic opinion – especially a good looking one like James, who can actually speak French – won't do the cause any harm.

'So you've memorised the list of everybody you've to talk to?' Dillon is whispering in James' ear in his sing-song Irish brogue; not all Jacobites are Scots, far from it. The powder from Dillon's wig makes James want to sneeze. 'We need to get round as many as possible before the gaming begins. Remember. On no account are you to sit down to cards. There is no money for a stake, and even less than no money for you to lose.'

James has, in recent weeks, come to see that Dillon has been handed an impossible task here in Paris, with very little financial support from the Stuart court, now in Rome, and thwarted at every turn by incessant spying and active interference by the Whigs in London. Still, Mr Dillon remains diligent in the pursuit of his mission. Yet James finds he cannot like him. A blinkered, dogged little man, with a wig too big for his head and who looks like an imposter in borrowed finery. Always doing the same thing; and every time expecting a different, better outcome.

Which is why James isn't listening – he is looking at the women instead. While it is true he hasn't warmed to being paraded for the cause, in a role at which he knows he is a charlatan, the presence of women at these salons has been the ultimate compensation.

James, the boy who grew up not knowing his mother, with no close female relatives, has never encountered creatures like them. James' only previous exposure to womankind on a grand scale has been the buttoned-up city societies of Glasgow and Edinburgh. On entering salons here for the first time, he stood speechless as an idiot farm boy before the sea of décolletage, the vast expanses of naked alabaster skin, the cascades of perfumed curls and the delighted trills of laughter.

These days, however, he has mastered all the juices that rise, and although this is by far the most fashionable, and ostentatious salon Dillon has brought him to, he finds he can control his deep, deep fascination sufficiently so as not too appear too gauche. He is concentrating on a small clique of women, a little older than he, who are noticing him also, and whispering behind fans.

Suddenly, at his elbow, he is aware of a shorter figure – a gaunt, pinch-featured, pale man in expensive silk brocade and fashionable stock. The face is framed in a full wig which, with the thin lips and their sardonic little side up-ticks, gives the impression of a nipping, sniping creature.

'You are recently come from the low countries, I understand,' says the man. 'I envy you. The Dutch have such a free and enlightened society. Every time I come to Paris, which every man must love, I find I long to be back there.'

James looks down on the man, startled by his presumption. 'Certainly, I liked it fine. The Dutch were very kind to me when I needed friends,' says James, who feels Dillon tugging at his sleeve on his other side. He is aware that Dillon is trying to get him away from the man, which fills him with a sudden contrariness. 'What, pray, took you to Holland?' he asks the pinched little man, simply to prolong the conversation, a move that feels likely to cost him a torn cuff from Dillon.

'I was once secretary to the French ambassador at the Hague,' replies the man, 'although I have had to return there on several occasions since officially leaving the post. The consequence of the regent's literary criticism, I fear.'

'You are a man of letters, sir? I, latterly, was a scholar also, of ethics and moral philosophy. Should I know your name, sir?'

'Yes,' says the man, with a knowing twinkle. 'You should.'

'Oh,' is all James can manage. A pause. 'Then I regret my ignorance.'

'See if you can guess. For my first play, a great critical success, the regent imprisoned me, and when I sought to publish my recent poem, I found the door of every publisher in France closed against me. That was when I last had to return to that haven of tolerance, the Hague, to find one who would bring out my work. But pah! I suppose Le Duc and I are reconciled now, as he has permitted the Comédie-Française to re-stage that first play later in the year. At least it will mean another purse of livres to help soak up the blood of previous wounds.'

'You are M'sieur Voltaire!' exclaims James, realising now, and bowing, despite one arm being dragged backwards by Dillon. James is genuinely impressed to meet this great man. The reputation of his dramatic satire, *Œdipe*, has crossed the Channel, along with the author into brief exile. James tells him, 'I have your poem, *La Henriade*, on my table. Your sallies in it against the political state of France and the twin evils of religious fanaticism and civil discord are as subtle as they are profound.'

M. Voltaire visibly preens. 'Such discernment,' he says. 'Tell me of your scholarly credentials.'

'I studied under Francis Hutcheson at the University of Glasgow,' says James, intending to explain further.

'M'sieur Hutcheson! I have heard of this gentleman. He maintains that man, even without prior knowledge of God, yet he has a knowledge of good and evil. So there is more to you, M'sieur Lindsay, than the emissary of your throneless king there would have us believe!' And he nods at Dillon. 'We were all here agog to hear of your epic tales of battle, but now I discover you have far more interesting thoughts to share. A scholar indeed. We must discuss further, but I fear the floor is being commandeered for dancing.'

And so it is. An assignation with Voltaire is promised and then James is off, freeing himself from Dillon, across the floor to where the covey of beauties have not ceased to be interested in James' presence. 'God bless you M'sieur Eugene,' he is saying to himself, remembering his childhood tutor, 'for every twirl you taught me!'

And then when he is among them, he is telling himself that such women exist is only the second-best thing to have ever happened in his life; and that the best is being able to dance with them.

Dillon, who has been left standing, fuming at James for allowing himself to be seen dallying with such controversial figure as that roué Voltaire, watches his protégé prance elegantly round the room with a succession of willing partners. It upsets Dillon because the boy is patently not job hunting – the reason he is here – but he is at least not causing trouble. Dillon idly follows the elaborate parade of dancers as they go bobbing round the room, his attention straying only to chase up crystal goblets of punch for himself, to his own steady rhythm.

It is then that he notices another pair of eyes on our young hero. The Comtesse de Boufflers. A regular of the salon circuit. The comtesse is a known collector of prize horseflesh – and other prize flesh, too. Possibilities suggest themselves to Dillon, but as they are jostling for position in his now alcohol-fuddled brain, events take on a momentum of their own.

He watches as the comtesse approaches another aristo grande dame, the Marquise de Veregennes, all rouged and caked coiffure, and a known socialite predator of infamous spleen. There are whispers.

The dance stops and partners step apart, and James, whose elegance on the floor has been admired, hands his lady her hand back with a bow. The exchanged moment is shattered by a bellow.

57

'Vous! Fantassin Écossais!'

It is the Marquise de Veregennes. It is obvious she is addressing M'sieur Lindsay. 'You! Scottish foot soldier!' she has sneered. It is an insult, calling an officer a common soldier.

Silence.

'I do not know you,' she says with imperious grandeur. 'But I hear reports that you entered this place exclaiming, "Ah-ha!" as if it were some Moorish souq. What do you mean by such remarks?'

Everybody knows – for they have seen it before – that la marquise is obviously setting herself up to humiliate the young man. They wait, breath held, to savour what mockery must follow.

James bows to her, and says in his best, courtly French, 'Ma'am, I have been misheard and reported falsely. I did not say, "Ah-ha!".' A deliberate pause. 'I said "Ho-ho!".'

And the room ripples with laughter. His riposte is nothing but a piece of ill-thought nonsense, but delivered with aplomb – and it has parried the old harridan's opening stroke. The space she sought to plunge her daggers has vanished like smoke in the general hilarity.

From aside, the Comtesse de Boufflers is regarding James through the crowd, with a greater interest.

Later, after tables have been set for cards and candles, brought in by the gross, have been lit, James is observing a game of piquet between two ageing, extravagantly accoutred men of substance. It is being played for very high stakes, notes piling up on the table. They have attracted a substantial number of the guests, and James is dimly aware that side wagers are in play among the crowd.

'You do not play yourself?' It is the voice of a tall woman at James' shoulder. He sees that in her heels, she is not far short of his height, but he perceives little else. James is still of an age where he cannot accurately guess the years of older women. All he knows is he can see the crinkle of laughter lines around her eyes; showing the otherwise smooth face is without the customary caking of powder. He thinks she has the most kissable mouth, especially the way she is letting the hint of a pout play on it. He does not know that the suggestion of rouge on her lips is subtle and deliberate. The confection of her wig covers the colour of her hair, but he notices her eyebrows are finely trimmed and chestnut. Her eyes, however, are too candid for a youth to measure what experience, what knowledge, lies behind them. Suffice to say though, he can't take his off them, and so he does not notice the jewels, all the riches that adorn her.

'The purse of an exile does not extend to the tables, ma'am,' says an ever-gallant James. He enjoys the attention of these beauties, even though he is yet too much the naïf to comprehend the calculations involved.

'Yet you have other attributes, I have noticed,' she says. 'The chief of which is that you do not mangle our beautiful language in the way most of your fellow countrymen do. Or at least, the ones I have met.'

'No ma'am. I had a good teacher.'

'Another attribute! La! The ability to learn. How uncommon in one so young.' She pauses, as if to regard him better. 'You dance admirably. I am sure there is not a lady in the room who has not noticed. However, having heard you, I say nothing to your wit, sir. And nor should you.'

James' eyes widen at her impertinence, but before he can recover himself, she says, 'You have, however … timing. And that is a gift. Tell me, do you love horses?'

'I could ride before I could walk, ma'am,' says James, wondering where this is going, but not really caring anymore. Curious, he adds, 'And often I have found a horse has offered me my truest friendship.'

She considers him a moment longer, then says, 'I am the Comtesse de Boufflers, Chevalier Lindsay,' arbitrarily bestowing on him the title of knight, and extending the crook of her arm for him to take. 'Come with me. There is much I would like to discuss with you, young man.'

James' life changed completely that night, and Mr Dillon's worst fears for the young man's future were rendered naught at a stroke. For a start, before the sun would set again, the Earl of Branter's youngest son found he had a new and infinitely more grand roof over his head and a heavy purse in his pocket. A path to fortune and pleasure was opened up to him that far outstripped even his wildest fantasies.

He took to his new life with a seamless grace.

Among the trappings of society that rested so easy upon him, had been the eventual granting of a commission in the royal army. And on the fateful day, he had been busy at his duties.

On that day, the sun had risen and passed across the firmament as it had done on all the days that had gone before, without a hint of the changes that were about to unfold.

James accepted his gloves from his servant, Bouvet, and gave his bright red uniform coat a final brisk flick before mounting his fidgety horse. The filly looked equally resplendent in her own red uniform of saddle cloth, blanket roll and tail ribbon.

James was in the uniform of a cornet of horse, in the King of France's Chevau-Légers de la Garde – the Guards' light cavalry, in other words. His red coat and breeches, like the horse's saddle cloth, were edged and seamed in gold lace, and his coat sported broad, black velvet cuffs and buttons of solid silver. He wore black cavalry boots and a tricorne hat, the latter trimmed with white lace and feathers, and – appropriately, he thought, given his ancestry – the white cockade of the Jacobite cause as well as of the French royal household.

Another Monday morning, and another drill with his entire company of horse across the Palace of Versailles' vast cavalry parade ground. This was no official review, only the company's colonel was watching. It was an exercise in maintaining standards, and the colonel had already cantered over to the far side of the ground for a better view. As cornet, it was James' honour to carry the squadron's royal standard. Bouvet handed the device up to him, fixing the end of the pole in the horse's stirrup pouch. Without a word exchanged, James turned his horse and cantered out on to the ground, where the company's 200-odd officers and men were shuffling themselves into military order. It was a splendid sight on a bright, sunny morning, with just enough breeze to make the company's white silk colours flutter, and the gold and silver embroidery sparkle.

The Chevau-Légers de la Garde only recruited young men of good family and comfortable means. That the Earl of Branter's youngest son was of good stock went without saying. As for his means here in France … the Comtesse de Boufflers had looked after all of that for some time now.

James had come a long way from that impromptu flight across the Nor' Loch and voyage aboard the *Hilde* to Holland. He had been lucky; any reasonable man would agree. Because how easily it could have gone the other way and ended on a gibbet. Gratitude should have been the appropriate response, as any reasonable man would also have agreed. But James Lindsay, now a little older, couldn't help but wonder whether there might have been *other*, other ways. Ways that, if he'd taken them, wouldn't have left him feeling like a pretty songbird in a cage, twittering for his supper.

Today he was on a royal parade ground, exercising with soldiers from another country's army. His company's mounted kettledrummers beat the time, and the bugle calls pierced the morning air with military urgency as the immaculate lines of mounted red soldiery wheeled and cantered, presenting sabres in one single flash of steel, and sheathing them again before peeling off into lesser units, and joining again, with balletic precision, to the beat of hooves and the cascade of tinkling bridles.

He couldn't help but wonder how else he might have spent this day if things had transpired differently.

It drove his thoughts back to the time he'd spent with Professor Pfuffenkipper in Leiden. That old man in his tasselled smoking cap, puffing away beside his huge black metal range, pulling at the crepe skin of his sunken cheeks as they discussed Hobbes and Spinoza and the nature of knowledge, and of course, Hutcheson. Pfuffenkipper had wanted to know *everything* about Hutcheson.

'You could stay, you know, young man,' he'd once said to James. 'You have a fine mind. Pursue your studies here, at one of the finest seats of learning in the world.'

'I have not the money, sir,' James had been forced to reply. 'Nor any means of getting it.'

When what he'd meant was that he was intent on joining his brother in Madrid; on donning one of those distinguished white uniforms he remembered so well from Glenshiel, and becoming like those dashing Irishmen. The Wild Geese, they called themselves. He liked that.

'Nonsense, young man,' the old scholar had pressed him. 'Where is your Scotch enterprise I'm sick of hearing about? The lectures are public. A little teaching, a little scrivening, the guilders will soon pile up to keep body and soul together while you learn. Enough anyway, to have your work reviewed, and to sit for examination.'

But James had kept on heading south – although it hadn't taken long for events to force his first re-evaluation of that decision. Three nights in a cell in the citadel in Lille had done that. Pfuffenkipper's letters of introduction to leading figures in Paris had been in Latin, a language the lumpen officer of the city's watch not only could not read and did not recognise, even though he was a Catholic. He was convinced it was Hapsburg code and that James was a spy. Matters hadn't been helped when it turned out James' French was also useless, since the idiot only spoke the local Picardy patois, which James found gibberish. He was only released after a local curate, dispatched to hear his confession, confirmed that James' letters were legitimate. The entire episode rammed home to the young man how parlous his situation was in these foreign lands. That, and how difficult it was to rid oneself of infestations contracted in gaols.

The drills always ended in a mock charge. It never failed to exhilarate; the bugle sound to canter eclipsing the sudden *shush!* of steel as 200 sabres were drawn from their scabbards; the kettledrummers wheeling away from the line; him, the cornet of the colours, reining back to let main body move past, dropping back to the second line and then the sound of the charge itself. The sense of being in the belly of this great thundering mass of horses and men; the pounding hooves, the reverberating earth and the peal of the bugle notes, the imagining oneself in battle.

Everything was there, except the sound of shot, the heady reek of powder and the cries of the wounded. He could remember those too, from Glenshiel.

And through the trees, to remind him where he was, sat the palace where Louis XV lived. Louis XV whom he never saw, despite being one of his majesty's guards.

It had surprised him at first, how many of his countrymen had preceded him into the French army – the most elite company of the Garde du Corps, the king's personal bodyguard, was named 'the Scottish Company', after all. It had been founded, he was assured, in 1440 – but was nearly entirely made up of French noblemen, these days. The Scots now tended to congregate in the lesser regiments. It had only been the comtesse's money and influence that had got James into the ranks of the Chevau-Légers de la Garde.

James was under no illusions that he fitted in.

His fellow officers were all cut from the same cloth. Wealthy younger sons in need of a profession to keep them out of mischief, although mischief they often found. They had practically no daily responsibilities to the troopers they commanded, nor did they seem to take any interest in their mounts. It appeared that NCOs attended to all the daily grind of discipline, and servants saw to the horses. Presenting themselves in a requisite state of elegance, whenever summoned, seemed all the duty required of these officers. For the remainder of their time they hunted, or frittered away hours at gaming-tables, or whored and drank.

James discovered he had a head for the drinking, but everything else held little interest.

'You must behave as a rich man! I insist upon it,' the comtesse often admonished him, throwing him another purse. 'D'you wish people to mutter behind their fans that I am consorting with a pauper, and a foreign one at that?'

So he played whist, and was moderately successful, finding it natural to count cards and hold the tallies in his head. However, his fellow officers were under no illusion as to where his stakes came from. Everybody knew of the comtesse, and her penchant for young stallions. Nearly all were jealous because of her beauty, but no acerbic asides, not even veiled asides, ever came James' way regarding his 'kept' status, or indeed on any other aspect of his background. Not after they had seen him at sabre practise. Watching him pass and thrust had made had it plain; provoke a slap of the glove from this young interloper and you could well end up skewered.

James might have had brothers, but in reality he had grown up alone, and like all only children, he had yet to develop any understanding of the effect he had on other people. But even he could not miss the general froideur with which he was treated in the Chevau-Légers. Which was why, after such exercises he seldom joined his fellow officers for their afternoon revelries, but usually saw to his horse's brushing down and feeding, before he rode her back into the city and to the comtesse's own enclave in Saint Germain.

On this day, as usual, he was lost in a reverie as he rode. His filly, another Sophie, practically knew the route herself.

Ségolène Raffarin was the true name of the Comtesse de Boufflers, his employer. She had first 'hired' him as the keeper of her stud after that fateful meeting in the salon. How appropriate, her society of friends had all thought, but never said, because she was too significant a force in her society to offend. Her husband, the Comte de Boufflers, dead some years ago of a calenture, had been fabulously wealthy. And now, so was she.

Ségolène, oh Ségolène, how had it all started? For her it began as a transaction, pure and simple. For James, the naïf? He hadn't known any better than to follow where she led.

And then, as it always did, his reverie drifted back over all the events that had brought him here.

Mr Crawford and Mr Dillon, his first, and so far still his only true friends in Paris, had certainly been pleased with how things had panned out.

Crawford especially, would never forget the evening his maid had announced there was a countryman of his at the door, seeking an audience, and handing him a note from the almoner at the Paris Faculty of Theology. 'One for you, I think, mon ami,' it had read.

'Show him in.' Crawford would always remember saying those fateful words. And then, there before him had stood a tall, rather unkempt looking lad, his long red hair in need of a wash, yet still managing to comport himself with dignity. Not rushing to blurt out his predicaments – for predicaments there must be, otherwise why would he be here, clutching such a note from a dispenser of church charity.

'I am James Lindsay, the third son of the Earl of Branter,' he'd said, once seated with a restorative brandy before him, 'and I am in Paris seeking a passport or other safe conduct that will carry me to my brother in the service of the King of Spain at Madrid.'

So, he wasn't there to deliberately sponge. Yet every word of his declaration spelled trouble.

'Mr Lindsay,' Crawford replied, 'it is with some regret I have to tell you that in coming here, you have stepped into a briar patch … a perfect tangled web of interests and prejudices, where what, on the face of matters, might seem simple, is not.'

For a start, the fact that James was asking for a passport from the French authorities meant he must be travelling without one, and coming from Scotland that could mean only one thing as far as they were concerned. Here was another Jacobite fugitive.

'My Lord Stair, the English ambassador, and an exceedingly irritating and ingratiating rogue catalogues every one of your kind who arrives here, or even merely passes through, and reports them to London,' Mr Crawford had assured him. 'France's current policy is for good relations with the English. Need I say more? Also, dear Lord preserve us! A safe conduct to Spain? You obviously do not know that very little time has elapsed since the King of Spain conspired, unsuccessfully, to murder Orleans, before Louis' majority and while he was still regent, in order to replace said Duke with himself … and that since then there has been a war. For you to be found in possession of any document with the word "Spain" in it, would see you immediately consigned to the Bastille!'

And even then, the depth of James' predicament had yet to be fully plumbed.

Because of the pretender's ostensible commitment to the Catholic cause, there were many in France still well-disposed towards his followers, which was why the almoner had sent James Lindsay to Crawford and not the Paris gendarmerie.

But Crawford had then gone on to assure young James that he should not take any great comfort from that, because he had little to offer him by way of assistance.

'My master is John Law of Edinburgh, a banking gentleman of some international repute,' Crawford told James. 'And I am his man of affairs in this city, where he retains considerable interests, yet can no longer safely reside.'

James had recalled the name, and some rumour of scandal.

Crawford had been good enough to elaborate. 'I know not whether it was common knowledge in the cloisters of the University of Glasgow, but the previous incumbent of the throne of France had all but bankrupted this country, even before the war that ended with the Treaty of Utrecht back in the year thirteen. Which was why Mr Law, already an established banker here, had proposed certain financial innovations to restore the nation's fortunes. They worked. Only too well. He created a boom, which greed soon transformed into bust. And Mr Law's name has suffered in consequence. So you see, I am no position to beg favours here. I merely stand guard over his personal monies that are not transportable ... and to help Mr Dillon, who is the representative of our rightful king, James, to disburse certain pensions to those of the king's followers still here who have fallen on hard times. These are not large sums however, I assure you. But there will be sufficient crumbs from them to keep your body and soul together until we find some way to secure you better prospects. So, Master Lindsay, while the path ahead will not be easy for you, do not wholly despair. There are friends at hand, who will at least do what is possible.'

If his aim was to get out of the country safely, be it to Spain, or, as Mr Dillon later suggested, to join the king's court at Rome, then an ally of greater influence must be found. For, Crawford assured him, 'It will not be long before my Lord Stair will mark your presence, if he hasn't already … then you will be watched, and all hope of a quick, safe, clandestine passage out of the country will be gone.'

And then, Ségolène had swept him from the shadows, and into the safety of plain sight.

She heard his horse's hooves on the cobbles of her courtyard, and the day's irritations immediately set in. He wouldn't just dismount, and come immediately to see her; he never did. What was difficult about just handing that dizzy filly of his over to a groom like everybody else did? No. He had to go and stable her himself, strip off the tack, do the brush down, whisper to it and stick an apple in its stupid mouth. Sophie, he called it. Honestly! Why would you give a girl's name to a horse? Why couldn't he call the damn thing something sensible, like 'Lightning' or 'Prancer' or 'Turnip'?

The comtesse was in her morning room with friends, sipping sherbets, chattering. She rationed these audiences to the other ladies of her set to keep them sweet. The little gatherings also had the other twin advantages of reminding her regularly of her own superiority, and serving as a low level intelligence trawl on all the doings going around her. To have James Lindsay come barging in on them, demanding her attention, would have sent just the right message, and provoked just the right twinges of jealousy.

But no; he couldn't even play the rough soldier when she wanted him to. She knew he'd be off to have a bath instead.

And he couldn't even do *that* like a gentleman, having a servant undress him while scullery maids boiled the water and carried it up to the tub in his rooms. No. He'd be down there in the sculleries; wandering in, saying hello, heaving the full jugs onto the range because they were, 'too heavy for slips of lassies like you!' Talking to the servants like they were people. She'd tried explaining, but it was like talking to a gatepost.

But the real fury was with herself; that she was even thinking these thoughts; that she allowed such clutter to enter her head. That she even cared.

James indeed carried up the water for his own bath. He would have got one of the ostlers, but they were busy. And he undressed himself; having some poker-faced, powdered-up dandy of a footman making free of his person was not something he would tolerate. He'd made that plain to Ségolène from the start.

He sank into the piping hot water, and he thought of all his nights on the hard ground to extract the maximum pleasure. He'd done that every time he'd got into a bath since his escape from Glenshiel. Now he had a more extensive repertoire to compare; the hard lying on the deck of the *Hilde*, the nights in that cell in Lille. And he reflected on how much was to be said for soft living – the good and the bad. Heady aromas might have assisted in the emphasising the contrast, but he drew the line at scented essences in his bath water. Just one more of the little things he had found it hard to adapt to in life as a gentleman here in Paris.

Take the servants, for example. He had grown up in a clan tradition. The true clans were all but gone now, the extended families where the chief was a father in the literal sense. Now, a chief merely presided over the folk who lived upon his land and paid him rents. But the notion continued. And a chief was still supposed to serve his folk as well as rule them, supposed to regard his people as a responsibility, not a chattel. Where James had come from that meant there was natural society between you and your folk. Unlike here, in this place of entitlement and licence.

He knew it made Ségolène angry, his talking to the servants, but it wasn't rebellion on James' part. It was that he didn't know how *not* to.

At first, it hadn't mattered to him. At first, there had been the utter, all-consuming immediacy of intimacy with a woman. He still smiled when he remembered Ségolène's exquisite squeal of delight when she realised she was to be the first to pluck him.

And there he was, back thinking about Ségolène again.

Having been denied the closeness of women since the death of his mother, whom he really did not remember in any concrete way, the idea of femaleness had absorbed and fascinated young James Lindsay since he could remember. But there had been nothing to fix his curiosity upon. The aunties were too far away, and there were no cousins of a similar age close at hand to play with. And certainly no beauties, when he'd reached an age to appreciate them, in the world where he lived. The only women he 'knew' were creatures from literature. The covey of ageing, sexless and physically remote aunts, and the females among their pudding-faced progeny, really hadn't counted.

Then he had moved to Glasgow, where the lowland ladies were very pretty and plentiful. But a wall of strict Presbyterian restraint surrounded them, precluding even the merest hint of social intercourse. The move did, however, reveal to him what an unprepossessing breed Highland women-folk had been. And then he arrived in Paris, where everything turned out to be *permis*. And no comparison made any sense.

Paris, where he had encountered Ségolène, Comtesse de Boufflers, a true beauty, and where he had found his way to the depth of her charms. The headiness of it all would have been enough to un-man the stoutest heart. For, as he was coming to realise, he *was* being un-manned, by every aspect of his current circumstance, so that every time he thought on it, it sucked the joy out of him.

'I have been betrayed by love!' he would exclaim aloud to himself, from time to time, when the weight of his own inexperience became too heavy. He was a young man, and keen to dramatise his own romantic tragedy. And of course, being the age he was, and entangled in all that luxury and emotion and sex, he had not the faintest idea what to do. All he knew was that he wasn't turning out to be the man he'd always wanted to be, and he didn't like it.

As for Ségolène, she'd started off being charmed by the way he looked at her, drank her in; this young man, so nakedly besotted. She was no stranger to that – but she was to the total lack of selfishness in him. My goodness, he'd been a lover without art or subtlety, but time went by and she discovered she wasn't becoming bored as usual. Instead, she found herself basking in his attention, mesmerised by the sheer, unalloyed joy it seemed to give him attending to her considerable needs.

It had started off being amusing to her, the way he never seemed to tire, and then it became something different, when she realised this young man was taking his time getting to know *her*. How unfair for the boy she'd always dreamed of meeting when she was a girl, to come along, now, after marriage and the older, bloated, richer Comte de Boufflers. After she'd learned so much about the world. How thoughtless he was, to come dragging with him his youth and pureness of spirit and that something ineffable she'd always yearned for, but was now too jaded, too corrupt, to fall completely into its embrace.

These days, when he looked at her in that way she loved, all she knew was that somewhere, out there, there was a young woman he did not know yet, nor she him, who one day would get it all, instead of her. Unless, of course, she destroyed him first.

There was no salon that night. The sniping started early. It followed a familiar routine; his lack of conduct dissected; his lack of social ambition disdained. And she was damned if she was going to let him go swanning off again to the Café Procope to spend another evening drinking coffee and consorting with that disreputable little scribbler, Voltaire. She even told him he was getting fat. Which, needless to say, was not true.

'Promise me sir, you will never swim in the sea,' she'd said, 'lest you emerge from the waves with harpoons protruding. Thrust there in error by some misguided whaler confused by your commodious girth!'

There was to be a salon the following night. 'You will have to wear a corset, if one can be found that will encompass you,' she said. And then a detailed itinerary of the conduct expected of him followed.

In nature, in human engineering, so in human society, there are structures. When they fail, they seldom give any warning, so one might prepare oneself for the catastrophe about to unfold. Façades might be maintained, but behind them weakening forces will have long been at work, chipping, eroding, exhausting … until everything holding it all together is down to but a thread, a filament.

And so it was with James and his comtesse that night. No special reason, no outrageous excess, just a tiredness in his restraint. He decided, this time, he would reply. Something he seldom did.

'Madame, sometimes I fear you presume too much.' That was all he said, and not even loudly or with menace.

'Presume, sir?' she whipped back, steel in *her* voice. 'And why should I not? I pay for you!'

Crawford and Dillon were in deep confab, in a booth at the back of Procope's, one of Saint Germain's more popular coffee shops. Crawford looked up and saw James Lindsay come barging through the door, like a man on a mission. The young man briefly scanned the crowded room, spotted them and came immediately to their table, sitting down without waiting to be invited. He was in uniform, and Crawford couldn't help but notice the young man was toting a sabretache attached to his sword belt. The 'tache looked unusually stuffed for a mere night's carousing.

'I have a service to request, Mr Crawford and Mr Dillon,' said James, without preamble. 'One that you may find stretches the understanding of our friendship.'

'And good evening to you, young James,' said Dillon, archly.

James' fingers drummed on the table. 'I make such a sweeping state-ment, sirs, as my request transgresses into the realms of criminality. So you will know I do not make it lightly, but only because it is of the utmost urgency and concerns my entire future, my life. I must leave the country, gentlemen. Now. Tonight.'

'Good grief, laddie! Why? And to where?' exclaimed Crawford. Dillon, however, was staring at James with a queer intensity.

James flung out his chest. 'I must join the king, at Rome!'

'Well, that is all of a sudden,' said Dillon, not looking at James, but quizzically at Crawford. 'Has the good Lord sent you a vision?'

71

Crawford helped James to a cup of steaming coffee, and gestured for him to drink. And as James did, his chest collapsed and he let out a sigh as deep as a death rattle. When finally he raised his bowed head, he said, 'The Comtesse de Boufflers. I cannot stay another moment. She ...'

Dillon, with a paternal smile, reached out and patted the back of James' hand. 'We are all men of the world here, Jaimie lad. You need not explain another word. There is, I take it, no hope of any ... reconciliation?' When he saw the look on James' face, he stopped. 'No, obviously not.'

James collected himself, 'It has long been my wish to one day resume my journey to join my brother at Madrid, as you know. And that was where I intended to strike out for this very night ... until I remembered what you told me, Mr Crawford, when you were dishing my chances of ever securing the necessary passports. You also said, should the comtesse wish to hinder me ... she had the powerful friends to do so. Well, let us say my parting from her was not amicable. I have only the briefest of head starts on her fury, so I'm sure you will agree it is only sensible for me to believe she is already moving to thwart my plans. She will suspect Spain, but I fear it is not only on the road to Spain that will be looked for ... it will be at the ports to the west, and the border with the low countries too ... obvious alternative routes to my final destination. But she has never heard a word from me of loyalty or support for James Stuart. And that is the sort of thing she will remember. So if I strike east, I have a chance. It will not occur to her that I might head for Rome, and King James' court in exile. Even though it is the only destination in that direction where I am likely to receive a welcome.'

Crawford and Dillon weren't looking at James as he made his declaration; they were studying each other, as if silently coming to a decision. 'Well, Mr Crawford, "many things prove to me that the gods take part in the affairs of man", eh? What do you think?' said Dillon.

'Herodotus,' said James, head hung, despondent. 'Why should you wish to quote Herodotus? Is this really a time to show off your erudition, Mr Dillon, or are you just practising on me?'

'You are right to think you will be detained,' said Dillon, brushing aside James' question and talking to him with a great intensity. 'I have told you all about King Louis' fervent wish not to antagonise the wee German lairdie any more than he has to. Especially when it comes to harbouring fugitive Jacobites. But you, living under de Boufflers' roof, have been granted many indulgences, not least the right to remain in France ... not to mention the commission in his own guards. Without the comtesse's protection however, my Lord Stair will feel free to report to London another renegado. So of course, you are right. You would be detained. Which means you must indeed get out of the country, and sooner rather than later.'

'I have not come without ideas on this,' said James, reaching into his sabretache and producing several sheets of writing vellum, each one carrying the regimental seal of the Chevau-Légers de la Garde. 'It is here, where the criminality I referred to comes into play, gentlemen. Mr Dillon, in your capacity as an ambassador, you will know the form of writing, and Mr Crawford, as a man of business, you will have the hand of a scrivener. I am proposing we forge a laissez-passer ... a deed I know will place us all in peril, but could well be the only thing that might save me.'

Crawford and Dillon grinned at each other. 'You are a canny lad, Mr Lindsay,' said Crawford.

'We must repair immediately to my rooms,' said Dillon. 'There is much to be done before they shut the city's eastern gate. And you Mr Lindsay. We have some news to impart on the way that, with the blessing, will result in it being *you* who will be doing *us* the favour tonight. *Us*, and your king.'

James was used to the press of people in Paris these days, but it still vaguely discomfited him how thronged the streets could still be even this late in the evening. He was picking his way through the eastern district of Faubourg Saint-Antoine. It was a rough, labourers' slum where the tenements sat hugger-mugger, the streets were narrower and the stench even greater than the crush of the Rue de Quincampoix, where he'd had his first lodgings. He sought the eastern gate on the King Louis XIII wall, or 'le mur des fossés jaunes', as it was known locally. The wall was more of a ditch and glacis topped with a stone revetment, than the imposing bastion its name suggested, and the gate was a mere toll booth for collecting taxes from merchants trading in the city. Trade done, the booth shut at night, usually about 10 o' clock, but if whoever was guarding it got bored, or too drunk to remain at his post, it closed earlier. The dark and shadow of the narrow cobbled streets that led to the gate – the only light was that spilling from shop fronts – and the press of people, meant there was no point in trying to hurry.

'The gate will be guarded, although God knows who takes responsibility for it there,' Dillon had briefed him. 'It might be some local gendarme or a night watch made up of hired louts. Try and get there before they close it, and if you have to wave the letter under their noses, try not to hand it over. The chances are they won't be able to read anyway, so the seal should do the business.'

Up ahead, in the spill of burning torches on the city wall, he could see the men guarding the gate were indeed preparing to close it; shooing people out of the way, shoving a tumbrel loaded with cheap furniture trying to get out before the stout wooden doors swung to. The men all wore the grey-white coats and black tricornes of French army infantry of the line, in other words, proper soldiers. And the one wielding the halberd to press back the crush, James recognised must be their sergeant.

He nudged his horse through the mob, calling, 'You there! Sergeant! Hold the gate. An officer coming through!'

The sergeant stepped into James' path holding up the halberd to stop him. 'State your business at this hour, sir!'

This was not supposed to happen.

'State my business to you, sergeant?' said James, summoning all the hauteur he could muster, but did not feel. 'Do officers often have to obey sergeants in your regiment?'

74

'Your excellency, it is a random l'attention de passage. It is my colonel's orders to check. I cannot disobey my colonel,' said the sergeant stiffly, but with all the rectitude and respect James expected of an old stager. He would not be able to bluff or bluster this man.

Nor would he be able to escape him, if the sergeant were to discover *all* the paperwork he had about his person.

Back at Dillon's rooms, the ambassador had drafted two laissez-passer on James' stolen vellum, and another letter of introduction, this one to King James' man at Vienna.

'This first laissez-passer will take you as far as the frontier fortress at Metz,' Dillon had said. 'It says you carry officers' personal dispatches between garrisons. Nothing official to attract attention, but it will get you an official change of horse. It is over sixty leagues to Metz, and you must travel fast. Faster than any other rider who might be carrying your details. Also, travelling within France, your bona fides will not be challenged too closely. I have smudged a wax seal to the letterhead, so that it will look official, but carelessly stamped.'

The other laissez-passer was to carry him as far as Austria. Relations between Vienna and Paris were currently good, Dillon had told him. James was lucky. The two countries were normally at war. Peace meant his journey through the German states between here and the Habsburg empire should be straightforward. Crossing the French border, however, could prove more problematic.

'You are not an official royal messenger,' said Dillon, 'so you must have a plausible excuse to be in possession of such a laissez-passer. I have fashioned this.'

And he'd pushed across a padded, fine canvas envelope, sealed with the royal stamp.

'In my communications with Versailles I have on occasion received one of these document sachets,' said Dillon. 'I always keep them … for times like this. As I never break the seal when opening it, but slice the wax horizontally with a thread, I can re-seal it to look as if it was never opened in the first place. Inside, I have placed a document for a

Mr Teviot, at Innsbruck, outlining what we have discussed, James. He is one of my correspondents, and you must seek him out here, at this inn, and show him this cipher when you arrive.'

Dillion passed him another slip of paper with a scribbled address and adorned with a wax stamp. James had no idea what Dillon meant by a 'correspondent', but he did not ask, as any explanation might have taken too much time.

'The seal on this sachet will appear unbroken,' continued Dillon. 'At the French border, if you are challenged as to the purpose of the journey, show them the sachet with its seal, and merely say you have been personally entrusted by his majesty's household to deliver it privately, to the French ambassador at Vienna, and that you know no more. That should put the fear of hell itself into whoever is asking. If it does not, and you are ordered to present the sachet for closer examination, then run like hell my dear fellow, for a noose awaits you otherwise. The same applies if at any time you are searched while you have all these other papers about your person, as they quite obviously contradict each other. In that event, run, Mr Lindsay, for your life will not be worth a fig.'

So James produced for the sergeant the laissez-passer that guaranteed his passage to Metz. 'I carry unofficial dispatches,' he said. 'See, here.' And he went to hand down the vellum.

The sergeant did not reach to accept. 'I shall have to summon my officer, your excellency.'

He could not read. Bugger, the man! Damn and blast!

'Damn it man! Where is he? I have over sixty leagues to ride and not a moment to lose!'

'Across the street, your excellency,' said the sergeant jerking his thumb. 'Momentarily detained.'

James could see he was gesturing to a bawdy house, light pouring from its open shutters, along with noise and music as well as all the customary squeals of intemperate laughter.

An officer meant questioning; especially a drunken officer upset at being prised from his carnal appetites. James forced himself to calm down. Then in a reasonable voice he said, 'So, sergeant, I wait while you summon your officer. Questions are asked, meanwhile the gate is closed. I do not know your officer. Maybe he doesn't like assuming too much responsibility. He refers the matter upwards. I continue waiting …' and all the time, he was reaching into his sabretache for the sachet with its royal seal.

He'd been sworn not to produce the damn thing this side of the border, as it would draw too much attention. But all he could do was look at that damn gate, which would've been shut and barred by now, if the sergeant's men had not become so distracted by the amusing little drama now going on with this high and mighty guards officer.

'And sooner or later, someone higher up, much higher up,' continued James, 'will demand to know why a royal guards officer, carrying a dispatch with this seal … you recognise the seal, sergeant? Don't you …?'

The sergeant didn't need to look twice.

'Will be demanding to know *urgently* in fact, why this officer has been subjected to an entirely pointless and insubordinate delay. And by whom. Or you can simply acknowledge what you see before your eyes, and let me damn well pass! Now!'

The sergeant, who as a younger soldier, had felt the lash for far less, stepped back and called to his men, 'Clear a passage for his excellency!'

He spent his first, short, night's sleep in a warm bed in one of the many inns along the route. Before he went to bed he sat down and wrote a letter to his commanding officer back at Versailles, Colonel Flahaut, a man who had always treated him fairly and like gentleman. In his brief *billet*, he resigned his commission, apologising for the abruptness of his departure which he put down to 'matters of the heart gone awry', and hoped he'd understand that he did it to spare the regiment any scandal. He also asked if the regiment might look after Sophie, and attached a note saying where she was and reassigning ownership

Another horse he had to part with. He did not like parting with a horse, he decided, and hoped it might never happen again.

As he'd been assured, his laissez-passer allowed him to sign army chits for new mounts along the route, so after entrusting his letter to the innkeeper for posting, he mounted up, and rode on. If la comtesse had raised a hue and cry, no alarm had out-ridden him on this road.

The remainder of his ride to Metz was uneventful. Beyond the fortress city he burned the first laissez-passer and unfolded the second. At the border, he was dismayed to see a large number of soldiers present. He toyed with turning back and trying another crossing point, but with the evening sun behind him, coming down a long straight road, the guards had obviously seen him and his uniform. To have wheeled his horse would have excited more than curiosity. It was only as he rode closer that the tightness in his chest relaxed. The soldiers wore the uniform of King Louis' Irish Brigade. He stopped at the post for a chat, as any Scotsman in the king's service would.

Brandy flasks were passed to and fro. 'I remember many a warm conversation with your fellow countrymen in the service of the King of Spain, at Glenshiel,' James had let drop.

'Officers with Don Nicolas Bolano's regiment? The Galicians?' one of the Irishmen had barked.

'There very same,' said James, and the next thing his shoulders were being hugged and he was surrounded by a great hubbub. 'Aylward's my name, sir,' one of them was saying, 'and sure, one of them there that day must have been an Alyward too! My cousin, a James like you … he's been in King Philip's service since the year eight.'

James said, 'Yes! Indeed he was!' while beaming; and all the while not having any memory whatsoever, of any name from among those fine Irish gentlemen – only remembering their generosity and their soldierly bearing.

When his new Irish officer friends heard where he was bound and why, no-one asked for further proof of his journey, and no demand was made to see the sachet. They understood he must press on immediately. But he must swear to call on them on his return journey. The Brigade was billeted at Strasbourg … not even a day out of his way. James swore, and felt guilty about his deception.

It was only after he crossed the Rhine and entered the town of Karlsruhe in the Margraviate of Baden that he decided it was time to use some of the substantial purse Dillon had handed him, and buy a horse. In fact, he bought two to carry him the further sixty leagues into the Austrian alps and Innsbruck. He even bought a suit of civilian clothes, but then thought better of changing out of his French uniform. A French guards officer in full regalia, carrying a dispatch in a sachet that was openly addressed to the ambassador of a friendly court and sealed with the French royal household seal, along with an official laissez-passer, was unlikely be mistaken for a spy. A strange civilian with a strange accent might be.

He kept up a steady pace now, through the breathtakingly beautiful and bountiful countryside, letting one horse regain its wind while he led it, and riding the other until it too, ran out of puff.

Onward he went, to the rescue of his king's future bride.

5

The Polish Princess

James was practically being bundled up the narrow tunnel of the inn's wooden staircase. The two Austrian officers, in their crisp white and gold braided uniform coats obviously thought they were doing him a favour, expediting his visit. Alas, James still had not the remotest idea of what he was going to say when he got to the top and had to bang on the Princess Maria Clementina Sobieska's door. Hopefully, there would be a lady in waiting of some description to intercept him so he could gather his thoughts.

After three respectful raps on the big, panelled door, it opened, and there before him stood a diminutive girl, no more than a teenager, in an elaborate, embroidered, full length peasant-style night coat of a richness no peasant could ever afford. But it wasn't her coat James noticed first, nor the pure, alabaster perfection of her face. It was her fine dark-blonde hair, that fell in one long tress, all the way down to her ankles.

'M'sieur?' she said, giving him a quizzical frown, then looking over his shoulder to the two Austrians, 'and the officers of my protection?' All delivered in a clear and lilting French.

'My protection' – this was obviously the princess herself. So, no lady in waiting to give him time.

He felt a push from behind and suddenly he was through the door and in the room, which was presumably the parlour of Princess Clementina's suite, with the more senior Austrian babbling away to her in a language James could not understand but guessed was German.

It was rather a grand room for a hotel, with several comfortably upholstered chairs, and a high-backed, three-seat sofa; all brocade, studded cushions and intricately crafted legs and arm-rests. There were blazing candelabras and closed drapes that could have defied an alpine blizzard, and a writing desk, from which the princess had obviously just risen.

James was fresh from his ride, having passed through Innsbruck's gates less than an hour previously. His body was heavy with fatigue and he could feel the sweat still drying on his skin.

He had approached Innsbruck from the west, after a long ride along the valley of the River Inn, and had entered some way into the city, heading for the establishment where he'd been told Mr Teviot would be waiting for him, under the name of Herr Domogala; a gentleman of commerce from the northern Adriatic dominions of the Austrian empire. In reality, this Mr Teviot was the emissary of the pretender, James Francis Edward Stuart, to the Habsburg court, travelling incognito. He would explain everything in detail to him, Mr Dillon had assured James, before James approached the princess.

Why he was going to be approaching an incarcerated Polish princess, in the name of James Francis Edward Stuart, was long story, said Dillion; but the essence of it was this:

When the pretender's mother, Queen Mary, died, her substantial papal pension had died with her. So, James Stuart had been forced by immanent penury to contemplate marriage. Several eligible brides had been suggested, including the daughter of the Duke of Modena. Alas, said Dillon, although Pope Clement regarded James Stuart as the rightful King of Great Britain, and in his exile as no less than a Catholic martyr, the Italian aristocracy were not so well disposed. The Pope might have agreed to fund him until a more secure income could be found, such as a substantial dowry, but the stipend was begrudged, because the aristos saw only a titled vagrant – not a king. Because, as they pointed out, that title was in name only.

No Italian family, and no dowry had been forthcoming, and so James Stuart's court in exile had to trawl further afield.

It was a move that produced the perfect choice.

Princess Maria Clementina was the grand-daughter of King John III of Poland – known throughout Christendom as 'John Sobieski', and the man who had raised the Ottoman siege of Vienna and saved the city. And when the suggestion was put to her family that she marry James Stuart, Clementina's father, Prince James-Louis Sobieski had thought the idea of his daughter becoming the Queen of Great Britain alongside a restored King James III a splendid idea; and so had the 16-year-old Princess Clementina.

Also, she came with the requisite, very impressive, dowry, Mr Crawford had added.

'However, the idea of it has reduced King George to an apoplectic rage,' Dillon went on to explain. 'Especially the idea that James Francis Edward Stuart might produce an heir from such impeccable lineage. When news reached George several months ago that the lass would be travelling from Poland to Rome for the wedding, he immediately sent word to his old friend and ally in Vienna, the Emperor Charles, demanding in the name of their future relations that he put a spoke in it. Charles, not really knowing how best to respond, and to buy himself time, had the princess met as she passed through Innsbruck, with an offer to stay awhile and enjoy the alpine air. And now neither he nor anybody else knows quite what to do about her, or the stand-off that has resulted. To deal with it all, the Emperor Charles has his best military man on the scene. Feldmarschall Heister. It was he who first met Clementina, inviting her to stay initially in the Schloss Ambras, an imposing fortification standing on the southern hills above the city, but her presence there looked too much like incarceration … and too much like the Holy Roman Emperor was dancing to wee Hanoverian Geordie's tune. Also, old Heister had fought with her grandfather at the siege of Vienna, so there is something of a sympathy between him and the girl, and rumour has it he does not enjoy his role as gaoler. Anyway, the old fellow has since moved her to a suite in the Kaiserhof, a rather grand coaching inn in the city. And the guards around her now are more a subtle presence than a ring of steel. After all, no-one intends her any harm. They just don't know what to do with her. And it's not as if she could escape, at least not on her own.'

And *that* was why Dillon and Crawford had wanted James to go to Austria.

Get to Innsbruck, meet with Mr Teviot, and concoct a plan, they told him. After all, there were any number of reasons why James, an officer of King Louis of France's guard, should request an audience, and be granted one. Not least the suggestion that King Louis might be offering to mediate over her future. The fact that there was no offer was irrelevant; just get an audience with her – in private – and test her reaction to the possibility of a rescue.

'It is inconceivable that old Heister won't fall over himself to let you in to see her,' Dillon had said. 'Even the remotest chance that Louis might be prepared to step in with a solution to this mess will be grasped with alacrity, or I'm a Dutchman!'

The only problem had been that when James' presence in Innsbruck had been detected, Old Heister had indeed *more* than fallen over himself when informed. He'd ordered that James, as a cornet of horse in the Chevau-Légers de la Garde, be rushed immediately to the inn where Clementina was quartered, without even the chance to change his linen, or the diversion of an interview with himself first.

And now, here he was, in the princess' suite, and not a clue what to say. The two Austrian officers stood resolutely behind him, as he introduced himself.

'You have a private message for me, sir?' said the girl.

'Yes, er, um, your, um, Princess Clementina,' stumbled James.

'Sie können uns jetzt verlassen, Meine Herren,' she said to the Austrian officers. A pause, then – with emphasis – 'Es ist eine private Botschaft.'

As the officers bowed and withdrew, she smiled at James and repeated in French, 'I said, "You can leave us now. It is a private message." Please step with me.'

With that, she drew aside one of the drapes and opened a huge shutter. When James stepped through it, he was in the night air, two stories up, overlooking the edge of an imposing square of tall, sober, five storey, white-plastered buildings, each one topped at their corners with little onion turrets. They were standing in part of a wooden balcony rising over three storeys of the inn. He'd noticed the structure above him as he'd been first ushered through the front doors. It was all balustrades and carvings and looked like a miniature house itself, grafted onto the stone.

'Now, tell me, you are not French, are you?' she said. 'Although you wear a French uniform. So, are you really from the French king as Uncle Siggy says?'

You might as well jump right in, James instructed himself. But it seemed such a great leap. He prevaricated a moment. 'Uncle Siggy, princess?'

She rolled her eyes, a very mature gesture for one so young, thought James.

'Sigbert', she said. 'Sigbert Graf Heister, the feldmarschall, who is my host at present, and who was my grandfather's friend and comrade in arms. He sent to tell me I was to receive a visitor, likely carrying a message. I take it that is you?'

'Ah …' said James.

'And you refer to me as, "your royal highness", on first address, and then "milady" thereafter,' she added, with a helpful nod. Still seeing confusion on James' face, she added, 'I'm sure nobody has their ear to my door, but they have all these listening tubes, and other such silliness … spy holes in the walls and ceilings. And floors. As if I've ever had anything to say or hear that's worth eavesdropping on. It's most tiresome. But I assure you, whatever we say out here will not be heard. Unless of course, you insist on shouting. I take it you do have something to tell me that *is* worth eavesdropping on?'

James, now much charmed by so much poise and confidence in a girl so young and pretty, drew himself up to his full height. 'I do bring a message, milady. And it is from a king,' he said. 'But the king is not Louis of France.'

And then he told her everything he knew. And that he was here to effect her escape.

'La! How romantic! How dashing!' she said, contemplating him coolly. 'Shall you now call on me to lean out and let fall my hair, like Persinette, so you can climb down to the street and catch me when I leap? Then whistle for your horse so we might ride off into the night?'

It wasn't until the morning of the second day that Cornet of Horse Lindsay managed to present himself to Herr Domogala, having finally found him as he breakfasted at his coaching inn in the city centre.

On hearing of James' first encounter with the Princess Clementina, Herr Domogala, or as James knew him, Mr Teviot, didn't look so much at a loss for words as reluctant to use the ones he wanted to, lest he sour their relations before they'd even begun.

Eventually, through gritted teeth, Mr Teviot said, 'Persinette is a French fairy tale of the last age. It is about a virgin trapped in a tower, whose prince comes to save her, repeatedly, by climbing up and down her long hair.'

'Is there a lesson for us, Mr Teviot?' James asked. 'Is the princess trying to communicate something I have missed?'

'Well, the fairy who'd been protecting Persinette took a dim view of all the saving that had been going on, and blinded the saviour. So what do you think?'

It was James' turn to sit mute, rebuked; while Mr Teviot called for another pot of chocolate and drummed his fingers, thinking.

'How did you leave it with the Austrians?' he asked. Had he met Uncle Siggy? And was he likely to?

There had been no talk of meeting Uncle Siggy, said James.

'No,' said Mr Teviot, 'I suppose not. Feldmarschalls don't normally have conversations with mere cornets.

However, James went on, relating how the senior Austrian officer had said a room had been taken for him at the Kaiserhof, to be near the princess, while he awaited any reply. Should James seek a further audience with her royal highness, the officer had said, he was in the first instance, to approach him.

'Good,' said Mr Teviot.

James had already divined Mr Teviot was prone to sarcasm, but otherwise he seemed a serious, reliable sort. Certainly he looked the part of an envoy, or even a man of commerce. How wealthy he was, was hard to tell that morning as Mr Teviot was not properly dressed for the world, even though he was dinning in a public room of the inn.

His hair – cut short to allow a full wig to sit easily – was silver-grey and on display; no wig had yet been donned. Nor was he wearing a stock or coat. The impression was of a man whose business was more important to him than how he looked.

'Well,' he said at length, having quite regained his composure. He even smiled, a little thinly, before continuing. 'That you delivered the sachet, with its seal intact, directly to the Princess Clementina instead of to me, actually helps our subterfuge. And that she let you bring away with you all that was in it, addressed to me, tells us she is not entirely opposed to us. As does the fact that we are still at liberty, and not denounced to Uncle Siggy.'

And at that he rolled his eyes in resignation before adding, 'On the other hand, from what you have told me of your conversation, I think it is safe to assume the girl is never going to take you seriously. So we have to open some other channel of communication that she will. Leave that to me. You, on the other hand, my young blade, must devise the practical plan that is going to get her out of the grand Kaiserhof and onto the road to Rome. A plan, sir, that has to have some reasonable prospect of success!'

The sun had already passed behind the peak of the Patscherkofel mountain when the coach and four overtook Mr Teviot and James, who were returning at a leisurely pace to the city after a country ride.

The coach travelled on a little then came to a halt in the shadows of a copse very close to the side of the road.

With the sun gone, the air was suddenly cool, and the light growing dull.

James and Mr Teviot cantered up beside the coach, James greeted the man on the box beside the coach's driver, and then turned to his own companion to make the introductions.

'Mr Teviot, this is Major Aylward of his majesty King Louis' Irish Brigade.'

Both men acknowledged each other with a touch to their hats, and as they did, two ladies emerged from inside the coach and walked away a short distance to stretch their legs, leaving the men to converse under the trees.

'Allow me to present my fellow officers,' said Aylward. 'This is Captain Patrick Tracey and Captain Colm O'Brian, who has brought his wife, Mrs O'Brian, to render the service you have requested. The other lady is Mrs O'Brian's maid, Teresa.'

The men were in the day attire of civilian gentlemen; subdued, comfortable and well cut. Aylward was a distinguished fellow, tall, with the weathered cheeks of a soldier. The other two were open-faced, younger men, each with a compact economy of movement about them that bespoke a certain seriousness. All three wore bobbed, un-powdered wigs beneath their hats, and were smiling broadly.

'We meet in the one true cause,' said Aylward. 'That the king shall have his own again!' It was the traditional Jacobite toast, and Aylward passed round a flask for them all to take a drink of what turned out to be excellent brandy.

Major Aylward, the officer who had waved James over the border at Metz not a month before, a complete stranger who had recognised a kindred spirit in a fellow exile, and entreated him to visit on the way back. His presence here on the road into Innsbruck was no accident.

After the near disaster of his first meeting with Princess Clementina, and Mr Teviot's reproaches, James' head had been fogged by self-recrimination. But once he'd got it all out of the way, James, the student of moral philosophy and logic, had found he was well armed to deal with the seemingly impossible task of getting a princess out of a prison. Once he'd applied some intellectual rigour, he knew that what starts out looking impossible, can quickly become all too feasible, if you break the problem down into its component parts.

He knew that he and Mr Teviot were never going to prise the princess out of the feldmarschall's clutches on their own, let alone get her all the way to the Empire's border and safety.

Step one must be to secure help. And that was when Major Aylward's parting words had echoed in James' head. Aylward, an Irishman in the King of France's service, was almost certainly a Catholic. From which must follow a degree of loyalty to who else, but the king over the water?

So James knew all he had to do to involve Aylward in his plan was to lay it all before him. The man would not, could not, refuse. He set his scheme in motion by writing to the major, care of the Irish Brigade barracks, jogging the major's memory of the young Scottish cornet of horse in the king's Chevau-Légers de la Garde, who had once passed his way, and the promise they'd parted on; that they should meet again. He suggested a date and location for such a meeting. The major agreed.

But it had only been after the two men had sat down at that travellers' inn just the other side of the major's border post, that James had unveiled his proposition. They were two soldiers of fortune banished from their homes because they refused to betray the king over the water. Now, however, there was a chance for them both to render their king an incalculable service. Was the major in?

Of course he was.

Needless to say, the Austrian feldmarschall and his staff had known all about James' meeting with Major Aylward. They had opened James' letter; had, in fact, been expecting one to be sent, and for Cornet of Horse Lindsay to ride out on receiving a reply. It was just what an emissary on such a delicate mission would do; such unusual, behind the scenes communications were to be expected. Especially after the plein pouvoir – the written power of authority – from Princess Clementina's father in neighbouring Silesia had arrived, appointing Cornet Lindsay by name to guide her in any future negotiations. Prince James-Louis Sobieski's communication had been under his seal, to be opened only by his daughter, but that hadn't stopped the feldmarschall from opening it, clandestinely.

What neither the feldmarschall nor his staff had thought to open however, was an earlier, nondescript business letter from a Herr Domogala, temporarily resident in Innsbruck, to an obscure lawyer in Ohlau, Silesia. But then, they weren't to know it had contained Mr Teviot's coded request to the prince that he 'instruct' his daughter on her future relations with Cornet Lindsay. After all, there had been no reason to suspect Herr Domogala was involved in any way in this matter of diplomacy. While the Austrian authorities were well aware Herr Domogala received a lot of letters, and wrote even more, that was what any man of business did.

In fact, the only concern the feldmarschall's staff had was the time it had all taken. But when they sat down and thought about it, a messenger would take time to cover the 200 leagues between here and southern Silesia; and even longer, the distance between here and Paris. Any helpful intervention by King Louis was always going to be a long, drawn out affair. However, as long as matters were well in hand, nobody should lose any sleep.

'And you have the Papal States' laissez-passer with you?' Teviot asked Aylward.

These were travel documents for a 'Comte and Comtesse de Cernez' and their staff, who were 'on a pilgrimage to Rome', that Teviot had written in his own copperplate hand, and stamped with a procured Papal seal. And he had sent them off with James when he rode out to recruit the major to their plan, so that major's party might enter Austrian territory without arousing suspicion.

'We do,' said Aylward. 'They barely glanced at it at the border.' Then he asked, 'And we meet our future queen tonight?'

'If all goes according to plan, major, you do,' said Teviot.

'And for that brilliant plan, we have you to thank, Mr Teviot,' said Captain O'Brian. 'And for my ennoblement, and my wife's, too! Ha! Ha!'

Because for now, O'Brian and his wife were not just calling themselves 'comte and comtesse', they had an official Papal laissez-passer to prove it – and much amused Captain O'Brian was by the idea, forged though his document may be.

Teviot shook his head. 'No, no gentlemen. I merely did the paperwork. The scheme is all this young man's here. Which I confess, I didn't think he had it in him.'

Everyone laughed and James smiled and bowed. Apart from all the academic logic he'd had drummed into him at university, he had also lived too long in the presence of the Comtesse de Boufflers not to have learned how to scheme, too. So he accepted the accolade gracefully, but he didn't like this kind of talk. Teviot might have spoken the truth, but too much could go wrong for them to be throwing plaudits around at this stage. He didn't like tempting fate.

So, before the self-congratulations went any further, he killed the conversation by observing that 'There are many other elements in this enterprise that must fall into place yet, and many leagues to travel, for us to call it a success.'

The enterprise's next element depended on young Heipke Remer, a chambermaid at the Kaiserhof.

If recruiting Aylward and his fellow Irishmen had all been about getting the Princess Clementina away from the Kaiserhof, then the role James had selected Heipke for was to be all about delaying the pursuit.

Heipke was a slim, comely, alert young serving girl who had embroiled herself in this conspiracy by having an eye for James from the moment he stepped through the Kaiserhof's door. After all, he was the dashing, foreign, young cavalry officer, with the flowing locks and the discreet wounds that announced he had been in battle. Right from the start, he had enjoyed all of her intimate inquiries – might there be anything else he needed? Then came that flash of her eyes, that she was so liberal with when it came to him. It was a flirtation he returned with pleasure, without even considering whether he might use it to his advantage.

Also, it helped they could converse. For although, like everyone else for miles around, she was a native speaker of German – a language James had not a word of – her mother had been Francophone Swiss, so their flirtation was not just a matter of stolen looks and secret smiles.

And that was why the idea had come to him; the role for her in his plot.

She had begun the conversation on the fateful day of her entrapment.

'That princess you wait on, upstairs in her grand suite, never talking to anyone. She is a haughty one,' Heipke had observed as an aside, as she cleared the coffee things from his table in one of the Kaiserhof's many snugs. 'You write her notes and inquire after her, and she just leaves you sitting all alone, never giving you a reply, or granting you an audience.'

'I wait on her, Heipke. I am her servant, ready here to do her bidding. Not she to do mine.' James paused to give her one of his smiles, 'After all, we lesser mortals cannot presume to know what forces govern the thoughts and wishes of princesses.'

Heipke loved it when James casually threw in such enticing little words like 'we' when he talked to her. So she was too busy basking in the effect of that last one to notice James was looking at her in a new way; as if measuring her height and build, noticing her blonde braids, far more golden than Clementina's, but no matter. By the time her hair was revealed, all would have been decided.

James had been at first surprised, and then dismayed by how little natural reluctance he'd felt when it came to subverting and then manipulating the poor girl.

'Heipke?'

'Yes, M'sieur James?'

'Do you know the story of Persinette?'

A squeal of delight. 'Yes! Of course. The beautiful maiden, with her long golden hair. Innocent, shielded from the evils of the world in a secret tower, by a fairy. But she's really a prisoner too. And then when her prince comes and …'

Heipke's eyes had gone so wide James feared they would pop out. She immediately shifted sideways, so her body blocked James, where he sat at his table, from the view of any prying eye; as if keeping him all for herself. Looking down on him, her face had been suffused with a confusing mixture of wonder and loss, as she'd mouthed, 'You are the prince … come to …?'

James realised it was the notion that she might be in a real-life fairytale that must have gripped her so intensely, there seemed a possibility of her swooning.

He'd given her a deliberately furtive, confiding, sideways look. 'No, Heipke, I'm not a prince … but I am a prince's emissary. Sit down, here.'

Heipke, her eyes never moving from his, did as she was told.

'The princess is here against her will,' whispered James. 'You must never tell you know that.'

Heipke shook her head vigorously.

'Her prince should be here to take her away himself, but he cannot. It is too dangerous. For him … for her. So he has sent me, to lead her to safety … to his arms …'

Heipke gasped.

'But they guard her closely, Heipke. The emperor's men. There is such high politics, and low motives involved, to thwart the lovers' dreams. That is why I must cut through all the intrigues that surround them with the blade of my sword, to bring the two lovers finally together. But I need an ally, Heipke. A friend I can trust. Can I trust you, Heipke? Will you be my ally? I cannot deceive you, Heipke, there will be danger …'

But Heipke hadn't bothered listening to his final words. 'M'sieur James! Command me!'

And it had been as easy as that.

Early evening in Innsbruck city, and the sky is dense with rain clouds. The stolid white stucco bluffs of the tenement blocks are all in shadow, and the few people in the streets all seem to be hurrying.

The Comte de Cernez' man has gone into the Kaiserhof to inquire about rooms for the night for his master's party. The coach idles in a side alley. The man, as he waits for service, does not acknowledge the passing of the red-uniformed French cavalry officer as he strides past him and into the back public rooms. There is nothing at all to attract the attention of the two Austrian officers lounging in the foyer; both men are imperial cuirassiers, and quite ludicrously, are all buckled up in the bulky metal breastplates and huge heavy cavalry top boots their full field uniform requires – uniforms more suited for a battlefield than the front of house in a fashionable inn.

James, once out of sight of the imperial officers, slips down the servants' passage and goes directly to where Heipke is stacking clean sheets before carrying them upstairs. With his eyebrows he gestures her to follow.

'It is tonight,' he whispers. 'Collect your cloak, place it in the sheets and follow me.'

Heipke, eyes now bright with excitement, obeys. They climb the back stairs to the princess' suite. 'I only managed to finish her hair this afternoon,' Heipke breathes, 'but it is perfect, M'sieur James.'

'Heipke. You are a marvel,' says James.

The only guards Princess Clementina has been assigned to mind her person are the two cuirassier officers downstairs. The feldmarschall had ruled some time ago that a full detachment would be too obvious, too oppressive. After all, no-one is threatening her. And the thought she might try to escape is ludicrous. So no soldier stands before her door. James doesn't bother to knock; he has purloined a copy of the key.

When she hears the door opening, Clementina hurriedly reaches for her cotton cap, sliding beneath the blankets to pull it on. She has been in bed, not to be disturbed, for two days now; it is a chill, she says, that she does not want to become something worse. So she has been seeing no-one. The cap is to hide the ornate braiding Heipke has been secretly applying to her long, flowing hair over those two days; it has been a time-consuming task, carried out bit by bit, every opportunity she's had to sneak up here from her duties. The braids are part of James' deception plan. For no gentlewoman would ever suffer to have her hair braided like a peasant girl; which is why Clementina is trying to hide it from whoever is about to barge in.

Clementina stifles her petulance when she sees who it is; her father's strict instructions to obey this young oaf have dictated her every move these past weeks, and she must swallow it.

Whispered instructions, and then James briefly absents himself as the ladies change clothes, and Clementina dons Heipke's cape. Heipke, her own hair under her cap, is free of braids today, and she lets it tumble on the pillow as she jumps into Clementina's warm bed. Only one more task to fulfil. James produces the ropes and silken strips, which he wraps around Heipke's wrists and ankles. The silk is to stop the ropes chaffing the girl; for James hopes it will be some time before she is discovered. Then the loose gag is tied behind her head.

'The bonds are loose, Heipke,' says James. 'But the instant you hear someone at the door, you must pull the cords here ... and here ... and that will tighten them, and you will not be suspected. But before you do, remember to tighten the gag first. Are you ready, Heipke? Are you sure you want to go ahead, my brave girl?'

'I'm sure, M'sieur James. Sure as sure.'

Going down the back stairs with James, Clementina is hissing in his ear.

'All this fuss with that stupid girl,' she is saying. 'Tying her up ... all this ... artisan's scaffolding you have placed around my head. What more theatricals are to come, sirrah?'

James turns sharply, halting her descent of the stairs, and stares hard into her face. 'You are checked in your room every hour, as you know. As long as they see you are in your bed, snuffling, they go away. So that is why we are leaving someone else snuffling in your bed ... so that *you* can get away. It is not difficult to understand. And that stupid girl you refer to, she has volunteered to help you win your freedom, at some considerable risk to herself. This has nothing to do with theatricals, madam. Can you imagine what might befall her if your Uncle Siggy ever found out she had been complicit in your flight? That is why she is tied up right now ... to show that she is *not* complicit, so that she will come to no harm. As for the *scaffolding* and the cloak ... princesses walking in the street attract attention. Serving maids don't. Now, may we proceed without you perpetually braying in my ear?'

They are out the city, and heading south for the Brenner Pass. Beyond it lies first, Bolzano, still within the empire, but far enough away; and beyond, the border and the Veneto, where at last they will be beyond the reach of the Emperor Charles.

Darkness has fallen, and James is riding a little ahead of the coach, there to ensure they stumble across nothing untoward. He hears its rattle behind him as he canters along. Until that is, he doesn't. James swings his horse at the sudden silence, and hears Aylward hissing for him to come back. He touches his spurs to the horse.

'The princess has forgotten her jewellery,' hisses Aylward, from the driver's box. 'She will not go on.'

'You are trifling with me,' says James, in an equally low tone. 'I would suggest, Major Aylward, sir, this is not the time to ...'

'Ask her, Seamus, me lad,' says Aylward, who has now taken to calling James by his Gaelic name.

James dismounts.

Clementina, when she sees his face in the door, turns away.

'Milady,' begins James, with a calm he does not feel. The quicker they put distance between them and Innsbruck, the less likely they are to be caught by a detachment of cavalry.

'I shall not be addressed by that loud and uncouth brute,' says Clementina, referring to James.

'She says we cannot proceed without her jewels,' says an obviously exasperated Mrs O'Brian, before adding in a monotone, 'their value cannot be calculated ...'

'Milady, you place us all in considerable peril ...' James tries again. 'And anyway, what possessed you not to have them to hand, before we left?'

'See? The brute does not listen!' says Clementina, still studiously ignoring James. 'First, he fusses over a stupid girl, while I have to stand by, fuming. Then he bundles me ... *bundles* me! ... down a cobwebby staircase as steep as an alp ... and then he complains about a moment's forgetfulness! Well, I say this only once! The loss of my jewellery is not worth the prize. There will be other kings who will wish to marry me. I wish to be taken at once to the nearest imperial officer so that I can hand myself over. I am in the clutches of madmen ... and I fear, so are you Mrs O'Brian. We shall not be safe until Uncle Siggy rescues us!'

Although still a young man, James, these days, is now much older in the ways of wilful women and knows instinctively this stand-off will go nowhere. He either turns his horse and rides off into the night, abandoning everyone, or he returns for the jewels. It actually takes a moment for him to make up his mind, and it is only the parlous fate that might await Major Aylward and his friends that swings it for remaining.

'Mrs O'Brian, would you please inform her royal highness that I would be eager to retrieve her jewellery, but only if she would undertake to continue her journey to the border. Oh, and please inquire of the princess where her jewellery might be found within her suite? The sooner I am on my way, the faster I shall catch you up.'

'They are in a velvet bag, in my bedside table, of course. And tell Chevalier Brute, his kitchen skivvy girl will be able to help if he has trouble finding that! As for this fiasco? If we must continue, then la! We must!'

A cold, simmering resentment consumed James as he galloped back up the coaching road to Innsbruck. It was the entitlement of these people. Their utter disregard for the rest of the human tribe; beyond even contempt – contempt requiring an acknowledgement that those thus held existed.

The distance passed in but blink, and before he knew it, he was striding purposefully through the front of house of the Kaiserhof, heading to the back stairs to the princess' suite. There was no tumult, or alarm in the air. The quiet meant they were still as yet undiscovered in their plot. In a moment he was up the stairs and at the door, unlocking it with a slow dexterity. He wanted in, and out again; no fuss.

The suite itself was dark and still. All he could hear was the measured, light breathing from beneath the bed's heaped blankets. Heipke was obviously asleep, and he smiled as he briefly marvelled at her cool.

He approached the bed. Knelt. Opened the small bedside night table. And inside he felt the knobbly, velvet shape the size of a cannonball. His fist closed around the neck and the sound of voices came from beyond the suite's door. Then a key in the lock. No quiet subterfuge this time. In a moment James was on his feet and across the room to the far wall and shadow, the brief hiss of his sabre as he drew it from its scabbard.

Damn and blast it! Why had he not grabbed the velvet bag before he leapt?

The door opened, and there was the spill of guttering light from candelabra. Two figures entered; the first an elderly civilian in a formal coat and breeches and the second, one of the Austrian cuirassiers, sans cuirass, in a white shirt, waistcoat and breeches, and his heavy cavalry top boots that looked even more clumpy and inappropriate in a bed chamber than they did of the polished wooden floors of the foyer.

'Your royal highness,' wheezed the elderly man, 'it is I, Doctor Lubbe, to inquire after your health at the feldmarschall's request.'

The game was up. James stepped into the light and said, in French, 'You have chosen an inconvenient moment for me and the princess, messieurs.'

The doctor turned, eyes wide with shock. James had no idea whether he had understood anything he had just said, but from the way the old man's be-spectacled eyes fixed upon his drawn sabre, that was enough to send him scuttling, with amazing agility from the room, dodging nimbly round the advancing soldier as he too drew his sword; a far heavier weapon than the one James brandished.

The Austrian, like the gentleman officer he obviously was, immediately assumed the en garde stance, sword arm extended, before getting ready to lunge. As he did, Heipke sat upright in the bed, a terrified yelp escaping from the muffling of her silken gag, which James assumed she herself had just tightened. The Austrian saw her rise out the corner of his eye. Three things snagged his gaze at once, and held it longer than they should have; the gag on the poor girl's face; the tightly bound wrists she'd raised to cover her face, and her golden, not dark, blonde hair; hair that fell only to her shoulders. That a princess whose safety he had been entrusted with should be lying bound and gagged in her own bed was not be countenanced any emperor's officer; and that the girl, bound and gagged and now lying in the princess' bed was not the princess, only compounded the already unthinkable for him, and made it harder to comprehend.

While all that jostled in his brain, James stepped forward. James, whose early handiness with the epee had been roundly honed in subsequent years. In an advancing flick of his sabre, he engaged the Austrian's raised blade, ran his point down it to the guard until the tip snagged the fretwork, and then he flicked the heavy steel of it right out of the Austrian's hand. All executed in mid-step, as he passed outside the Austrian's sword arm and careened into his back, forcing him to pirouette, so his face was now to the wall; whereupon James then promptly slammed him with the full weight of his body into it, before standing back and pressing his sabre point to the base of the Austrian's spine – just nicking the skin and no more, to gain his attention, and make his own intentions clear.

'What have you done with her royal highness, you scoundrel?' said the Austrian, in a perfectly acceptable French, delivered in a voice of steel as cutting as the blade of the sword he no longer held.

James didn't answer. The doctor would be summoning this officer's entire squadron of heavy cavalry. He needed to get to the bed-side table, get the velvet bag and be gone. But if he moved his blade from this man's spine, he'd be on him in a flash; and it wouldn't be to negotiate his surrender. He couldn't ask Heipke to get it; she was supposed to be his victim, not a co-conspirator.

Princess bloody Clementina, that bloody woman. All this bloody

98

trouble was likely to get someone killed, not least him. He gave the Austrian another prick for want of something to do.

'T'were best if you stick it in entirely, m'sieur,' said the Austrian. 'My honour shall not survive this. But then, nor will you, you whoreson.'

The insult sharpened James just enough. He found himself looking at the single strap of material descending from beneath the Austrian's high-backed waistcoat to the buttonholes at the top of his breeches; the back support of his braces.

'You presume, m'sieur, to involve my lineage?' said James, flicking back his blade. 'Those are not the words of a gentleman. M'sieur, you do not deserve the honest point of a sword.' And he made a tight, hard swipe, severing neatly the brace's strap.

The Austrian's breeches immediately dropped, tangling around his knees in the down-turned tops of his heavy boots. As the man stumbled, James was across the room, and the velvet bag was in his hand. He looked back to see the victim of his swordplay forfeit all dignity as he struggled to stand, move and untangle his breeches from the substantial folds of boot leather where they had become hopelessly wrapped.

The Austrian roared something Germanic and incomprehensible at James, who was now opening the balcony shutters. James replied, laughing. 'Your honour will survive that much faster than a skewered liver, mein herr!'

Then he gave him a smart salute with his blade, and added as he was about to disappear into the night, 'And untie the poor fraulein, you boor! The bastard who did that to her ... a damned scoundrel!'

And then he was gone.

Even before he was leaping into his saddle, James knew the way to head out of the city was to go west. For France. Where else? He wore the uniform of a French guards officer, was widely believed to be an emissary of the French king; if he was heading that way, then so must the fugitive princess be.

As for why the feldmarschall might believe the French king had wanted to kidnap Clementina, James could conjure up not a single argument. And fleeing now, he had not the time to dwell on it. Let all those court sophists divine the reasons; debate upon what vital vested interest must this month be steering the ship of state. Let them blame the entire charade on Louis' marriage to a Polish noblewoman. There must be some shady intrigue buried there that had made it all so necessary. That was the way the world worked, wasn't it? Nothing to do with an ordinary soldier like Cornet James Lindsay.

Except he wasn't even that, anymore. Just another of those Wild Geese now, with no state to claim him. So, on, into the night, at the full gallop, going so fast he could feel the horse's pleasure beneath him; so fast he knew it was a pace he could not long sustain.

He gave the horse her head until he felt her begin to blow, then he wheeled her directly south off the road that followed the line of the River Inn, up into the forested foothills, and there he dismounted, and lay down to snatch a half hour of sleep.

He was up again, and already doubling back along a small woodsman's path that followed one of the lower contours of the Stubaier Alpen range where it corralled the south western approaches to the city, when he heard the pounding of many hooves below in the Inn valley. The clouds of earlier had cleared, and there was a moon somewhere behind the mountains, so although there was light enough to ride, there was not enough to see down through the gloom of the trees to the valley floor. Only the shiny snake of the River Inn peeked through the branches from time to time. It must be the pursuit, he reckoned, but could not see them. They had not been very fast in getting moving. But that was not a comforting thought – what if it meant they had sent a fast courier on ahead, carrying all the necessary dispatches to raise every military post along the route and to block the border? None had passed him, certainly. But there might have been one, riding not so far behind. He'd be long gone towards the posts opposite Metz, or Strasbourg, or both. And what if they'd sent a rider in every direction? What if they hadn't just assumed that yes, they are gone to France, and nowhere else? What if they'd covered all options;

just to be safe? A fast courier heading for Bolsano could already be overtaking Aylward and the coach.

The thought put the urgency back into his progress. There would be no more sleeps or stops. The poor horse would just have to endure.

6

The Palazzo del Re

All the glory and the fussing that had followed the success of James' epic dash from Innsbruck had long since faded. There had been much rejoicing that Princess Clementina had been delivered safe, and there had been the lionising of her saviours. Now she was a familiar face at James Stuart's court in exile, and the face of James Lindsay was that of just another courtier. Routine had returned.

And so it was this night. The candles and the roaring fire made the king's private chambers look much warmer than they felt. A very apropos metaphor for the entire Stuart court in exile, thought Chevalier James Lindsay, as he looked down on the chess board and yet another impending defeat at the hands of a better player.

The Roman winter's evening chill permeated the room, and rain could be heard lashing the shutters. His opponent made his move, and Chevalier Lindsay lost his second knight. Three more moves and it would all be over. Young Lindsay didn't lose all his games to the middle-aged man before him, the pretender to the throne of Great Britain; over the two years he had been at the Palazzo del Re he reckoned he'd probably won at least three out of every ten games he had played, which was exactly how his opponent liked it. Because the man who would be King James III liked to win, but would have been disdainful of anyone who let him.

It was the custom among the 100-strong court here at the palazzo to treat the man as if he already was king. Everyone always referred to him as, 'your majesty', to his face, and 'his majesty', in general. So quite quickly James had settled on thinking of this man before him now, purely and simply as the king. And why not? For James Francis Edward became the title far more convincingly than the current incumbent, Georg August, the short, fat, florid and very German son of the not long dead George I. Georg August was widely known among his subjects as 'the rump', either because of his reputed martyrdom to piles, or his habit of flicking his coat-tails and showing his backside to anyone who disagreed with him, but officially he was to be known henceforth as George II.

Thinking of Georg August always made James smile. However, if he wanted to frown, all he had to do was think about what he himself was doing, still here at the Palazzo del Re, and the court of James III, in exile.

James' arrival here – or rather he should say, the arrival of Princess Maria Clementina Sobieska – had been greeted with much fanfare – or at least, as much fanfare as the king's impecunious court could muster. After all, she was the king's betrothed, and with her she brought the political sway of the Catholic kingdom of Poland, a sister married to Louis of France and a dowry handsome enough to transform the court's finances.

That it had been down to James Lindsay and his three now-renegade Irish officers, that she had arrived at all, served to include them in the general celebrations. The king had knighted James in the tiny courtyard of the palazzo on the day. But the honour would be no more than a scrap of paper until he regained the throne.

As for Aylward, Tracey and O'Brian … there had been baubles too, but they could only be paper titles until the king was restored. And as they had forfeited their commissions in the service of the King of France, they had been rendered penniless. A grateful Pope, however, made James' position more formal, by creating him a Knight Commander of the Order of St Gregory the Great, with the title 'chevalier'. He also conferred on the three Irishmen the Order of the Golden Spur and the hereditary title of count, with an annual stipend – which had particularly thrilled Mrs O'Brian, who'd henceforth be known as 'comtesse'.

As for James' future; the king had taken a special interest in him, appointing him as his personal aide de camp, which came with its own modest living direct from the king's own purse. Given that James was young, and a mere third son of an earl of no influence, and had so obviously deserved favour for his rescue of the future queen, the title of chevalier and appointment as aide had excited no jealousy at court – at first.

It would take a little more time for him to learn about court jealousy and how it worked, and its place amongst all the other vices; and how viciously they all worked themselves out.

Thus had begun his long journey into the disillusion that was now his life. He had arrived a hero, and now he lived on in a state of boredom. He had been feted, and was now in obscurity. 'At least the chevalier keeps the king from pestering you to play him at chess,' they said – if they said anything about him at all.

Because he was seldom noticed in that nether world where he lived, James could observe and hear things he was never meant to hear. And he did. So as time went by, his discretion became more apparent to the king. To the point where the king came to rely upon him, and confide in him too; impressed by how he never tried to lever power or influence. It cemented a bond of trust between the older, powerful master and the younger, powerless servant. And that in turn had made it all the more tragic for the disinterested James to realise the rot at the heart of the king's cause.

The king lifted his bishop and held it poised over the board. James could see the move but had been powerless to prevent it. But the king paused, and instead used the piece to tap the end of his prominent nose.

'I have had bad news, today James,' he said, looking into space.

James wondered what particular bad news the king referred to; nothing ever remained secret at this court and there was always some unfortunate thing arising. Was it the queen's latest tantrum the king was talking about? Apparently, there had been a bad one that very afternoon. Or was it the letter that had arrived overnight, announcing another catalogue of catastrophes in the king's endless striving towards restoration, that he'd overheard the Earl of Inverness, the king's current secretary of state, discussing openly?

The king began a tale of some obscure Baltic commonwealth whose elected king had died, but James wasn't listening. He'd stopped listening long ago, too depressed these past months to care anymore about labyrinthine foreign power-plays and how they'd contributed, again, to the endless litany of Stuart failures.

He'd arrived at the Palazzo del Re – he'd forgotten how many years ago – with his faith in the 'honest cause' ready to be restored. The hard work and continued dedication of Dillon and Crawford, then his encounter with Mr Teviot, and their crowning success freeing Clementina had seemed to point the way. The petulance of the princess, now queen, had been a disappointment, but actually meeting the king himself, not to mention his own knighthood, had filled the chevalier James with hope and sealed his loyalty.

James remembered his first impressions of a considered, courteous man, of immense personal dignity and – he'd thought then – of sound judgement. The reek of the Earl of Mar's disastrous tenure as secretary of state had still clung to the court, but the king himself had presented an undaunted face to the world.

Mar had been an assiduous courtier, apparently; always present, flattering, obeisant, earning himself the title 'Bobbing John' from the jealous and keeping a meticulous note of every plan and conversation that passed between the king and his agents – one for the court archive, and the other, alas, for Sir Robert Walpole, the Hanoverian usurper's prime minister. Yet the king had appeared to have risen above that betrayal, his will to fight on as tenacious as ever. Here, James had thought, was a king in every sense – apart from his possession of a throne. James had believed his years in the wilderness were now over.

But the reality of the king's true position could not be denied, at least not by anyone with eyes to see and ears to hear.

On the face of it, King James' court had still been a vibrant one when James Lindsay arrived; and indeed it remained so. The palazzo, no more than a baroque, four-storey town house in the shadow of the minor Roman basilica of the Santi Dodici Apostoli, held musical soirées twice a week, and balls every weekend. Every gentleman from Great Britain passing through on his grand tour was encouraged to call.

But behind the settled façade was a writhing, seething struggle for personal gain and favour. Some came from vanity, most from greed. Factions constructed grand strategies, abased themselves at courts from Madrid to Paris to St Petersburg, seeking diplomatic backing, the promise of troops, guns, the promise of future treaties with a restored Stuart monarchy – and always, their hands out for money.

Sometimes the corruption and self-interest was so blatant, James had felt sick. How could the king not see? Not act? Sometimes he wondered if it were not just a throne the king was lacking, but the dynamism necessary to seize it.

'He just seems to always want to see the best in people,' the Comte de Valençay had once observed to James at one of the palazzo soirées, long after the all the initial shine of James' heroic rescue had rubbed off. De Valençay was King Louis' man at the Vatican.

James would never forget how the French aristo had first introduced himself that evening.

'Chevalier Lindsay, I carry a message for you from Colonel Flahaut ...' a man had said, suddenly at James' elbow, out of the blue. Colonel Flahaut? James was stunned; his former commanding officer of the Chevau-Légers de la Garde? How could this man know that? Who was he?

'The colonel still remembers you, despite the passage of time, chevalier. When we last conversed, and I told him you and I now shared the same city, he asked to be remembered to you. He also asked me to thank you for your parting *billet* ... most courteous, he said, although obviously hastily written,' continued the man, 'and he said to tell you that knowing *la* de Boufflers he quite understood your reasons ... and applauded your

106

discretion in sparing the regiment any subsequent discomfiture. Oh, and he added that your commission still sits upon his table against the day you choose to return.'

For want of anything else to say, all James had managed was, 'I do not believe I have had the pleasure …?'

'Oh! Pardon! The Comte de Valençay, King Louis' ambassador to the Holy See, at your service. I do so enjoy attending the Stuart court here in Rome, so far from its natural home. They do put on such wonderful entertainments; one almost forgets they are merely doing it to distract themselves from their pain … they certainly distract me! And the people you meet are invariably fascinating.'

After that, de Valençay often button-holed James to renew their 'diverting conversation'. James had always found him a most discomfiting man; very tall and languid yet precise in all his movements. His limbs were most eccentrically elongated, so that he seemed to move like a praying mantis, but he was compelling in his charm and wit. James always looked forward to their meetings, despite himself, always feeling uncomfortable, as if he was in the presence of a superior intellect. Grateful for the attention, yet recognising that he was in the presence of something dangerous, too.

It had been what else de Valençay had gone on to say at that first meeting that had first snagged James' interest in the man.

'Resigning your commission, chevalier … do you ever wonder whether you swapped a sound horse for a lame one?'

'I don't understand the question, comte. I had no …'

'Choice? Of course you didn't, but I ask it in terms of your king, and seeing the best in people.'

James frowned.

'We live in a world today of great power relationships, that produce causes for war and strife ad infinitum. France, Spain, Austria, Russia. And Britain, behind its moat. Alliances, interests … who is with us today, and not, tomorrow. In this world the periods of peace are merely truces, and human bloodshed only suspended. But a truly powerful

Britain, in an unknown future, what role might she play? A Britain, despite her moat … bound to the continent, but not of it … using her diplomatic skill and her commercial might to direct and control in an intelligent fashion? Her current king is a fat German farmer. But on the other hand, do you think a king who only sees the best, is a king who is equal to the task of controlling and directing … *in an intelligent fashion?*'

James had stared at him, dumbfounded. He had only recently begun a new correspondence with his old friend Davy Hume, and it was on this very subject – of how man might break the endless cycle of bloodshed and war through a new philosophy of moral conduct – that they were exchanging letters. Their old lecturer and mentor Francis Hutcheson had returned to Glasgow University to take up the chair of moral philosophy, and his work was stimulating much thought. Both James and Davy had agreed they were living in an important time. How had this Frenchman known? Indeed, how had he known anything, and why had he lit upon James to share his thoughts?

'I merely throw these thoughts out,' de Valençay had continued, with a smile as sweet and innocent as a child's. 'They are but the musings of a diplomat with too little to do, who likes to peer into the future … but by employing more earth-bound, empirical tools than your gypsy astrologer. I'd be intrigued to hear your thoughts, chevalier. We should converse often, you and I. People who think as we do are rare beasts in this city of God.'

It hadn't taken James long to work out that de Valençay was probably reading his mail. But why? Why read the mail of a lowly courtier? He almost certainly had other spies at the palazzo; like all continental monarchs Louis would want to keep a close watch on what James Francis Edward Stuart was up to, in case he actually succeeded. And that was when James worked out the why. De Valençay would know of all the hours that James and the king-who-was-not spent together in the private chambers; the young, loyal aide de camp and the monarch in waiting who had no-one to trust. They were going to talk. It was only human nature. The only question was; what about?

Life at court. It was why James had shut his ears to its noise these days, why he was so sick at heart.

The king, meanwhile, was droning on. And James was composing in his head his next letter to Davy, while contemplating snuggling in under the quilt of the Duchesse de Villars. She was young, her husband old and fat and always at cards, drunk. She was James' latest *divertimento* on the endless merry-go-round of courtly dalliances that helped the days go by in the palazzos and villas of this city that was every bit as decadent as it was holy.

'But that is not why I have asked you here tonight, James,' the king was saying.

James looked up; his reveries instantly shelved. The king was peering at him closely. 'I have a mission for you.'

James' preparations for his journey were well in hand, so the *billet* from de Valençay, to join him for a promenade along the banks of the Tiber, was tiresome. But de Valençay had intimated he had some information for him that must help him in his forthcoming mission. So much for the secrecy of the king's chambers. So, out into the early March chill he'd gone.

And there he was; de Valençay, bundled in a fur coat and wearing cavalry boots and a full, insulating wig. Ambling aimlessly, tapping and prodding with a walking stick he didn't need, along the paved, tree-lined path.

'A-ha! *Colonel* Chevalier Lindsay!' he said, on sighting James. How on earth had he found out about his new status? How did he find out about anything?

'You have heard of my appointment, m'sieur le comte,' was all James said.

'How could I have not? It is the talk of the salons …'

It was not.

'Well, among the ladies of the salons.' And with that, de Valençay gave his customary conspiratorial grimace. 'Tell me, is your new regiment fashionable?' he asked. 'When I tried to make out its name, all I saw was a preposterous profusion of consonants I could not begin to pronounce.'

'All Polish names are difficult to pronounce, comte,' said James, equably. 'As for whether it is fashionable, you'd have to ask the queen. She arranged it for me.'

'So you are off to the north. To the Polish and Lithuanian commonwealth. To lend your service there, in their time of grief at the death of Augustus the Strong, King of Poland, and Grand Duke of … the other place. We do not know how long you might be, but we do know it gets cold in the winter, which was why I wanted to alert you to my little gift being handed in to the palazzo's concierge for you, probably as we speak. It is a trifle, but I am sure you will welcome it, if you come to feel the cold. And look! You are making me tell you what it is!'

James wasn't.

'Ruining the surprise! Oh, very well. It is a coat, not unlike mine. Made of the pelts of sable. Very rich. And comforting.'

James, eyeing de Valençay's coat, said, 'You are most generous, comte. But my departure many hundred leagues to the north is going to make it difficult for me to repay such generosity.'

James knew a fellow like de Valençay did not dispense gifts like that for nothing.

'On the contrary, colonel,' said de Valençay. The tone of his voice had changed. It brought James up. This was business now. Except de Valençay went into a long, silent reverie that James knew better than to interrupt.

Then, with his mantis smile, he said, 'You know King Louis in his latest missive to me … its chatty postscript … was recalling how highly he'd thought of you when you were in his service.'

James snorted. 'You are practising upon me, comte. You are suggesting the King of France even knows my name? I very much doubt it.'

It was de Valençay's turn give a laugh. 'You'd be quite right to doubt it, my dear James. Louis, as God's direct appointee on earth, has neither the time nor inclination to remember the likes of you. But the men he employs to think his earthly thoughts, most definitely do. I have been asked to speak to you today, not to interrogate you on the nature of your mission …'

'Just as well,' said James, 'For I would tell you nothing.'

'How gallant, James. But your loyalty is as misplaced as it is irrelevant. I already know more about where you are going, and why, than you do. No, it is to ask you for a favour. When you compile your reports for your king … what some people might call *spying* … I would like you to forward a copy to me.'

James spoke rather too harshly in response; but then de Valençay's accusation had angered him greatly. 'Spying? How dare you, sir!'

'My dear James. I know you are going to claim that you have merely been asked to offer your service to a foreign court, and of course, while there, report … no, too formal an instruction … *reflect*, let us say, in letters home. Ones you might write on a cold and lonely evening with nothing else to do … on all you hear and see around you … dip into the general mood … little sketches of the players … colourful accounts of balls and soirées … what is being said by whom, and to whom. On the surface, tittle-tattle, but believe me … each page would be a treasure trove. You young blades with your heads full of romance, you think spying is all about invisible ink and stolen documents? You're wrong. Just having someone tell you what is round the corner is worth far more. Your king is sending you into what is likely to become a hotbed of political intrigue and power-plays, and as likely as not, war – because he wants to know what is going on behind all the formal communiqués, and because you are unofficial and therefore more likely to hear and see … more. Much, much more than you could ever steal from a rifled bureau. In God's name, sir, what else do you think spying is?'

James stood for a moment, crestfallen. Played upon again. 'And I thought I was escaping all these games,' he said, trying to sound droll. 'What a flat they must take me for, to play my strings with such ease?'

'Oh, it's far worse than that, my dear James. Far worse,' said de Valençay, with a sardonic guffaw. 'Let me tell you what awaits you in Poland. The death of Augustus II has re-opened all the old fault lines in Europe. So I will summarise. Polish kings are elected by a council of nobles. Augustus, while he was alive, tried to abolish the tradition by announcing that he was going to settle the crown on his son. He failed. So now that he's dead, the crown is up for grabs. My liege lord Louis' wife is Polish, and indeed her father Stanislas once held the crown ... for about half an hour, or at least that's what it felt like. He wants it back. And my liege lord Louis wants him to have it back. However, Russia – and Saxony, for what that's worth – want Augustus' son to inherit. Austria probably wants the same, but isn't saying ... for the moment. Ditto, King Charles of Spain. They all have vested interests ... a Poland friendly to France might discomfit our old enemy, Austria. If Russia puts Augustus' son on the throne, it gives the tsar a little bit more leverage in mittel Europa, and then there's the endless opportunities for the players to nibble at each other's territorial extremities ... all the ones they've always coveted ... if it comes to war. Contemplating it is like overturning a stone and watching all the insects wriggle. I'm sure that was the gist of what your king had to say to you?'

James nodded, glumly. All the things he'd come to detest in the mindless churn of empires.

'Well, he hasn't told you everything,' de Valençay went on, idly whacking at a twig with his walking stick. 'There's been talk of a compromise candidate. One who would ... defuse matters ... for the time being. They have lit, in secret, upon some sixth, seventh, tenth, God knows what, son of King Peter of Portugal, would you believe? Some barely breeched little brat, called Manuel. Nobody's ever heard of him. Eminently manipulable. And the whole idea, likely an anathema to the Poles. But who cares about them? That's the *official* secret one. But there is another, *unofficial,* secret contender. One who would really set the cat among the pigeons. Who would not entirely displease Louis ... but only unofficially ... because he would not want to upset Hanoverian George in London, who would be apoplectic if he ever got wind. Nor would this candidate entirely displease the tsar, or Charles of Spain. Can you guess who it is, young James?'

'Why would I want to bother?' James replied.

'It is James Francis Edward Stuart,' said de Valençay. 'Your king.'

James stopped walking. It was as though someone had punched him in the stomach. Why would King James want the Polish throne? And if he was considering it, why not say? If James was going into the lion's den to report back to him on who was favourite to win, should he not know James Stuart's name was in the pot? James' sense of being manipulated himself, in this whole adventure, never mind poor little Manuel, filled him with a rare anger.

'Of course he didn't tell you,' said de Valençay. 'Your king may appear the essence of the open, straightforward, decent man, but he cannot have been playing this game for so long and learned nothing. If you didn't know, then there is no danger of you letting it slip. Also, you being such a blindly loyal aide, if someone else let it slip, it is the first thing you would report ... unalloyed ... a full account of how the gathered reacted to the very idea of it. The astonishment ... or maybe hilarity? Contempt? Serious calculation? He'd get a purer picture.'

'But why? Why would he want the throne of Poland?'

'Oh, come now,' said de Valençay, with a snort. Think about it – once you've finished luxuriating in all your resentment. For a start he would get a whole new, national exchequer to play with. No more begging bowls. Then he'd get a seat closer to the top table. He would have something to trade in terms of alliances, instead of just future promises. He insists now, he is not interested. Just one throne interests him, Great Britain. His own. He must say that, because what if people laughed at the idea, or worse, he shows his hand, and loses. Those are just two arguments. There are more. That is why I, and my liege-lord Louis, are so keen for you to listen for any mention. *Any* mention. And then to tell us. It is why King Louis remembers you. Or rather, the men who think his earthly thoughts do. Not for all the services done, but for the one you might yet do.'

James' head was spinning. When he looked down, he could see de Valençay dangling a full purse. He looked up at the man's gaunt, unknowable face. 'You presume to bribe me, m'sieur?'

113

De Valençay held the purse steady now. 'The coat I have sent you has deep pockets that need filling. And the float your king will give you, won't do it.'

'What kind of man do you take me for? To betray my king … for silver?'

De Valençay sighed, and palmed the purse. 'A wise young man once wrote, … *these kings fall out and kiss and make up again with a gay abandon that shows no interest in the societies of people over whom they hold complete power. That this world should be ordered so, ruled by the whims of creatures selected through random accidents of heredity is an outrage to all justice. Man, by our advanced nature, should be capable of so much more. That is why the pursuit of reason and law, and by way of our intellect, penetration to the very essence of what raises us above the beasts, is now, today, the only worthy goal of humanity …*'

'You read my letters, m'sieur? You read my letters, then taunt me with them?'

'Do not insult me with your faux outrage, m'sieur. You know I read your letters. Everybody reads everything in that palazzo. And then sells everything. Its entire architecture is designed around *douceurs* … and not just from your allies. It is well known that Sir Robert Walpole has an open purse, and a deep one too, for the right hand that chooses to dip in. My God, m'sieur. If you ever wondered when your king last sat at stool, why, ask Sir Robert – he'll even be able to tell you its colour!'

The two men glared at each other, then de Valençay's face mellowed.

'And I'd like to point out, m'sieur,' he said, 'that I read *all* of your letter to M'sieur Hume of Edinburgh, and most fascinating it was too. Where you discuss your own future … where you assert that cruel fortune and Hanoverian George have conspired to render you incapable of pursuing the only goals you call worthy … but that he, Mr Hume, must press on in their pursuit, never faltering … while you, in the exile you have been condemned to, not chosen, are left with only one path … to turn your back on the corrupt life of a courtier and become one of the Wild Geese … a soldier of fortune … "I will make my way in this life by my sword alone," were your words, I believe. Very dramatic, chevalier, and romantic, and noble. I am sure the soldiering bit will come easy to you.' And with that, de Valençay raised the purse again. 'But don't forget the fortune bit. You are so right about the corruption of this world. And to wonder, where is honour? But it takes a man who knows how to look after himself, to assign them their rightful places.'

James couldn't help the smile that was spreading across his face. He reached out his hand and took the purse. 'So, you are saying, m'sieur le comte, that the coat and the purse aren't bribes, but merely there to keep me warm, while I practise my honour?

'See. As I said. A wise young man … Oh! One more thing,' and he passed James a slip of paper. 'A name,' he said. 'If you should ever find yourself in need of … guidance up there.'

'Someone I can trust?' said James. But de Valençay's baleful look cut him short.

'Please. Never utter that word in my presence again,' he said, with a wry arch of his brow. Then with a little more grace, he added, 'There is a world of difference in this business, my young chevalier, between accepting guidance, and … that silly word. No, let us just say someone who might be of use. And do please, give her my regards should you chance to meet.'

7

The Road to Poland

What a journey it had been. It felt like he had traversed the entire globe.

Then, suddenly emerging from the dense sea of silver birch, with the land slowly rising before him, there it was. The city of Warsaw, its spires and towers all bathed in late summer light.

The newly-minted Colonel Chevalier James Lindsay had started out from Civitavecchia, the port of Rome, with a servant, two mounts and a pack horse, and sailed aboard a Venetian brig to Marseille, disembarking only to ride the few leagues to the river port of Arles on the River Rhone, then aboard another vessel, a sailing barge, for the long, slow creep up into the belly of Europe. The bargee had complimented him on his timing.

'You have made it before the end of March, m'sieur, just in time to beat the spring melt. You would not like to see this river in spate with all the snow of the Alps turned to water, rushing south to summer in the sea!'

Up the river to Lyon, and then onto another barge to follow the River Saône to Dijon before he and his little convoy struck east to Colmar and then onto yet another barge to take the Rhine to Mainz. From there it had been a long ride up through the valleys of the Electorate of Hesse.

'The country is nominally within the sphere of influence of the Holy Roman Emperor,' a senior secretary at the Palazzo del Re had told him, while stamping and sealing all his passports and letters of introduction, 'by which we now mean Charles of Austria. However, Frederick, the Landgrave of Hesse, is apparently somewhat detached, and professes to Calvinism, although others say he is a more enlightened figure than that might suggest ... but whatever, it means you should not have to answer too many questions there.'

Austria, he had been informed, would likely be no friend to his mission, or to him, after Innsbruck.

In the event, there had been no questions to answer, as he travelled through what appeared to be a magical, medieval fairyland; through mountains and forested valleys, through towns like Fulda.

Fulda was a wonder; a tiny confection of the medieval and the baroque, where all roads seemed to meet, nestling in rolling farmland. Another hub of wealth, in a rolling countryside so verdant and productive, it brought a memory and an ache for his own damp, scratchy home; all moss and ancient rock, a place of grind, existence and ignorance, but only because so great was the contrast.

And then it had been over the border into Thuringia and beyond, onto the eastern bend of the north German plain; endless flat, with the city of Leipzig and towns like Cottbus rising out of it like islands. Ever eastwards, into the Polish forests, where the landscape and the people became poorer, and the sullen wastes of it broken only by the city of Poznan, with its bustling markets and twin-steepled St Peter and St Paul Cathedral on an island in the Warta River.

And now, here was Warsaw. Finally.

His stomach clenched again. It was this thing that had been gnawing at him all those weeks and all those leagues; the prospect of what awaited him here – the young chevalier whose repute lay in battles fought and daring deeds executed with panache, but whose truth, he knew, was just one long anecdote of chance and bluff.

He was on his way to command a regiment of dragoons in the name of a king who was not his own. Him, a young man who had so far commanded nothing, not even his own destiny. And on his shoulders sat the expectations of two other kings, his own and that of France. Expectations that he discharge the roles of diplomat and spy in their names, in a great game he'd never played before. In foreign lands whose languages he did not speak and whose religion and politics were alien.

James Lindsay of Branter, a young man heading towards his thirties, an age at which so many others had achieved so much more.

His ambition to be a scholar had been thwarted, then his decision to place his sword and honour in the service of a noble cause had been dashed when that cause had eventually turned round and mocked him with all its shabby, shallow posturing.

These thoughts had haunted him the whole journey. But James Lindsay had never been one to let things discourage him for long. Stepping forward was what he'd always done. Yes, the future was filling him with trepidation, but then he could hardly remember a time when it hadn't. All he knew was that acting was always better than fretting. So, although his stomach was all a-churn, he was full of resolve too.

How hard could a soldier's life be? From what he'd already experienced, it was just a lot of marching to and fro, a lot of griping and whining and waiting, and from time to time maybe a little running away. And as for challenges of command? He'd seen on the field of battle the likes of Tullibardine and Lord George Murray, men he had once worshipped. How hard could command be?

And when it came to the great game – if those procrastinators, deceivers and self-serving scoundrels at the Palazzo del Re could play it, then why not him? If he chose to.

It was time to serve himself, like that rogue of a Frenchman had suggested when he'd handed over the purse and the sable coat. He hadn't quite yet put a name to this new resolve, but he knew where it was taking him – or at least, he thought he did.

He was contemplating a future free of any loyalty to the House of Stuart, free of all future obligation to any foreign crown or duchy or principality – a future that was purely mercenary.

His little convoy was eventually swallowed into the constant tide of busy people heading in towards the city gates. No-one turned a head, they were used to strangers passing through, this being a place of commerce, and of learning too.

Once in the city James sent his servant, Silvio, off to find a comely inn somewhere near the middle of the town, while he set off to find the military headquarters and report to his regiment.

Silvio, his servant, was short, squat and swarthy in his shapeless hat and leather surcoat that he'd worn in heat and cold. He had not been a companion in any way. James had long ago given up on any conversation with him, the man being practically monosyllabic. All he knew was that Silvio understood French and spoke a guttural Italian. Apart from that, James had no idea where in the world he might have come from. He was a mongrel, who was not quite sullen and had been just efficient enough. He would be rid of him directly and replace him with a soldier who knew his duty – and his new regiment's customs, too.

It was only a matter of time. One of those things you know is coming but that no amount of steeling yourself can ever prepare you.

Colonel Lindsay had set out at the head of two squadrons of his regiment to scout the roads to the north east of Warsaw early the day before. Last night they had bivouacked around a series of copses off the main road to Zambrow, some eight leagues from the city. And now, today, they were wheeling south across low rolling fields beneath a still hot, early autumn sun.

The fields had been surprisingly empty. No peasants working them, no livestock grazing, the roads, or rather packed-dirt tracks, had been deserted. The land knew something was coming.

He had breasted the rise first, his men ranged out behind him in two long, skinny lines, one squadron up, one back. Three hundred dragoons in their dark blue uniforms all faced in red, walking forward at a steady pace, covering the ground, looking for a Russian army.

And now, here they were, the Russians, spread out in a carpet of mostly green and white – the foot soldiers – that seemed to ripple through its own cloud of dust as it marched across his front. The Polish nobles at the electoral *sejm* who'd favoured the Russian candidate had said 20,000 were coming. James, looking down the gentle slope towards this host, could not gainsay them. He had never seen such a press of men, or one that stretched so far – further than he could make out.

His chest tightened, and his mouth shrivelled to dryness. Beart, the Frenchman who commanded one of his squadrons, came up beside him, regarded the sight and then turned to order the two lines to halt.

Beart, who could give classes in sangfroid, made no spurious comment regarding the magnificent tableau they had just stumbled upon. His only words were, after a long moment, 'Your orders, excellency?'

James thought: My orders? The only sensible order he could think of right then was, run! The thought that he might actually give it, made him laugh to himself. That he did so would become regiment lore after this day was over, and attach about his reputation like a mantle. 'And what did Colonel Lindsay do, when he first saw the Russians? Why, he laughed!'

James' eyes drank in the terrain. And in his sweep, he saw the more colourful bodies of cavalry, guarding the flanks of the Russian column of march. One unit, in sky-blue tunics and breeches, and black-fur edged pelisses, detached itself and began to deploy into its component troops. His presence had been noted.

Hussars, he guessed; even at almost 2,000 paces he could tell from those short jackets, worn over the shoulder. Light cavalry. Most of them were forming into line to face up the rise towards him, but at the back, there was at least a troop that was not.

James' horse was on top of a crescent hill that curved shallow to his right, but a few hundred paces to his left, the curve was sharper. The detached hussar troops were galloping that way, while the bulk of them, now deployed in line, were walking up the rise directly towards James, as they would if they were coming to chat. He took it all in, and knew immediately what the enemy were intending, the moves revealing themselves just as if he were looking down on a chessboard and James Francis Edward was manoeuvring him into another drubbing.

He reached down into his sabretache and withdrew his notepaper and pencils, then he scribbled his orders. No dictation for Colonel Lindsay, no misunderstandings left to chance. He tore off the written sheets and handed them to a teenage cornet with a curt, 'Rapidement!'

Much had happened since James had ridden into Warsaw mere weeks before. For a start, he had assumed command of his promised regiment, with a proud local name, the Dzików, or Wild Boars – or, if you were Beart, Les Sangliers. Some 750 dragoons, or mounted infantry, they formed the only cavalry among the mere 2,000 regular Polish soldiers in the city.

Then he had been introduced to the Polish aristocracy, but as a welcome ally, nothing more. The French minister to Poland, le Marquis de Monti, had told him not to take offence. 'Be grateful they do not want to be friends,' he had assured him. 'They are an acquired taste, hard to assimilate en masse.'

For they were all gathered there, the entire Polish nobility, in the city of Warsaw. For the *sejm*, so great was the fever among them at the prospect of a fight for the succession.

There were endless receptions in the city. Morning and afternoon receptions, evening receptions that went on until dawn. There were frequent duels. And all the while, James had been left on the fringes, or in the ante-chambers, twiddling his thumbs, waiting for he knew not what.

He'd used part of the time to sell off the indifferent nags that had carried him here, and to set off to find a mount more suited to his tastes. He found her in another chestnut filly that he named Estelle; a calm, settled, elegant beast who had responded with grace to his whispers and his apples.

If he'd remained committed to his duties to keep in communication, he'd have found himself seriously stuck for anything to write about to Paris, or Rome, on which way sentiments were swinging. The only thing that was obvious was the rabble wanted Stanislas. You only had to listen at the windows to hear. But from the halls where the debates among the nobles took place – and there were many – there was only dispute, and the odd sound of swordplay, with more wounded bodies emerging than clarity.

It was while he languished in this wilderness that the Gräfin Dorothea von Kettler appeared. Hers was the name de Valençay had handed him in his scribbled note.

Looking back from his vantage on the hill, James watched as the first line of his dragoons dismounted and marched up to form a line, a little over 300 paces behind him, below the hill's brow. The second line closed up into troops, and cantered off to his left, staying hidden behind the contours of the rise. Beart stole a look at his commanding officer, and was relieved by the satisfied jut of James' chin. He had witnessed many times the chill fury of his colonel as these lumpen peasants had had to be drilled again and again, to drive into their brains the relatively simple evolutions and manoeuvres he demanded of them. They appeared to be performing satisfactorily today.

When he turned to his front, the Russian hussars walking up the hill towards him and Colonel Lindsay were markedly closer. Beart wasn't exactly sure what his officer was going to require of him, but discipline prevented him from asking.

James was watching the Russians, too. But he was thinking about the Gräfin Dorothea.

He remembered standing in the shadow of de Monti at some rout, with the din of the place so oppressive as to inhibit all speech, when he first saw her without knowing her name. It was later, on a patio, shuffling, trying to disengage from one of Stanislas' entourage, that she had approached him, all coquettish, with a fluttering fan – the late summer warmth had rendered many of the more agricultural nobility as fragrant as their livestock.

'You look lost, my pułkownik Dzików,' she'd said, the first in French, the latter in Polish. And when he looked blankly at her, she added, 'Mon colonel des Sangliers.' Then she'd introduced herself.

Here was the lady who might offer guidance.

'Ah, m'selle gräfin,' he'd replied with an innocent smile. 'May I present myself. The Chevalier James Lindsay, colonel of the Dzików dragoons, as you obviously are aware, formerly in the service of King James III, the rightful sovereign of Great Britain, and now in the service of the King of Poland …'

'Whoever he may turn out to be,' she interrupted, with her coquettish smile, and James had bowed at her wit, smiling.

'Indeed,' he said. 'I was told to look out for you, gräfin, by someone I believe to be a mutual acquaintance.'

'It is my turn to say, "indeed". To whom do you refer?'

'The French minister to the Holy See, the Comte de Valençay.'

And at that her gaze had turned to steel, and she'd recoiled from him.

'Tell me, chevalier,' she said, her voice cold as ice, 'be candid, I beg … has the comte sent you here to kill me?'

The dismounted rank of his dragoons had now reformed themselves as infantry; two solid lines of musketeers, one standing, one kneeling, their officers, swords drawn, on either flank and their weapons pointed up towards the brow where James and Beart sat, minding the advance of the Russian hussars.

James looked to his right, where his detached troops had now wheeled, and were dressing their line. Looking most martial, yet facing nothing but a field of grass, sloping gently from their right to left. James had spent many a day in his father's library, studiously reading the accounts of Marlborough's campaigns on the Danube and in the low countries back in the first decade of the century, and as he sat up to see if he could catch any glimpse of the detached Russian troops, he hoped he'd remembered the great general's tactics correctly.

The Russians to his front now were becoming perilously close; he could even make out the individual mustachios on the front rank's troopers. He turned to Beart, and said, 'M'sieur, I think it time we judiciously hid behind your squadron.'

The two officers cantered down the back of the rise, and behind the double rank of dragoons, James calling out in a parade ground voice, 'The first rank will fire only when the enemy begins his advance! The second rank will step through and kneel, while the first rank re-loads! The second rank will fire! The first rank will step through while second rank will re-mount! The first rank will fire, and then re-mount!'

He looked along the grim, dumb ranks of his men. They had practised this often enough, and initially their drills had invariably turned into Bartholomew's Fair, which James had never attended but had seen etchings enough. But the men before him today looked a lot more capable. It was not them he was worried about. It was the deployment of his detachment, under that young Polish captain, Poinatowski.

No sooner had he and Beart wheeled behind the ranks, than the Russians breasted the rise, a long line of sky-blue, their horses still walking. James was convinced he sensed a flinch as they confronted the Dzików dragoons' double line of muskets.

This was the moment. There was the enemy. He was about to lead men in battle for the first time. He swallowed hard. He'd always imagined his mind would be wonderfully focused when the time came, except that now that it had, his mind wasn't. He couldn't stop thinking about who he was about to start fighting for.

Stanislas. The man the Russians didn't want to assume the crown of Poland. It was him who had the quarrel with the Russians, not James Lindsay. In fact, James Lindsay felt no animosity whatsoever for these poor bastards in front of him.

But then that was, of course, the point of this new life. He wasn't supposed to be fighting for a cause or a king anymore, he was fighting for gold now. So you'd better get used to it, he said to himself; and the idea seemed so ridiculous it made him laugh, a loud, sardonic laugh, for the naive youth he used to be, intended only for himself. But the Dzików heard it too.

They also heard the bellowed, incomprehensible orders coming from the Russian line.

They were a little over 300 paces away – nowhere near enough distance for the Russians to get some momentum behind their charge, but far enough for the Dzików to fire two volleys into them. There was the sudden swish of sabres being drawn, and James caught the flash of unsheathed steel along the Russians' line. Then nothing, no movement, no sounds but the odd snort of a horse, or the sound of others being restrained. And above it all, birdsong in the vast, vaulting sky.

The two lines stood, immobile. James held his breath, until the sound of a distant bugle forced him to look to his left, where over the curve of the crest came another body of Russian hussars, in line, and advancing directly towards James' troops at a brisk canter. Here were the Russians he'd watched detach themselves earlier, and who were now executing exactly the manoeuvre he'd hoped they would – charging to cut him off and pin him against the hussars to his front.

And then Poinatowski's bugler sounded off too, high and tinny – a rhythmic run of notes he knew so well. The charge!

But he couldn't watch. A bugle from his front announced the hussars in front of him where moving. James imagined their officer; what he was thinking now … Handed his orders to 'go and drive off that Polish patrol!' – and him thinking, he'd do more than drive it off, he'd roll it up. And now he was watching his bravado and flourish turn to shit.

The Russians in front of him charged. James felt his bowels turn to water, his knees crimp tightly against Estelle's flanks and his breath rasp in his throat. A throat so dry he wondered if he'd ever be able to give the order when the time came.

Until the Russians had got into their stride and he felt the earth tremble even up through his horse, too late to stop now, and the time *had* come.

'Ranga przednia, ogień!'

'Front rank, fire!' In Polish. There were some phrases he'd thought it best to memorise, even if he was never really going to master the language.

He'd hardly recognised his own voice before there was a loud, rippling crackle and the world to his front vanished in a billow of white smoke.

He ordered the second rank forward, in Polish, and the first rank to re-load, aware now that he was yelling, so loud he could feel his throat rattle with the effort.

Mid-roar, the Russians burst through the smoke, no longer in regimental line, but a shambles, with riderless horses, and riders, tattered and bloody barely clinging to their saddles, but still coming on.

'Drugiej rangi, ogień!'

The second rank fired.

Another ripple of cracks. More smoke, and then the men who had fired suddenly breaking their ranks and running back, muskets shouldered, for their horses, following their drill to the letter. James felt an unexpected rush of pride. But it didn't last long. The front rank was now in place, and before the smoke had thinned, he yelled again.

'Ranga przednia, ogień!'

His dragoons discharged another volley into the smoke bank. The same cacophony of screaming horses and men came back at him, and the dead thumps of meat hitting ground came echoing back too. And then his front rank were running back, and as his second rank troopers, now mounted, were wheeling into line. What was left of the hussars' charge came bounding out of the second bank of smoke, sabres reaching for the backs of the dragoons still on foot.

James' heavy cavalry sabre was in his hand – a fearsome lump of steel, long, straight and with a terrible heft to it that he gripped through a solid, utilitarian steel guard. He yanked Estelle's head round and sank his stirrups into her, and they raced straight towards a Russian trooper trying to hack down one of his running Dzików.

James would never forget the face he saw; time telescoped in reverse for him. He saw every tiny detail in crystal clarity, every movement precisely as if he was gifted to predict where it would go. The man hatless, his long hair tied back with ribbon, skin gaunt, sun-weathered, peeled back in a killing rictus, the eyes suddenly all whites as he caught sight of James coming at him. The bad teeth beneath the huge, preposterous moustache, like a breaking wave. So dandy, in his hussar blue.

And James – aware of his own heartbeat and the rhythm of his breathing and the blood pumping through his veins and Estelle between his legs, the living, pounding force of her carrying him like a force of nature.

The Highlander's battle cry. He remembered the stories. He never heard it at Glenshiel, there had been no Highland charge that day. But the stories of the battle-yell echoed in his head as he felt each individual thud of Estelle's charging hooves reverberate through his own body, carrying him inexorably into the killing space and his Russian hussar. How you sucked the yell up from your very bowels and spewed it out with all the rage and fury of every wrong ever done to you, right in the face of the man you were going to kill, so that he would know, so there would be no doubt that it was him who was going to die here, and not you.

He felt himself reach for it, into his bowels.

And he heard the voice in his ear, warning that when you found it, it would be the only one you'd ever own, so it'd better be good, something to curdle blood.

And he sucked it up, and let it explode.

The Russian, just an ordinary trooper, was raising his own light sword from stabbing to parry to try and avoid James' heavy blade.

And James' Highland yell came forth.

He felt the sound of it in his own chest, rather than heard it, and what he did hear was like nothing that could have come from a man at all.

He saw the Russian's expression change in that instant, saw his thoughts. *It's not supposed to be happening like this.*

Then the Russian slashed down, tried to pull his horse's head around to get out of James' way, but he moved as if his muscle had been rendered flab. James watched as if in slow motion as the Russian's sword hit his, and didn't waver it an inch, merely bounced off the grip guard as the forward edge, with all of Estelle's charging weight behind it, sliced right into the Russian's left rib cage, smashing bone and ripping through lung and heart and then out the back of him.

James charged through, leaving the Russian's burst corpse, half cut in two, to flop from his saddle; and as he did so, there was only one thought in his head. *My first man. By my own hand, my first man.*

In a momentary flash he saw all the life the Russian had lived, that had just ended right here, right now, extinguished in a heartbeat by James Lindsay. He felt his own heart beating as he knew his enemy's did not. And an animal elation, that almost instantly shocked and appalled him.

But no time for that now.

He wheeled Estelle round, ready to charge back into the fight, his heart pounding, his life more real than he'd ever known it. But there was no fight left. All he could see were the backs of a scatter of sky blue uniforms, galloping away, up the rise; with even more riderless horses, resplendent in their sky blue saddle cloths, cantering in circles and making terrible noises. Bodies on the ground, some dead, some not. In a heartbeat he saw none of the dismounted were Dzików, although from the several slashed dark blue coats he could see some of his men were wounded. He left it to Beart to rally them and headed out of the fug of powder smoke, the reek of it strong in his nostrils, so redolent of Glenshiel, and went riding to find his other body of Dzików.

That was when he saw Poinatowski, a huge, beaming smile spread across his face, with his troopers behind him in column order, galloping back to re-join. James silently registered satisfaction; he hadn't needed to worry about the flashy young Pole after all. He'd kept his troop in order, no charging after their fleeing hussars as cavalry was always wont to do. And from what he could see, his men had seen off the Russian detachment without suffering a casualty, caught them square on their flank and scattered them before they could turn and fight.

James turned back and ordered one of his cornets to tell the bugler to sound the recall, so he could re-form the two squadrons quickly. He wanted away before the Russians sent others to seek their revenge. He was still breathing hard as the Dzików cantered from their tiny battle-field, a tumult of emotions tumbling through his breast.

It was then that the full horror of what he had just done welled up, threatening to smother him, but failing. He'd wanted to feel revulsion but was powerless to – not against these waves of what another might think of as dark joy, but he knew to be something far deeper, far, far more visceral. He became aware of an ache in his face and was surprised to realise it was from a smile he couldn't suppress.

8

The Retreat from Warsaw

The Gräfin Dorothea pushed her way through the press of people to where James had just appeared between the entrance columns. They were in a high-ceilinged hall on the edges of the city centre that was serving as a spill-over from where the main *sejm* was in session, in a pavilioned park, the numbers attending being too many to fit into one building.

The din of from all the chatter was too much, so when Dorothea reached him, she ensnared his arm and led him out onto a large patio area with camp tables and chairs set out in random clusters. The area was no less busy, but the noise was bearable.

'Where have you been?' she said. 'Have you heard the news?'

'I've been to report,' said James. Which was true. He had just spent the past three hours in a confused and bustling ante-room in the Ujazdów Castle, trying to tell someone in command of the encounter his dragoons had just had with a substantial Russian army marching south of the city.

'You need General von Bittinghofen,' he'd been told. Where was he? Nobody knew. 'At the *sejm*, probably,' or 'at the Zamek Królewski' – the royal palace.

James had eventually sat down and scribbled out a detailed report and handed it over to some aide who obviously had no idea of its importance. As many as 20,000 men, he'd estimated; infantry and cavalry, but he'd seen no evidence of field guns, just a small battery of horse artillery. Then he'd left in disgust, heading into the city to join the throng, to look for a familiar face, to get a drink. All this he told an impatient Dorothea.

'Stanislas Leszczyński is in the city,' she said.

Stanislas, the once, and hopefully future, King of Poland. 'So, he's decided to turn up,' James said, and Dorothea ignored him.

'Why were you not here?' she said. It was an old refrain in their short acquaintance. She was endlessly asking him that. Why was he never at the debates or the fringe meetings or the routs? How did he expect to learn anything? Why was he not trailing his coat, dispensing little nuggets of his own, to gather bigger ones in return? Information was the only currency here, she'd told him, and you had to gather it. Presumably he was going to want to write something in his letters back to Rome, otherwise why was he here?

'Who said anything about writing back to Rome?' James had replied.

'If you're anything to do with de Valençay, you're gathering information,' she had come back at him twice as fast. 'And why would your own sovereign manqué have sent you here? Because his queen thought you'd look nice in a Polish uniform?'

'I've been drilling my soldiers,' was James' usual answer. This time he said, 'I have been on patrol with my soldiers.'

'That's not your job,' Dorothea had replied.

'As a colonel of cavalry, I think you'll find it is.'

'Are you really so naïve? I think you'll find for colonels of cavalry it is usually drink, cards and whores! As any colonel of cavalry in any army here for a thousand leagues will tell you! But we both know your real job isn't being a colonel, is it? It is gathering information. And as far as I can see, you're not very good at it.'

'So why do you flutter about me, like a moth to light, if I am so useless?' asked James, all smug from believing he had topped her argument.

'Dear Lord, preserve me! So pretty, yet so dense!' Dorothea was the synthesis of frustration. 'Because people know who you are and where you've come from. They're curious where the future King of Great Britain

131

stands … what he might offer … what he might ask for … so when you plough your furrow, I want to see what you turn over, you idiot!'

A pause for the emotion to leave her voice, then, 'And I want to know what de Valençay's going to know, after you tell him.' Then another pause, during which she allowed her icy stare to melt a few degrees, before she airily observed, 'And I am standing when there are seats to be had, and my hand has lacked a cup of punch this last age.'

The electoral *sejm*, when it finally took place, was in the same large open air pavilion they'd used for the debates, bounded by hedge boxes, with a long, raised dais at one end, standards bearing family arms and crests all the colours of the rainbow fluttering and snapping from ranks of poles that surrounded the gathering. The noise of the crowd was fearsome, with trumpets and bugles being drowned out. But in the din there was dispute; the numbers of the pro-Augustus lobby were too few, with those who were there, intimidated into silence.

The decision of the gathered nobles was clear, though announcing it had been difficult above of all the noise. Stanislas Leszczyński was declared Stanislas I of Poland. At least that was what James and Dorothea assumed, given the deafening cheer that went up. A contrary result would have almost certainly led to instant bloodshed.

That would come later, James suspected. Dorothea agreed. Conflict with Russia and Austria was inevitable. Tsarina Anna, and Charles VI of Austria, would not allow the defeat of their candidate to stand.

It amused James Lindsay no end however, that his namesake, the pretender to the throne of Great Britain, could ever have imagined his name might have entered the ring as a possible compromise. Now that James had been here and seen it all as it had unfolded. How else could he have understood how intensely parochial it had all been? Or how all the outsiders had only eyes for the pot being stirred before them, too much so to have even considered there might have been a contender in the man who pretended to the throne of Britain?

It made him chuckle when he reflected on how deluded the great could become, and how incapable they were of ever imagining their own irrelevance. All it took was a little distance from reality and a coterie of flatterers to drown out the truth, and it was easy to hear what you wanted to hear, and imagine thusly.

But then, James had decided early on in his journey here that this was a game he was not going to play. Dorothea had been wrong when she accused him of being, 'not very good' at it. It wasn't that at all, it was that he no longer cared.

The Gräfin Dorothea. What a woman she was. Not a classic beauty, her face was too full of character for that, but mesmerising, nonetheless. Pale, with a golden mane of hair and ice blue eyes. Once she'd satisfied herself that the Chevalier James Lindsay had indeed not been sent by the Comte de Valençay to kill her, the eyes had lost their lethal edge. Once seen, that edge was never to be forgotten. And especially because she had refused point blank to explain why she thought the comte might actually want her dead.

He'd not been alone in being disposed to feel wary of her.

'She's a von Kettler,' di Monti, the French minister to Poland had once whispered in James' ear. 'Out of one of the litters of the ruling family of the Duchy of Courland. Who, for the uninitiated, are quite a tribe in these northern marshes. Also. She is a player, chevalier. And she always, in the end, plays for her own side. I merely mention it as she seems to be quite taken with you.'

Right now however, it seemed that it was James who was feeling taken by her, as she steered and manoeuvred him around the post-vote celebrations, looking demure and doing her utmost to stop her ears from actually flapping, eavesdropping or openly listening, all while hanging on her chevalier's arm and trying to affect an air of not taking a blind bit of notice.

'And who are you gathering information for, milady?' James had asked her after one particularly boring exchange with some minor aristo.

'Why do I have to be gathering for anyone? Cannot a lady be curious as to the goings on of the world?'

'I refer you to your earlier comment regarding any known associate of the Comte de Valençay,' said James.

His words drew an instant, venomous look, then a sigh. 'My land is very small. A tiny little haven, surrounded by big, lumbering beasts that do not care where they plant their hooves. So it is as well for us to know who it is who might wish us well, or ill, or even be indifferent, or careless, at any given moment. Knowledge is power, chevalier. Watch, and listen, and learn.'

James Lindsay decided he liked her, but he also remembered the word de Valençay had warned him never to use in his presence.

And then it was their turn to be accosted.

A boy in a cornet's uniform was at James' elbow.

'Excellency! Excellency!'

James turned to snap, but the boy's face was so full of eager urgency all he managed was, 'And what can I do for you, young man?'

'Colonel Chevalier Lindsay is to report to the Zamek Królewski, forthwith, excellency! A carriage is waiting outside, excellency!'

At the mention of 'the Zamek Królewski' Dorothea's eyes blazed.

'Then lead on, young man,' and James steered Dorothea towards the tall doors. The young cornet's brow furrowed as he saw the grandly dressed gräfin sweep past him. 'I, em, I …'

'Do your orders specify Chevalier Lindsay, *alone*?' said James.

'No, excellency.'

'Then let us all proceed.'

The meeting with King Stanislas I was a low key affair, in a small ante-room of the palace. The king was wigless and had obviously come out from his wardrobe, in mid change, to greet this colonel of his famous the Dzików dragoons.

He cut the jowly, rubber-lipped figure of a middle-aged baker or cobbler or some other such artisan, and he looked tired, but with a determined set to him.

'Colonel Chevalier Lindsay, come, embrace me!' he said, in perfect

French. 'Let not two fighting men stand on foolish ceremony!' And without more ado the king stepped forward and threw his arms around James, who could only imagine the look on Dorothea's face. Who's well connected now? he was thinking.

'And Gräfin von Kettler,' said the king, standing back, and holding out his hand to be kissed. 'So pleased to see you at my court in these times. I trust your mother is well?'

Dorothea touched her lips to the back of the royal hand, and retreated one step. 'She is, your majesty.'

'And I see you have already made the acquaintance of our hero of the moment,' he added with a benevolent smile that said he knew this young woman well. 'I would have expected nothing less of you, Dorothea. Hah! Hah!' And his great laugh boomed out.

'Hero, your majesty?'

'How demure of you to pretend you do not know,' said the king, archly. 'Only this very morning he has defeated a Russian army of 18,000 men in the hills to the south of the city, with only two squadrons of the Dzików dragoons!'

Then he turned to James and said, 'A great victory for our cause, which we shall *never* forget!'

James was on the point of interrupting him, to point out that it had been only a minor cavalry skirmish, which had indeed gone well, but mainly because his two squadrons had probably marginally outnumbered the Russian hussars, and the Russians had been inexpertly handled. But something in the looks all round told him it would be wiser to keep his mouth shut. All he said was, 'Your majesty is too kind. Any of your officers would have performed with as much zeal.'

'But chevalier,' said the king, overflowing with benevolence, 'any of my officers were not there. You were!' The king then commanded, 'Dorothea! Embrace the chevalier for his bravery! Kiss him!'

Dorothea turned her head so as the king could not see the sudden wickedness in her eyes as they met James', and she obeyed, with a relish James could not fail to experience.

'Now, chevalier!' barked the king, once Dorothea had disentangled herself. 'General von Bittinghofen has orders for you. We are on the move this very night. We cannot stand against this Russian army; we have not enough men.'

James, with a little ironic smirk to himself, found he was reflecting on how short a time the fruits of his morning victory had lasted, when just two squadrons had been enough Poles to see all those Russians off, apparently.

But no such reflections were assailing the king. 'However, the city of Danzig we can defend, until assistance arrives from our friends. So go now and prepare your men. And see that the gräfin is provided with a comfy coach too. I'm sure I can depend on you for that, you gallant fellow, eh?'

They were all the same, these kings.

9

The Siege of Danzig, Part One

The cold defied belief. James had never felt anything like it, where your breath condensed and froze on your face and the end of your nose and in your eyelashes, and the air you breathed burned your throat and caused your teeth to ache. And it had been like this for days now, with no sign of it lifting. When he'd complained the locals had laughed at him and told him to get used to it; it would be like this now, until April.

He was out riding along the sluggish stretch of water the locals called the Martwa Wisła, or Mottlau river, a tributary of that great river, the Vistula, which emptied into the Baltic several leagues to the east of here.

There was ice in the water, drifting on the flow, and the water that was flowing looked almost viscous, with vapour curling up in wisps, so much colder was the air above it. Estelle's hooves crunched the snow in a rhythmic syncopation with the plodding of the other horses following on behind. Their sound was sharp in the cold air, utterly echoless, deadened by the endless muffling carpet of white. James was not alone. Immediately to his rear was a young cornet of the Dzików dragoons he'd co-opted as an aide, and behind him, three troopers, one carrying his personal guidon.

The cornet was an eager young man whose noble family name was another of those consonant wastelands that, when he'd tried to pronounce it, he'd drawn only barely concealed smirks from all within earshot.

Since then he referred to the boy only by his intelligible Christian name – Casimir.

They were riding out onto the white, flat peninsula of Westerplatte, which jutted out into the equally flat, grey Baltic, stretching grey upon grey until it merged with the featureless grey sky on an indeterminate line that was the horizon. Everywhere was dull, bleak, dead, cold. This ride was a ritual now, since he'd received word from Stanislas' court and headquarters in the city of Danzig itself, that their cause was shortly to be reinforced by ships of the French navy.

The garrison James commanded at Weichselmünde, a stout, modern, star-shaped fortress built to the design of the famous French military engineer, Vauban, of course had outlying posts on the Westerplatte, to monitor all shipping entering the Mottlau river and to act as a warning tripwire against anyone attempting to force the river in men-o'-war. But James liked to ride out anyway, every day, to take in the lay of the land, to show his men in the posts they were not forgotten and to break the daily monotony of fortress life. And to breathe fresh air, no matter how cold.

He and the Dzików dragoons had been at Weichselmünde since October, sent to secure the approaches to Danzig from the sea. Since then, not even a Russian patrol had sought to disturb their idyll.

Not so upriver. A force of about 12,000 Russian infantry and cavalry had encamped in the countryside to the south west several weeks previously. There had been a number of probing attacks towards Danzig, but no attempt had yet been made to invest the city properly. Stanislas' current royal capital was as yet not under siege.

In fact, after their hasty quitting of Warsaw in September when Stanislas and his 2,500-strong 'army' had marched away the day after he had won the vote, the Russians had displayed little urgency in trying to topple him militarily from his throne. There had been no pursuit whatsoever, so that the retreat to Danzig had been entirely uneventful. The only thing that had chased them was the news the Russian general, Peter Lacy, had reconvened the electoral *sejm*, but this time with only pro-Russian Polish nobles, and voted in the big, fat Elector of Saxony, Frederick Augustus II, as the new king of all the Poles instead.

It was this delay by the Russians that had allowed Stanislas' military commander, General von Bittinghofen, to review the state of the walls that surrounded the city and reinforce its defences. It had also allowed him to raise a substantial number of locals to form militias that would bolster the 4,500 regular troops he now had under his command. It was at that time von Bittinghofen had issued his special orders to the Colonel Chevalier Lindsay, 'Take your dragoons to Weichselmünde and be our eyes on the sea!'

At least it had got him out of the usual sink of muddle-headedness and sycophancy that all courts, and headquarters, seemed eventually to become. But it also meant he saw no more of Dorothea. Irritating and dangerous woman though she was, he regretted this state of affairs, as he'd enjoyed being irritated by her and it had been a long time since he'd encountered a woman who made him feel as though he was playing with fire.

He smiled to himself as he thought about her and snuggled down into de Valençay's sable coat. James had never been so thankful for a gift as he was now, with all that voluminous fur around him, and the fact that Dorothea had been jealous of it, coveted it – burying her face in it and moaning with pleasure when she first laid eyes on it – that made him smile about her even more.

He'd paid her coach many visits during the march north from Warsaw.

'You'll like the north,' she'd said to him, on the journey. 'You'll probably know half the merchants in Danzig, and be relatives with half the bandits in the countryside around.'

James remembered asking her why she always talked in riddles.

'Where is the riddle? They are all your people. You Scots. You've been coming here for 300 years, with your swords, offering to fight our wars for us for money, and when the wars were over, not going home. The ones who were too lazy to live by trade and barter just stole and robbed. In fact, they were probably the more honest of you. Scots, Scots, everywhere, with your drinking and your heretic, democratic church!'

And she'd been right. Well, the bit about the, 'Scots, Scots, every-where …' In Danzig he'd heard more than a little Scots brogue amongst its merchant class, and there was even a Presbyterian minister and a kirk. The accusation of banditry, however, he could not talk to; suffice to say there appeared to be no Scots bandits on this coastline.

And then, in her more wistful moments, she'd even told him about her lands.

'We are really a German people, rather than Slav,' she'd mused, only half paying attention to him in the jolting coach, half back in her own forests. 'Our lands were called Livonia until they were partitioned by war. The usual carving up by the victors. The duchy is all we have left, from the Daugava River to the Baltic. The duchy itself is barely 200 years old, and has always been a vassal to someone. The Poles … the Swedes at one time … the Austrians, through those whelps of the House of Wettin in Saxony … but mostly the Russians. And most of the time we ignore the vassalage, but we never forget the strength of our neighbours and the ease with which they could do us harm. We von Kettlers, always watchful, always cunning in the protection of our people.

'What about you? You are a small land with a big neighbour? A neighbour with big friends to help it, too. Like the Holy Roman Empire and all its vassals along the Rhine? Yes? So what are you doing here? On the other side of Europe, fighting other people's fights? Surely you have fights of your own? You have big friends too, that can help you, don't you? Like Louis, and his Bourbon cousin in Madrid, and the Pope, although I do not understand why he continues to support a pretender king who refuses Mass.'

Which was all true. And not just for the Scots. The strife was not just Scot against Englishman, no matter how much it was dressed up that way. Across all the British lands, from Ireland and the West Country to Cumbria and Northumberland, entire tracts of the Midlands, there were people who believed there was a fight still to be fought, to put a Stuart back on the throne instead of those wee German lairdies. And yes, Dorothea was right again; they had powerful friends. The quarrel between the Bourbons in France and Spain that had once thwarted James' attempted flight to join his brother in Madrid had long since been patched up. Louis might only be lukewarm yet, but the Spanish court was fully behind the Stuarts. Peter I, Tsar of all the Russias, had been an ally while alive, and the King of Sweden, too. And, of course, the Pope. First one, then when he'd died, his successor. Both had stood four-square behind the pretender's claim. James too, had often wondered why. Given James Francis Edward's religion now. But then, maybe under this pretender king the Catholic church would no longer be *totally* banished from those islands where it once held hegemony, and that was why two Popes had kept faith, and kept financing.

But not that James cared. Not anymore. He only had this to say in reply to Dorothea's question; why was he here, in Poland?

'Things are different in my land. Those whose job it should be to protect us, have all the cunning of a deaf and blind sow, and the level of their watchfulness depends on who is wafting the deepest purse under their snouts.'

She had liked that answer, and had made an appreciative moue. 'So the soldier of fortune's soul is not so jaded,' she said, 'that it can no longer recognise injustice.'

He'd liked hearing those words about himself; although admitting it to his new self made him feel uncomfortable. So instead he went back to picking over what he always went back to, when he was thinking about Dorothea; the kiss the king had told her to give him. Nothing had felt less like duty. But then, nothing had followed its promise. He knew he could pick over that one for ever and still be no wiser.

So he snuggled down deeper into the coat, and tightened the muffler he had around his head and ears beneath his hat, and stretched his mittened fingers inside his huge leather riding gauntlets. No ships on the vast grey nothingness today. He touched Estelle's flank as she walked along, and turned her. It was time now to head back to the fortress and its blazing hearth fires; time to go back to the hunkering down and the waiting.

* * *

It was late afternoon when James, accompanied by one of his squadron officers, Poinatowski, who had performed so well during their skirmish with the Russian hussars, and James' aide, Casimir, were rowed into the city from a landing on the west bank of the Mottlau, across the river and up one of the waterways that flowed into the centre of Danzig. The entrance into the city was through a line of low, bluff stone bastions, between two overhanging fortified gatehouses from which were suspended an intimidating chain-linked barrier of floating logs. This waterway not only led to numerous wharves in the city centre, but supplied the substantial moat into which the continuous star-shapes of the bastion works were sunk.

James admired the defiant solidity of these walls, and as they passed, their improbable thickness. Even the heaviest siege cannon could blast away here until judgement day and barely chip them. He had been summoned by General von Bittinghofen, who was now commanding the city's defences, and he had asked Poinatowski to come with him because he wanted him to put his ear to the ground and get a feel for the defending garrison and a sense as to how things were going. And Poinatowski, being a Pole, was obviously suited to keeping his ear to the ground. Also, he was fluent in a most elegant, diplomatic French, useful when it came to explaining Polish things to James.

The air froze their breath, and the snow, now largely dirty on the streets, was held in ridges and drifts by its frozen crust. From one of the central wharves, the party trudged to where the general kept his headquarters in a large three-storey merchant's town house.

Pyotr Poinatowski had become something of a permanent fixture by James' side since the dragoons had been posted to garrison Weichselmünde. To look at, he was every inch the Polish nobleman. Tall and dark and in possession of those distinguished high cheek bones so typical of the Slav people – so it had come as no surprise when James learned, but not from Pyotr himself, that his father had been castellan of Poland's almost mythical Wawel Castle in the south eastern city of Kraków. But those were not the main reasons James had decided to keep him close. It was because he had proved to be a sharp, witty, companionable young man, who obviously had a firm grip of cavalry tactics and knew his men. He also seemed to know everything about the politics of Poland, and everything about everyone who played them.

It was Pyotr who had told him all about Dorothea, and her uncle, the Duke of Courland.

'He's here in Danzig, and has been for some time,' Pyotr said. When James had pressed him further, he'd replied with a wry smile, 'Be sure of what you wish for, excellency. Some people say trying to understand the feuds and bonds of the families of mittel Europa … that way madness lies.'

'I am still curious, it cannot be any more convoluted than the Bourbons,' James had replied, 'and I had to live under them for more than a few years.'

Pyotr had nodded, and then began his tale. 'The current Duke Ferdinand's predecessor, Frederick William, was married to Anna of Russia, the current tsarina, whom he left a widow, some time ago. Tsarina Anna thought to replace him with one of the Saxon Wettins, but they turned out not to be to her taste, so the duchy remained in the hands of the von Kettlers, the title passing to Ferdinand as it should have. He is a very old man now and lives here because on balance, he prefers the Poles to be holding his strings in Danzig than the Romanovs in St Petersburg. Dorothea is living in his house now, and helps keeps him up to date … among other people.'

'Among other people? What does that mean?' James had inquired.

'If the Russians decide to fight it out over this succession, and oust Stanislas, and they will if they fight, their preferred successor for the moment is another Saxon, Augustus. The Saxon involvement means the Austrians will get a say in the running of Poland, and of Courland too, which for Frederick is not quite so bad as the Russians in charge on their own. There's more room for compromise with the Austrian emperor, Charles. But another successor – someone other than Augustus – that could mean unforeseen complications for the von Kettlers. That is what makes Dorothea continually vigilant. Why she trades her information with many people, so she knows who is thinking what. It is all a great game, as I am sure you know, excellency, having been sent here on such a mission yourself.'

'And what does that mean, M'sieur Poinatowski?' James had promptly replied.

'Aren't you here as the eyes of the Stuart pretender in Rome? Everybody says so.'

'I am here in the service of the King of Poland,' said James with all the hauteur he could manage.

'Ah-ha! Keep them guessing. Good tactics, excellency.'

And then a thought had entered James' head; one he didn't reflect on before blurting out the words, and perhaps he should have. 'And what if one of the alternative successors was the Stuart pretender?'

Pointatowski had been good in his response; no obvious surprise, merely a long, considered look before saying, 'Nobody would have any idea how to react to that one, excellency. Astonishment? Laughter? Fear? Everyone to pause to re-box their compasses? Why do you ask, excellency? Is that the real reason you are here?'

'I told you the real reason, M'sieur Poinatowski.'

That conversation had been long ago, while they'd kept watch by the hearth fires in Weichselmünde. There had been no more mention of the Stuart pretender between them since, or of who Dorothea might or might not be talking to. But now they were in Danzig, and as James and his party trudged through the snowy shadows of the narrow streets, he found himself wondering which house might hold the old duke and Dorothea, and if he'd get the chance to call on her, once his military obligations had been discharged.

If he was honest with himself, international diplomacy had nothing to do with that.

The meeting with von Bittinghofen took place in a long dining room, gloomy with dark wood panelling and guttering candles, and a fire that was poor in fuel. 'We are rationing the kindling against the day when the Russians complete their ring around the city and firewood becomes short,' the general had explained, hugging his own heavy coat tight.

Before him on a grand table lay maps of the city, its defences and surrounding countryside. To the south and east on the map were placed card squares, representing various Russian formations. To the east, marshes were marked, but to the north, and all the way west of the Mottlau river, the city was still open to the rest of Poland.

'A 10,000-strong army is assembling in north Saxony,' said the general. 'And another Russian army is marching from the east, with siege artillery. By the new year, the Russians will be in a position to begin the siege properly.'

The men standing round the map regarded it gravely. The general then went on to outline how he planned to use James' Dzików dragoons to attempt to interfere and delay the Russians' build-up, and a puzzled James leant more intently over the map.

The next day dawned bright, but cold. James walked Poinatowski to the ferry wharf for his trip back to Weichselmünde with orders for the Dzików dragoons to march back with him to Danzig.

As they crunched through the frozen snow, James drank in the wealth and cosy security that radiated from the narrow streets of this prosperous Hanseatic city. No city like this existed in his home country, no riches the likes of this had ever yet been accumulated. But then, home was no longer home. He belonged now only where his sword could bring him wealth. That had been the decision.

He craned back, admiring all the buildings. They were mostly wooden with expensively carved fronts; some commercial, the rest dwellings. There was expensive cobbled paving everywhere, from the narrow wynds to the more substantial streets with their larger town houses. And on the waterfronts, the warehouses with their vaulting double door fronts, and high, protruding goods gibbets for winching cargo, all busy as hives.

Once he'd seen Poinatowski off, he had an appointment with a banker in the city who'd been named to him by the court at the Palazzo del Re as a 'Mr MacDougall' – an auspicious name, he thought, for a man of business with contacts in Hamburg and who would see what wealth the Polish exchequer afforded him moved there in thalers.

Meanwhile, he had something on his mind he wanted to raise with Captain Poinatowski. 'If General von Bittinghofen wanted our regiment in Danzig, why didn't he order us all here in the first place, instead of all this to-ing and fro-ing?'

'I imagine he wanted to see how you'd react, excellency,' said Poinatowski.

'React? To orders? How did he think I'd react? Do I give the impression of being insubordinate?'

Poinatowski laughed. 'I understand your question, excellency, but I fear you are not yet attuned to our reality here in Poland. Our army is not the army of France, nor of Great Britain, excellency. Most of our officers are a mongrel corps of displaced persons. We sweep them up for gold, for we have no large cadre of our own. So we get the disgraced, the failed, the just plain greedy, often the incompetent, but all of them, invariably, with a great conceit of themselves, who see orders as more of an advisory matter, to be disputed, usually for no other reason than their own pride or contrariness and seldom through any greater tactical wisdom. So I am presuming the general asked you here to see how you would react to his plans first, before making his ideas actual orders. For as I am sure you can understand, to be seen having to coerce one's officers to one's will is not a look any general would wish to be known for. Nor would the chance of them downright disobeying you, be one you'd be willing to take, too often.'

'Good grief,' said James, shaking his head. 'Well, here's hoping he knows me better now.'

'Oh, I think you can depend on that, excellency, given the very great honour he has just bestowed upon you. All implicit, needless to say. But no-one in the army will have missed the import of the mission that has been entrusted to you.'

'Why does everybody in this damned country speak in riddles?' snapped an irritated James.

Which drew another indulgent laugh from the Pole. 'I warned you. Do not ask. That is the way madness lies. But, just this once as you have already embarked on your questioning, I will attempt to give you a context, so be patient please ... Just because you march in the military traditions of the Duke of Marlborough ...'

James knew nothing could be further from the truth.

'... the military traditions of the Duke of Marlborough ...' James thought back, dully, to the field of Glenshiel and to all the chaos of leadership that had surrounded and blighted that day. But he said nothing, and instead wondered whether having read about Marlborough could count in any way towards marching in his military tradition.

'... most armies of mittel Europa are forged from a baser metal,' Poinatowski was continuing. 'Lumpen, illiterate peasantry, who can barely speak their own language, let alone understand any complex instruction issued in it. They are closer to the horse or bullock that pulls a plough than to a thinking man. So they are whipped and bullied into lines and columns, basic commands send them right or left, forward or stand ... load, point, shoot. They are not required to think for themselves, for they cannot. They have no culture in it. Nor are they encouraged. What foolish general, or even a king, would wish upon himself an army of soldiers capable of thinking for themselves? Imagine what democratical terminus might lie at the end of that turnpike? No, all that is required of a soldier is that they be more afraid of their officers than the enemy. In fairness, we Poles have had to be a little more fleet of foot than that to survive down the centuries, with our nation's borders re-drawn with every war or dynastic marriage that comes along. We have acquired a modicum of self-awareness – a few building blocks of understanding – as you demonstrated to yourself, with your orders that day against those Russian hussars.'

'My orders? And they demonstrated what, exactly?' said James, trying not to sound exasperated. 'No orders could have been simpler, or more straightforward, that day.'

'To you maybe, excellency,' said Poinatowski. 'But think. You required a substantial body of troops to hold more than one order in their heads at a time, and then execute them in a sequence that required timing and concentration. I do not know any other body of troops here capable of such complexity, on our side or the enemy's. But your regiment managed it. And are now famous for it. Everybody knows it, including the general. Imagine how he feels today. Not only has he a senior officer he can rely upon to obey his orders, he has a commander who actually, just might be capable of successfully conducting irregular manoeuvres against the enemy without his command collapsing into a confused rabble. What joy! What prospects for breaking the wheels off the Russians' sedate encirclement! Which is why we speak in riddles ... so as not to lend ourselves hostage to fortune.'

'So I am now the favourite, am I?' asked a now sardonic James. 'Thank you for your most enlightening lecture.'

'It was my duty, excellency, and I give you joy of your new status, with only two further words to add, by way of an advisory – *professional jealousy.*'

After James had bid farewell to Poinatowski, he went off to settle his affairs with the banker. It transpired Mr MacDougall knew the house of Ferdinand von Kettler – apparently the old man did not use his title in the city – so, his business done, James set out to call on Dorothea.

She was not there. When he asked when she might be back, the old duke, in a full wig that dragged on him like a pack-mule's panniers, said absolutely nothing. James was not actually asked to leave the house – it was just that the ensuing total silence had made remaining pointless.

It was not total silence that James encountered from his fellow senior officers in the days that followed, but in their company, conversations quickly descended into the monosyllabic. Poinatowski, right again; professional jealousy. James found he was not concerned, and frequently spent his evenings writing. The days, he spent walking or riding the walls and defences of the city, familiarising himself with the ground over which he would likely have to fight. He seldom found his fellow officers similarly engaged.

Then there were the evening concerts given by a lively and talented chamber orchestra, sponsored by King Stanislas for 'the diversion of the population in these troubled times'. It was at one of those that he chanced upon di Monti again, the French minister to Stanislas' court.

'I have inquiries after your health, chevalier colonel,' di Monti had observed to him. 'From one Comte de Valençay.'

'Really? And how is the comte?'

'La! At his obscure best, chevalier. His letter referred to the wounds you have suffered to your left hand, and inquired whether similar or worse injuries had been suffered by your right. He is a most arch character, the comte. I am assuming that he must have extracted a promise from you to write to him, and that you have not lived up to it. N'est-ce pas? I merely pass on the message, of course, knowing better than to inquire any further into the comte's affairs. Good day to you, chevalier.'

James understood perfectly; his reins were being jerked. It did not signify. He had nothing to write, never having paid any heed to the politicking all around him. But the comte's name being uttered gave him a twinge; that he had even mentioned the name of Stuart in connection with the Polish succession, if only to Poinatowski. It mattered not a jot that the chatterers might speculate on all manner of reasons for his presence here. But in that one unconsidered moment he had let slip a genuine morsel to be chewed upon by all who might come upon it.

He liked Poinatowski, instinctively. But what did *that* signify? The young Polish noble might know of all the currents in play in his world, but there had never been anything about him to give the impression he was an intriguer. One might assume the titbit would be safe with him, that he would never trade it for gain. But then it would only take James' indiscretion to form part of some anecdote Poinatowski might unthinkingly tell over cards, or round a mess table, and then the idea would be free, with a life of its own in an unsympathetic world.

There was nothing to be done. He would never mention it again. Or write it down. Certainly not in his letters to his elder brother, still in Madrid, or the oldest, still in Edinburgh. Nor to David Hume, to whom he wrote the most. Not that any spy here in Danzig would ever get to read a letter written by him if he did, because he always now handed them personally to trading ship masters about to sail.

It took over a week for the Dzików dragoons to start arriving in the city. Beart, his second in command, had done little to plan the movement in advance, so the men and horses had come dribbling in, in great disorder, on whatever barges had been randomly commandeered. However, once they did arrive, their billeting was seen to with great efficiency by Poinatowski. Even so, it took another two weeks before the regiment was ready to execute his orders.

'Bugler!' James gave his battlefield bellow. 'Sound the charge!'

The brassy, urgent blasts were in his ear as he prodded Estelle's flanks with his stirrups, and behind him, two troops of dragoons in a single rank moved as one from canter to full gallop, sabres drawn, towards a very agricultural line of wagons. Their peasant drivers, dressed in all manner of skins and woollen bundles, began leaping from them, before they realised they'd nowhere to run.

James drank in the scene, leaning forward so his head was practically between Estelle's eyes; the road ahead of him winding across a packed, old-snowy waste. Everything grey-white apart from the wagons, most of them no more than rolling hay-ricks – fodder for the Russian cavalry, and the few artillery horses around Danzig. Then there were the high-sided wagons, canvas tied tight across their open tops; those could be anything from powder barrels or shot to delicacies for the senior officers' tables.

There was a score or so of Russian dragoons, scattered along the length of the convoy, about thirty wagons in all. No gay coloured uniforms here; it was too cold. Like James' own men, the Russians were all in long grey coats, their bicorne hats scrunched down over mufflers, and in as much alarm as their civilian charges. Bolt upright, reining their horses, not knowing where to turn. No chance to draw a sabre or a musket, they nearly all just wheeled round and fled up the rise where their fellow troopers had already ridden, in tight troop formation, to see off a half a dozen Dzików that James had placed there in advance to draw their attention.

The Russians and all the local waggoneers had been looking at the enemy on the crest of the rise, and their own charging fellows, so nobody was watching to see the three-deep column of Polish horsemen ride from behind a bare, leafless copse of birch on the other side of the road; or to see its troopers, once clear of the trees, immediately swing from column into line with the precision of a sweeping watch hand.

Estelle carried James, careening through the gap between two wagons, with Casimir galloping fast in his wake. Out the corner of his eye, James could see one of his troopers battering down, with the flat of his sabre, one of the drivers who had raised a hay fork in his own defence. Stupid man, he thought of the driver, either hide under a wagon or run! Nobody is interested in you!

The Dzików had all been warned in advance ... leave the drivers alone! And if you have to strike out, do it with the flat of your swords, not the edge! Because if all went according to plan, he was going to need the drivers. But then his troopers all knew that by now. This wasn't their first raid on the Russians' supply train.

James was gaining on a trailing Russian, whose nag just would not carry him any faster no matter how hard he whipped at it with the barrel of his drawn horse pistol. Poor beast, he could see her ribs. These Russian cavalry mounts were having a hard winter before Danzig, the horse fodder being all eaten up for miles around, and what there was, having to be carted in like this.

Grunting, his breath billowing in clouds with his exertions, pushing Estelle onward, he was within half a bound of slashing at the Russian's back when the poor wretch, instead of turning and discharging his weapon in James' face, hurled it away and yanked his horse's head round, throwing up his hands and begging for quarter.

Still in mid-bound, James edged Estelle to the side with his knees, and as he hurtled past the supplicant enemy dragoon, he put his entire weight into a fierce back-handed swipe, so the flat of his sabre caught his enemy square on the side of his head and sent him cart-wheeling into the snow. And on he rode, after the next one, his eyes fixed on another retreating grey-coated back.

Casimir was at his side, yelling something, as his horse matched Estelle's tearing pace. James looked up and immediately understood.

It was all over. The disciplined ranks of Russian dragoons that had been heading to drive off his six Dzików were now just a dissipated scatter of fleeing horsemen, galloping along with the score he'd just driven off the convoy of wagons, all of them going in any direction, as long as it was away from the now stirrup-to-stirrup lines of charging Dzików.

'Have the bugler sound the recall!' ordered James, as he reined in Estelle, and waved down Poinatowski and his half dozen troopers from the top of the rise. It was time to organise the convoy for its new destination — the clutch of barges waiting for them on the south bank of the Mottlau river, less than three leagues away to their north west – before any of these fleeing Russians raised the alarm, and a far stronger force came out to put matters right.

'I do not know the manners of your wild, barbarian people when they are at home, chevalier,' said Dorothea, sitting very prim and erect in the wonderfully warm and cosy reception room of her uncle's townhouse. The steady candle glow in the draughtless air gave her skin a peach-like softness that James found it hard to take his eyes off.

'But,' she continued, 'in civilised society it is not considered gallant to question a young lady. When she says she has been indisposed, that is considered sufficient reply for any gentleman who aspires to the name, sirrah!'

While James had been on his latest raid, Dorothea had sent a note to his lodgings, thanking him for his previous visit and advising him she was at home and receiving. He had, by return of messenger, requested an appointment to call on her. And now, here he was. And all he had said was, 'I trust your indisposition was not serious … did not confine you to bed, or place you in need of physic.'

He made his apologies, begged forgiveness for the barbarian he so obviously was and promised to do better; all the while thinking he had never seen her look so healthy.

'You are forgiven, James.'

He liked the way she said his name so much, it quite banished his intellects from his brain.

'After all, it is always a little beguiling to a young lady to have a hero of such repute inquire after her health,' she said, with a smile beguiling to any young man. 'Especially when all one hears is concern for that hero's own health. From friends one might assume the hero should be in constant contact with. How can this be so, James?'

'You lose me, Dorothea.'

'Our mutual correspondent, of course. The Comte de Valençay. He writes to me expressing astonishment at your silence. Deep worry over what affliction might be the cause. Eagerness to hear your news. Especially concerning the matter you talked of in Rome. You never mentioned to me, your confidante, that you had talked of *that* with him, in Rome. That anyone was talking of *that*, anywhere.'

And suddenly, all James' intellects returned to him in rush.

'The comte talked of many things in Rome, Dorothea. I merely listened. Until I stopped. I was not aware you were still a correspondent? Indeed how can it be, since your first reaction to the news he was known to me, was your assumption he had sent me to kill you.'

'You are showing your barbarity again, James. How could a gentleman possibly repeat such an allegation … that I would say such a thing? La!'

Here was a woman who was used to trifling with men, and getting away with it. For all her subtlety elsewhere, he was surprised she was signalling it so obviously. Perhaps, he thought, she was in a hurry. She had often told him, in their past conversations, that knowledge was power. Well, let us see, thought James, who as a much younger man had been trifled with by the best. He gazed candidly at her, but the flash of her eyes said she was not so much angry with him, as frustrated. Good, thought James. I can dance too.

The winter dragged on. Several times more James led his dragoons out on forays against the Russians' lines of communication. Some of these actions were more successful than others when it came to plunder, and on only two did he lose any troopers killed. The dragoons themselves, he felt, had become more confident, although it was hard to tell from their flat, dull, Slav faces, drilled down the generations to never betray an emotion or inner thought – or so it sometimes seemed to him.

Christmas came and went; a drab affair by Polish standards, he was assured. It was the siege's fault, people said. Except this wasn't a siege, at least not yet, General von Bittinghofen had kept telling him. It was just a lot of Russians hanging about outside their front door. He'd know when the siege started, proper. Nobody would be in any doubt.

James continued to call on Dorothea, and they conversed on matters ranging from the state of the city's defences and the progress of the Russian works, to the performances of the king's chamber orchestra, with only the odd upbraiding from her at his failure to communicate with their mutual acquaintance, de Valençay. He had the impression her heart was no longer in that particular hobby-horse. She seldom flirted with him now. It was all too apparent that her manner had become far more serious, although the precise forces at work behind this new gravity, she studiously never discussed. And James was wise enough not to pry.

His fellow officers among the king's small army in the city continued to keep their distance, apart from Poinatowski, who continued to shoulder a substantial role in the running of the regiment. In Beart, his second in command, James began to see an officer who was there not because of his abilities, but because he had probably failed at home. A plodding, unimaginative man who, however, did not seem to harbour any malice and who could at least be relied upon to get on with all the administrative business of soldiering.

Then the tempo of the skirmishing around the Russian siege works stepped up, and James and his dragoons found themselves drawn in.

The fruits of this despotism are like a poisoned windfall, writes James, seated at a desk in his own lodgings, his quill scratching to the light of a candle constantly guttering in the many cold draughts. *It blankets the land and rots everything it touches …*

He is writing to David Hume, in Edinburgh.

In an age when the chances of a letter finding you on a foreign shore were slim, the busy shipping lanes between the ports of the Baltic Sea and the Port of Leith have rendered their correspondence routine. A state of affairs that James is becoming increasingly grateful for. Quite simply, he needs someone to talk to, to help him come to terms with this new world in which he now lives. And in this letter, he is fulminating on the injustices of man in his current state; a topic on which he and David have long debated.

The countryside here is nothing like the land that bred us both. It is flat; an endless flatness from horizon to horizon with no mountains for 100 leagues and only ripples in the ground for hills. This soulless view is broken only by scant patches of birch and impoverished settlements of peasant hovels that do not deserve the name village. All the ones we pass on our patrols have been stripped by the occupying Russian army. The livestock stolen and slaughtered to feed their horde, the food stores emptied of grain and hay, the food lifted even from their plates, and the fit male peasantry carried off to be used as beasts of burden digging trenches and battery revetments for the Russian besiegers. Those that are left, are left to starve in the cold that grips this winter landscape. While I have not seen or heard of any deliberate atrocity or ill-usage of women folk as in the great religious war of the last century, I fear that is only because the Russian officers make their men so busy that they have not the leisure for such daemonic diversions.

And then you come inside the walls of Danzig, and commerce and industry proceed as if all around were normal. With its outlet to the sea, trade continues and great profits are made, buying and selling. Trade even continues in its own convoluted fashion with the Russian enemy, especially in goods that suit their officers, such as wine and other fine provender.

He is particularly upset this evening because of the events of the previous one.

He and his Dzików had been placed under the command of one of von Bittinghofen's subordinates, a particularly stupid man convinced that he is the new Achilles. For several weeks it has been this senior officer's mission to harass the enemy's trench building to the south of the city. Last night, his plan for disruption envisioned trapping a significant number of the enemy engineers in one of their own covered trenches, and burying them alive. Or at least, that was his stated intention.

James' revulsion on hearing the plan almost drove him from the room, and indeed his service as Dzików colonel. But he kept his own counsel, and listened, incredulous, as to what this officer, one General of Brigade Karol Vytautas, a Lithuanian apparently, had in mind.

He stood over a huge map of the city and its surrounding terrain, and with great sweeps of his hand outlined his plan. 'The Russian engineers have pushed saps through the village of Schidlitz to here,' – saps being covered trenches that allowed the engineers to get closer to the city's walls without the city's guns being able to fire down on them – 'and this is where they are digging gun batteries from where cannon will be able to shoot up the slope of the glacis and command our battlements on the Hegelsberg bastion.' The glacis being a rising earthwork in front of the city's walls, to protect them from direct siege artillery fire.

Another of General of Brigade Vytautas's dismissive slaps hit the map, again explaining nothing.

'Tonight we will disrupt their work, and ensure there will be no-one left to continue it,' he said with a conceited flourish, again failing to expand on his claim that he intended to 'bury' them; no mention was made as to exactly how.

Nonetheless they all set off into the night; an entire company of Polish grenadiers to directly assault the half completed batteries, and two squadrons of the Dzików to enfilade the saps where the engineers were expected to flee.

James' quill scratches fervently on across the paper, each slash of ink a mark of his anger.

From my saddle, secure in all the privileges my rank bestows, I have an Olympian view of this comedy playing out around me, and what I see tells me men are cheap. Only those prepared to prostitute themselves to power, or useful idiots, prosper. There is no justice for the rest. The only rule is that of the strong over the weak, and no law but that of the wild. And all of this is happening today in the heart of Europe, in the cradle of what we call civilisation.

The Dzików approached the saps down a series of culverts in the land to the west of Hegelsberg, where Russian trenches had yet to reach. With them was a young Polish grenadier officer, wearing a padded leather jerkin instead of his regimental coat, and a forage cap instead of his usual mitre. Mud-spattered and haunted-looking, he was to be their guide.

Alas, also with them, having suddenly materialised out of the night, was General of Brigade Vytautas himself, come 'to see the entertainment.'

Only the dull reflection of snow lit the landscape. The horizon ahead of them was marked by the distant campfires of the Russian army proper. The first trouble occurred with an argument between Vytautas and the Polish grenadier guide; except it was not so much an argument as the young grenadier merely pointing out something on his map, and Vytautas raging at him. James was too far away to hear what was said, but close enough to see Vytautas turn away triumphant.

The mounted dragoons then resumed picking their way further down the culverts, the snorting of horses and the jingling of bridles sounding like a regimental band parading in the freezing darkness.

It was then the rattle of musketry reached them, from back towards the city walls. The Polish grenadiers had launched their attack on the unfinished siege battery.

Another altercation between their guide and Vytautas quickly followed, something to do with exactly where they were. It ended with the general of brigade shouting that they must press on, and quickly. So they did. It was then that James became aware the guide was no longer taking the lead. So James reined Estelle in and dropped back to talk to him. Leaning from his saddle, he asked, 'Can you explain how exactly my men are supposed to "bury" these Russian engineers in their saps, without shovels?'

The grenadier looked up at him as if he was mad. 'I do not follow you, excellency.'

'The general of brigade's orders. If we are to "bury" them in their covered trenches, how are we supposed to do it?'

'What he means is "kill". With musket ball and bayonet, excellency. The way the general of brigade always does it.'

Even before they set out, James had never intended to 'bury' these Russians, always supposing he was ever to come across them on this gimcrack adventure, but to take them prisoner instead. That plan was no longer an option after Vytautas turned up. But James was not unduly worried. Amused rather, trying to imagine how the general of brigade was going to effect the sealing of the hapless Russians in their covered trench. By having his dragoons ask them first for *their* shovels, so they could start digging them in?

He'd never imagined his men would be drawn into bloody murder so directly and felt his gorge rise with fury. At that moment, Vytautas arbitrarily announced it was time to dismount.

James, controlling his rage, ordered his men to deploy on foot and form up in three lines. From that point they left their horses tethered and marched, or rather stumbled, through the dark to the line of the saps. Alas, when they got there, they discovered they were in the wrong place. Instead of covered trench, the cuts in the earth were open, and closer to the Russian infantry lines than had been planned. Too close.

James became aware of Vytautas behind him, berating the grenadier for his incompetence, when a stampede of feet could be heard coming down the trench. Vytautas had heard it too and appeared at his side.

'March your dragoons to the lip of the trench and prepare to fire by ranks,' he ordered James. But James had already decided: not while I command them! And then the charging mob had appeared round the zig-zag of the trench, and even in the dark, the nature of the running, shabby, disorganised men was plain to see; local peasants, farm labourers and herdsmen – forced labour from the surrounding settlements. Not a military engineer among them. Or a Russian.

'Issue your orders, colonel!' Vytautas hissed in his ear.

Sitting at his desk, as all the images of the previous night crowded in on him, James is aware of his pen scratching on. He remembers standing close by the flank of his men, looking down on the running peasants below as they realised what stood over them; the groan that rose from them and the way they'd half recoiled, half tried to speed on. Arms thrown up as if mere flesh and bone might provide cover. And the plaintive cries for quarter.

'Your orders!' Vytautas again.

Useless to point out these were Polish folk. Vytautas could see that just as well as James.

He cannot remember if he even looked at General of Brigade Vytautas as he bawled one of the parade ground instructions that he'd learned by rote in Polish; bawled it in his best parade ground voice. 'Three ranks, about face!' The crunch and stamp of boots until the dragoons were facing the way they had come; away from the trench lip. Then, 'Forward, march!'

And he remembers marching away with them, in step.

That was when he heard the shout behind him, and then the report of a pistol, very close. In the second that followed, he tensed for the impact of the ball. He was in no doubt who had fired, and that they had fired at him.

But no ball struck. Yet when he turned, there was General of Brigade Vytautas, pistol in hand, the barrel pointing in his direction. Except the barrel was wavering in increasing circles, and when James looked to the man's face, a gout of blood came spouting from his mouth, and his figure slowly toppled to measure its length on the cold, hard snow.

Behind Vytautas had stood Poinatowski, calmly holstering his own long cavalry pistol.

Poinatowski walked past James to join the marching dragoons. As he did so, he stopped briefly, coming to attention, as if making a report. 'Only if anyone asks first, shall I speak, and then all I shall say is that in the heat of battle, I saw a soldier pointing a gun at your back, excellency. How could anyone recognise it was the general of brigade, in the dark? If indeed it was. Do you wish to collect his remains or leave him? I personally would leave him, excellency, and let the Russians announce that he died gloriously, surrendering his life before he would accept defeat.'

The tide of its squalor licks everywhere, even almost to my own boots, but it is to my eternal relief I feel able to report to you I remain un-tainted, and hope I speak true, at least for now.

The scratching of James' quill is interrupted by a knocking at his door, which is then thrown open before James can reply. It is Poinatowski, breathless. 'It is the French, excellency,' he gasps. 'Their ships are in the offing, off the Westerplatte!'

10

The French Squadron

James had the great masts of the French warships in sight from a distance, towering over the flat landscape in the crisp, grey northern light as he rode at the head of General von Bittinghofen's delegation. But it was only after he had finally passed through the gates of the Weichselmünde fortress, and mounted its seaward bastion, that he had a full view of their majesty, anchored there in the fairway of the Mottlau river. Two ships; *Achille*, a two-decker of some sixty guns, a frigate, *Gloire*, and a clutch of Baltic transports.

From the busy tent lines they had passed outside the fortress, it had been obvious that the troops the French warships carried had already disembarked. Some 2,000 infantry accompanied by three light field guns, he'd been told. When you tallied them up in the ledger of war, it was not much to add to the barely 4,500 regular troops King Stanislas I could already number. Especially since the word from the Polish irregulars out in the country was that another 10,000 Saxons had just added themselves to the Russian order of battle, which itself had been growing steadily over the winter. By James' reckoning, some 40,000 enemy troops had now massed in the countryside around Danzig in an arc from the east at Fort Sommerschanz on the mouth of the River Vistula proper, to the southern banks of the Sasper See, a lake just south of the Mottlau in the west. All they lacked was a siege train of heavy guns for this battle to commence properly. And according to von Bittinghofen's aide, it was on its way.

Only one or two boats plied between the French men-o-war and the fortress now, and James could see *Achille*'s captain's barge was still alongside the magnificent warship. A council war was scheduled, but it was obvious the French delegation was still aboard their ship. When James turned from the battlements with a grunt of frustration, his eyes were drawn down to a carriage parked by the entry-port to the fortress' jetty below. Coachmen were lounging about it, passing a flask – local eau de vie, no doubt – so the coach, which he certainly recognised, was obviously empty of its passenger. It was the location that caused his moment's hesitation in failing to identify it immediately. It was the Duke of Courland's coach, the one he never used because he was an old man and never travelled beyond the city gates these days.

It was not until late in the evening that French set foot in the fortress, very late for their appointment. The officers' dining hall had been prepared, except that the candelabras were all now defaced with dripped wax, and their candles low, and the wine warm from a blazing fire, which was now just a collapsed centre of white hot embers. When the French officers walked in, James slipped out. He was not needed for confabs at this level, but mostly he wanted to see who else had come ashore with them. And sure enough, there she was, a figure moving through the shadows, muffled in furs, yet instantly recognisable; about to step into her uncle's coach. Dorothea, the Gräfin von Kettler.

James stepped forward and gripped her arm to help her board. He felt her stiffen, and then felt the blaze of her eyes on him before recognition tempered her fury, but only a little.

'It is you, chevalier,' she said. 'La, but you have a talent for materialising everywhere.'

'Dorothea, what are you doing here?'

The arch of her brows said she had marked his forwardness in using her given name; not to mention questioning her.

'I am a subject of Stanislas the First, chevalier. I live here.' And with that she stepped inside the coach. As she did, a coachman was coming round to secure the door, so James was forced to step back. He wanted to say more through the window, but before he could open his mouth, she had leaned forward and tapped the roof, and the coach lurched away.

The council of war did not last as long into the night as James had feared. Yet from it a great plan was devised. No endless debate, no caveats. Decision had been the order of the night. The French infantry and guns would be ferried across to the west bank of the Mottlau river and would then march to a line of entrenchments Saxon infantry were throwing up between the Sasper See and the coast. They would drive these Saxons off their defences and then march to turn the flank of the entire Russian army at a small village called Zyakendorff, which lay around a road junction to the south of Danzig. All were agreed. It would be manoeuvre and daring, and speed and élan, that would trump numbers in this coming battle, and so render the Russian General Lacy's position untenable.

As the council broke up, the leading French officer casually, and truculently, upbraided James for '… not having brought your dragoons with you, chevalier. Who would have imagined Polish cavalry were shy of glory?' James did not know his name, had not even been introduced to him.

'His name is Chapuis,' said Capitaine de Vaisseau Perouse of the *Achille*. 'His written commission describes him as a "brigadier d'infantrie". During the voyage here I found him to be a gentleman of very strong opinions, especially when it came to his own military genius.'

The French capitaine, who'd already insisted James call him Claude, was referring to the senior French army officer who had so insolently addressed James after the council of war.

Claude and James were perched high in the air, in *Achille*'s main topmast crosstrees, with an arm and a leg each wrapped around the topgallant shrouds. James' telescope rested on one of the shrouds' ratlines as he gazed intently across the west bank of the river and over the league and a half of flat fields to the far side of Sasper See.

It was a crisp, bright morning with a bitter chill still in the air, no hint spring was approaching. James was here at his new friend's invitation. For, when the French capitaine had heard there was a Scots officer, of equal rank, among the Polish forces in the Weichselmünde fortress, he had immediately sought him out.

'Twice I have sailed to your country, chevalier James,' the capitaine had rhapsodised, pumping James' hand. 'Carrying soldiers and arms to help you throw off the yoke of that preposterous German usurper. And what a beautiful country, and what people, and what a welcome!'

It was an occasion to share flask of cognac, he had insisted, and promptly ordered one from his personal stores. That had been three days ago. Since then, James and the capitaine had been watching the spectacle of the two French regiments and their battery of light artillery attempt to transport themselves across the Mottlau river.

Towards the end of the second day of their observations, the capitaine had remarked idly, 'You did say you heard M'sieur Chapuis declaim the essence of this operation was to be speed and manoeuvre?'

'And daring, and élan,' added James.

Now it was the morning of the fourth day, and the two French regiments were no longer a chaotic shambles, but immaculate, marching oblongs of grey-white uniforms and black tricornes, bayonets flashing in the weak sun, snaking slowly towards the earth-coloured scars in the snow that marked the enemy's earthworks.

'You think he will attack before lunch?' inquired the Capitaine.

'Speed, as well as manoeuvre,' said James, dryly, his eye still firmly stuck to the telescope. 'Those were M'sieur Chapuis' very words, were they not?'

'Mais oui. But he *is* French after all. So probably only after lunch,' said the capitaine with a wry smile. Then after a delicate pause, 'So, he is to throw these Saxon newcomers out of their trenches 'How many are there? A regiment?'

'Apparently,' said James.

'So how does that defeat an entire Russian army tens of thousands strong? With just 2,000 French fusiliers? I am not a master of land warfare, my friend James, but I can count.'

'… *and* three six-pounders … *and* daring and élan,' James said.

'And speed, as well as manoeuvre,' added the capitaine.

The two men started laughing.

Time passed. James passed the capitaine the telescope. To make conversation, he said, 'Chapuis has been confiding in General von Bittinghofen, apparently.'

His friend trained the instrument on the advancing French column.

James continued. 'Chapuis told him he's met the Saxon army in the field before, and has respect for their fighting qualities. Respect, mind you, not fear. So he is confident he will overcome them … seeing as he will outnumber them two to one. The Russians, however, he has not met. Nonetheless, he has arrived at several conclusions. Their army might march in step, and disport itself in elegant uniforms, but it is not a European army. It is no more than a horde from the east … no more than a dandified barbarian mob. And once confronted by modern European troops, it will melt away in fear and awe, especially if those European troops have recently triumphed over the troops of a superior ally. He is convinced that victory is assured.'

'Dear God almighty,' said the capitaine, handing the telescope back to James. 'I do not know if I can bear to look.'

As darkness fell that night, James and the capitaine watched as the shattered remnants of the two French regiments began trickling back to the far bank of the Mottlau for re-embarkation across the river and the safety of the Weichselmünde fortress.

Throughout the day the two men had followed Chapuis' every move as he deployed his men on the snowy plain on far side of the Sasper See. It had been like watching an invisible hand play toy soldiers on a bed sheet.

They had complimented Chapuis on the precision of his drill as he marched his troops up to face the enemy, on a two regiment frontage in three ranks. But then, their admiration had waned and they were consulting their timepieces. Chapuis took his time, pacing the spaces between each company and battalion, dressing the lines, then dressing them again, then marching the colours to the front and then calling forward the fifes and drummer boys. And in all that time, the French fusiliers had not moved one step forward.

Then it had been time to roll out the three cannon, one on the left flank, one on the right and one between the regiments. The little match-like figures that had started running forward, James recognised as the skirmishers Chapuis had borrowed from one of von Bittinghofen's Polish militia battalions, obviously being thrown towards the Saxon trenches to cover their cannon.

It had been mid-afternoon before they saw the first puff of smoke billow from one of those French artillery pieces, signalling that the action had commenced, the distance too far however for them to hear any report. The paltry cannonade did not last long. Then the grey-white lines of French fusiliers began to move, their colours like tiny white and gold smudges preceding them. Mounted officers, too. Then they came to a halt, and the colours and the mounted officers dropped back into the solid block of each regiment. Everything looked frozen, like a painting, until a sudden wave of white smoke erupted all along their French line and the fusiliers who had just fired marched into it, and were lost. The powder smoke from their muskets clung to the ground in the windless air, like a strand of cotton wool stretching out towards the coast. That events were unfolding within it was all too apparent from the way it seemed to wheeze and convulse every three or four minutes, as each succeeding volley of fire added to its volume.

And then it was over.

At first it was only a few tiny, stick-like figures lurching from the smoke; then they came in confused gaggles, streaming away; eddies of grey-white uniforms, some like clots around the colours, with the officers on their horses, turning and wheeling like ineffectual dams trying to stem the flow.

Chapuis had been the first back across the Mottlau river, and into General von Bittinghofen's forward headquarters in the Weichselmünde fortress. He had raged across its hall, denouncing all and sundry as he went. First, it was the general's worthless uhlans who were to blame.

'They said they had reconnoitred the earthworks … mere scrapes in the ground, they said!' Chapuis roared.

Von Bittinghofen's uhlans had reconnoitred the earthworks, but they had not described them as 'mere scrapes in the ground'.

'I found parapeted trenchworks worthy of Vauban!' Chapuis ranted. 'They said I faced only a tired regiment of foot, exhausted after their march from low Germany! I faced a brigade at least, maybe even a division!'

He said that when it came to estimating an enemy force, von Bittinghofen's 'blind peasants' were only good for, 'tallying a sow's litter!' He then accused them of treachery; of lying to lure his fusiliers to their destruction. That was when von Bittinghofen's low, steely-edged warning about who Chapuis was trifling with had hit home. The Frenchman, forced to give pause when it came to insulting the honour of Polish uhlans, began venting his spleen along another axis.

At least, he declaimed, his attack had achieved something the Poles had been incapable of so far; demonstrating beyond doubt that the enemy's encirclement of Danzig was now complete.

'So here is a message for you, general! Paid for in my men's blood!' he railed on. 'Your position is now untenable! The Russians are free to bring up their siege train, their big smashers, and they are going bombard you into dust. You have lost, m'sieur general, and so has your so-called Polish king! Once my men are back across the river, we are embarking and sailing away from this, this, *prison*!'

The next morning, while Chapuis' men began forlornly filing back up the gangways onto *Achille* and *Gloire* and the worn-out rented transports, James had himself rowed back upstream to Danzig. He found the city in ferment. One of the first to accost him on his way to make his report to King Stanislas' aide was the rodent-featured French minister, the Marquis de Monti.

'I have Chapuis' dispatch in my hand!' he whined. 'How can it be? How can it be?'

The Frenchman was waving several sheets of vellum. James eyed them incredulously; how could that wretch Chapuis have penned such a detailed document and had it here in the city so quickly? Obviously, there were circumstances where he indeed was capable of speed and manoeuvre.

'How is it he was sent off to face the entire Saxon army, alone?' begged di Monti. 'He swears the Poles knew, yet let him march to his death! Have we been betrayed, chevalier? Has France been betrayed?'

James sighed, and turned to face the wheedling diplomat, whose Quai d'Orsay sangfroid had so totally deserted him. The little Frenchman recoiled before James' hard stare, yet with a defensive flourish he added, 'He says the Saxon army is advancing on the city as we speak.'

But his voice trailed away when he saw his words were having no impact; so that his final bleatings were delivered without conviction. 'And they are intent on storming us off the march … that we can expect them before the evening gun … that the city is doomed.'

James let his words hang in the air. Then, quietly, but with great precision, he addressed the marquis. 'M'sieur Chapuis marched his force against a single regiment of Saxon line infantry, established behind prepared positions. Unfortunately, his tactics in the ensuing engagement did not reach beyond exchanging musketry with them at close range. I say "unfortunately", because M'sieur Chapuis brought with his force no planking to traverse the ditch before the Saxon position, so that his men might attack it once their volleys were discharged, nor short ladders so that his soldiers might ascend the Saxons' earthen palisade once across the ditch, nor sacks of grenadoes they might throw to keep the Saxons' heads down while effecting such manoeuvres. As for M'sieur Chapuis being left to march to his death, I can assure the marquis that when I saw M'sieur Chapuis yesterday evening, he was still very much alive. And as for what the Saxons might be doing now, as we speak … I rather think they are drinking coffee, as safe behind their earthworks as they were yesterday before M'sieur Chapuis so rudely disturbed them.'

James went on to deliver his short account of what he knew to von Bittinghofen's nearest staff officer. The glum aide thanked him for his duty, especially for his independent interpretation. It accorded entirely with the official dispatch, which had landed within the hour. James accepted a stiff tot of warming local eau de vie from the functionary, and for a moment they both gazed silently into a peat hearth fire, the insipid flames of which seemed to be drawing cold air into the room more efficiently than it was heating it.

When he returned to his lodgings there was a letter waiting for him. For an excited heartbeat he thought it might be the one he was expecting from David Hume. But the envelope bore the Stuart seal instead. The dwindling reserves of combustibles in the city as a result of the siege meant a fire in every room was a luxury no longer possible. So he sat down without shedding his topcoat, or mitts, poured himself a stiff brandy from his personal flask, and began to read.

It was the usual turgid prose James had come to expect from the palazzo; dry and devoid of any intimacy one might expect from a liege lord to his trusted confidant. After all the usual inquiries after health came the litanies of disappointments; how he, his king, had been expecting to hear James' analysis of events in Poland, the real news behind the bland diplomatic communiqués. Had any negotiations between Stanislas and the Russians taken place? And how was Augustus of Saxony faring in extending his rule as king, since the Russians installed him as their choice at that elaborate coronation in Krakow? Was anyone discussing a compromise candidate, even at this late stage, who might be agreeable to both sides and who could put an end to the fighting? And if not, was anyone even prepared to discuss such an option?

Although it did not specifically betray a definite stance on the part of the Stuart court, or set out any instructions to him, James thought the letter remarkably frank in its questions. An uninvited third party to this correspondence could draw all manner of conclusions from what the writer wanted to know.

A dull weight descended upon James. All those decisions made during his journey to Poland, his determination never to look back, to never again put his trust in princes or submit to being the useful idiot, and still the past dragged on him. He let his fingers feel the smoothness of the paper, imagining how the man who would be King of Great Britain must have held it, to approve it before signing. No ordinary document, but a letter of supplication from a sovereign to his subject; a king begging his servant for service, playing on his loyalty, seeking to use the better parts of him. He folded the letter and placed it in a box he never bothered to lock. Experience had taught him that anyone who would want to read the letter's contents had probably done so already.

11

Encounters with Russian Generals

James lay in the long, reedy grass, peering down towards a huge, primeval carpet of birch trees that seemed to stretch from observable horizon to horizon, and at a substantial road of packed, dusty earth that snaked along its edge.

Along the road trotted several troops of Russian cuirassiers, their white tunics bright beneath the highly-burnished steel of their breastplates. The spring rains had come and gone so the going beneath the horses' hooves was free of the rutted mire puddles of even a few days ago, and the column kicked up myriads of little clouds as it passed. They weren't the first heavy cavalry detachment he'd seen that morning.

The previous night he had led two squadrons of his Dzików on another cavalry sweep along this corridor between the Mottlau river and the sea. They were now several leagues to the east of Danzig, towards Fort Sommerschanz, which had, finally, recently fallen to repeated Russian assaults. However, that he and his Dzików had managed to patrol out this far was testament to the fact that the Russian encirclement of the city was not quite complete. And from the number of Russian patrols he'd seen every time he'd probed this far east, it appeared they were all too aware of the gap; which was why they were using a regiment of cuirassiers to try and stop the hole.

James wasn't looking to fight this imposing-looking lot of hard nuts;

he was after booty first and foremost, and failing that, to disrupt any new workings being thrown up in support of the siege, like supply dumps, or new tracks being laid to carry besieging troops in towards the city's walls.

The latest word from the countryside was that the Russians were about to begin their work proper on reducing the city. Their heavy guns had arrived, and were waiting in artillery parks in the countryside to the south and west, before being rolled up to the newly dug battery positions facing Danzig's walls. And a new general had arrived, one Burkhard Christoph Graf von Münnich, another German in the service of Tsarina Anna, and a noted army engineer who was reputed to have been placed in charge of the inner circle of Russian forces.

But James wasn't thinking about that right now. He was tutting away to himself over the lack of targets for his dragoons. The Russian cuirassiers trotted round the curve in the road and vanished into the wall of forest. But as they did, from the other horizon, from towards Danzig, appeared an altogether more promising cavalcade.

A coach and four, escorted by a dozen hussars in the same sky blue uniforms he remembered from a previous tussle. The coach looked as if it carried officers of some significance.

This road was the main artery from the mouth of the Vistula at Fort Sommerschanz to Danzig, and where the coach was passing was where the Baltic's featureless, flat and sandy coastal plain ended, and the road curved into the forest and rolling landscape that was now offering James and his Dzików all this dead ground for cover.

James reached for his telescope. The coach was coming to a halt.

Strange.

Why?

Then, six officers were clambering out of the coach. He turned his focus on them, the lens of his glass picking out all too clearly the gold braid that bedecked their uniforms, and the feathers flowing from their equally braided tricornes.

A field table was produced, and was being unfolded, and map tubes were being laid out. Were they here to survey some siege-supporting site? Actually, he didn't need to know any more; he had already decided he was going to grab them.

The Dzików were at their leisure in a dip in the terrain, the horses from the two squadrons tethered and minded by the young buglers, and the troopers squatting and nattering in small groups, taking the odd fortifying chug from their eau de vie flasks. This departure from the usual rigid discipline was highly uncommon. Soldiers did everything in files and columns. It was universally understood; for every movement, an order. It was modern way of fighting; how you bent uneducated masses of men to your will.

It had taken a long time for NCOs, and even the men, to become accustomed to stepping out of that world, no matter how briefly. But James had decided rested troops, and rested horses, fought better than ones who'd spent all the day's long hours stuck in meaningless regime; men sitting to attention on their hard saddles, and their mounts standing motionless in strict lines with a trooper's weight on their backs.

Once his lumpen, usually deeply stupid, troopers had overcome their astonishment at being allowed to loll about from time to time, they had responded well, despite all the additional drills – and discipline – involved in learning how to re-mount and form up fast, in an emergency.

So nobody needed calling to alert when James and Casimir came galloping over the brow of the hill.

'Captain Poinatowski! To me!' cried James as he pulled Estelle to a halt.

James' plan was simple. Poinatowski would take a troop of dragoons and ride down to secure officers who had emerged from the coach. He and James agreed, the mere dozen Russian hussars covering them would not be capable of putting up much of a fight against seventy charging Dzików; so capturing the Russian gentlemen should be a mere formality.

James would take the rest of the two squadrons and watch the road lest another of those cuirassier patrols turned up from the direction of Fort Sommerschanz. The flat terrain towards Danzig meant James could offer no cover from that direction without them losing surprise. So Poinatowski would just have to take his chances when making his grab.

The units parted, James leading the bulk of his force up out of the dip and on to the rising ground overlooking the road to the east.

He and Casimir went ahead to scout, dismounting again, and crawling to the lip of the rise. When they popped their heads up, there before them, deployed in four ranks across the road, facing back to Danzig, were at least 200 Russian cuirassiers, their big heavy cavalry mounts snorting and stamping billows of dust as they waited, officers conferring at their head.

From James' position, he was looking diagonally towards their backs, and he could easily see the curve in the road that masked them from the Russian officers' coach and equally, any cavalry unit intent on attacking it. But it was not the whole picture. Maybe 1,500 paces back up the road towards Fort Sommerschanz was another mounted group. James retrieved his telescope. Another dozen or so Russian cavalry. Most of them cuirassiers, but one officer in particular so be-decked with braiding he must be a general at least; as if there to watch the ambush the Russians so obviously intended for anyone attacking that officer-filled coach up ahead.

James smiled, and said to himself, so you're just going to sit there, just close enough to say you were present at your victory, but not so close you might feel the swipe of a sabre ... well, we'll see about that.

'Casimir,' said James, 'tell the captain of second squadron I have ordered that he give you command of half a troop.'

'Excellency!' breathed Casimir, his eyes wide, fit to burst, and a manic grin splitting his face. 'Immediately, excellency!'

'Casimir, please wait one moment ...'

'Excellency!'

'... to hear what it is I want you to do with them.'

James was aware of the lad physically straining to master his excitement, and paused while he did so. 'Now, Casimir, listen here ... when you have all those doughty troopers under your command, I want you to ride down there to where that officer with all the finery is sitting with his escort. And I want you to sound the charge as you go. And when you arrive amongst the Russians, pull up, then I want you to invite him, the one with all the finery, to dine with me tonight in Danzig, and if he declines, insist, with your sabre. His escort … drive them off, and if *they* refuse, then make them wish they hadn't. But before you do all that, Casimir, I want you to tell Captain Wajda of second squadron that he is ordered to bring forward the remaining troops to me. Now go!

Casimir, his chest expanding to equal the honour he'd been thus accorded, said in a choking voice, 'It shall be done with all dispatch, excellency!' And was gone, racing back to his mount.

James looked back to the 200 Russian cuirassiers through the blades of grass in front of his nose. His throat felt suddenly dry and a strange, cold electricity ran through him – a feeling of being super-alive, the blades of grass suddenly becoming magical wonders in the super-clarity of his gaze and the beat of his heart in his chest like a drummer marking ritual time.

Behind him, Captain Wajda would be coming forward with a little over a full squadron of dragoons – more than 150 troopers – and when they got here, he was going to lead them in a charge against those 200 cuirassiers.

He'd been in many actions with the Dzików; been aware of the way they looked at him afterwards when they thought he wasn't noticing, how he'd not understood at first, especially since staring at an officer in any army on this continent could end with you tied to a triangle and flogged. But then he'd realised it was his often inappropriate laughter that was to blame – his reaction to the random thoughts that were forever crowding his brain before a fight – so that his men must have thought he'd been laughing in the face of the enemy, when really, he was laughing at something else entirely. He knew it was too late to explain; as if a regiment's colonel would ever explain … anything. Maybe it was no bad thing his men now thought him fearless, the hardened warrior who found the battle fear so amusing. Little did they know.

But he knew. Everything until now for him had been mere skirmishes. Nasty, bloody little roadside scraps, over in minutes. Not many dead, and the rest run off. But what was about to unfold here would be his first full cavalry charge, in anger – a full squadron gallop into battle; as in a *real* battle, not like that mere bout of schoolboy taunting that had been Glenshiel. Or even the day he took his first man. There might be no vast collision of armies exploding around his ears right now, but if you added up the numbers, it was going to be the same as any cavalry clash on the field of Oudenarde or Malplaquet, with all the same violence and savagery. Stirrup-to-stirrup, horses lunging, troopers, their sabres levelled, thundering headlong into an enemy charging back.

Wajda was there behind him. James didn't have to look; he could hear the jingle of the bridles. Too late to worry now, he told himself. Mount up James, m'lad, and lead them over the skyline.

A Russian officer, inspecting the straightness of the cuirassiers' ranks, saw the Dzików first.

From the moment he was aware of the commotion his dragoons' arrival had created, James ceased to pay attention to the Russians and turned to his own men, issuing his orders to dress their two ranks, looking back as he coached Estelle backwards into the front rank between the skinny, barely pubescent bugler and a cornet of horse clutching his squadron's guidon. Wajda would lead the second rank; he would know just how much to space its advance behind his, so that after James' rank had collided with the enemy, Wajda would be there to fall upon any cuirassier who had beaten his man or hacked through James' front rank, or had eddied round its charging flanks and was trying to get at his rear.

James looked quickly to his left and right. The front rank was one long, continuous line of snorting, nodding, bridled horse muzzles. And then he looked to his front, so as to see what all his troopers would be seeing.

What he saw almost choked off his command. The Russians had all but reversed their ranks, and were now facing him, dressing off under a barrage of clipped commands that he could hear from here, at the top of the rise. He remembered that fatuous Frenchman, Chapuis, and his insistence that the Russian army was a mere rabble of dandified barbarians, and wondered what he'd have had to say about this performance.

Disorder in the enemy ranks would not be assisting him today. He covered his dismay with a bellow of his own.

'Rysować szable!'

Draw sabres!

Then he ordered the bugler to sound the advance.

Time telescoped. The rational departed, and all feeling, thought and focus collapsed to a single point.

At first the opposing lines coming together was all but imperceptible to a bystander, and then, after a discordant trilling of bugles, the horses began to trot, and then canter, so that the lines converging speeded up like two objects falling.

He was aware that he was yelling an order, though he himself could not hear it, and then it was if a sound was filling the whole world ...

Ta-da-tada-da-da-da! ta-da-tada-da-da-da ta-da-tada-da-da-DAAA! ... blaring in his ear.

The bugler, blowing the charge, and Estelle suddenly becoming a force of nature under him; power and lightness, like wind under a bird, straight and sure, so, even pressed between the bugler and the cornet, they hardly bumped or touched, the entire line moving headlong together, with its direction now beyond James' power to control, so that in the leisure now granted he was even able to realise the man he would collide with, to pick him out in the onrushing Russian line, to even guess how many more thundering bounds until their horses smashed together and their steel clashed; and how verdant the trees were behind him, and how blue the sky was, peeking through their upper branches.

James could pick out every detail of the Russian cuirassier's potato face; the cracked brown teeth told him the man was screaming his battle cry, just as James was, but the yells of over 350 men, the sound of the bugles, and the thundering of their horses was drowning individual sound so that the world was become just an avalanche of noise.

The telescope snapped shut.

All things happened at once.

The deep, reverberating thump of horse flesh impacting at a closing speed he does not want to think of; it is a sickening glancing blow he feels up through every bone in his skeleton as his knees gouge into Estelle and he clings to her for dear life. To his side, James is aware of a figure flying from the crash of horses, then his Russian is in his face, the man's sword arm drawn back for a downward slashing, killer blow; James, throwing his whole upper body down, flat against Estelle's neck, sabre arm still outstretched, and the Russian's blade slicing the air above him as his own sabre connects with the Russian's cuirass, and glances into the space between his enemy's throat and shoulder …

… and they are locked.

James' arm, and the Russian's, entwined in a grip. Both their tricornes are gone, and the force of this death embrace slews their mounts. The Russian's head comes toward James in a butt, but the momentum of their horses lets James take the blow on his shoulder. It stuns the Russian. But their arms are still locked. As the Russian writhes, thinking it might break him free – the fool – James has his short pistol in his hand … and presses it against the Russian's armpit, in the space where the front and back plate of his cuirass buckles, and he pulls the trigger … and in the smoke … so he cannot see … James is free of the wretched man; and Estelle from the Russian's horse's tangle.

But they are not free of the fight …

The charging ranks have crumpled into a slashing melee; Estelle and the bugler's horse jammed tight by the pressure of Russian ranks. Before he knows he has done it, James has raised his sabre to ward off a downward slash against the poor lad's head. But from the corner of his eye, there is another Russian, pressing against his other side, for some reason his horse turned, so he is facing the same way as James, and he is pulling his sabre back to slash.

James finds he is looking quite candidly into the Russian's face as the Russian prepares to kill him; he knows he cannot move to avoid the blow, because he is pinioned by his bugler, and by horses behind him and to his front; all of them Russian cuirassiers. But his own sabre arm is in the air, free of all encumbrance; free to be drawn right back and stabbed into the Russian's guts, long before the Russian's blow could ever hope to cover all that air between them.

James, his sabre hand now slick with blood and his uniform's arm saturated in it, from the hole he's sliced open in the Russian, now turns back to his bugler, who has his own sabre out and is brandishing it wildly about him without tactic. James sees a face mad with panic, and grabs the boy's free wrist. Words are pointless, the din about them too great. Their eyes meet, and the bugler, his flailing abruptly ceases and he understands, calms, smiles a quite horrible rictus as he realises that his duty now is to defend his colonel. He faces away from James, and they both begin to fight for each other's backs in slashes and stabs in the heaving mass of men and horses; in the smells of horse and man sweat, and blood; and the noise. Horses' and men's noises, that they make when they're in the grip of fury, or they're being cut or they're dying; and the clash of steel. A din without rhythm so that there is no time; on and on, as though it will never end.

And suddenly it is all over around James; he and his bugler are left standing, with no white tunic or burnished cuirass left to slash at. There is only space around them. Eyes bulging, they drink it in, both of them drawing deep, deep breaths; both of them stunned, wheeling their horses to face any new threat. But there is no new threat.

Any semblance of rank or line for both cuirassier and dragoon is gone. Where once were ordered formations, there are random knots of men milling together, still isolated little fights, sabres slashing in the sun. The smothering din has been silenced however, just the odd scream and savage oath. The Russians have broken off, streaming to their rear. And then James sees why; back towards the road, a tight group of Russian officers around their squadron guidon, are rallying their troopers to form up again. If they do, they will charge back, and their formed line will cut down the scattered clots of Dzików still scrapping on.

James has the bugler sound his own recall, and the weeks and months of dunning new drill into them pays off in a moment. Without being whacked with sword flats or cowed by abuse screamed into their

179

faces, James' Dzików break off their scattered melees and gallop to slide into together in a single line, facing down the hill towards the still milling cuirassiers.

One brief glance along his own forming troopers; their line will do. But when James looks back to the cuirassiers all he sees is still a dull, lumpen rabble of peasant soldiers too stupid to order themselves quickly enough, who are being belaboured into some semblance of a formation by their own knout-wielding NCOs.

He turns again to his own troopers. No lumpen mob here. James gives the order.

Ta-da-tada-da-da-da! ta-da-tada-da-da-da ta-da-tada-da-da-DAAA!
… the blaring in his ear again.

And the charging Dzików hit the Russian troopers at full gallop, while they are still just a seething mass.

The recovery point for James' dispersed troopers was back in the dead ground north of the road. When he led the tattered remnants of his squadron back into the dip, Poinatowski was already there, the senior Russian officers' coach and its bored set of four horses accompanying him. But Poinatowski wasn't paying attention to his prize. He was laughing with Casimir, slapping the lad on the shoulder, and then ostentatiously bowing to a mounted man whose horse's bridle Casimir was holding.

The figure on horseback was a very grim, hatless, portly little man, his green Russian uniform all bulging epaulettes and smothered in braid, and him still gripping the hilt of his sheathed sword with a tenacious fury.

James trotted up. When he was closer, he could see the man's face was quite red. James edged Estelle closer still and introduced himself. The man merely gave him a venomous look, then continued staring straight ahead.

'He says he will only speak to an officer of equal rank,' said Poinatowski, unable to keep the laughter out of his voice.

'And what is his rank?' asked James.

'Ah. There's the rub, excellency. He says he'll only tell an officer of equal rank.'

James' brow furrowed as he looked back to his seething prisoner, and when he saw his puffed up jowls actually quivering with outrage, James started laughing too. 'And his sword …?' he asked.

'He'll only surrender it to an …'

'… an officer of equal rank …' James interrupted, still laughing, but this time in the puffed up officer's face.

'Captain Poinatowski,' said James in his best colonel's voice, 'Form the squadrons in column of march, prisoners in the middle. Time to get our guests home.'

Back, safe behind the walls of Danzig.

The clutch of Russians Poinatowski had rounded up with their coach-and-four turned out to be no more than middle ranking staff officers; but the puffed-up, portly Russian Casimir had put in the bag was no less than a major general.

James had stood smiling, to one side, while the young cornet was much feted by General von Bittinghofen, and by his staff officers, who then, regardless of previous enmity, went on to wine and dine the Russian with all due deference to his rank. The Russian staff colonels from the coach were to dine in the officers' mess, and as they all spoke French, James found them to be a convivial bunch.

'Alas, our acquaintance is destined to be short lived,' one of them told James during the second night's dinner. 'I saw Major Saratov go into your general's office this afternoon.'

'I don't understand,' said James. 'Another Russian officer? Here? How can that be?'

'By a letter of safe conduct, chevalier,' said the Russian, equally puzzled that James did not know of such documents. 'Both our staffs issue them every day. How else would we communicate?'

'Communicate?' said James.

'Or negotiate … or whatever other gentlemanly accommodations our

181

leaders wish to make. We are neither of us animals after all, chevalier, are we? We may fight, but we can still converse.'

James just stared back at him. He had no idea there was a regular traffic between von Bittinghofen and Lacy, the Russian army commander.

'Saratov is here to negotiate our parole,' continued the Russian staff officer. 'A simple process, but a timely one for us. You will understand we do not wish to be here in the city when the bombardment begins.'

'Parole …?' James was aware he was endlessly repeating the Russian's statements but couldn't help himself.

'Yes, chevalier,' the Russian replied, his voice now heavy with impatience at this idiot before him. 'We sign a bond – in other words give our parole — not to take up arms again, against you in Danzig. And on that cognisance, we are allowed to go free. It is a time-honoured custom, chevalier, never to be *dis*-honoured. You must have heard of it?'

James did not wait for the after dinner drinking. Waiting for him when he'd returned from his last patrol had been a letter from David Hume. He'd read it immediately, and it had left him disturbed. So now that he was back again, he wanted to return to his quarters and go through it once more, with greater diligence.

When it came to matters of the mind, David was his compass. He might be a contemporary but James knew that his friend's penetration of mind and understanding surpassed anything James himself possessed. All through his time in Paris the two had corresponded; James reporting on his conversations with M'sieur Voltaire, and David sharing with James his own groping towards what was shaping to be new and original thought; a path that might one day go beyond that of their mutual hero Francis Hutcheson, whom even Voltaire had held in high esteem.

The letter had started out plainly, and with all the wit James had come to expect from his particular friend.

… and because we do not specifically address the question of the succession at the university, whether in favour of the House of Stuart or of Hanover, they think we do not talk of politics, and leave us alone. They are the fools we always suspected. What is moral philosophy, if it is not politics at its most profound?

But then David had gone on to confide in James that for years he had been working on a book, an exploration of the basic nature of man, apparently. And now it was ready for publishing. *I intend to call it 'A Treatise of Human Nature' and it is an attempt to define what innate senses man is born with, and then how we can best shape those senses; those drivers; to create a being capable of living within a system of government that is both mutually beneficial and moral.* So David had written. All well and good.

Their mentor, Hutcheson, had already declared that although man might be driven by his passions, he was also born with the ability to tell good from evil, and thus capable of comprehending not only the power of reason, but its necessity if he was to rule his baser instincts and therefore be able to live together in harmony.

David's letter, however, had let it be known that although he could not disagree with the initial sentiment, his own belief now was that – and here James always quoted to himself the original text when thinking on it – *experience tells us in the long term, any appeal to reason must be hopeless, because reason is the slave to passions too!*

The original text because this was where James had begun to feel disconcerted.

Lord Kames, our other great teacher, asked us: why does society exist? David had written.

To protect property, was his answer. But it is self-gratification – man's greatest passion – that drives us to acquire property in the first place. So it must be reason's role not to conquer passion, as Francis Hutcheson tells us, but to facilitate it; canalise it so that man does not have to live his life merely plundering and being plundered in return, but can exist in a mutually beneficial contract with his neighbour. If it be money you desire, why rob a bank, when you can open one?

Reason; the facilitator of the passions.

His friend was proposing to turn Hutcheson's teaching on its head; the teaching of two millennia of philosophers, right back to Aristotle, that reason must govern the passions. No it isn't, David was writing. It

183

is only passion, self-interest, that drives us to gain what we want; and reason is merely the way we can achieve it without hurting ourselves or anybody else.

As far James he could see, the consequences of untrammelled passion and self-interest were working themselves out all around him right now and being borne by ordinary people, from those poor, wretched peasants who'd been dragged ignorant from their village serfdom on some remote steppe into a foreign army so that he, James Lindsay, from an obscure Highland backwater, could slay them for no good reason, to the prosperous burghers sitting, waiting by their hearths in this prosperous city, for the Russian shells to start landing; firing their warehouses and their wealth and their very homes.

Right here, right now, on this far Baltic shore, thought James, we could be doing with some of that directing reason or yours, David. When you publish, I hope there will be people prepared to listen.

It wasn't until much later, sitting alone in the guttering candlelight of his quarters after several bumpers of burgundy, that James realised the ache in his chest was pride for his friend; that he could know such a noble mind. He could barely imagine the intellectual backlash David was going to face for his temerity to think such original thoughts. But then the whole world was living through a new age, where it was time to smash the old icons, and even some new ones, and view all life anew, through a more enlightened prism. So what if young Hume made a few old men choke on their porridge? That there was a mind greater than all these grubbing ones around him; somewhere at work in this senseless anthill, striving to make some sense, trying to map a path to a better future, was enough for him, for now.

That, and the fact that Davy Hume's letter was serving another purpose; putting a stop to the brooding that stalked him. A moment's distraction and he would lurch back there in his mind, charging the Russian cuirassiers, and all the blood and mayhem that had followed. All those images in his head, and churnings in his guts, clinging to him ever since, like scabs itching to be picked at.

Like all men, he had always wondered how he might behave when it came to put it to the touch. Would he fall apart or would he stand? Which was why he had kept repeating to himself, well, now you know! ... in order to drown out all the other clamour.

12

The Tsarina's Emissary

The following day, James was summoned to von Bittinghofen's quarters.

'General Peter Lacy, the officer commanding all the Russian and Saxon armies before Danzig, would like to meet you,' said the old general, squinting at him with a suspicious eye.

'Me? Why?' It was the best James could do by way of reply.

'We are sending back his officers tomorrow,' said von Bittinghofen. 'They have all signed their paroles, there is no reason to detain them. And he has requested you to command their escort. He says he wishes to meet the enterprising officer who managed to capture one of his major generals, and to thank you for your gentlemanly conduct towards him.'

James was about to remind the general that it was the young cornet of horse, Casimir, who had actually effected the capture, but quickly realised such a response would be redundant. Other matters were in play here.

'I do not wish to go, sir,' said James.

This gave the old general considerable amusement. Laughing, he said, 'Well said, chevalier! Telling the great General Lacy, "your compliments be damned", eh? Shunning even the remotest chance for a purse full of silver for your troubles. Or maybe even gold, should you wish to be of further service to him. Alas, what you wish is irrelevant.'

James felt himself bridle at what had just been said. 'Make your meaning plain, sir!' His voice was frigidly polite. He watched von Bittinghofen closely, as he in turn gave James a long, shrewd look.

'No, you are not the man for that, chevalier, are you?' von Bittinghofen said at length. 'I apologise.'

James, now emollience itself, asked, 'For what, sir?'

'Implying betrayal.'

'I do not understand, sir.'

'A man like Lacy, requesting you present yourself at his court? Just to say thank you for returning a fool who is only going to be sent back to St Petersburg in disgrace? Or maybe to talk about the weather perhaps? Or the fishing in the Mottlau river? I thought maybe you had somehow made plain to him you were open to offers … to spy maybe … or to swop your allegiance and command his cavalry now he's lost his original commander, our major general whom young Casimir collared. You are, after all, a soldier of fortune, chevalier, a sword for hire. But then you are not that calibre of man, are you? I see that. Always have. I can only think it is the damned siege that has rotted my brain and provoked me to suggest otherwise. I offer my most humble apologies, chevalier. But you still have to go. Refusing would be discourteous. It is a matter of honour for you. And for me, as your commanding officer. Sorry, but there you are.'

'Put like that, sir, I of course will obey. But on one point, I do not see how you could have possibly thought I could have made myself plain to General Lacy. How could I have managed that, sir? I know there is a channel for correspondence between our armies, but I am equally sure your staff must know everything that goes into communications between our two camps.'

'Courtesy of the Gräfin von Kettler, of course. She passes to and fro with a tedious regularity. Negotiating between her uncle and the Russian court, she says, but God knows what else she trades.'

James felt a weight settle round his heart. His intuition had from the beginning warned him the woman was dangerous; even to just stand next to. But this?

'Dorothea von Kettler might have given an impression of a certain intimacy between us to some,' he spelled out laboriously, 'but I can assure you general that we are not so close that I would entrust her with any such message, even if I was so disposed to send one.'

The old general laughed a knowing laugh; and with that, their interview was over.

The Russian major general refused to travel in the coach with the other senior Russian officers, and insisted on his own horse. The instant he mounted, he shouldered the beast to the head of the parole column where it had been arranged James should ride with another Russian officer sent to conduct them through first the Polish lines, and then the Russian ones.

The major general studiously ignored all his junior comrade's pleas to move aside, and as the column set out. James was happy to drop back and chat through the coach window with his new friends.

The journey was little more than two leagues, through the Bischoffsberg gate and out to the south east, winding through the Russian lines, on a route James guessed had been specifically designed to give him a view of the enormity of the Russian build-up; something to give him nightmares as he waited for the artillery bombardment to commence.

The headquarters of General Peter Edmond Lacy, Knight of the Order of Alexander Nevsky, senior figure in the Collegium Militaire – or Russian general staff – and favourite of the Tsarina Anna I of all the Russias, was in an imposing, rambling manor-cum-farm house, with its own wall and courtyard. The general was not there to greet them at the gate. In fact, there was no welcome committee whatsoever. Just one colonel, standing in the middle of what was obviously ordinary, day-to-day bustle. He curtly dispatched all James' Russian guests to various doors and outhouses as they tumbled from the coach. He was even more abrupt with the major general – despite the man being his senior officer – not even offering to hold his horse's bridle while he tried to dismount.

James' small escort of six Dzików meanwhile were bustled away by a couple of Russian cavalry NCOs, presumably for restorative chugs from their bottles of the local eau de vie, judging by all the bonhomie. That left James standing alone with nowhere to go – until he saw a small civilian in a fustian coat looking for all the world like a butler. He offered to take James' tricorne and cloak, and pointed the way into the main house, all in serviceable French.

They went through a huge, vaulted entry hall with a tall, leaded and stained glass window at the back, and then he was led from the hall down a dark, winding corridor, past open doors leading to much larger rooms, all of them busy with staff officers. Finally they came to quite a commodious snug, all dark wood panelling with four huge, luxuriously upholstered wing-backed chairs and lots of little tables for resting your drink, or book, or for holding candle sticks. A small fire blazed in a grate, and James was offered a seat and asked if he cared for any refreshment. He asked for a cordial.

After only a brief few minutes General Lacy arrived, unannounced, not that anyone could be in any doubt who he was, thought James, rising to accept his hand. An imposing figure indeed: tall, late fifties probably, although a mite old-fashioned in his full wig and shoes that were a bit too big in the buckle and the heel than was in style these days.

No aide or other officer accompanied him, so they sat down without ceremony and the man inquired, speaking French, if James had been offered anything. A shrewd face, with a laconic eye; not much would pass this man, and everything else would in some way or another amuse him. The first thing to amuse James was when he thought he caught the Irish in the general's voice, and when James mentioned it, also speaking French, Lacy replied in English, so the Irish really did come through.

'Aye, even after all these years I still have tongue I was born with. Killeedy, County Limerick, nearer to sixty years ago now than fifty. You have a good ear to pick it up.'

He was another of the Wild Geese.

'You look surprised,' he said.

'There are a lot of us, it would seem,' said James. 'Fled the depredations of the ill-natured and unjust regime that sits in London.'

'I fear the ill nature and injustice I turned my back on long predates yours, chevalier,' said Lacy, without giving any indication he intended to elaborate. 'Now to you. Thank you for returning my officers in person, but then we both know you didn't have any choice.'

James nodded and smiled an acquiescing smile.

'And well done on your excellent little action. A three-pronged attack in three disparate locations with two entirely different objectives, each executed with determination and timing, and each wholly successful. Too successful, as far as my plan for the outcome went. But then still as fine a piece of cavalry manoeuvre as I've seen.'

'Your plan, sir?' said James, not understanding, and forgetting to show due deference and modesty for the compliment.

'Yes. I wanted you to capture that coach load of pen pushers and cartographers. They were a handsome catch, sure, but at this stage of my operations more or less useless to me. Because I wanted to have cause to summon you here. For there are matters I wish to discuss. My major general of horse was a bonus for you. The fool of a man was not supposed to be there. I blame myself, of course. It is what happens when your subordinate officers feel it appropriate to use their initiative. When news of my orders for the coach to trail its coat reached him, he was bright enough to determine that such a foray might tempt your most tiresome dragoons, and decided to set a trap to catch you. Presuming, I imagine, that I would be effusive in my gratitude and admiration once he'd succeeded. Alas, he was not bright enough to inform me first. No matter, the Collegium Militare will supply me with another quick enough while he goes off to grow potatoes.'

'I cannot imagine what matter you might wish to discuss with a mere colonel of dragoons, sir,' said James, trying to imagine all manner of matters, furiously.

'Chevalier James Lindsay of Branter, formerly in the service of James Francis Edward Stuart, King James the Third of Great Britain … in waiting. Currently a cavalry officer in the army of his king's wife's divided nation. Surely such a man of parts as you should have another, more influential role? But no, apparently. The people my staff correspond with inside Danzig – who are friends of M'sieur Stanislas, the future Duke of Lorraine, if only he would listen to reason – tell me you do not discuss affairs of state. Not with him, nor anyone else of import for that matter. Indeed you do not even correspond with the Palazzo del Re in Rome … although on occasion, it has with you. And mightily grumpy they have sounded, I'm told.' And with that, Lacy gave a laugh, before continuing. 'No, it would appear soldier of fortune is indeed your only calling up here on the Baltic's shores. Would you say that was a fair summation of your circumstances?'

For a moment, James contemplated feigning ignorance of any involvement in affairs of state, and then thought better. Not with this man. Wiser just to say as little as politeness dictated.

'Fair. Yes, I would, sir.'

Lacy smiled at the reply, and then went on. 'Normally your progress through these concerning times would not concern me, chevalier. But I am not only a soldier, I am also the emissary of her majesty, the Tsarina of all the Russias, and when intelligence of other, graver matters reach me, I must inquire.'

'Indeed, sir,' said James, holding fast to his reticence.

'Although I always take notice of fellow soldiers of our caste, whose mastery of our trade brings them renown,' he added, eyebrows arched, to see if a compliment would bring his guest out.

'You are too kind, sir,' said James.

'The tsarina would *not* look with approval on James Stuart putting his name forward as a compromise king for the throne of Poland to end this inconvenient war,' said Lacy, leaning in slightly to better scrutinise James' reaction. 'There. I have said it outright to you, soldier to soldier. What do you intend to reply, or to do with the information?'

Startled, James did not even try to qualify his reply. 'I would do nothing with it, sir! For I know nothing of compromise kings, sir, nor of anyone who does!'

Which, James knew, was strictly a lie.

The Comte de Valençay and all his insidious implication on that chilly day in Rome; he had been very keen on the idea of James Francis Edward Stuart and the crown of Poland. James found himself wondering – abstractly, with a little quiet smile to himself, that he kept buried deep, down inside – if this had been his first, proper diplomatic untruth; and how easy it had come, and if maybe a new career might indeed beckon.

But to the world he continued his denial with what he felt was a reasonable vehemence. 'And I carry no instructions from my liege lord James Francis Edward Stuart on any matter that might so pertain. Upon my honour, sir.'

Lacy flopped back in his chair with a sigh. 'No, no. I never for one moment thought you did. If you had, there would have been a trail a mile wide. And there is nothing. Nothing, except this tedious woman spreading dangerous ideas. I am sure you know to whom I refer. The Gräfin von Kettler.'

'I do, sir. Except I think I can say with some certainty she does not speak for the court of King James,' said James, thinking it wise now to engage with this conversation given the turn it had taken.

Another long suffering sigh came from Lacy. 'Indeed. But for such a notion to become common currency would still be demeaning for his royal personage. A smear against his name. The very thought that he might have acquiesced in his royal self being mentioned in the context of a raffle such as the Polish succession *sejm* would be seen as vulgar beyond redemption in every court across Europe. But consider … for any such bid to be actually launched … and then to be unsuccessful … for unsuccessful it would surely be … that would be beyond disgrace. A humiliation from which your king in waiting could never recover. Indeed, it would be a smear against the entire reputation of the Stuart dynasty and a great gift to the fat German farmer who currently rests his commodious buttocks on Britain's throne. I tell you all this of course, not because they are my own thoughts, but those of the tsarina and her ministers.'

James had often thought as much himself since his conversation with de Valençay. But what he said was, 'Are you suggesting the Stuarts act to prevent such rumours, sir? Surely by their nature they are like a virulent disease and all but impossible to stem?'

'Oh that would not be for the Stuarts to attend to,' said Lacy with a dismissive wave. 'Their friends would see to that. What I am saying, and what you might say should you ever resume your correspondence with the Palazzo del Re, is that my mistress the tsarina looks forward with much complacency to a Stuart on the throne of Great Britain once again. It would suit her most admirably and she would do as much in her power to facilitate it.'

And with that, Lacy's smile disappeared, and his voice took on a timbre of menace. 'Which is why she takes such a hostile view to any machination that might besmirch James' name and consequently his prospects. Which is also why she is adamant his embassies should not be looking for a part-time job for him in a place where his interests would be better served by alliances with people who are well disposed towards him, and not in direct intervention into politics he does not understand, and thus might jeopardise that affection.'

Taken aback by the tone the general had now adopted, James bought time. 'I am not involved in King James' political circles, and am not party to the advice they tender, sir. Nor do I seek to be.'

'Yes! Yes! And it is a wise position to adopt, for it is pure silliness for a soldier of fortune to involve himself in such matters. And dangerous. But it is even sillier for him not to be aware that they exist. This is middle Europe, where the imperial dynasties of the Romanovs and the Hapsburgs are neighbours. We have a way of organising our affairs here that suits us very well. And in that spirit, we have chosen Augustus of Saxony to be king of the Poles. He is a very fine fellow and one who is most accommodating to us and the Hapsburgs. We know what to expect of him and he of us. France and their Bourbon cousins in Madrid are supporting this Stanislas fellow against him as an act of pure diplomatic vandalism. Mostly to irritate the Hapsburgs, for there has long been bad blood between France and Austria. But the tsarina is upset too. Allowing a Pole to sit on the Polish throne opens all sorts of possibilities for outbreaks of waywardness in the very place where *we* all live. Not the French or the Spanish. And believe me, the Poles are a people much given to waywardness. No, Augustus suits all our purposes admirably. That is why we fight. For stability and peace to get on with our affairs, not some manufactured notion of nationhood, or collective destiny and so-called rights. And that is why your king entering the fray would be such a distraction, for us, and for him.'

James nodded sagely, but all the while thinking, stability for whom? And exactly what affairs will they be getting on with? And what is so abhorrent about a people wishing to rule themselves? But he said none of that. Instead, he said, 'Do you wish me to mention all this to Dorothea von Kettler, sir? By way of impressing upon her she must desist from her indiscretions in future?'

The stern glint came back into Lacy's eye. 'I do not advise it, chevalier. We shall take her aside the next time she pays us a visit.'

James suddenly saw where this was leading. How best to ensure someone desists? Kill them. He found himself wondering how they would do it. But then that would depend on all the politics he did not understand. How strategic was Courland? How important was Russia's good name in all this? Those considerations plus ones he could not guess at, would determine whether it would just be cold-blooded murder, or if she might accidently, fatally, collide with a cannon ball while passing through the lines.

From the start James had found Dorothea von Kettler a fascinating woman, and a most definitely desirable one. But equally he'd always known that trouble and danger lay down that path. A red flag waved about her head, telling him, 'stay away!' But could he stand by while she was casually rubbed out, her life extinguished because it had become inconvenient in the great diplomatic game? Or was there something he was prepared to do? He wasn't sure.

'So tell me, chevalier, how does this service you are now embarked upon suit you?' Business done, Lacy had changed the subject. 'Is the work rewarding? In rank and compensation?'

'You are surely not inquiring if I am here to haggle for a better commission, sir!' said James, with what might be construed as a faux archness, but then again, might not. 'I would have thought that quite beneath you.'

Lacy laughed out loud. 'Touchy when it comes to your honour, chevalier! What a likeable chap you are! No, I would never suggest such a thing my good young man. Nor, as we both know, would it be friendly to your reputation for you to even consider such an offer. In the trade we ply, reputation, like honour, is everything, is it not? No, I was merely leading up to asking you to speculate on your future career once all extant duties have been performed.'

'I would need to survive all my extant duties first, sir,' said James.

'Before you give yourself over to reflection in any direction?' asked Lacy. 'How very wise and contained of you. But perhaps I can tempt you to un-contain yourself just a little, chevalier, for the evening, and dine with me. I have another guest I think you would be fascinated to meet.'

There was little space around the dining table that evening, such was the press of senior officers; Russian, Saxon as well as Polish, to James' mild surprise. 'Yes, there is a pro-Tsarina Anna faction amongst the Polish nobility,' Lacy had whispered in his ear on noticing. 'They are the ones who have the brains to take cognisance of the obvious … that life is more rewarding under her imperial majesty's patronage than going all giddy over some romance of "la patrie Polonaise".'

The table was most grandly presented, with a cloth, various regimental silver and ranks of serving knives and cutlery, and it groaned with food and wine and spirits, so that by the time the boar was being carved a level of boisterousness prevailed that was more fitting to a junior officers' mess. A quintet of bandsmen struggled to make their oboes and trumpets heard above the babble. It was then that Lacy introduced

James to an elderly gentleman in a uniform he did not recognise. And he did it, James noticed, in English. That made him study the old man more closely. He wore a full wig that accentuated a long nose in a long, leathery face. It was a face that looked used to command in the most extreme of circumstance, but also it had a familiar set to its features. Not as in James might know the man, personally; but that he might know his ilk.

'This is Colonel the Chevalier James Lindsay of Branter, currently in the service of M'sieur Leszczyński in Danzig.' Lacy addressed the elderly gentleman first; Leszczyński being King Stanislas I's family name. James did not miss the snub to his boss, but knew it was intended for amusement, not insult. 'And, chevalier, please meet Admiral Thomas Gordon of the Imperial Russian Navy. Not a Russian name, you will have noticed. However, when my particular friend addresses you, I think you will determine Russia is not his birth home.'

'I dare say ye shall, young chevalier,' said the admiral, with a warm smile, 'but that country is ma home now. I am at your service.'

James put the old sailor's age as at least his mid-seventies, but there was no doubt of his accent; it was pure Doric, straight from the streets of Aberdeen. The long nose, the deep upper lip, the sardonic droop of the eyebrows – he had recognised the ilk, after all.

'My lord admiral, it is I who is at your service,' said James, with a reverential nod. 'Especially as we both find ourselves a long way from home.'

'Admiral Gordon was an officer of the Royal Scottish Navy until your Act of Union, when he passed over to the Royal Navy …'

But Lacy was interrupted.

'Where I might have bided, but ma conscience wouldna' thole swearing an oath to that Hanover fellow,' said the admiral. 'And so I found gainful employ with Tsar Peter while he was still with us. And it is here I've bided.'

Another of those Wild Geese, thought James. We are indeed many. And for a moment all the unacknowledged yearnings he'd felt – always there below the surface, unarticulated through all those exile years – left him. Just went. And he felt part of a greater fellowship. A benign wave washed over him; he wasn't aware of it, but it must have shown in his expression, because when his eyes came back and he was looking at Lacy and Admiral Gordon, he saw they were looking back at him with broad smiles that were as knowing as they were friendly. As if they'd looked right into him, and were familiar with the view.

After a distinguished career at sea under Tsar Peter, Lacy told James, Admiral Gordon was now Governor of the Kronstadt fortress, which guarded the roadstead of St Petersburg, and he was here as Lacy's guest to witness the opening bombardment of Danzig. 'That, and because many of the larger siege guns, the real smashers, are manned by Admiral Gordon's sailors,' said Lacy. 'It is sad, but they will do great damage to property, and to life. Because M'sieur Leszczyński will not budge, no matter the generosity of the terms. Perhaps when you return, you might enlighten him as to the full weight of shot and shell about to descend on this tiny patch of ground, which is all that is left of what he still insists on calling his kingdom.'

'I am a colonel of dragoons, sir,' said James, not stuffy despite the seriousness with which he wished his reply to be heard. 'I came here to execute my orders, not to spy, or set myself up as military advisor to King Stanislas. I hope you will understand that, sir.' The 'king' he added pointedly, just as Lacy had with his 'M'sieur Leszczyński'.

Lacy and Admiral Gordon looked at each other, sharing impenetrable smiles. 'I understand perfectly,' said Lacy, with another of his sanguine nods. 'It was ill of me to press you otherwise.'

The next day, Lacy was up early to see James and his small detachment escorted to the Russian lines

'Needless to say, I am sad that the next time we shall meet will likely be on the field of battle, but that is the fate of men like us,' he said. 'So please do not think it presumptuous if I offer a piece of advice. We are soldiers of fortune, you and I, and in our trade there is one rule we all do well to observe … and that is never to have anything in our lives that we cannot turn round and walk away from, if fortune dictates. Now, all this we find ourselves embroiled in shall one day pass, and when it does, then remember me chevalier, as I shall remember you.'

And with that, Lacy shook James' hand and watched him mount. He even waited to give a wave, as James and his men cantered out of the courtyard.

13

The Siege of Danzig, Part Two

The main Russian siege batteries commenced their bombardment an hour after dark that night. The mortars opened up first. For those watching from the walls between the Hegelsberg and Bischoffsberg bastions, it was as if tiny clusters of faeries had sprung briefly to life, before their lights vanished in the smoke and scores of tiny sputtering slivers of fire arced into the black sky. The noise of them followed, out of synch; a delayed series of reverberating booms, running together in a wave so that the sound quickly turned to one continuous rumble. And then the screaming of the shells before they began to land in crumps and flashes, blossoming all across the district of the city around the canal wharves.

In the hours before the bombardment commenced, James had called at the Duke of Courland's town house, on the southern edges of the wharf district, to seek an interview with the Gräfin von Kettler. He sat in one of the large, high-backed chairs in an upstairs reception room. Dorothea sat in a similar chair opposite him, so they faced each other like an old married couple before their hearth. No fire blazed there however, the late spring evening being so balmy. In a corner of the room sat a meek and pensive parlour maid; their chaperone, there also to serve them chocolate from a bowl that sat on a small spirit stove by her side.

The poor girl gave the impression of trying to shrink further and further into her own clothing as the atmosphere in the room grew ever more brittle, and the voices of the couple by the hearth ever louder.

James had come to the house not to accuse Dorothea, but to warn her. But at his first raising of the purposes of her visits to the Russian headquarters, she coldly erupted in a measured fury, so that quickly their tryst had descended into a shouting match.

James had never felt such tumult of emotions in his breast over a woman as he did with this one. He didn't know why he bothered, why he didn't just walk away and leave her to her destiny. He knew her to be headstrong and calculating. But then there was all that ladylike grace on the surface, like a fast frigate in full sail, the complexity and beauty and sheer speed of her as she charged through the world. It kept tugging at him, even though knew there were tempests churning beneath; in a flash of anger, all that grace could vanish in the blink of an eye. But what was revealed was just as tantalising. The naked intellect, her drive and determination, and a fearlessness in the furtherance of her cause. All of it drew him as much her beauty.

'Have you no idea what you have done, with your careless talk?' he said, half placatory, half in reproach. 'What on earth possessed you to tell General Lacy that James Stuart might seek to offer his royal person as a compromise for the throne of Poland? Because that is what you did, isn't it? I cannot believe you magicked the idea into being yourself. Who put you up to it? Who planted the bad seed? And why on earth did you think it a good idea?'

But after he'd said it, James knew he had gone too far, with all his imagining this and questioning that.

'Yes, I said all that, and why not?' The deep chill in her voice was as cutting as a sabre fresh from the armourer's stone. 'As if you could understand. Your people and your land do not live in the shadow of a great bear, where learning to dance with it is never enough … because it can step on you without even knowing. You must learn to dance *round* it if you are to survive. So I dance and dance and dance, all the time. To protect, to save … and because I am loyal.'

'Dear God almighty, woman, what are you havering about …'

But she cut him off. 'You do not understand, because you do not think it necessary to clutter your mind with it … because it is not a matter of life and death for you. But it is for me, and for Courland. So I will explain and then we shall talk about you, and then we shall see if you wish to continue being so wilfully obtuse.'

James' brow furrowed; what was all this, 'then we shall talk about you' that she was saying? What was there to 'talk about' when it came to him? He was not the problem here, it was *her* wayward, headstrong charging about … to call her a bull in a china shop was not even close!

But Dorothea was not finished.

'I would love to see Stanislas reign as King of Poland. Courland would love it. To have a neighbour free of the pernicious intrigues and ambitions of the Hapsburgs and the Romanovs. But I came to Danzig to drip into Stanislas' ear that it would be better if he accepted their consolation prizes and slipped away. This Augustus they intend to put in his place is a puppet – even he knows it. The Poles might not want a puppet, but Austrian Charles does. Especially one who will give him stability on his eastern frontier. Tsarina Anna would rather just swallow Poland whole, but with Austria in the game, she cannot. However, if a compromise can secure her western frontier, and allow her influence to extend a little further along the southern shores of the Baltic, and even further into Europe, then she will acquiesce. After all, such an accommodation means that she and Austrian Charles can concentrate on scratching at their mutual itch to the south – the Turk. For Poland, it is an arrangement that means she is no longer in any danger of being merely gobbled up by the bear, and Courland with her. Both get to live a little longer, and not to end up just booty in a bag. That is why I came here, to do what I had to, to prevent that, with what I had to hand.'

James, dizzy with it all, had wondered if maybe the ordinary Courlander, or Pole, might have settled for just being allowed to get on with their lives.

'And then you turned up, chevalier,' she sneered at him. 'Or rather, not so much you, but who you represented. You were bound to attract attention with a *sejm* in full call … but you proceeded to do nothing. The man you would call king had sent you, must have sent you. No other meaning was credible. Yet you did nothing in his cause, not even listen! Not even after the letters from Rome arrived – which everybody read, obviously. How could you imagine they wouldn't? And so everybody then knew that you *had* been sent with a mission, a mission you betrayed! You stand in judgement over me, for what I have done. But all I have done has been out of loyalty. Something you obviously do not comprehend. I asked you why you were here, so you might help me save my people, but you wouldn't tell me. So I asked where answers might be had …'

And in a flash, James knew who had put the whole Stuart notion in her head. De Valençay. She had been communicating with her old partner in intrigue. Of course she had! She would not have been able to resist, regardless of the wisdom of it. If James shut his eyes, he could practically see the letters passing to and fro between Dorothea and de Valençay, and he wondered how many other fingers must have handled them those confidential communiqués. But he wasn't allowed to wonder long, for Dorothea hadn't finished.

'James Francis Edward Stuart,' she said the name with a malicious precision. 'Of royal blood. Married into Polish nobility. And a friend to Louis of France, also married into Polish nobility. A Stuart on the Polish throne puts a Polish consort there beside him. Not quite what the *sejm* voted for, but almost there. It also brings France into Poland. The most powerful nation in Europe … what a buttress against the east. And for France herself, a strategic gift that allows her to close the pen on the troublesome Hapsburgs. And for Courland, we get a powerful friend on our doorstop, and overnight we cease to be a mere bauble for a Romanov to dispense as reward to their latest favourite. I want James Stuart on this throne. And I have a way to sell the idea to the Russians that will suit them very well, if I can prevail upon your General Lacy to place it before the tsarina.'

James added hubris to the mental list of her qualities that he had been composing just a moment before. He had no wish to hear what notion she wished to sell to the Tsarina Anna. Just as he had no idea whether all her other constructions had any truth to them. He'd come here for one reason only – to tell Dorothea one thing only; that as fine and grandiose, and oh so subtle her notions might sound to her own ear right now, as far as her future was concerned, they were but flotsam. Because Lacy would never listen to her, because the Russian tsarina didn't want to listen, and when her soldiers got here, they were going to do away with Dorothea von Kettler, and that she had to leave immediately. There could be no more secret safe conduct passes beyond the walls for trysts with Lacy's staff. If she tried again, she would not return. Nor could she wait idly while the siege around the city closed, because it would seal her inside with nothing left to do but await her executioner.

He tried again to explain, but she'd have none of it and was in full retort – on how events had moved beyond his shabby betrayals, how he knew nothing, and in his shabbiness, had changed nothing; and 'thank you for your concern,' she said, but her own safety no longer signified in this latest swing of the pendulum of power.

And that was when the first Russian mortar shell plummeted through a warehouse roof at the end of the next street and exploded.

The initial barrage continued for over two hours, with the huge mortar shells plunging into the close-packed canal district with a sickening regularity, the sheer weight of them shattering tiles and battened floors until the huge, fuse-sputtering balls came to rest deep amongst all the combustible produce stored within, before detonating, sending flame and red-hot iron splinters into all the tarred cordage and barrels of turpentine and bales of wool and the wooden fabric of the buildings themselves. Then the shelling stopped. But it turned out to be only a pause. To let the mortar barrels cool? To bring up more shot? More powder? For the expenditure of both had been prodigious. Then it started again. By midnight, the fires had turned the city centre night into day. Only a lack of breeze stopped the embers swirling in the huge up-draughts of air from spreading the flames to other parts of the city. Down each narrow street you could see the glow from the fires throwing dancing silhouettes as men fought the fires throughout the night. Like armies of matchstick figures in relief against the walls, in and out of the flicker and smoke.

James and Dorothea stood for a while, mesmerised by the spectacle and the noise, and soon, the heat. Until one shell, its dull metal intrusion actually visible, seemingly coming towards the house in slow motion, the tiny fire dance of its fuse growing perceptibly larger in the sky; and in an instant it was tearing in so fast it forced them both to step back, before it went plunging into the back of the house opposite. They could hear it crashing through floors, then a bright, white flash appeared, illuminating every window in the instant before every window blew out, and the shattered glass from them pattered against the walls of their own house, and the heat and concussion hit them in the face.

James pulled her back into the room. 'Downstairs, into the cellar, now,' he said, manhandling her. He felt her stiffen as if to object, and then her will went with her recognition of the mortal peril they both were in, the whole city was in. And down they went.

The dawn brought a brief respite. Then, the bombardment resumed; different guns now, hammering the defences instead. And when the mortars resumed, it was the two southern bastions they rained their shells down on.

The fires in the city continued to burn throughout the day, and the bombardment's incessant crump and rumble became as ubiquitous as birdsong. Always there.

Through it all, James had business to attend to, before he returned to the Dzików colours.

As he made his way along the debris-strewn streets of Danzig that morning, he could see that the Russian gunners were operating to a plan. Different areas of the city were coming under sustained bombardment only for a set number of hours, then the guns and the mortars would shift. Different ordnance was also being used; the mortars dropping their fizzing shells into the inner city, and the big howitzers demolishing the defences. A solid pall of black smoke continued to hang over the wharf district, and from billowing smoke above the roofs to the south west he could see the fires were in control there.

The Russian gunners obviously had detailed cartography of the whole area within the outer bastions, for them to be consistently dropping all that ordnance so accurately. But then given the wholly porous nature of Danzig's defences until now, it was hardly surprising; all the trading that had gone on, and the regular negotiating missives that had constantly passed between Stanislas' court and Lacy's requisitioned farmhouse; not to mention Dorothea's frequent forays.

James was on his way to do something he was not proud of, but if he was going to save Dorothea from her own foolhardiness, he had convinced himself it was absolutely necessary. Do the deeds men do have names in and of themselves, or can they be justified into more noble repute? That was a question he knew he was about to put to the test.

Was it an act of betrayal he was he about to commit? Something she'd assured him he was good at. Another banner portrayal of his disloyalty? A confirmation of all those low traits she had listed to his character, to himself and the world? Well, if it kept the silly bloody woman alive, then he'd just have to live with it.

The big hall below von Bittinghofen's private offices was in confusion. Aides trying to put together information on a huge cartographer's plan of the city as to where the shells were landing and the damage being done. The general himself was there, besieged by muddle of staff officers, all obviously gathered in hurry, many without coat or wig.

James needed urgently to speak to someone in authority; someone who commanded the walls and the city gates. He dived into the fray. But it was not long before it became apparent that his mission might now be redundant. He had been on his way to denounce Dorothea as a Russian spy to von Bittinghofen. Privately, so her sin might be obscured and no retribution follow. Not a hard task, given her nobility. No commoner, general or not, would ever put her up against a wall. But at least von Bittinghofen could restrain her; confine her to the duke's town house. Because her movements in and out of the city had to be stopped, even if it meant falsely accusing her of what would be, for anyone else, a capital crime. General Lacy had personally assured him that, 'she cannot be allowed to continue …' It really could only mean one thing. And even if there was a chance that it did not, was that a chance worth taking?

But as he waded through the melee and heard the snippets of shouted orders and passing information, it quickly became obvious that all the churning in his guts over what he was about to do had been for nothing. Yes, he had stepped forward, determined, but it was becoming apparent his decision to betray – if that was what it was – had already been taken from him; that this great revelation of his character was cancelled for today. It was, it transpired, now no longer safe to venture beyond the walls or through the gates. To do so was to invite musketry and cannon ball against your person. But what had she said about her own safety, and how much it counted? Before he could start fretting on that, a passing aide finally put an end to all his fears that she might yet find a way to continue pursuing her wilful ways. There were no safe conducts out of the city anymore, he said. Danzig was sealed off, the siege proper had begun. With Dorothea still inside, said James, with a sigh, to himself.

He turned around and left the headquarters without another word. Getting her out of the city would have to wait. He headed back to the banks of the Mottlau to be rowed across the river. When he finally arrived at the Dzików lines, he found Poinatowski and Beart in great spirits. With the air to the east still full of the din of the continuing bombardment, and a black pall continuing to hang above the city, the two officers led him into their mess tent and poured him a stiff brandy.

And Poinatowski, beaming ear to ear, said, 'There is a French squadron in the offing, waiting to land infantry and artillery. At least a brigade, we think. Maybe more. And no Chapuis this time. They have Louis' minister to the Danish court, Count Plélo, aboard … a king's minister leading them. This is business, excellency, is it not?'

And suddenly all Dorothea's going on about, 'latest swings of the pendulum of power', became clear. A French squadron and French troops; was Louis XV really intending to keep Stanislas on the throne, or was he preparing the way to force a new compromise candidate on the warring factions? And if the latter, had Dorothea von Kettler divined matters correctly? Had she been right when she asserted that Chevalier James Lindsay knew nothing, and that she knew all? His heart sank at all the dispute, confusion and sating of honour that must follow; and the bloodshed, too.

The confined streets of a city were no place for cavalry, which was why the dragoons were still camped on the wide flat terrain to the north and east of the Weichselmünde fortress, between the Mottlau river and the sea. They were there, along with all the grenadier companies from the few regular Polish infantry battalions inside Danzig, and three battalions of militia, to block any attempt by General Lacy swinging the right flank of his army round to occupy the Mottlau's west bank and finally seal off Danzig from the Baltic and any hope of relief. They were not much of a blocking force, to face a massed Russian infantry assault in open battle, but they were all General von Bittinghofen could field.

'Drill,' James told his officers. 'In full regiment formation. Up until now we have been manoeuvring in penny packets ... companies, half troops, troops and squadrons. From now on, we drill as a regiment, all three squadrons in concert. Drill, drill and more drill.'

The following morning, with the early summer sky still red from the sunrise, the Dzików, with Captain Poinatowski at their head, formed up three ranks deep, with a squadron frontage of 150 troopers, plus all their officers and NCOs, and their colour party and buglers – over 500 men and their mounts – and they trotted out onto the flat sandy soil of the Westerplatte, their colonel watching from atop the only rise in ground for miles. Bugles sounded the commands, and the trot went to canter, and then came the urgent rising notes of the 'Charge!', and the earth shook as each trooper gave his horse its head. Meanwhile to the side, each troop's corporal of horse, at full gallop, minded the ranks, looking to their cohesion, noting those to be cursed and corrected later, because no order shouted could ever be heard above all that din; and when the whole charging box was on the edge of disintegration, the bugles sounded once more, ordering the 'Recover', and the charge collapsed in chaos.

James, with Beart beside him, made his notes on what he had witnessed, and then called Poinatowski forward. 'Captain,' he bellowed in a stern, parade voice, 'that was a disgrace to the honour of the regiment. Once more, if you please …' and leaning forward he passed his notes to the young captain, but with a knowing smile, and said, sotto voce, 'some observations for you to attend to, but really not bad for a first time out, Pyotr … by the time you have executed another dozen or so, I'm sure we'll start to look like a cavalry regiment should. Then we can graduate to the complicated manoeuvres, eh?'

The day wore on, and the air grew thick from all the dust their horses kicked up, so that it clung to the fields around them like a cloud fell to earth. Sitting high in his saddle, Colonel Lindsay studied their progress, certain what he was driving them through would prove vital in the days to come. There was the creak of leather beneath him, and the smell of it, and of horse, and the dust of a campaign in his nose, and grit in his mouth; and the clarity that it all brought to him. How everything was made simple by the ordinary, and how it focused the mind. He was commanding men he would shortly lead into battle. There was nothing else to think about. Just drill, and more drill, until they could move in their sleep, or better, through all the smoke and noise and mayhem of modern war, without thinking.

And every time the drill was paused, to water the horses and the men, to tighten straps and dun more lessons into each trooper's peasant head; and the noise of pounding hooves and bridles and bugles died away, there, to the east, was the never-ending grumble of the Russian guns bombarding Danzig; to remind them all why they did this.

When the Dzików trotted back to their lines outside the wall of the

Weichselmünde fortress they could clearly see a forest of masts. The French squadron had obviously entered the river and was now anchored in a line opposite the fortress' jetties. As the troopers rode closer it became apparent that the soldiery carried by the ships had now disembarked, for the fields leading up to the fort's glacis were a milling mass of grey-white uniforms, all industriously employed in throwing up tent lines and digging latrines. An artillery park had also appeared, with a row of half a dozen six-pounder field guns and their limbers neatly pegged down, and the barrels of shot and powder being stacked.

As they trotted by, James counted five separate infantry regiments' colours planted in amongst the growing sea of canvas, their fleur-de-lis-speckled folds barely shifting in the calm evening air. Cooking pots were also much in evidence in the French lines, and limp ribbons of smoke were starting to rise vertically from several corners of the new camp.

James' personal quarters were in the fortress, and once he had Estelle shoulder her way through the press of soldiers clogging the main gate, he dismounted and walked his horse to the stables. He felt like a stranger in the crush of new faces; bustle and organising was going on every-where, a mad tumble that offered no apparent path to order he could see, but then he was too tired to be paying proper attention and sought only a bath and sleep. He feared, however, a summons to meet his new commander, whomever that was going to be. The only name he'd heard so far was this Count Plélo that Poinatowski had mentioned, but he was just some politico, and James fully intended to steer as far away from him as he could.

The other thought that drifted through his mind as he fed Estelle her usual two apples before seeing to her being rubbed down, was whether one of those French men-o-war out there on the river was the *Achille*, and if he would be seeing his friend Capitaine Perouse again. Then it was up the stairs to his rooms, where one of the servants was already filling a hot bath for him. When the waft of the steam hit him, it vanquished all other concern from his mind, and he cast off his sweaty uniform in a dream before sinking into the oblivion of the near-scalding water.

That there were two letters waiting for him, delivered courtesy of the French men-o-war, was something he would deal with later.

James watched the water's reflection dapple on the great cabin's deck-head as Claude Perouse helped himself to a pinch of snuff. Both men were reclining in deep, upholstered chairs more befitting a country house drawing room than a ship of the line; enjoying the last of the evening sun streaming in through the huge gallery window that stretched from beam to beam across the *Achille*'s broad stern.

They had just dined on a huge dish of ortolans, a large turbot and jugged boar, washed down with a fine gamay from Capitaine Perouse's own family vineyard near Tours. The conversation had been just as rich.

'The word from the flagship is that this Comte de Plélo is under orders to seek early battle, and deliver an early victory,' Capitaine Perouse had confided in him. His information was not first-hand, he said, and he'd had no opportunity to evaluate the comte himself as he'd sailed on the squadron's flagship. But he'd been told King Louis' emissary had seemed an educated man, if a little enthusiastic.

'He is not the military commander, that is a major general called Estaing de Sailland, who I have met and who strikes me as a capable man, but this Plélo has the political power. What he says is writ. You say Lacy has 60,000 men before Danzig, and Plélo arrives with 5,000. And you, and the Polish troops, that makes what? Twelve thousand? Those are not odds for an early victory. It looks like it might be the Chapuis fiasco all over again.'

As James studied the dapples, he wasn't so sure. He was no general, but he knew enough of how battlefields worked to know they were not talking about a straight fight. Lacy could not put all his 60,000 men into the field against Plélo, because he'd need the vast majority of his army to maintain the siege lines around Danzig, lest the garrison sallied forth and destroyed his guns and his supply dumps and magazines while his soldiers were off fighting battles elsewhere. The Russians and the Saxons might be hard pressed to field an army equal to Plélo's 12,000, especially if Plélo and his tame major general decided to seek battle on this side of the Mottlau river, and all the communications and transport problems that would entail for Lacy.

An early victory was certainly possible, and would deliver a position to bargain from, and as the expedition was under the command of a politico, that made sense. He wondered what the Comte de Plélo had been sent to bargain for; then decided it was none of his business.

Balloons of cognac now nestled in each man's hands as they sat there, comfortably digesting, and James was grateful when Capitaine Perouse abruptly changed the subject, enquiring if the two letters he'd carried to him had brought good news, or bad. The capitaine had to take a further pinch of snuff to help him recover from the hilarity of hearing who one of James' correspondents was.

'So you actually write to that dog,' asked the capitaine, smothering a sneeze. 'You know there are respectable people in Paris who would horse-whip him on sight? What on earth do you write about?'

'Yes, my dear Claude, I do write to him, even though I know his reputation,' said James, who could still remember from his own days in Paris the dichotomy of opinion regarding his old coffee house friend. 'But there are others who would welcome him at their table,' added James. 'We write to each other about ideas. The world of the mind. And better ways to govern ourselves.'

'And that interests you? How fascinating. How have you, a simple soldier, come to be so embroiled?'

'I was not always a soldier, Claude. There was a time when my ambitions lay in an entirely different direction,' said James. And then he told his friend of his time at Glasgow's university, and how he and his friend there, a lad his own age called David Hume, had aspired to an academic life; and of their teachers, inspirational men who were becoming famous thinkers in certain circles across Europe. He rehearsed that whole heady time for Claude, and then he abruptly wound up his lyrical waxing, by saying simply, 'and then Jacobite politics intruded and stole it all from me.'

The capitaine's countenance was a picture of concentration. Eventually he said, 'No. I cannot see you in a scholar's robes, choosing dry debate above adventure and another purse of gold for all your adoring women to spend for you. The man I see before me, wigless, waistcoat unbuttoned, contented, cradling his brandy, it would sit ill on him if he was condemned to be behind a pile of books. But enough of such drole notions, my brother James. To your correspondent, the celebrated M'sieur Voltaire … what bon mots from the world of *his* mind has he sent to stimulate you to further thought? Has he offered guidance, or sent your reeling brain reaching for the decanter?'

James smiled at his friend's amused mocking, too full from his table to take offence. 'Sadly, M'sieur Voltaire's grasp of my affairs is wildly astray, I fear … for a man who claims his drama reflects the state of man as he really is.'

'How so?' said the capitaine, taking a gulp from his balloon, eager to hear of the follies of the famous.

'We have been discussing a book, M'sieur Voltaire and I, a book that my friend Davy is to publish this year and that I had ventured to predict must become significant to the way we view our world, my friend being such an original thinker and great mind for one so young. And M'sieur Voltaire was remarking in this letter why such works, far from being original, are become so commonplace in our current age. He wrote, I believe …,' and James furrowed his brow to recall the actual words, '… *such mental meanderings are possible in this modern century because to its credit, in it we see none of the barbarity and cruelty that has disfigured earlier ages. Nowadays we have less trickery and fanaticism, and more humanity and good manners, which allows our society to indulge such flights of* … and so on. There. I think that is a fair rendition I have given him. In other words, he pooh-poohed the entire idea of a man from Edinburgh having an original thought. Which, in other circumstances, would not have sat well with me.'

The capitaine laughed. 'I can hear the sneer in his every word!'

James laughed too. 'Quite. I was particularly fond of his general observation that there is *less trickery and more humanity* in our modern world. He has obviously not been here before Danzig came under siege. But that is not where I fear his error lies. There was more. Our poet then turned his peregrinations onto me. While he could see no utility in my friend's work, he foresaw much potential for my role in our new renaissance age. It was the mood in Paris that James Stuart would soon regain all that divine right decreed should be his, and when that happened, a man like me, in his service, must be of far greater influence when it comes to advancing knowledge and virtue in the world. And again, I will seek to repeat M'sieur Voltaire's very words … *you will be on hand to guide him to the path of the philosopher prince. With a man like you at his side, a man who thinks, who loves truth and detests persecution and superstition, who can show his prince how to penetrate deep into the true nature of man so that as prince, he can better know how to justly rule … such a man must be seen as invaluable. If he is wise, and people say he is, James Stuart must know that no king can be truly sanguine in his power unless he binds a man like you to his cause with bands of steel!* There! Again, I believe!'

The capitaine nodded sagely. 'He flatters you, James. How can you say M'sieur Voltaire is in error if all your joint philosophising is supposed to be bent towards the very enlightenment of absolutism he defines? I do not understand, why do his words amuse you?'

'Because,' said James, with a mischievous smile on his lips, 'the other letter your ships brought to me was from the court of the said king in waiting, James Francis Edward Stuart, dismissing me entirely from his service, declaring me unworthy of the House of Stuart's patronage, branding me disloyal and decreeing that forthwith I am banished from his majesty's presence, properties and any territories he rules now, and those over which he might rule in the future.'

'Ah …' said the capitaine. And for a moment both men gazed at each other with great frankness, until, without the slightest hesitation, both of them spontaneously burst into gales of laughter.

The next day, head thick from all the wine and brandy, James was back on his horse at first light, and the Dzików marched out again to drill.

The letter from the Palazzo del Re had flung in his face all the same accusations Dorothea had, and in between watching his regiment blunder and learn as it thundered and wheeled across the grass-tufted sandy soil of the Westerplatte, he reflected through the dull throb in his head what it all made him feel.

The short answer, he concluded, was nothing.

Regardless of whether his friend Claude had been right, and a life of books was no future for a man like him, it was his choice to make, and James Stuart and his dynastic ambitions had no right to take it from him so arbitrarily. His deluded father and his enthusiasms in that direction had contributed, of course. But it was that man Stuart, and the despotism of his birth right, that had dragged them all into this mess of contest, dispute and disharmony, when all he, James Lindsay had wanted was to get on with his life.

He imagined himself a faculty member at Glasgow, or even Edinburgh – he did not fancy Aberdeen or St Andrews, the east being too cold and dark in the winter, and too far from truly polite society. His days would be spent reading and debating; other hours set aside for deep thought and other hours yet in writing them down. As the years passed, he reflected, maybe a chair; certainly tenure. Then marriage one day; a house and children. His own hearth and a sturdy kitchen table, covered with his notes, as he supped his coffee and marked them up while his children clamoured, mewling and puking over them; their cries, when not disturbing all thought, keeping him awake, especially when the pain of the previous night's excesses lay upon him, like now. And how their discordant noise would form a hellish harmony with his wife's endless scolding over how little money his bookish career was delivering … until he found himself laughing again like he had with Claude. His friend, whom he could rely on to never mewl or puke, or scold, and who was probably right on his choice of career.

Mainly because he realised now there was another truth to be acknowledged. Something that he had long suspected, but after their growing correspondence, he now knew, was that he would never be as clever as his friend Davy. The fact was, David Hume had a finer brain than he. It was not something he could find any jealousy in his heart over. Rather, he was proud to know such a man; relieved even, that he existed. That somewhere in the world, an intellect such as Davy's was there to grapple with the big questions

That evening, the Dzików returning after drill, James followed his officers into the regimental lines. Poinatowski watched him dismount and lead his horse Estelle towards the farriers' station. He called after him, 'Excellency! May we pour you a flagon of our Polish beer after your day's exertions?'

'As long as there is a chance of others to follow it, captain, I am your man!' James called back.

There was already a huge excitement abroad in the fields surrounding Weichselmünde fortress; the to-ing and fro-ing among blue-and-white striped tents of the French regimental streets and the dull canvas of the Polish militia lines; this newly cobbled army had an air of something pending about it. Close to 12,000 men were pressed into this small bubble of Baltic coast. Everywhere there was evidence of preparation. Even though James was sure none among them knew for what, or why.

The French had been here three days now, and James, as colonel of the army's only heavy cavalry element, had not even been introduced to the major general who would now command it, let alone been informed of what might be expected of him. No posting of any chain of command had been made, nor any orders issued. The bustle of the encampment pressed these thoughts on James as he settled Estelle, even though he knew fretting over it all was pointless. They'd all learn soon enough. He walked back to the regiment's mess tent, and only managed a step through the flap before Poinatowski thrust a wooden beaker, brimming with foaming beer, into his fist.

'For your refreshment, excellency!' said the grinning captain.

James had come here because he felt he had to tell his officers *something* about what was going on; the sudden arrival of the French, and all this military build-up.

He remembered all the ignorance and uncertainty that had preceded Glenshiel, and felt it was wrong to repeat the mistake. That he was almost as much in the dark as his own men however, seemed an even worse omen. What did he know? That this war had extended beyond their own narrow horizons. But then rumours running rife about the camp and all the conjecture that followed had already dealt with much of where they now stood in this war. Which was precisely why James now feared a repeat of what he'd witnessed on the evening of Glenshiel; whether he was going to see his dragoons just melt away, just as the Highland army had that evening, astride the road 'tween Eilean Donan and Inverness.

Maybe if he could give them some reason to fight, even an invented one, they would stand. Because, right now, he was thinking he could do with a reason to fight, himself.

He invited his officers to sit and charge their own wooden beakers. Then he plunged straight in. 'I think we are all aware, gentlemen, that this war has progressed from an internal Polish matter to a general confrontation between those old foes, Bourbon France and Spain, and the Hapsburgs and their mittel Europa neighbour and Holy Roman Empire ally, Saxony.'

James had not mentioned the Russians; the Russians who were currently bombarding Danzig and threatening to drive them into the Baltic. But then, nobody seemed to notice. He pressed on.

'Since King Stanislas has retreated here to Danzig, he has secured support from King Louis of France, who has in turn concluded an alliance with Spain and the Kingdom of Sardinia to come to Poland's aid against those who support the usurper Augustus of Saxony. Troops of this alliance have already overrun the Duchy of Lorraine and are advancing into Austrian possessions on the Rhine. Another army, led by the Spanish infante, is already advancing on the Austrian-controlled Kingdom of Naples. This is a Europe-wide conflagration, gentlemen. But while that might make us look like a mere side-show, I am assured we are not.'

There had been no such assurance. In fact nobody had told him anything. All he knew had come not from their army command, or from Stanislas' court, but from the gossip and the idle guesswork over dinner of a mere middle-ranking naval officer who was probably passing on more than he knew himself, namely his friend Claude; in his own words, a simple sailor.

James continued: 'The strategy here on the Baltic, is to hold Danzig as thorn in the enemy's side …. a diversion that must force him to split his forces … and ultimately in any future peace negotiation, the prize that will wrest Poland from both Austrian and Russian spheres of influence.'

All utter drivel, of course.

But what else could he say? He couldn't have the poor wretches going into battle thinking they might be about to die just because someone had over-played their hand in another man's fight.

Yet that was likely the case. His friend's guess was that the Comte de Plélo had come with a power to negotiate. But from what James had heard from Lacy, the Russians had no interest in talking about anything apart from surrender, which meant that they really were all about to become victims of an over-played hand. He would have certainly been very upset himself right now, suspecting what he did, if it hadn't been for all those thalers Mr MacDougall was currently transferring from Stanislas' treasury to a Hamburg bank on his behalf. A cold detachment crept over him at his own duplicity. Suddenly he'd never felt so far away from the boy he used to be, and the man he'd thought he would become.

Later, outside the tent, sitting in companionable silence with Poinatowski, the two men listened to the persistent guns, and watched the sky over Danzig glow red in the falling darkness.

'You never really mentioned the Russians at any length, excellency,' observed Poinatowski, idly. 'Seeing as it is them we shall be mostly fighting.'

'No. I didn't. To be honest, no appropriate tosh to spout about them came to mind.'

Poinatowski laughed. 'Tosh, excellency?'

217

'Pyotr, when it is just us, in conclave, discussing the doggerel of life, call me James.'

'Ah. You realise here, in this culture, such familiarity is not common … excellency …' and he stuttered to a halt under James' saturnine glare. 'It would make me feel uncomfortable,' he concluded, his eyes down.

'Then feel uncomfortable, Pyotr … for my sake,' said an unblinking James. 'It would mean a lot to me to have someone in the regiment to talk to me as a human being again.'

'As you wish, excel … James.' And with that, Poinatowski's face crumpled into the complicit grin James had come to enjoy.

'Tosh?' said Poinatowski, returning to his initial question. 'You mean your address was not sincere?'

'What do you think? How would I know all that grand strategy? I had to tell them something. I just didn't want …'

Poinatowski interrupted him. 'You know it is a fact that you astonished everybody that you bothered at all? We are not a people who are used to having things explained to us. That is something that makes us uncomfortable, too.'

James sighed. 'If I am to order them to fight, do they not need a reason?'

'We are not a people who are used to wondering why, either, or indeed wondering about reasons for anything, James. Our princes speak, and we obey. To do otherwise has in the past, always proved dangerous.'

'Maybe I just want the world to be a fairer place.'

'A dangerous aspiration. Who put that idea in your head?'

James smiled at him. His friend was right. This was a different world. *The dead hand of despotism you and Davy long used to rail against over your claret, is far deader here, laddie*, he said to himself. Suddenly, Hanoverian oppression seemed an infinitely more civilised affair. A beast you could at least argue with. He laughed and said, 'I suppose I'm still wishing myself back home, instead of getting on with being a long way from it. And *that* is a dangerous aspiration.' He gave a wave of his hand.

Poinatowski, gazing off into the night, said, 'Only one home for us soldiers, eh? The field we pitch our tent in. But going back to the

Russians, and why they're here. If I might offer *my* explanation to *you*. It's because of Courland. It stands to reason. Word will have travelled from Vienna to Saxon Augustus on his new Polish throne back in Warsaw, that the price of the Russians helping keep him there, is the duchy. Augustus is not a stupid man, so he will happily throw it to the bear, once he's won. It's the currency of our politics in this world, betrayal, gain, the exercise of power just because you have it. Now, your officers being mostly local lads, if you'd told them that, they'd have understood.'

James had forgotten his friend Pyotr's grip of the game. He gave him a look of candid appreciation. Poinatowski said, 'No great mind required to see that coming, I assure you ... James.'

'Exactly. But you have explained a matter that had been troubling me.' Because it let him see the chain of cause and effect all too clearly now; Dorothea and her flip, from believing the Austrians to be a benign influence, to her desperation that a Stuart candidacy be true. Courland.

'You know, Pyotr, I think your people's way is better. No thinking or explaining needed. If we are told to fight, we fight. Trying to unravel all this politicking is making my head nip.'

14

The Battle of Westerplatte

Poinatowski found his colonel sitting at his folding campaign desk, inside his tent. He'd been called there from the mess tent where all the other officers had gathered after the day's drilling. James gestured for him to sit, and handed him what looked like a folded letter.

'Our orders,' said James. 'For tomorrow. It is a great honour. We lead out the army.'

Poinatowski read the half dozen lines of precise penmanship, and coughed apologetically. 'I believe you may be putting a false gloss on matters, excellency, when you talk of an honour.' They were talking military matters now, and there were formalities to be observed. 'It is merely how it is done. No honour there, I fear, excellency.'

'Quite, captain. I was being ironic. That is a thing we do in my country when confronted by the likes of that.'

He gestured at the letter.

'You refer to the precious little explanation, or detail it contains, I venture? But then that is how it is done, also.'

James reached for a bottle of brandy, one of the cases gifted to him by Capitaine Perouse, and poured large measures into two glass before carrying them to where a map was unrolled on a larger version of his own desk. Poinatowski followed, collecting his glass on the way. Both men stood gazing down at the terrain they were to fight over the next day. The map was more an impression than a military cartographer's precise document, but it was good enough to show all they needed to see of the corridor running east from Weichselmünde fortress, between the Mottlau river and the Baltic.

'We lead, in column of march, down this road through the open fields north of the Mottlau,' James drew his finger along what was really more a cartoon of a road, than something they might take scale or measurement from. Then he added, 'What happens here, d'you think?' And his finger this time jabbed at row upon row of tiny, thinly drawn, rolling lines and tufts to the north of the road, representing a serried run of scrubby sand dunes that ran inland from the sea. 'All of it broken ground, and soft going too. No use for cavalry in formation, and hard going for infantry. Bad ground. But how bad? We have not reconnoitred it. So my flank is to just hang in the air?'

Poinatowski didn't answer.

'All the orders say is that we are simply to march forth, until "such time as it becomes apparent a halt must be called, and deployment begun." What on earth am I to understand by that, pray tell?'

Poinatowski went back and sat down. He finished his brandy in a gulp, and gestured to the bottle. 'May I, excellency?'

James felt his jaw drop at the presumption; but then he was never done encouraging such familiarity in his friend. He smiled to himself at his own bumptiousness as he too stepped back over to his desk and flopped onto his camp seat. 'Fill mine up too while you're at it, captain. You look as if you are about to tell me something I won't like.'

'Ask you something, rather, excellency.'

James gestured for him to go ahead.

'No-one doubts you are a soldier of considerable experience, excellency,' said Poinatowski, carefully picking his words. 'The evidence has been for all to see these past months. But there is a question I must ask.'

'Oh for God's sake, Pyotr!' But James already knew what question he was about to be asked, and his irritation stemmed from a churning stomach.

Here he was again, having to face down that dread he refused to name again. Like he had before his first charge in anger. He knew how to do it, but those orders he'd just opened spoke of something to be dealt with of a far greater magnitude than he'd faced before; a beast wholly unknown to him, and potentially un-manning. He knew he was being asked again to put it to the touch, but the stakes seemed so much higher this time. He found himself idly wondering how many times a scholar might be so challenged in his lifetime.

Poinatowski asked his question, 'How many battles ... have you fought in, excellency? Not skirmishes ... actual set-piece battles, where field armies meet ... battalion against battalion ...?'

Poinatowski was about to say more, but realised he'd probably said too much; not sure how wise it had been to point out that his colonel might lack experience.

James could see from Poinatowski's face that he too had a gift for already knowing the answer to questions he'd just asked.

But he could also see his junior officer wasn't asking the question out of contempt, or even fear, or doubt. He just wanted to have matters straight, so their discussion could continue. He liked Poinatowski even more for that; risking his colonel's ire to achieve a better understanding; when the man could just have let James hang in his ignorance, and be damned. A petulant response from him would ruin everything now, whereas good grace would take them forward. James liked the idea of being a man of good grace. He took a deep breath and tried to imagine the expression on the face of a different James, one in a university gown, being asked such a question, and laughed before he replied.

'Not a one, captain. Not a one.'

'Then there are things I would like to explain, excellency ...' said Poinatowski, all brisk, and smiling now himself, before James interrupted him.

'If we are to sit here drinking all night, while you give me, *your* colonel, a lesson in war, then I think it is only fitting you feel uncomfortable too. No more "excellency" now. We talk as men.'

'James,' said Poinatowski pointedly, with his complicit grin again, 'there is nothing I can tell you now that can ever really prepare you for what will happen tomorrow, but there are things you should know about battle anyway … truths you should know so that you will not be distracted when you encounter them. In other words, a brief description of what a modern clash of armies is really like. Because it is always very easy to be distracted on a battlefield, something that can end most unfortunately. So let us begin at the beginning. You will already know that where there is an army, there is also a manual. Every state, every prince, who fields an army, has one, and they exist so no soldier has to think.'

James nodded that he was following. Poinatowski continued. 'The consequence is that a modern battlefield has become a very mannered, stylised arena, or at least would appear so, if you could see it. But you can't. No-one can, not even if he were lifted up by an angel to look down upon it. Because of all the smoke. Gunpowder makes a lot of smoke. In fact, smoke is the guns' principal manufacture. More than death. It blankets everything, right from the opening cannonade. Great, clinging, stinking clouds of it, so that in the thick of battle it grits up your eyes and you can almost chew it.'

But, said Poinatowski, all that happened after the shooting started. Before it, there was much James might expect to see; before all the smoke got in the way. 'The whole extravaganza is more akin to a courtly gavotte than a fight, and it all begins with the approach to battle,' said the captain.

'A general marches his soldiers onto the field, and then he must deploy them, from column of march into lines, hopefully without any interference from the enemy, for that would be impolite. The infantry, in battalions, usually forms up three deep and in the centre of the general's line; the cavalry in squadrons, also three deep, but to the side, protecting the infantry's flanks. The artillery, in batteries of seldom more than three guns, are then be run up between the battalions to take up positions usually about half a dozen paces in front.

'Long before all that, of course, the general's orders would have been written out and carried by aides to all his units … so everybody knows what is, generally, to be expected of them. Because,' added Poinatowski, more pointedly, 'from the moment the general orders his artillery to open fire, he generally has very little control over what happens after that.'

'The smoke gets in the way?' asked James.

'The smoke, indeed,' said Poinatowski. 'And the noise. Don't forget the noise. Sometimes the din is so great you can blow a bugle sounding recall until you are purple in the face, and no-one hears a damn thing.'

Poinatowski paused to gulp his brandy, then resumed. 'After a brief cannonade, the infantry battalions whose written orders say they must go forward, start to march, in their rigid lines, towards the enemy lines, which are, by custom, a mirror image of their own. They perform such manoeuvres with parade-ground regularity, the sergeants keeping the fronts straight with their halberds. Until they come within musket range of the enemy line, then they stop, the front rank kneels, and fires. The second rank fires over them and the third rank, over the second rank's shoulders. It goes without saying, the enemy ranks return their fire, and thusly they both continue until one side breaks and runs away. But none of this you see ...'

'... because of the smoke,' said James.

'Again, indeed,' said Poinatowski. 'And that, in essence, is a modern battle. A machine for delivering firepower to the enemy. It is very rare they will fix bayonets, and even rarer will they charge. These are peasant soldiers, most of them, devoid of imagination, but not so devoid that they will stand in line to face a naked blade if their delivery of firepower fails. A cavalry charge in a modern battle is even rarer.'

'I do not understand,' interrupted James. 'I would have thought the shock of a regiment of cavalry hitting you would ...'

But Poinatowski interrupted, in his turn. 'Cavalry seldom fight in regiments. Mainly because there is rarely the room for them to deploy. A modern battlefield is usually a small arena, otherwise what minimum control a general might have would be lost altogether. No. The manuals agree cavalry must number off into squadrons, free to range the battle-field plugging gaps. A wise general will always hold them back to head off any enemy flanking attempts or breakthroughs, always assuming his opponent is clever enough, or lucky enough to be able to assemble such a movement in the confusion of battle. The defending general will then counter by using his cavalry as mobile infantry. Trotting them up to within range of the threat, where they can open fire with their carbines, either from horseback, or in the case of dragoons like us, they will dismount and form an infantry line of their own. Think on it. In a pitched battle, any cavalry squadron deciding to charge a line of infantry would be riding into their muskets. They would be shot to pieces before they could lay a sabre on them.'

'And cavalry against cavalry?' asked a pensive James. 'Our forays against those Russian hussars ... against the damn cuirassiers ... the charges there performed their functions.'

'Skirmishes, James,' said Poinatowski. 'Where there was space for a gallop to gain momentum ... for a squadron to manoeuvre in good order. There is no space on a battlefield. Which is why the manuals dictate that cavalry should fight cavalry in much the same way as infantry fights infantry.'

A glum James pursed his lips. 'Which explains all the furrowed brows at my new drill regime, and the shambles that followed every time I ordered a charge. Why did no one say?'

'You were the colonel. We obeyed. And then we saw how effective we became. No-one wanted to say anything after that. Walking your horse up to your foe and then just sitting there exchanging carbine fire is a wretched way for a cavalryman to fight. You made us look like supermen, and the Dzików liked that. Thank you, excellency!'

James gave him a dark look, but let that one pass. 'Don't mention it,' he said.

'And that is it,' said Poinatowski, winding up with a stiff gulp from his glass. 'It is all about fire and movement, by rote. And the first one to break his opponent's line wins. It is how we fight war in the modern age.'

'And how does the churning in your guts the night before fit in?' asked James, who had hardly touched his brandy.

'Oh, that comes in, in just the same way before your sixth battle as it does before your first,' said Poinatowski, and he nodded at James' glass. 'One more word of advice however, my friend, drink that up … so you can have another.'

James' chest felt full, and his throat tight. Back straight, upright in the saddle as his body swayed to easy rhythm of Estelle's measured pace. The sun was up, and he was starting to feel its heat. Behind him, well back, he could hear the massed drummers beating time above the sound of marching soldiers; above the hoof-beats of his Dzików dragoons, and the jingling of their bridles. In front of him was a simple road running into the morning haze, across an endless expanse of empty, flat grazing land – with not an animal in sight.

The boy James, a lifetime ago, playing soldiers in the grassy butts of the Kirkspindie estate, had never in his wildest fantasies dreamed that when he became a man, he might be here now, colonel of his own regiment, leading an army of French and Polish soldiers, 12,000-strong, into battle. For in that morning haze, somewhere, was a Russian army, waiting for them.

The churning guts and the cold sweats of the night before had long gone, banished from the moment he swung into the saddle. His written orders, now tucked in the breast of his uniform coat, had said, 'the Dzików shall form the vanguard', so he had turned Estelle's head towards the front of his regiment standing patiently in column of march, the horses' heads tossing, their tails flicking, eager to be moving, and walked her into position, ahead of the lead troop's officers, ahead of the colour party, of even the bugler and his aide, the young cornet of horse called Casimir, whose second name he could never pronounce, until he and Estelle were the spear-tip of the entire army. Then, in the unquiet silence of a host before it moves, his voice had boomed loud, but thin, in the echoless morning air, 'Avant!'

And in the crunching first noises of the thousands of stirring soldiers, crows had risen in a black cloud from the dumps behind the army's lines. But he did not see them, his eyes were to the front as the Dzików stepped out, and battalion after battalion marched behind them, the French in their grey-white and the Poles resplendent in blue, regimental colours flying and drummers beating the pace.

Several times now, James had stood up in his stirrups and looked back, but the flatness of the terrain meant he could only see an overlapping wall of marching men; that they were in three columns you could only tell by the leading files of drummers and regimental colours. Only the rising dust, rippling into the distance, gave any impression of depth. Even so, James hadn't seen so many men gathered together and moving with one purpose since the Russian army that had marched on Warsaw.

There was a thrill to it he could not articulate, even to himself.

Somewhere in the mass was the army's general, this Estaing de Sailland fellow whom James had yet to set eyes on; and the French minister, the Comte de Plélo, who was apparently riding with them too. Command was theirs, but as the army paced forward an unspoken conviction settled upon Colonel James Lindsay, that the actual responsibility for it, right now, was his.

It was he who was leading this army, after all, and whatever destiny was holding for it upon this road, it would be he who would touch it first.

The knowledge settled a terrible quiet on him; as if all the strands of his life were about to come together on this nondescript reach of sand and grass; the sum of him so far, about to be tested.

Battle.

He had listened closely to his friend Pyotr Poinatowski; was conscious now of a deep gratitude to him for what he'd tried to tell him. Much of it he'd guessed, so steeped he was in the stories of Marlborough's victories in the previous age, when his country had been one under Stuart Queen Anne; the victories of Blenheim, Ramillies, Oudenarde, and the slaughter that had been Malplaquet. Just words on a page, until today, when he too was about to learn what battle really tasted like.

Pyotr had uttered one true thing last night, that nothing he said would prepare him for this.

So many firsts for him, these months past, to test him. He was still here, but now was coming the ultimate rite of passage. Now he was about to find out whether all his presumptions to being a soldier were mere arrogance. He thought back on every step that had led him here, and he knew he would accept the judgement of this day, and with that, he found he was smiling to himself, because he was content.

Battle. So be it.

He was looking forward to meeting the man he would be after this day – if he was allowed to survive. And with that, he consigned his fate to God, saying the words in his head: I am ready then, let us put it to the touch once more.

What caught his eye appeared at first as a mere an anomaly against the horizon; nothing more than a tiny disfigurement of the land, as if a stretch of field had been too eagerly ploughed, so that the earth stood proud on the shoulder of a too-deep furrow.

Then he wasn't sure; was that a glint of the sun off steel? Or what had first appeared as boulders, did he just see them begin to bob and move? Were those the shapes of tricorne hats? But the questions were rhetoric; he knew what he was looking at, instantly. The movement of soldiers behind a trench line.

He did not rein in Estelle, or pull her round so he might more conveniently yell or gesticulate wildly to the rear. The trench was still far off. He let Estelle maintain her pace, while he retrieved a pencil and paper from his sabretache and scribbled a note to the general. Then he handed it to Casimir.

'Cornet, I want you to deliver this with all dispatch personally, into the general's hand,' said James. 'And on your way, seek out Captain Poinatowski, present my compliments and inform him his presence is requested here.'

James watched as Casimir's horse carried him, in the most tearing hurry, back down the column of still advancing dragoons. From that moment on, all the terrible events of the day began to unfold with an almost mechanical inevitability; like watching a series of interlinking cogs and wheels grind wheat in a mill, but with blood instead of dust.

To his left, James was aware of a tiny knot of militia uhlans, appearing and disappearing in the grass-tufted rises of the broken ground. Perhaps his general was not so clueless after all; these Polish irregular cavalrymen were acting as his flank guard, there to give warning of any Russian attempts at harassment.

Poinatowski arrived. 'There,' said James, pointing towards the scar against the horizon. The long smudges of green running well behind the trench line were more distinct now; demonstrably not the hedge rows he'd first assumed, but rank upon rank of green-coated Russian infantry – still; rigid in the shimmering air.

'I would advance no closer than double cannon shot before you deploy, excellency,' said Poinatowski, taking it all in.

James shook his head. 'Nor yet so close, captain. I believe I will throw out our screen now. If the general wants us closer, then I am sure we can accomplish such a move in line. Have the bugler sound the left wheel. We shall form in line to the front, two squadrons up, one in reserve.'

'This instant, excellency.' And Poinatowski wheeled away himself, and cantered off to make it so.

James turned to watch the parade precision as his troopers walked up to where a corporal of horse marked the turn, and then they peeled, in single file, trotting to their left on an angle one could measure by a set square. James led his colour party a short distance along their walking files to a point that would stand as the centre of the line, and there he halted. He could not help the tiny frisson of pride as he watched his men execute his orders so precisely.

Then he turned back to face the enemy, un-slinging his telescope for the first time to survey the Russian positions. At first, the only movement he could discern was a galloping aide; like a tiny equine banner moving in a wake of dust behind the trench line. Then he made out the Russian guns. Nothing heavy; much like the French artillery coming up behind him, no more than six-pounders, clutched together in batteries of three. Another mirror to the army marching to oppose them. Such fussy etiquette, he thought, for such gory purpose.

And as he thought it, another notion descended on him; a powerful one, from out of nowhere, that here today they would be facing the Russian general in chief himself, Lacy. It sent a shiver through him. But events behind him would not let him dwell on it.

His bugler was sounding 'Halt, and wheel!' and he turned, just in time to see the fragile single file of walking horses step right, as if a wire running under them had been pulled, so that in an instant they had become one continuous front, over 300 troopers in length, presenting towards the enemy. He gave the order, and the bugler sounded, 'Advance', and the line resumed its slow walk towards the Russians. No written order from his general was required; he knew what was expected of him at this stage in the dance; to screen the main body of the army while it too deployed in line behind him.

At their slow pace, it took what seemed an age for the Dzików to cover the remaining distance to what James reckoned was just beyond the Russian's effective artillery range. And there he raised his left arm and brought the line of troopers to a halt. Looking to his left he could see the considerable distance that lay, wide open, between his flank troopers and the grassy dunes. There was an even greater distance on his right, to the bank of the Mottlau river. But as he looked in that direction, he could see French infantry marching towards the river in a solid block, two regiments deep, with a third wheeling in behind. Turning right round, the vision that presented itself to him was of rest of the French and Polish regiments filing off their columns of march to deploy as laid down by their manuals. The mechanical metaphor that had first struck him earlier was all too obviously continuing to play itself out, except it had taken on a much more grandiose, theatrical aspect now. As he watched, he found it difficult to tell whether he was just a member of the audience or part of the cast. And he felt all the dignity he'd experienced marching at point, drain away from him as if the sheer mass of trudging soldiers was acting like gravity upon him, dragging him back, subsuming all his personal glory.

The deployment of the army dragged on for hours. Behind him, the machine ground on through its cycle, but to his front only the sun moved, climbing slowly ever higher in the sky, until James started to feel the sweat forming under the silk shirt he always wore to a fight, lest a blow or a bullet carried any material with it into the wound. There was dust in the air now too; he could feel it gritting on his teeth. He took a sip from his water canteen, careful not take too much, knowing what lay ahead would be thirsty work; not knowing when he'd get a chance to refill it. Checking for the umpteenth time his brandy flask, guessing he would likely need that too before the day was over. Endlessly cluttering his mind with such trivia to pass the time.

And there, from nowhere, was a French officer reining his horse to halt to face him, resplendent in a finely tailored uniform of the Grenadiers à Cheval – obviously a staff officer – and from his braid, if James recalled his French army marks of rank correctly, a captain.

Without taking the trouble to present himself, the man took in the Dzików and their immaculate line in one long evaluating glance, then, not even looking at James, his eyes still lingering on the farthest dragoon, he addressed James, a superior officer, with calculated insolence.

'Major General Estaing de Saillard presents his compliments and requires me to present you with your orders.'

James could barely understand him, such was the high-flown and formal nasal throttling of his words. Then, to James' astonishment, the young French captain handed the orders to Casimir, and not to him.

Before James could say anything, the officer stepped his horse back a few paces and sat up in his saddle. 'The major general intends to drive the Russians off the Mottlau river,' he said, with a grand, sweeping gesture, 'and then pin them against the sand dunes, where they will be given the opportunity to surrender. Complete victory is his goal. To that end he requires your cavalry to take up position behind our left flank with all due dispatch. Once there you are to prevent the enemy from taking advantage of the fact that our line falls short of a suitable anchor there in the dunes. The Polish militia uhlans will support you. God grant us victory!'

And with that, the French captain wheeled his horse and sped off back to his master. James, a colonel, had not even been given an opportunity to open his mouth. He knew what had just happened of course – he had served long enough in the French army to remember the contempt in which they held the soldiers of lesser nations. He felt he should have been seething, but as he sat there, Estelle beneath his rump, her head down to crop at the long tuft grass, he found himself absently wondering instead whether the arrogant little arse would survive the day or end up a bloody smear on the sandy soil. Then he was distracted by Casimir, offering him the folded set of written orders.

The sun was long past its zenith now and James sat there, mildly irritated with himself for not checking his fob watch for the time the French cannonade had begun. It had seemed an age, but he knew only too well how time can play tricks with you in a fight; if this exercise in tedious waiting he and the rest of his Dzików were enduring could be called a fight. Poinatowski had been right about the smoke, however. Way over towards the river, there was already a roiling grey bank of it, all but unmoving in another listless, windless afternoon.

The Dzików stood in three squadron ranks, their mounts shifting and shuffling, and facing away from the sound of the guns. At an angle, to their right, were the backs of the collected grenadier companies of all the Polish battalions, so all you could see was the rows and rows of coloured felt at the back of their tall mitre hats, like they were a field of tulips. They too seemed to be shuffling with boredom. And all the time, the endless, out of rhythm, drum-like roll of the French batteries firing, and the Russian batteries replying. Even if they'd all been allowed to turn and look, there was nothing to see. Not even the flash of the cannon was visible through the cocooning smoke.

As James had led the Dzików walking in column across the massing front of the army, he'd had the thrilling sensation of watching something unimaginably powerful being drawn tight; cocked, ready to be unleashed in a terrible blow. The grey-white of the French uniforms, picked out in all the gaudy colours of their regimental facings – the blues and reds and yellows – tramping in determined, eerie silence to their mark. Except, there had been no silence, really. Everything was unfolding to the thin staccato of shouted orders; the relentless *tum-tee-tum! tum-tee-tum!* of drummer boys leading every company in every battalion. It was just that there were so many men, and yet an utter, desolate absence of talk that made it seem like a silence.

And then they had swung round the end of the army's line of battle, and into their position as ordered. And now, they waited.

That was when the *tum-tee-tum! tum-tee-tum!* of drummer boys started up again. The beat came drifting to them out of the smoke along with the booming of the guns; and then, suddenly, the intensity of the artillery fire abruptly fell away and the beat of the drums rose. Somewhere in the smoke, battalions were on the move. This time, James remembered to check his timepiece.

'What time is it, excellency?' It was Beart. The first words he had spoken since they had formed up here at the edge of the dunes.

'It is almost three of the clock,' said James. 'M'sieur Estaing de Sailland moves at his own pace, eh, Beart?'

The two men smiled thinly at each other while time resumed its treacle drip.

In the dense swirling of the smoke, the regiments Gensac and Royal-Comtois stepped out, side by side, each one three ranks deep, colours in their front ranks, their colonels leading them on foot, drummer boys beating the advance. Experienced sergeants, a pace or two ahead, their eyes measuring the distance to bring them to musket shot of the enemy; the dull *thud, thud, thud* of 2,000 men's boots on the ground, marching to the same step.

James couldn't see them, nor hear the beat of their boots, but he could hear their drummer boys. And when they suddenly stopped, the absence of their sound made him flinch. For a moment, then a moment more, there was nothing; just the background noise that masses of men make even when they are doing nothing. Then a different sound; like ripping linen, and again, and again. Separate rips running together, volley after volley of musketry.

And it went on like that, for an age; the intensity rising and falling in random crescendos. James could not imagine what was unfolding in that smoke.

What was, did not bear imagining.

The regiments Gensac and Royal-Comtois had come to a halt just shy of 270 paces from the Russian trench line, and their front ranks had, on the order, 'Kneel!', dropped onto one knee. The two ranks behind had closed up on them, and on the order, 'Present!' had as one pointed their Charleville-pattern muskets at the enemy.

On the order 'Front rank, fire!', 300 or more kneeling soldiers from each regiment pulled their triggers, and their flints ignited the black gunpowder in their firing pans, creating a small explosion that sent the those 300-odd lead/tin balls shooting towards the enemy at a muzzle velocity of over 1,200 feet per second.

Even at that relatively long range for muskets, any ball hitting a man did the most appalling damage, penetrating deep into the flesh, the soft metal distorting as it went, opening horrific wounds, splintering any bone it hit and carrying with it tiny torn patches of coat and shirt, which if left the soldier's body, would later cause infection and death.

The French front rank's volley hit very few Russian soldiers, safe behind their earthwork. The second rank fared no better, or the third, as they delivered their volleys too. As the Frenchmen fumbled to reload, the Russians replied; their volleys ripping and tearing into the bodies of over seventy French soldiers along the frontage of the two regiments, crumpling them in heaps for the men behind to step over and fill the gaps.

The drummer boys, lying flat to be fired over, stood up and began their *tum-tee-tum! tum-tee-tum!* again. French line was once more advancing, another fifty paces. Line upon line of faces, smeared now with powder smoke; not men really, although they marched the way men march. No room to be men here, pressed shoulder to shoulder, so nowhere to run to the side; with rank upon rank of others behind, so nowhere to run back, and with an enemy and their muskets and bayonets to their front. No room for flight, only fight. So, on they marched, towards the fight. Line upon line of faces, many, frozen in probably the last expression they would ever wear.

The volleys began again. The French fired, paused to reload, then marched forward, another fifty paces. And all the while the lead/tin balls reaped their harvest. So that the lines following behind could see where the line ahead had absorbed each Russian reply; the bodies neatly arrayed and the ground beneath them beginning to slick with the blood flowing out of all those commodious holes. From the groans and the screams, here, at last, it appeared there was room to be a man again, or at least to suffer like one.

James saw none of that; he just watched from his saddle at the other end of the army's line as all the smoke down towards the Mottlau continued to cling to that corner of the pale blue sky; an indifferent pall with only the continuous *tum-tee-tum! tum-tee-tum!* and the musketry, suggesting anything at all was unfolding; just that the rip after rip after rip.

James cantered back to the rear squadron to talk to Poinatowski.

'Your insistence that nothing you said could ever prepare me was true,' James observed, reining in Estelle so they both now stood looking towards the Mottlau and the smoke.

Poinatowski took one look at James' weary countenance and started to laugh. 'If I had come out and said battles could also be boring, you would not have believed me,' he said. Both of them looked at the lines of grenadiers in front of them. Their officers had stood them down so that they were now all sitting in rows instead of standing as if on parade, muskets across their laps; some had even doffed their tall mitre hats. No mutter of conversation, though. None of the soldiers had anything to say.

That was when the hubbub started further down the line. The next battalion was standing, too. James and Poinatowski stood on their stirrups for a better view. It was another Polish battalion; fusiliers this time, no longer just an extended blue line, their individual platoons separating, being marshalled by sergeants pointing halberds, directing the soldiers back into column of march.

'Looks like our general needs reinforcements for his fight on the riverbank,' said Poinatowski as they watched. Scuffling sounds and yells broke out over their shoulders and when they turned, the grenadiers to their front were being slapped and cajoled back to their feet. And when they looked back the other way, the fusiliers down the line had started marching ... *tum-tee-tum! tum-tee-tum!* ... into the smoke.

That was when the two men saw, coming the other way, what looked like a convoy of peasant refugees and agricultural machinery – until they saw the marching uniforms behind the oxen and cart horses drawing the wagons. And then they could see that some of the wagons were actually artillery pieces. A mounted officer on a very un-military looking horse trotted up, and introduced himself.

'Messieurs, I have the honour to command this battery of light field guns,' he said, raising his tricorne. 'I am to reinforce your flank.'

Then he saw their looks of astonishment and alarm. 'Ah!' he said. 'We use local carters and labourers to draw the battery. My gunners do the firing!' Another winning smile. 'And they all know their duty very well, I assure you, sirs! Where would you wish us to deploy?'

James sent Casimir to bring down a troop of uhlans from off the dunes, and introduced their officer to the gunner. The three 6-pounders would go to where the dunes started to rise, and the uhlans would cover them.

'Should any enemy attempt to turn out flank, m'sieur,' ordered James, 'you are to pour fire into theirs.'

All while Poinatowski watched, chewing his lip, as the grenadiers extended their line to just two ranks deep. The manoeuvre was completed with little trouble, but this time the men were not allowed to sit.

And to the east, and the river, the crackling of musketry, shot and shell laboured on, while here, where the flank hung in mid-air, the waiting laboured on also.

* * *

James saw the uhlan charging in from the dunes while he was still some way off, his dust cloud haloed out behind him. By the time he got to where James and Pointowski stood, James was practically as breathless from anticipation as the uhlan was from hard riding. The man slewed to halt, removed his czapka cap and bowed in his saddle, trying to catch a breath. But when he spoke, James understood not a word.

'He is a Lithuanian Tatar, excellency,' said Poinatowski, translating. 'And has no command of diplomatic French … or Latin.' The latter, he delivered with his arch smile.

'Very funny, Pyotr,' said James, in no mood to trifle, but still able to see a joke. 'Now, what does he say, man? It's obviously urgent.'

'Not so urgent as it can't out-run a marching Russian column, excellency,' said Poinatowski. The uhlan's message; a Russian column was marching across the front of the grenadiers. 'Positioning to turn the grenadiers' flank, I believe, excellency,' said Poinatowski. 'It is obvious.'

The fug of boredom vanished from James' head.

A brisk gallop took James and Poinatowski to the open ground on the grenadiers' left.

'Everything's so damn flat!' said James, to no-one. The terrain gave him no view. All he could see was open grazing and a couple of stunted, wind-bent copses. And yes, there, in between, was a line of marching green; shouldered muskets prickling along like a porcupine's back. And in the midst, mounted officers; poles sporting regimental colours hanging lank in the still air, the only way for him to estimate numbers. One set of colours, one regiment; one regiment, 1,600 men. He could see two sets of colours. But there was no sense of the direction of march; was the line coming at him? Or marching across his front, like the uhlan had said?

He turned back to the grenadiers. A senior officer, he guessed from his braid-trimmed tricorne instead of a mitre, was stomping about, gesticulating. Their great general had appointed no-one to command the left flank. 'Stand and hold!' had been his only order. James cursed the belligerent stupidity of the man. The grenadier officer was likely a colonel, too. Was James going to get into an argument with him over who was senior? That way battles were lost; he'd read it in his histories. What was happening here, he'd also read in his histories.

'The Duke of Marlborough, have you ever heard of him?' he asked Poinatowski.

'Yes, excellency,' he replied, eyes rolling.

'That's what's happening here,' said James, holding his telescope to his eye again. 'But the wrong way round. The silly arse!'

'Excellency?'

'Marlborough tactics,' said James, while trying to concentrate on what he could see. 'He would always open with an attack on one section of the enemy line … and then keep battering away until the enemy was forced to reinforce. The section of his line he weakened to do so, Marlborough would then throw *his* reserves at it … and break through. Our general keeps throwing more reinforcements into his attack on the right … weakening us here on the left …and so here are the Russians, throwing *their* reserves at *us*.'

Poinatowski looked back at the 500 Dzików dragoons behind him, then across at the 800 or so grenadiers formed in their fragile two lines; and then out to where as many as 3,000 Russian soldiers were manoeuvring to sweep them up.

'So we stand and fight, excellency,' he said.

'We stand and fight, Pyotr,' said James, 'but time to tinker a little with exactly where we stand, and how we fight, eh?'

Another uhlan came galloping in from the dunes. Brief, breathless words were exchanged with Poinatowski, who turned to inform James. 'Cavalry too, excellency,' he said. 'Advancing from the east in column.'

'Tell Beart to order the dragoons to dismount and stand by their bridles. Then he is to assemble all the officers by the colours. I will join you there, Captain Poinatowski,' said James, snapping his telescope shut. 'But now, I am going to inform the grenadiers' colonel of my intentions, which is only polite, as I'm sure you'll agree.'

And with that, James spurred Estelle, and was off.

The small clutch of Dzików officers began replacing their tricornes and walking back to their mounts. The sound of battle to the east was still in their ears, unchanged, but now the smell of powder had reached them, despite the listless day.

They had waited until Colonel Lindsay had returned from the grenadiers' lines, and listened as he, grim of countenance, had then issued his orders.

They were to stand by their mounts so the advancing Russians would not see them there, sitting tall in their saddles behind the vulnerably thin line of Polish grenadiers. And yes, there was more waiting to be endured, but it would not be long now. Control your mounts and hold your lines, he had told them; do not let the cohesion of the squadron fall apart into rabble. When the moment to re-mount arrives, you will have to move fast, for it will be in your swift and diligent response to orders that the battle will likely be decided.

Colonel Lindsay's language had been clear and concise, spelling out everything they had to do; then he spelled out exactly what would unfold – and when had he ever been wrong? The blood was thrilling through their veins now.

Beart walked his horse out to the front of the first squadron to lead it; the second squadron formed the line behind him. Poinatowski was walking his to the command position at the front of the third, well to the rear; it would form James' reserve. Meanwhile James and Casimir, and his bugler, had remounted and were galloping off, way beyond the left-most platoon of the grenadiers' line. For James wanted to see if the Russians were going to do what he wanted them to; he wanted to be there to see how they would commit their infantry. And when they did, he would gallop to the French artillery battery nestling on the first rise of grass-tufted dune, and tell them his plan.

The first Russian regiment had all but fully deployed; three lines deep and facing the Polish grenadiers like a mirror, at maybe a 400-pace distance. James had watched as they came peeling off their column of march as though they were dealt onto the field by some giant, invisible croupier; their half-platoon frontages coming off the column at an angle in choreographed step, into single line and then pacing out so that on the order, 'Right turn!' they would face the enemy. Poinatowski had been on the button when he described modern battles a courtly gavotte.

Their drums had fallen silent, but he could still hear the steady beat of the other regiment of Russian fusiliers, still on the move. The first regiment had fulfilled his wishes; he was crossing his fingers the second would do the same. As for the Russian cavalry, he'd worry about them later.

He waited, aware of Casimir fidgeting behind him. The boy was a tense bundle of energy. He found himself absently wondering what was going through the lad's head.

No great feat; it was easy to guess what Casimir would be thinking – or rather, would be feeling – in every fibre of his body. There would be a burning conviction, that his country's future likely depended on this battle today. That he was here to fight for his king and for Poland; to place his life on the line for things he believed in.

How like that young James Lindsay of long ago he was; who had stood on the field of Glenshiel, eager for glory in the cause of his own king and his own country. God, there had been a fire in his belly on that day. He couldn't imagine Casimir feeling any different now.

And then he wondered whether Casimir was going to experience all the disappointment and disillusion he had when his day was over. Whether, in the end, Casimir would come to see that he had been practised upon, his youth and faith just chips to be played, the way James had. Were all the Casimirs on this field today being practised upon? Was there any point in this fight, and could Stanislas and his rule be defended? Or was this all just small part in a whole other game, being played for stakes entirely different to the ones these Poles were betting on?

He didn't really need to ask those questions; he knew the answers already. The Poles here might be fighting for their idea of Poland, but none of the other contenders on this field gave a fig for it, or for Poland's fate. Russia, Austria, France, Saxony, and beyond this horizon, all the others with an interest in the outcome, each with reasons too labyrinthine and arcane to list; Sweden, their neighbour Prussia, remarkably silent in this war so far, and across the German sea, remote Hanoverian Britain.

And James Francis Edward Stuart, in his fading palazzo in Rome, and Maria Clementina, his scheming, manipulative, Polish queen-in-waiting. It was all about spheres of influence and scoring points in their great pan-European power play, and nothing to do with idealism of the Casimirs of this world. Poor, sad, deluded boys.

Not that Colonel Chevalier James Lindsay cared. Not now. The young man who'd stepped out onto the field of Glenshiel really was no more. And if there had ever been a vestige of doubt, the way his eye was sizing up the ground where his fight this day would unfold, confirmed it. There was no fire in his belly anymore, no cause burning in his breast, no champing at the bit to vanquish a mortal foe. He was more like an artisan builder, working to construct a victory from a plan he had in his head, just like the builder constructs his palace. There was no moral cause at stake for him, nor even glory; just the thalers he hoped Mr MacDougall had successfully shifted by now. A cold, steadying satisfaction settled about him at the thought. It seemed altogether wiser to be pursuing his destiny these days as a journeyman, rather than as a dreamer.

As for Casimir? The boy was going to have to look after himself on that front and get his own wisdom as best he could; always assuming, of course, that he was left standing after all this. That they were both left standing.

The second Russian regiment, in marching column, was coming on – colours to the front, drummers beating. Stepping out, a four-man frontage, their line snaking back, drill immaculate. What had that French fool Chapuis called them – 'dandified barbarians'? James didn't think so, not looking at them now. As tight and disciplined a body of troops as he had seen. But then, Chapuis had never faced a Russian soldier in anger; no French general had, nor any French army.

As he watched their determined step, a volley of musketry exploded to his right. The first Russian line had advanced to exchange fire with the Polish grenadiers. A ridge of grey powder smoke had risen beyond the Polish line, and as he looked at the grenadiers' backs he could see gaps open up where some of the Russian balls had hit men in the second rank. Another ripple of fire, and another rising billow of smoke; this time it was from the grenadiers, returning the volley.

It was time for his dragoons to remount and prepare. James ordered his bugler to sound the order, and the boy blared it out with gusto, so it would be easily heard by the standing Dzików troopers to his rear.

Then the Russians fired again, as James had expected them to, noting that there had been no delay, no time for them to have advanced to close the range before they fired. Because, as he'd predicted to himself, the Russians had no intention of advancing on these hapless Poles, no wish to absorb their punishment at closer range; they only had to pin them to their position in order to seal their fate.

But he had no time for smug satisfaction. When he looked back to see if his dragoons were ready, he saw how far the Russian column had advanced. There they were, in all their military splendour, having marched clear now of the flanks of the two duelling lines to his right, and halted, as he'd hoped they would. In perfect position to advance on the Polish grenadiers' flank. Just where he wanted them to be.

Except part of the Russian column was still marching on; marching on too far, instead of coming to a halt too. For a moment, he could not figure out what was happening. Then he saw it was the flat terrain that had robbed him of perspective, that had tricked him into thinking he'd been looking at one regimental column, when all the time his Russian foe had been coming on in two battalion columns, marching in echelon instead of one after the other.

And with that one little deviation from parade ground form, they had out-manoeuvred him and his plan, leaving him to stand and watch while his failure played itself out to the relentless beat of the Russian drummers, before even a shot had been fired.

His plan had been simple; he would let the first Russian regiment advance to face the grenadiers. Indeed, there had been no manoeuvre he could have used to stop them. Instead, he would wait until the second regiment marched to outflank the thin Polish line, which would be then fully engaged to its front. And once the second Russian regiment was committed, he would have the Dzików advance from the grenadiers' cover and take *them* in the flank, the first two squadrons advancing to discharge their carbines into the enemy, one after the other, throwing the Russians into confusion; then the leading squadron would pass through, charge, and roll them up.

But only one Russian battalion had marched into that position on the grenadiers' flank. The other had marched wide. And once it was in place, the Dzików would not be able to approach the first Russian battalion without taking withering enfilading fire from the second. The Dzików's manoeuvre would be shot to pieces.

Unless he went now. Right now. Before the second Russian battalion had marched far enough to deploy and face him. He yelled at his bugler to tuck in behind him, and spurred Estelle, hell-for-leather for the Dzików's lead squadron. Casimir, stunned by the swiftness of it, merely turned and galloped after.

It was a race, and James was winning. He reined in by the Dzików's colour party, and immediately ordered them to the third squadron. 'Inform Captain Poinatowski I wish him to hold in position,' he barked at the cornet holding the regimental banner. And as he did, he watched across the thousand paces to the marching column of Russian fusiliers, and the frisson of alarm as their mounted officers galloped to confer, and hundreds of eyes followed his every manoeuvre.

He turned to a strangely calm Beart, sitting to attention as if he were on parade and not a battlefield. 'Squadrons one and two will draw their carbines,' he said, and Beart repeated his order in a parade ground bark.

'Forward, at the walk,' said James. Again, Beart repeated the command, and as one, their carbines gripped at the trigger guard, the butts resting on their thighs, over 300 Dzików dragoons stepped off into battle.

The order to 'Trot!' followed and the two lines of dragoons moved from behind the now-wilting line of Polish grenadiers, advancing directly on the flank platoons of the Russian line now advancing to begin their volley fire into the grenadiers' flank.

The smoke ahead was thick, He couldn't see the entire length of the line of grenadiers anymore, and only a rump end of the Russian line they were trading fire with was clearly visible ahead. As for the other Russian line, still advancing to flank the grenadiers, their flank appeared to be starting to collapse. He did not understand. His dragoons were still only a distant threat. No fire had been exchanged yet; contact was not imminent. But what he'd at first taken for confusion turned out to be sergeants man-handling the Russians' flank platoons, to turn from their front to face James' advancing dragoons. The second Russian line halted. He needed to close that distance, fast.

He ordered, 'Canter!' and the dragoons' pace picked up. The number of paces between them shrank, visibly, with each thud of hooves. And then the individual features of the Russians started to become discernible; the distance down to 200 paces, right where he wanted to be. He reined Estelle, and gestured Beart and Casimir and the bugler to do the same, so the front squadron passed through them, and as they did, he stood on his stirrups and bellowed his commands.

'Halt! Present! Fire!'

The Dzików's front rank discharged their carbines as one; 150 weapons going off in a single crash and gout of smoke, so that the oddly bent Russian line vanished behind it. James led his command party galloping to the flanks as the second squadron came cantering up. He left it to Beart to make the oft drilled-for call.

'Second squadron, pass through!'

And the second squadron rode through the first's open order line and into the smoke, and was lost. His teeth crunched on the grit of the powder smoke; it stung his eyes, and the reek of it cloyed in his nose and mouth and throat. His ears were filled with the noise of men; shouting, screams. He patted Estelle's flank to calm her, and leant forward to whisper his familiar sweet nothings in her ear. As he did, his stinging eyes could see down the line of the first squadron as its troopers reloaded, mechanically. Then he craned back, straining to see through the smoke, to where the other Russian marching column was. Through the swirling tendrils it was all too apparent that column had now come to a halt, too.

He could see sergeants were running, dressing the line; mounted officers, nudging their horses into position. The battalion's colour party too, marching to occupy what was about to become the centre of their line. James knew that somewhere in that press of gold braid and feathered tricornes was some Russian colonel or major, who'd found himself in command of this battalion simply because he had been able to afford the rank, or it had passed to him by hereditary right. Just as he knew the time left to him and all his troopers on this earth now hung on the eye of that Russian colonel or major, and whatever degree of drill aesthetic would satisfy him. Because only when he was satisfied, would he issue the orders, 'Left turn! Present! Fire!'

The longer the Russian delayed, the longer James' dragoons had – because when the Russian did give his orders, that was when his battalion would start pouring volley after volley into them; and there was nothing James could do.

His two fine squadrons of dragoons had nowhere left to go, no choice worth making. He had led them here out onto this battlefield in a bid to seize advantage, and now they stood exposed between fires; enemies to their front and enemies to their flank.

His first command in battle, and he had plunged them into a killing cauldron.

Two ragged volleys rang out from the smoke to his front, like an angry stutter; it was his second squadron of dragoons discharging their carbines, and the clumsily-turned platoon from the Russian flank returning their fire. He could see nothing of the effect of the duel, all he could see was his first squadron, now reloaded, stepping forward into the smoke, still obeying his orders, walking to pass through the second squadron's line to deliver another volley.

And once executed, their orders were to charge the Russian flank.

James wondered at the odds of their succeeding before the other Russian battalion raked them with their musketry. He needn't have bothered. The crash of the enemy's volley rang out. When he turned to look, a wall of powder smoke had already obscured the far Russian line. Except the smoke was far closer than it should have been. Since he'd last looked, the Russian line must have advanced to close the range before unleashing their hail of lead. Standing at the back of the Dzików's own fog of powder smoke, he did not see the enemy's musket balls hit home – but he heard the chaos; the cries of horses and men and the sickening, unmistakable slap of flesh hitting the earth. The heavy thuds were the horses, the lighter, liquid thuds, their riders.

The Russian battalion was reloading. He was watching them, transfixed, with a feeling of utter powerlessness, when a bugle sound echoed out the smoke to his front, above the cacophony of the dying. His troopers were supposed to discharge another volley into their heap of Russian soldiers. But that was the 'Charge!' he was hearing. Beart must have decided to order it now. He caught himself starting to wonder why, just as it became obvious why. If the charge was going to hit home and scatter that Russian line, it had to go before that other damned Russian battalion loosed another volley, otherwise there might not be enough Dzików left standing to deliver a killer blow.

The bugle's tinny blare cut through everything, even the sudden pounding of hooves; even above the ragged cheer his men were sending up from somewhere in that opaque roil of smoke. James spurred Estelle to follow his troopers into the battle.

When he caught up, there was no first squadron or second squadron. All he could see were troopers' backs, and corporals-of-horse urging troopers forward to fill the gaps in the first line as the advancing mass of dragoons picked up their pace.

James' two squadrons, now collapsed into one mass of men, hit the Russian's kinked line at a brisk canter, sabres drawn. Fewer than two dozen of the fusiliers had managed to deploy back to face the Dzików, and even then, they only stood two deep. Their raised muskets, bayonets fixed, managed to skewer a couple of dragoons as their lumbering mounts carried them through, but nearly all those Russian fusiliers died or were maimed under the dragoons' relentless slashes.

The main Russian body, three ranks deep, then took the Dzików's full blow. Horses ran into and trampled the green-coated infantry, splintering the ranks, some of the Russians falling under the horses' hooves, others under their riders' sabres. Others just turned and ran. For those closest to the flank, they ran into dragoons whose mounts were carrying them curling round the back of the Russian line, and went under their hooves too, or fell to flashing steel. The others, on pumping legs, were simply fleeing to any open space not filled with dragoon chargers or other Russian soldiers liable to get in their way.

The entire Russian line began to disintegrate, like leaves from an autumn branch, and as it did, the Dzików's cohesion collapsed, too. Their line split, and clumps of them, and then individuals, broke away to chase down the fleeing infantry, slashing and skewering as they went.

So the next volley from the enfilading Russian battalion sent its lead balls mainly into open space. James felt the whiz of them in the air and the draught of a couple, as Estelle carried him over the carnage. He was aware of the trampled and sliced bodies beneath him, but he would not let his eyes linger there, and anyway, the blood was too dull a colour in the washed out, lightless, smoke-choked air to assume its full horror. He must not dally, for confusion was everywhere, and he needed to ride through it to find thinner smoke – to see if their charge had saved the pinned line of Polish grenadiers.

As he rode, he rallied lone dragoons, until over a dozen Dzików were clustered around him as they exploded between banks of smoke to find themselves already in amongst the flank platoons of another Russian regiment, the one facing off against the Polish grenadiers.

James had been desperately trying to keep a picture of the battlefield in his head when he was confronted by an astonished Russian sergeant's face where only smoke and shadow had been. He'd had no sense of his own speed as he rode forward, and now the man's solid mass seemed about to flash past him – which was when he saw the sergeant's halberd coming up to meet him, the spike of it right in the path of his trajectory, like a wrong angle getting in the way of his solving an exercise in trigonometry. Too fast; everything too fast. He hadn't even his sabre in his hand, and his left hand – gripping the reins too tight to his body – was in the way of him reaching across to draw it. No time. His right hand went for his long saddle pistol; the left hand reached to parry the halberd and then the pain of the blow as his heavy gauntleted hand and halberd staff connected. The pistol out of its holster and up, pointing in the Russian's huge moustachioed face, a hand's breadth from his bared teeth; and then his finger squeezing as his aim and the weapon's barrel and the Russian's face went disappearing behind him, out of his field of vision. And the explosion as the powder ignited and the ball travelled from the barrel into the Russian's mouth; so fast no human eye could see – so fast, even the wreckage of its passage was gone and James was slewing Estelle so as not to collide with one of his Dzików troopers stabbing into the back of a running Russian fusilier, right in his path.

Another rending, deafening, rippling crash; another volley, from out of the smoke to his right. The fleeing fusilier and the pursuing Dzików went down in front of Estelle's pounding hooves, like some invisible cheese-cutter had sliced them away below his vision. He felt Estelle rear, and leap beneath him as she cleared the flailing legs of the stricken horse and its thrown, tumbling rider.

The volley had been the grenadiers' reply, and it took Russian and Dzików alike. More fleeing Russians to be sabred, but their mounted officers were coming into view now; halberd-waving sergeants trying to halt the flight, and dense clusters of blanco-ed cross belts and green coats dimly perceived, marching in formations James could not make out in the smoke. The drumbeats coming thick and fast. He had not enough dragoons with him to roll up this press of enemy soldiers, and they too must realise it, soon. But the drumbeats were coming from his right, not his front. The Polish grenadiers were advancing.

James realised Poinatowski had been right in his assertion; that generals must lose control more or less from the first exchange of fire. More than right – because he could see now that colonels did, too. He had orders he needed to shout, but who was going to hear them above this mayhem? Right now his command extended only to the length of his arms, and to those he could physically grab as they went barrelling by.

He had reined Estelle in, and halted, and was yelling – so his throat felt about to tear – for the Dzików to form line on him. But he could barely hear even himself against the noise of battle. Where was his own bugler? Where was Casimir?

Then a bugle did sound; tinny and distant, but being belted out with great insistence.

But since it wasn't close, he quickly shelved the knowledge of it at the back of his battle mind; there were other matters to attend to, closer by. He began waving his sabre as if doing so would somehow make him better heard. As he whirled and yelled, five dragoons rallied to him, one at a time, out of the murk; he gestured them to close up, stirrup to stirrup, and walked them forward again into the smoke and the melee. Then at the trot, until they were again trampling on Russian soldiery trying to bundle themselves out their way, not knowing whether to run or to stand and fight. The yelling and screaming, and only the odd pop of musketry now. But no more volleys; for an age, no volleys at all.

That was when James and his small gaggle hit against a solid wall of green coats three deep, the front rank kneeling, presenting their bayonet-fixed muskets, butts in the earth, points at an angle, pointing directly at his dragoons. No more than a dozen paces away. He could see the line in front of him clearly, but not where it ended – in either direction. The rear rank Russians, immediately to their front, then fired. A wave of powder smoke, and two Dzików went down. The rest were still standing, he couldn't work out how. They were never going to break this line. They didn't have the reach for their swords to slash down over the raised line of bayonets, presented by the men kneeling at the front, while all the men behind them had to do was load and fire, load and fire. At point blank range.

He yelled for the remaining dragoons to withdraw. He never knew if they heard him, for when he turned again in the smoke, he was alone; apart from the groaning men on the ground, tangling Estelle's hooves.

The distant bugle was still blaring. Someone was sounding the charge, frantic and insistent – somewhere. With a chill that gripped his innards he realised he was completely disoriented. No idea in what direction his front lay or where the enemy were. Or his own lines. Just smoke, and noise that never dimmed.

He had no idea how long he sat there in the smoke, breathing hard so the powder seared his lungs, not knowing which way to ride, having lost in his exhaustion the power even to make a decision. Conscious only of Estelle's reins in one hand, and his sabre in the other.

And then the volleys began again, behind him. Crashing out; then the reply. And again. Close. The Russian regiment and the grenadiers still slugging it out – it could only be them. Just as he knew the second volley, the reply, could only have come from the grenadiers. Much more feeble, ragged. They would not stand to take many more. He did not want to be caught up in their rout, so he wheeled Estelle and galloped in the opposite direction.

And suddenly he was in all but clear air; on the edge of the almost viscous clouds of burnt powder where there was only haze, and he could see for what seemed miles. Alas.

Soldiers were everywhere across the landscape, in blocked masses and running rabbles; no coherent shape he could work out in his first sweep of the visible battlefield. Only one thing seemed settled from this vista. He was not looking at his side's victory.

To the east, towards the river, he could see grey-white uniforms streaming, disordered, from the smoke banks. Coming out of them at an angle, heading back up the Westerplatte, as if intent on forming up to march back to the Weichselmünde fortress. In front of him was just the same impenetrable wall of smoke. It was when he looked north west, towards the rising dunes and the tuft grass, that he felt his heart sink.

One vignette caught his eye above all the others. There was the Russian battalion, the one that had marched wide and blown apart his entire plan for the day. It had formed a neat infantry square. James had thought forming square had become an archaic manoeuvre in this era of modern war; too time-consuming on a fast-moving modern battlefield. Although God knows, nothing had seemed particularly fast moving on this battlefield; not until the very end, at least.

Forming square was a tactic from the last century; from the ancient world even, or so he'd read. It worked because if infantry in line, in the open, when attacked by cavalry, marched the flanks of their line back until they formed a box, or square, then with the soldiers' bayonets facing out on all sides, they would be safe. At a stroke, cavalry were denied the advantage of taking the infantrymen from behind and breaking their ranks. But it was a complicated manoeuvre, and took time, especially under fire. So it was seldom practised in European armies, because in modern war an infantry line was usually 750 paces long. Too long for any head-on cavalry charge to ever overflow or envelop. Also, modern firepower meant any cavalry unit attacking such a line would have to face at least two, or possibly three, full volleys before it closed, and would be cut to ribbons.

But the Russians had used a square today, and from the debacle playing itself out against the rising dunes there, James could see it had worked for them.

For there was Poinatowski and his reserve squadron, being chased in disorder by a formed regiment of Russian dragoons, the Russians' dark grey coats advancing in neat line before pausing to discharge another rolling wave of lighter grey powder smoke; then on they trotted, walking down the tumbling, collapsing rabble that was all that was left of his Dzików dragoons.

James could see what had happened. When the Russian battalion marched out to enfilade James' and his regiment's other two squadrons, Poinatowski had formed his reserve in line and moved them up to threaten this Russian battalion's flank.

Even from his disadvantaged view over the flat terrain, James could see that it should have been an inspired move, leaving the Russian commander only one alternative; to wheel his battalion 90 degrees away from James to meet the new threat to his own flank. Poinatowski wouldn't even have to charge, just maintain position in order to force the Russian into such an exhausting manoeuvre, and pin him there with carbine fire.

But the Russian colonel or major or whoever he was, had not obliged Poinatowski, just as he hadn't obliged James. The Russian had formed square and continued to advance, forcing Poinatowski to close him, dismembering his squadron formation into half-troops to cover each front and ensure the square remained shut tight. And that was where the regiment of Russian dragoons had entered the fight, catching Poinatowski's men in their penny packets. And now they were trying to carry out a fighting withdrawal, like the rest of this flank of Estaing de Sailland's army, to the Weichselmünde fortress and the mouth of the Mottlau river.

They had been beaten. James had no idea what had befallen Estaing de Sailland's other flank, but right now it was plain to see it did not matter; because his army had been split in two. The battle was over, and Peter Lacy had won.

The sun was low over the flat of the Westerplatte by then, a large rust orb dipping slowly down through the vast corona of powder haze, quite separate from the lingering banks of smoke proper; it filled the entire sky to the south. There was no rumble of guns anymore, what fire there was, was random.

When James looked back on the chaos, he held no coherent memory of those last hours, just a jumble of impressions. He found it better not to pay attention to the carnage, or to wonder what would befall the wounded and the maimed. He shut out their moans.

And then he found Casimir, filthy from smoke, but otherwise unmarked, his big round eyes just this side of hysterical laughter, but still in control of himself. And the colour party too, although nearly all were wounded, he was certain of that from the blood that slathered them. James also sported a fair amount of blood on his own coat and breeches, and clotted in his hair – for his hat was gone. None of the blood, however, was his. Just spatter. All that was left of other men's lives.

He led their small party from the field, collecting the odd Dzików stray as they went, from among the many, many strays.

Nobody intruded on their flight. The Russians who had just defeated them here, on this flank, were obviously too spent for hot pursuit. So, as his Estelle rocked him with her steady pace, James' mind was left to its clutter of thoughts.

He felt physically and morally stupefied. No words came that seemed appropriate to what had just happened. It felt as if a great rent had been torn in the fabric of human society, and that they had all collectively stepped through into a world where the worst of man was permitted. For a moment, he glimpsed a future him, sitting down to write to Davy Hume, to try to tell him of the day. But when he looked at the page, he could conjure no words to put there. No language to describe his experiences had made it back through the rent. No words to make the transition and still hold their meaning.

He remembered Poinatowski before the battle. It was only the previous evening; even that seemed so far from credible. What had he said? 'There is nothing I can tell you now that can ever really prepare you.' How right he'd been.

And then there had been the image that he would remember forever; the sight that, when he finally comprehended it, stuck. That smacked him back to the here and now with something akin to a physical blow. It was the skyline above the Weichselmünde fortress. It had come clear into their view as they marched numbly towards it, but there was not a ship's mast to be seen. A forest of rigging had clogged the Mottlau there only this morning. Now it was gone. The French squadron had sailed.

James never remembered entering the fortress, fighting his way through the chaos there. Civilians, commissary men, Count Plélo's diplomatic entourage. He only remembered finding one of the fortress'

Polish gunner officers – sitting, methodically drinking the local eau de vie – who was only too happy to describe the precipitous departure of the French ships. 'There's a Russian fleet in the offing,' he said. 'So they didn't like to hang about.'

And suddenly James was seeing again that venerable old Scotsman sitting at Lacy's table; Admiral Thomas Watson of the Imperial Russian Navy. He wondered if the old gent would remember him, if he would be happy to offer him a drink, now. Probably, he thought. No. Not probably. Almost certainly. Theirs was the world he now inhabited. And that realisation told him it was time to absent himself. He had entered a contract, and discharged his duties under it to the best of his ability. On that, his conscience was clear. But the contract did not extend beyond the other signatory going out of business; and after what had happened on the Westerplatte today, the master in this master and servant relationship was most assuredly no longer trading.

He sat down at the Polish gunner's desk and began to write a note. 'How would you like to own a horse?' he asked. 'She answers to Estelle and she likes apples. Take this to the officers' farrier, and she's yours.' And he handed the dumbfounded young man the paper.

He'd miss Estelle, but where he was going, he couldn't take her.

With the French army defeated, and the Russians about to take Weichselmünde fortress – for take it they must, with nary a soldier left to hold it – Danzig would become untenable, and the short unhappy reign of King Stanislas would come to an end.

Colonel James Lindsay was a soldier after all, not a cleaner, and what was about to unfold here was no longer a war, but a mess.

'Sweden, I think,' he said to himself. But as he stepped out onto the fortress' jetty, into the mass of frantic scrabbling figures there, another thought hit him. One that stopped him in his tracks.

The Gräfin Dorothea von Kettler.

She must still be in Danzig. And the Russians still at the city gates.

James didn't have to look very far into the future to know what the Gräfin Dorothea von Kettler's fate would be. One way or another the

Russians were going to enter Danzig, and when they did, Peter Lacy would execute the Tsarina Anna's will, and the Gräfin Dorothea von Kettler's flapping mouth would be silenced.

The bloody woman. What was she still doing there when he'd warned her? Stupid question, he knew.

James did not employ a rational chain of argument to arrive at his decision. How could he? There were no rational arguments for what he now did.

It did not take him long to find one of the fishing boats he did business with. They knew him to be a good customer; a gentlemen who never tried to haggle them out of their profits, and always had the time of day for a fellow, not to mention a few jokes and lots of gossip. At the first boat he asked, 'Will you to take me up to Danzig?' the skipper said, 'Aye!'

Remarkable, when you considered all the other boats were heading out into the Baltic before what breeze there was changed, and the Russian fleet in the offing could enter the Mottlau, and start bombarding Weichselmünde.

It was only once he was under way that he had time to reflect on what he was doing. He was under no duty to this woman; he had no connection at all to her, save that of a brief travelling companion. She certainly had shown no consideration of him. Yet here he was embarked on a course that could easily cost him his life. He supposed it all came down to that pressure in his breast every time he thought of her.

An all-too-possible, alternative future was him bobbing happily away aboard this fishing smack, as it plied its way across the Baltic to Karlskrona and safety, while behind him, in a Russian-occupied Danzig, was her lifeless, garrotted body lying in a heap in some tawdry basement.

There was no breeze on the river; the fishermen had to pull mightily, through the narrow irrigation canals and shortcuts that cut across the big bend and brought them out opposite the city wall's Mottlau bastion. The journey took him through the shattered rear areas of the right flank of Estaing de Sailland's army. From where he sat on the bait-encrusted gunnels he could see how comprehensive the defeat had been. The mostly

French battalions were now pressed right back against the riverbank, penned in by a ring of Russian infantry and guns. Small boats of all description swarmed back and forth across the river to the city, but there would never be enough of them to evacuate the French, or even to supply them. James' little smack had to jostle to get under the river gate and into the city proper.

He directed the fishermen rowers up through the canals to the wharf nearest the old duke's town house. Everywhere they looked on shore, people were busy. Their main occupation seemed to be stockpiling their basements. Before he stepped ashore, he passed the boat's skipper a heavy purse, and promised him more if he'd only wait. Two hours at most.

The fishermen were grumpy in their nervousness now. All the good grace had gone. But they agreed.

15

A Future of Learning and Wisdom

She paced up and down in front of the mantelpiece as a caged bear does, awaiting its baiting.

The old duke was in his sitting room, and the servants they had left were nowhere to be seen. No chaperone for this meeting. But then, even James could see Dorothea was most definitely not at her provocative best. No inflaming décolletage, and her hair was un-powdered and merely pinned back; delicately done, but no confection, and no delicate waft of scent. She looked very self-contained and powerful, and throat-catchingly gorgeous.

'Your great General von Bittinghofen is already negotiating to surrender the city to Lacy,' she said airily, 'so I shall, I'm sure, be a sub-clause in some treaty and therefore quite safe.'

James decided to forego pointing out von Bittinghofen was no longer his general, the contract having technically expired. Or that he doubted that her fate, or even that of the entire Courland dynasty, would feature at all in a simple 'terms of surrender'.

'I have a boat at the wharf,' said James, repeating himself, still in measured tones. 'It lacks a lady's comforts, but it will, if you agree to step aboard, save your life, milady. So speed, milady. Speed, please.'

But she would not budge.

It had taken an age thundering his sabre hilt off the door to gain entry to the house. She'd known who was banging; he'd seen her face at a window looking down at him with an expression he could not read through the mullions. But she took her time unbolting.

She had already known the battle over the river had been lost, that surrender of the city was inevitable. Not to surrender would invite its sack. It was a custom of war. If a besieging army had to take any fortified bastion by storm, it was understood that once through the breach, that army's commander would give his soldiers a day and night of licence. A bounty, if you like, for all the blood they would have paid for the victory. Because storming a bastion was always a bloody affair. Certainly, the Russians' one previous attempt at taking Danzig's walls had been most bloody, and that had been repulsed.

Everybody in the city knew that defeat on the Westerplatte meant no-one would be coming to relieve them. Better to surrender the city than have it taken, and then handed over to an army of blood- and loot-crazed soldiers for a day and a night, while they slaked themselves.

And in that mayhem, what an opportunity for a tsarina's loyal servants to rid her of a tiresome gräfin of no significance, said James.

But there was going to be no mayhem, said Dorothea. And so no danger. What there would be however, was an opportunity.

That was how she'd been goading James for the past half hour.

'You seem determined to go down with your dynasty,' he said.

'We shall not be going down, chevalier! Let me explain the ways of diplomacy in a civilised world. The city will be surrendered, yes, but that is when the talking will begin. For this war to end, and wars always end, there will negotiations and then a treaty. Stanislas will have to abdicate, but it is not automatic that Augustus will succeed. Not if there is another, legitimate contender …'

'There is no other contender,' James interrupted. 'Legitimate or otherwise.'

'Oh, but there is … and we both know who it is!'

'There is no other,' said James, all too aware of whom she meant. 'There never was. I have tried to tell you that. The man you refer to does not seek the crown of Poland.'

'Then he must be made to!' hissed Dorothea, stamping her foot. 'His wife must make him, for the sake of her country, and my duchy!'

James paused for a moment to reflect on the likelihood of mad, resentful, Polish Clementina ever making her husband do anything. Dorothea was clutching at a fantasy. That fantasy had to cease now if he were to get her out the door and out of the city. Bloody woman!

'You are clutching at something that is past, milady,' he said, sitting down to emphasise he meant to be heard. 'The Russians will not hear you. Neither will James Stuart. The tsarina wants Courland back in her gift, and this war has been her opportunity. Not only is no-one listening, you have become an irritant. More than an irritant, to the tsarina. If you really want to do something for your people now, don't throw your life away. Live instead, to fight another day, with new weapons, on another battlefield.'

'What are you talking about, you tiresome man?'

'You come from a world where power is its own currency. If you have it, it is always there. You do not have to go to it, or wait while it is summoned. It is at your fingertips to exercise or contest. What is yours, what you believe history says should be yours, or that which you simply covet. You snap your fingers and you are in the game. How could the world be any other way? But you, Gräfin Dorothea, do not have any real power in this game. You merely strut through the corridors of power bartering in the crumbs from its table. You talk of your people, but how does your game bring in their harvests or prevent rampaging armies passing like locusts across their land? You do not change or influence the machinations of these great despots; you are merely a counter in their game. Those are the rules, and always have been. But the world does not have to be that way. A wind of change is blowing. This is an age in which natural philosophers are proving the natural world is not governed by man's dogma or superstition, but by natural laws – that can be proved by measurement, that are observable. Our human dark age of myth and magic is debunked forever – instead of spells, there is mathematics. And if we have now proved the natural world is governed by science, then might not the life of mankind be also? Might the lives of men one day be governed by reason and not obscurity, by law and justice and not the random exercise of inherited despotism or crude force of arms?'

'You are a dreamer, chevalier, and I am not even sure of what it is you dream,' she said.

'Great men are pondering upon just such questions all across Europe,' said James. 'Whether by philosophical inquiry we might plumb the very nature of man and by so doing, design laws and societies that channel our better character to the greater good of all. I know some of these men. I correspond with them. And what I am proposing to you is, do not die today, Dorothea, and let me introduce you to their thought, so you might regroup and renew the struggle for your Courland, but this time better armed, with new, irrefutable arguments instead of just intrigue.'

'La!' she said. 'Great men, indeed! And great their great thoughts! What nonsense. Men are nothing but instinct. And base, at that.'

'Really? Man is no more than a collection of instincts, before which he is powerless? Well, then, explain this ... it is my instinct right now to land a blow on your stubborn jaw, thus rendering you insensible so that I might carry your person to safety. But I am managing to overcome that instinct because I realise it would be a pyrrhic victory, never to be forgiven, so I am trying reason instead.'

She threw back her head and laughed, her shoulders rocking so she had to steady herself against the mantelpiece. James began to smile too, until her laughter turned to sobs, and he rose to help her to a chair where she buried her face in her hands and began to cry.

'I am out of ideas,' she said in a low voice. 'I do not know where to turn, what to do. I am defeated, chevalier. They have won. Do with me what you will.'

Word from Weichselmünde was that the Russian fleet had arrived and had opened its bombardment. James and his fishermen, with Dorothea now in their company, would have to follow the Mottlau the other way, to the estuary of the Vistula itself.

They took very little from the old duke's townhouse. The old man himself would be safe there; there would be no gain for the Russians, or anybody for that matter, in treating him harshly. Indeed his physical presence might even prove a bargaining chip for whoever held him.

It was dark when James and Dorothea settled themselves, and the fishermen, eager to be away, rowed the smack out the city and turned right. For the first part of their voyage, the far bank of the Mottlau was illuminated with a myriad of campfires, lit to warm the defeated French soldiery, and in the reflections close to the water, they could see some of their grimy faces eying them with a sullen indifference.

The near bank, from early on, was occupied by Russians, who paid them not the slightest attention. A fishing boat heading to sea. Who needed the stink on them of having to check?

And then, both banks were held by Russians, and eventually came the barked orders from shore. The Russian search was not particularly onerous. The young, pimply officer spoke German to Dorothea, who assured him they were Scottish merchants, on their way to visit their other investments. James offered him a purse as a bribe, and seeing it, the officer ordered a further search where another purse was duly found. After that, they didn't bother to search in the bait barrels where James' real cache was; or in the skipper's bunk, where James had stowed his pistols.

The fishermen were happy to go along. There was the money he'd paid them, and after all, the gentlemen wasn't a damned Russian, or a Pole – he was a Scot, just like the minister at the kirk in Tallinn, who always kept an open door for any distressed sailor – so they were happy to sail James and his lady to Karlskrona.

James still had his original letters of passport from the Palazzo del Re in the breast pocket of his tunic, and Dorothea had documents of her own. Both sets satisfied the old Swedish harbour master's brief inspection. He directed them to the local inn where a bath could be had, and a decent supper.

Dorothea had had little to say during their uncomfortable but otherwise uneventful voyage. But she had clung to him, especially when she slept. Only once had she asked, 'What are we going to do when we get there?'

The 'we' did not escape James, and when he looked at her, he knew it wasn't meant to.

James had had no answer. 'We have coin, and I have a letter of credit,' he said, referring to Mr MacDougall's little missive naming James' bankers in Hamburg, also tucked away. 'So we shall not suffer.'

Now they were on land, the questions seemed more pressing. As she waited for her bath to be filled in her bedroom, Dorothea fidgeted. James sat in the room's small gallery, smoking a pipe and looking out over the neat, flat countryside.

'So this is it?' she said. 'You snatch me from my doom, you offer me a future of learning and wisdom, then you hold me, comforting, in your arms across the sea. And now you just sit there. So now what? Eh, sir? Now what?'

James stood up, his train of thought on that very question, shattered. He glowered at her but before he could open his mouth the chambermaid came bustling back lugging her last, now empty bucket, all steam and dripping water. As she went out, she sang words in her strangely lilting language that neither he nor Dorothea understood, but assumed were that the bath was full now.

When James turned back to Dorothea, her look was so wanton and surly, he felt that familiar constriction in his throat, and a distinct lack of it in another part.

He had intended to say something to her, but all the events of the past days, weeks, months even, came crowding in on him, taking away any words, leaving only action to speak for what he felt right now. So he just picked her up and carried her through the bedroom door, pausing only to kick it shut, with the heel of his cavalryman's top boot.

Epilogue

The count had not a moment's doubt where he would find the king. He would be on the other side of the Gamla Stan, picking his way across the site that one day would become his new home, getting in the way, and irritating the all the French craftsmen. For the simple reason that it was a beautiful morning with the sky a deep azure, dappled with high scudding clouds, brilliant white in woolly clusters, and a blustery breeze that would blow away all the masonry dust and keep the day fresh.

The king was always there on good days.

It was not a long walk from the Kungshuset on Riddarholmen islet – where the king and queen lived for now, and where the count had his private offices – up to the new royal palace on Stadsholmen, overlooking the main Stockholm harbour. But there would be enough time for him to compose his thoughts before approaching His Majesty King Frederick I with this latest matter arising.

Count Arvid Bernhard Horn of Ekebyholm was the king's president of the privy council chancellery – in other words, his prime minister. He was an older man, of seventy years, fierce of countenance and short of temper when dealing with lesser mortals, which encompassed most of humanity. When dealing with those who had the power to thwart him, however – such as the king – he was a man possessed of an almost other-worldly subtlety and patience.

To look at, he was tall, gaunt and all nose. And today that nose led him unerringly to the king's presence, facing the southern aspect of the

263

new palace, where Frederick I of Sweden was watching the raising of a cast-bronze relief depicting the booty of war.

Frederick was a roly-poly, pudgy-faced man in a coat, all blue velvet and brocade, with a huge feather in his huge hat, and he was leaning back to look up at the industry taking place above him, quite enraptured.

The irony of the scene was not lost on Count Horn; the huge palace under construction before him was of a grandeur in inverse proportion to the failed glory of the country now building it, and the intricate frieze Frederick was so taken by depicted booty he could never hope to amass in his reign.

There was no love lost between Count Horn and the younger king, nor even a master–servant relationship. Both men knew Frederick was a weak king, in terms of the power he could wield abroad and the respect he commanded at home. Also, at the age of 58 he was childless, and when he died, his dynasty would die with him.

It had not always been so for Sweden or its royal household. Under the last king, Charles XII, Sweden had been the major power in the Baltic, with an empire along its southern shores stretching intermittently from Karelia and the Baltic states to Pomerania and the Duchy of Bremen. Until impetuous Charles went to war with Peter the Great at the beginning of the century, and lost it all.

Which was why Count Horn was under no illusion as to his role these days; it was managing Frederick's – and Sweden's – decline. And a grim, dogged, unrewarding struggle it often proved.

That war had lasted twenty years, and Sweden's final defeat had been almost a decade and a half ago. Both Charles XII and Tsar Peter were long dead now, but the Russia Peter had left behind now dominated the Baltic. Yet the Swedes and their new king had remained ever reluctant to let go of the trappings of their country's former glory. The palace was probably the grandest example of that denial; a huge brick and sandstone rococo confection begun three years before the outbreak of that fatal conflict, when Sweden's power was at its height. Yet it was still being built, even though the victorious Russians and every other scavenging neighbour had taken advantage of Sweden's fall to snap up her previous conquests, and all the revenues that had flowed from them.

Given half a chance, they'd try to snap up more. Which was why poor, weak Sweden these days needed Count Horn and his cautious diplomacy – of that, the count was convinced.

'Your majesty,' said the count in the king's ear. The king did not flinch, or indeed show any sign he'd heard. He was used to Horn sneaking up on him, pestering him with stuff, which was why he seldom listened.

'Your majesty,' Horn continued, undeterred. 'We have received intelligence from the collector of customs at Karlskrona that a close relative of the Duke of Courland has landed on our shores in most unusual circumstances.'

Now, news that a von Kettler had come to visit – that was interesting. Enough to make Frederick turn and look at the count. 'Unusual? How do you mean unusual?' said the king.

'She appears to have arrived in some state of disarray, having come on a fishing boat. From Danzig.'

Neither of them needed any further explanation of what coming 'from Danzig' meant. News of the city's capitulation to the Russians had already reached them. But that was a fight that Count Horn had steered Sweden well away from. Ask him what was happening in Danzig and he'd say, 'none of my business.' Privately, however, Count Horn dissected every move the Russians ever made, much as a Roman augur would pick through a fallen eagle's innards.

'You said, "she",' said the king. 'And "in disarray". You've lost me Horn, as you usually do. Why on earth would any "she" from the house of von Kettler be arriving here, "in disarray?'

'Quite, your majesty. Which is why I draw it to your attention.'

Both men regarded the men at work and the play of their intricate system of pulleys as they swayed up the next cast frieze.

'The woman is the duke's niece, the Gräfin Dorothea,' said Horn. 'And why she is here concerns me, your majesty.'

'Hmm,' said the king.

'My informants assure me the Duke of Courland continues to reside contentedly in his Danzig town house, and is unmoved and undisturbed by the Russian occupation of the city,' the count added. 'Indeed, there is no reason why he shouldn't. The Russians have no quarrel with Courland. In fact his presence, under their protection, could be of political advantage to them now that King Stanislas has been forced to flee. Which begs the question, why has the Gräfin Dorothea not remained there with him? Her arriving here on a fishing boat implies she must have departed in some haste. Which in turn implies an escape. And if that is the case, the only people she can be escaping from are the Russians ...'

'Oh, do get to the point,' said the king, while devoting all his attention to the frieze dangling above him.

The count was too old to bridle at such casual insults from his monarch. He continued with his customary, dogged patience, leading Frederick down the path he'd mapped for him.

'As your majesty appreciates, we do not wish to upset our Russian neighbours these days any more than we have to,' he said. 'So it may come to pass that, if indeed she *is* escaping from the Russians, they might wish us to send her back ...'

'Well, why don't you just get on and ...' said the king, interrupting, as the count interrupted him in turn.

'... therefore I counsel it would be wise that we speak to her first. To ask her, why? Why she has felt it necessary to flee?'

Oh, but did Count Horn want to know the answer to that question. Gräfin Dorothea's reputation long preceded her; the secrets she held, the information she always had to trade and all the back doors to knock on. A treasure trove had washed up on his shore, and he would be loath to give it back before he had properly inspected it.

'If we know that,' he continued, 'we will be better able to judge whether it is wiser to give her succour, or send her packing. Before news of her arrival here reaches General Lacy's ears, and thence the tsarina's.'

'You wish me to order her brought to Stockholm?' said the king. 'You could have done that yourself, count. You have the stamp.'

The count ignored the remark. He did indeed have the stamp – a custom-made seal used to legally approve all royal documents that in normal times would require a royal signature. But such was Frederick's indifference when it came to the administration of his much-diminished kingdom, he rarely could be bothered signing anything. So using the stamp was considered by all parties to be an acceptable compromise.

'There is another aspect to this matter, your majesty, that I fear would require your specific attention,' said the count, following his gaze up the palace wall.

A sigh escaped the king. 'How much of my attention?'

'There is a senior Polish officer accompanying the gräfin,' said the count. 'A Scotsman, who had been at the court of the James, the pretender to the British throne, but latterly has been in the service of Stanislas. An arrangement promoted by James Stuart's wife, as I understand it, who as you know is a Sobieski.'

'Ah, the noble John, hero of the siege of Vienna and slayer of the Turk, how they do trade on that glorious reputation,' said the king, distractedly.

'This officer, James Lindsay his name is, is the third son of minor Scots aristocracy and might be of some use to us, your majesty.'

'Use, count?'

'His nationality, your majesty, is the same as Graham's, the Russian admiral. Then there is General Lacy, the Russians' Irishman. All three are Wild Geese. All three speak the same language. And all three have already met, face to face, during the siege. Or so I am informed. Now, this Colonel Lindsay is a soldier of fortune whose contract with Stanislas has obviously lapsed. If we were to offer him employment, he might be of considerable assistance to us in the future.'

'Assistance? What possible assistance could a renegado Jacobite possibly be to me here in Sweden?' snapped the king. He was getting bored with this conversation.

'Clandestine assistance, your majesty,' said the count, his patience not flinching for a moment. 'I speak of course, in terms of a possible back conduit to the Russians, should ever such a diplomatic channel be needed. Consider it, your majesty. With all three of them speaking English, the chances of misunderstandings appreciably diminishes. And we both know how easily misunderstandings arise with the Russians, your majesty.'

'If I say yes to what you want, will you leave me alone, Count Horn?'

'A written royal commission in your horse guards, your majesty. I should like my secretary to have it with him when he goes to detain the gräfin. It will be offered to him couched in terms he might find difficult to refuse, and then we shall see what he says.'

'Very well. Have it drawn up, count, and bring it to me for my scrawl.'

Historical Note

By My Sword Alone is a work of historical fiction set in the first half of the eighteenth century – with the emphasis on fiction. If you are a student of the period and try to use it as a crib, you will fail. So be warned.

While much of the backdrop to the book is factually accurate, when it comes to timelines and certain events, I have driven a coach and horses through the whole shebang – just as I have taken terrible liberties with the characters of many of the real life protagonists I have lifted to populate my story.

Needless to say, there was no James Lindsay, or any Earl of Branter with an estate called Kirkspindie in Breadalbane. There was, however, a Marquess of Tullibardine and a Lord George Murray amongst others, all loyal to a very real pretender, also known as the king over the water, namely James Francis Edward Stuart, or as he would claim, King James III.

Just as there was a General Joseph Wightman in King George's army. And they all fought at the Battle of Glenshiel in 1719, which unfolded largely in the way described.

Also, the various acts of retribution visited by King George on those loyal to the Stuart pretender are all equally true.

As is the character of David Hume, James' student friend in the novel, who would in reality go on to become one of the leading thinkers of the Enlightenment. Their teacher in the novel, Francis Hutcheson, held the chair of moral philosophy at Glasgow University from 1729 until his death in 1746.

Obviously, the figure of Voltaire is anything but fictional, and his penchant for collecting a large and diverse cabal of correspondents has been recorded in great detail.

That the pretender, James Francis Edward Stuart, sought the hand in marriage of the Polish noblewoman, Princess Maria Clementina Sobieska, is also historic fact. As is the story that the Hapsburg Emperor Charles had her detained at King George's request while she was en route to her wedding. And group of errant Irish 'Wild Geese' officers did indeed free her as a service to James Stuart, although the exact circumstances of that event are not quite as recorded in this novel!

James Stuart did maintain a court in exile in Rome, largely funded by the Pope, and it was notorious as a hotbed of intrigue and treachery. However, it would have been historically impossible for a real life James Lindsay to have been there at the time of Princess Maria Clementina Sobieska's arrival, let alone to have been involved in her escape from the Emperor Charles. In the real historic timeline, all those events were unfolding barely three months after the Battle of Glenshiel.

Also, in the real world, there was no Dorothea von Kettler, although the von Kettler family were the hereditary Dukes of Courland, and they did conduct a generational struggle for independence from their over-bearing neighbours, imperial Russia, and to a lesser extent, Poland. So it would be no surprise if a von Kettler was known to the Stuart court, especially since the pretender's consort was such a senior Polish noble.

However, there is no historical basis to the idea that the pretender ever considered putting his name forward as a contender for the Polish throne, or sought to become involved in the subsequent War of the Polish Succession, which broke out in 1733, more or less in the way described.

There was a King Stanislas I of Poland, and he was elected by the Polish nobility. Austria, Saxony and Russia did indeed object to his ascending the throne, and did drive him from Warsaw to Danzig, where a Russian army did indeed besiege him. And, as described in this fiction, Stanislas had high hopes of being relieved, namely by his father-in-law, the French King Louis XV. However, while the French did send ships, and troops, to relieve Stanislas, they were too few and were subsequently vanquished. But not at any 'Battle of Westerplatte'. No such clash took place, and is an invention of the author.

The real end of Stanislas was far more prosaic. The siege of Danzig ended with the defenders capitulating, and Stanislas, intending to fight on, fled to the countryside to conduct a guerrilla war. All his noble resolve, however, was eventually bought off by the offer of the Duchy of Lorraine, and the war ended with the signing of the Treaty of Vienna in 1738.

That James Lindsay and Dorothea von Kettler made it to Sweden in the aftermath of the Danzig surrender, would not however have guaranteed them any long-lasting peace. A war was brewing between Sweden and Russia, and when it broke out in 1741, James would find the Russian armies were again being led by his old friend from the siege of Danzig, Peter Lacy, and its navy, by a Scottish admiral called Thomas Watson – both men very real life characters from history. But that is for another story!

Acknowledgements

I'd like to thank Alice Rees, who liked the idea for this story so much, she commissioned it; my editor, Cate Bickmore, for always getting it right, even when I don't; Imogen Streater, who got me all excited with her cover design, and my publisher, James Faktor, for taking the trouble to keep me in print.